SWEET DELUSIONS

STUCK WITH YOU SERIES
BOOK ONE

BEA MILLER

Edited by
LP TVORIK
Cover by
MAÏTÉ CAYUELAS

AUTHOR'S NOTE

First of all, thank you so much for giving this indie author a chance! Before you dive in, I'd like to let you know that this story includes sensitive topics, including but not limited to: alcohol consumption & abuse, anxiety & panic attacks, car accident (off-page), death of parents (off-page) , domestic abuse & violence, explicit sex, violence, home invasion, kidnapping, light choking, and attempted sexual assault.

"It isn't what we say or think that defines us, but what we do."

— JANE AUSTEN, SENSE AND SENSIBILITY

To my family and friends, for believing in my
dreams even when I didn't.

CHAPTER ONE

The doors swung open in front of me, giving me only a split second to straighten my spine and school my features into a neutral expression before camera flashes blurred my vision. The moment we stepped out of court, reporters crowded us, shouting questions at a deafening volume.

"Mr. Maxwell, over here!"

"Tell us about the account in Luxembourg."

"Do you feel bad about costing your clients millions in lost retirement funds?"

"Mr. Maxwell, can you answer the questions?"

"Miss Leigh, give us a statement!"

"No comment," I answered in my most professional voice. My client, William Maxwell, walked beside me with his head down as reporters tried and failed to get his attention. He'd been given strict instructions not to address the media.

I'd be damned if this guy ever opened his mouth to speak in public again.

A secret account in Luxembourg. Under his daughter's maiden name. An account that his ex-wife knew about and had no scruples sharing with the judge, of course. An account that *I* didn't know about.

I was beyond fuming.

The hearing had been going perfectly fine until Maxwell's ex-wife dropped the bombshell that had both sides of the aisle in a frenzy. While the prosecutors reveled in this new information, I watched as my career as a criminal defense lawyer suffered its first major blow.

We shoved reporters left and right. The police helped create a path to our car while reporters kept badgering me with questions. Once Maxwell was safely in the car, I turned to address the gang of jackals.

"The events of the last few months have caused my client a lot of pain and distress. You cannot blame him for being on edge when the prosecution leverages such egregious accusations against him." My voice was cool and collected, my tone professional. Not a soul watching me, or filming me, could suspect how angry I really was.

My client had lied to me. And because of that, I was about to lose my first high-profile case.

"Miss Leigh, do you have anything to say about the millions of dollars' worth of embezzled money found in Maxwell's daughter's account?"

Nope. Not going there.

"Is Maxwell going to settle?"

"Did Maxwell's daughter know where the money came from?"

I raised my hands in front of me to silence them before I spoke. "It's been a long day. Mr. Maxwell has been put through a lot. Right now, our strategy is to take some time for our client to recover emotionally, and then we will refocus on his trial. Thank you for your questions."

I ducked into the car, shutting the door on a cacophony of questions. Relief flooded me when the sounds faded as the car started to move, but it was short-lived. At least Maxwell had the decency to hang his head in shame. I just hoped he had the wisdom to not open his mouth right now.

We had won. There was no trace of the money, and we'd established reasonable doubt that Maxwell had stolen it. He was going to get off scot-free, like millionaires usually did. His ex-wife was meant to be a character witness, to speak highly of her ex-husband despite their divorce. She was supposed to gush about how he was a great father, responsible, reliable, honest. And in a way, she had. Ex-Mrs. Maxwell told the judge about how kind Maxwell was, what a generous man he was to have given his daughter over thirty million dollars.

There was no evidence of this transaction in his financial records, something the prosecution was quick to point out. From there, everything went to shit. Now the trial had been adjourned pending investigation into the new evidence.

She was good. Ex-Mrs. Maxwell had sounded completely innocent when she mentioned the money, clueless even. But it takes a liar to spot a liar, and the satisfied gleam in her eyes when she spoke was enough to tell me she had known exactly what she was doing.

I didn't know the complete history between the two, but it felt like she'd been biding her time until an opportunity like this presented itself. I'd be impressed by her act of revenge if it didn't have the potential to ruin my career.

Maxwell didn't say a word the entire car ride. He kept his focus on his phone, furiously texting someone, his puffy face growing redder with each minute that passed.

The car stopped in front of my apartment building, and although I was dying to leave his presence, I had to give Maxwell and my team some encouragement.

"All right," I started. "We had a minor setback today, but nothing to despair over. Granted, the situation is not ideal, but Mr. Maxwell remains an innocent man. As long as they can't link the money in Miss Maxwell's account to the embezzled money, we will be fine."

I paused to watch their faces, to let my words reach them before I continued. "Mr. Maxwell, we need everything you have on this Luxembourg account, and any other accounts that are not included in the official financial records."

"But—" he said, but I held a finger up to stop him.

"We don't care whether you are innocent. We've told you this before and you didn't believe us, choosing instead to withhold important information. You might face some real jail time, and your only hope of avoiding it is to be completely honest from this point forward."

Maxwell nodded, sinking back into his seat.

"We need everything you have, legal or otherwise, so we can come to court prepared. You cannot lie to us again." I spoke firmly, staring straight at him. Silence stretched between us for what felt like hours before he finally nodded.

I turned towards Peter and Stacy, the dejected look on their faces an accurate reaction to the clusterfuck that had been today's session in court.

"Find everything you can, reach out to Monty if you have to. I'm sure if there's anything you can't find, he'll be able to dig it up."

"Of course, Miss Leigh. See you on Monday?"

"Yes, we'll regroup and see where we go from there."

Before I could step out of the car, Maxwell grabbed my arm. "You better fix this. I'm paying you enough." His grip on my wrist tightened, and I internally recoiled. He didn't release me until I nodded.

I got out of the car with the weight of the world on my shoulders, eager to put this day behind me and push forward. At this stage, the best I could hope for was to settle out of court in exchange for a reduced sentence.

Not that Maxwell deserved it, the lying bastard.

I climbed up the steps leading to my building, the red brick facade a welcoming sight after this disastrous day. The elevator ride to the third floor seemed to take forever, but at this point I was just relieved I didn't run into any of my neighbors. I didn't think I had the energy for small talk.

As soon as I pushed the door to my apartment open, I abandoned my heels by the door. The cold hardwood floor felt great against the soles of my feet, cooling me from the feet up. I poured myself a tall glass of whiskey and sat out on my small balcony, willing my brain into weekend mode.

New Yorkers sped by below me, the city buzzing with energy as another weekend rolled in. Unfortunately for me, my brain was also buzzing, going over Maxwell's case, wondering how my team had not found this Luxembourgish account, hoping that we hadn't missed anything else....

I refused to be mad at my team. It wasn't their fault our client had decided to hide crucial information from us.

I would have to double check everything on Monday.

Or I could do it now and be done with it.

The urge to call Monty, my regular private investigator, overcame me, and before I knew it, my phone was pressed against my ear.

"Hey, this is Cassie."

"Ah, who else would be calling me at seven p.m. on a Friday night?"

"Is that how you greet all your clients? By calling them out on their workaholic tendencies?"

"Only the special ones." I could hear the laughter in his voice, the background noises fading as he probably went somewhere quiet to talk.

"So, what can I do for you, Cassie?"

"William Maxwell. I need to know about any international accounts he might have. We already know about one in Luxembourg, under his daughter's maiden name. If there are more that could be linked to him I need to know."

"Will do, kid. I'll get back to you as soon as I've got something."

"Check the ex-wife as well. I have a hunch she might be hiding something."

"All right, I'll call you when I find something"

"Thanks, Monty."

"Anytime, kid. Take care."

The line went dead, but I stayed frozen in time for a second, the phone still glued to my ear, my mind churning. I needed something, anything, that might help me win this case.

Knowing that I was too wrapped up in it to see clearly, I set my phone aside and padded towards the bathroom for a shower. I'd hoped the scalding hot water would cleanse my body and my mind, but fifteen minutes later I was putting on clean clothes, my relentless brain still turning over the details of the case.

Ignoring this morning's breakfast dishes still in the sink, I refilled my whiskey and plopped down on the couch to watch some reality TV.

The girls' trip my friends and I were planning in a couple of months crossed my mind. I should call Daisy to see if she wanted to go shopping together before the trip. Maxwell's case would probably be over by then, so I'd be able to truly relax.

If I somehow managed to win, then I could use this trip to celebrate, and if I lost… well, the trip would be an excellent distraction.

One of the housewives on the television screen mentioned something about Europe, and my thoughts immediately drifted back to Maxwell. I should tell Monty to check Switzerland. Like Luxembourg, it was known for discreet banking.

When I noticed where my thoughts had led me, I flipped off the TV and grabbed a book. But I caught myself staring blankly at the letters in front of me as thoughts raced through my head.

Frustrated, I tossed the book aside. At times like these, there was only one thing that would get me out of my head—a mind-blowing orgasm. I went to get my trusty vibrator, took my time scrolling through videos until I found one featuring two girls and one guy, then settled back on the couch.

I watched the video for a bit to get in the mood, letting my hands explore my soft skin before I removed my shorts and panties.

Closing my eyes, I imagined someone touching me, caressing my stomach, fingers brushing against my heavy breasts. Then, Imaginary Dude squeezed my breasts, and a gasp escaped my lips when he pinched my nipple.

He ran his palm over my taut nipple, sending shocks of pleasure to my spine. One of his hands traveled down past my hip bone to caress my inner thigh, his touch growing more daring.

Finally, he reached his goal, cupping my warm pussy, the heel of his hand teasing my clit.

For a second I was thrown out of my fantasy by the physics of how our bodies would fit on the couch, but given that he was imaginary, I let the logistics go and grabbed my vibrator from the coffee table.

Imaginary Dude ran his hands all over my skin, feeling the soft curves of my waist while his throbbing head teased my clit. I pressed the vibrator against my clit, focusing on the pleasure warming my insides. Deciding to go for a quick first orgasm, I clicked the little button on the side of my vibrator, upping the intensity to three.

I spread my legs wide open, resting my feet on the coffee table, finding my sweet spot again and pressing the vibrator right there. I told myself I would keep this position to intensify my pleasure, but my hips jerked up and down, my legs shaking as pleasure gathered in my center.

Imaginary Dude was still on top of me, his super defined eight-pack contracting and relaxing with each thrust. I was close, so close. A moan escaped me, warmth spreading all over my body.

And then, right as my body tensed, and I could no longer stop my orgasm, Maxwell's face invaded my mind. I climaxed to his puffy, red face, disgust overtaking pleasure.

Fuck no.

In a fit of anger, I put on some loud music, grabbed a wine bottle from the kitchen, and sat in front of my vanity to get ready. I knew the girls would be at Oasis tonight, and although I wasn't exactly in the mood, dancing the night away would be a good distraction from my thoughts.

In half an hour, the bottle was gone, I had done my makeup, and my long hair flowed freely down my back. I texted the group chat to confirm they were at the club. Once I got the confirmation, I slipped on a little black dress and checked my reflection in the full-length mirror.

"Perfect," I said out loud. "If my brain doesn't want to shut up, I'll soak it in alcohol and dance until it does."

If I couldn't relax at home, I would choose a night of chaos at Oasis instead.

CHAPTER TWO

Bright neon red letters flashed before my eyes as I stepped out of the taxi. Familiar and unfamiliar faces stood in line outside the club, all eager for the same thing as me.

Escape.

Oasis was the perfect place for that. The chaotic atmosphere of the club, with its flashing lights and hypnotic music, suited my brain. I was too overstimulated here for my mind to wander. I strutted towards the bouncer, infusing my steps with every bit of the confidence I wished I felt, the Maxwell case still weighing me down.

The burly man's face broke into a smile when he saw me. "Cassie! Didn't know you'd be coming tonight. The girls are already inside." He unclipped the back velvet rope and stepped aside to let me through.

"What have you been up to, Jax?" I asked, smiling back at him and deliberately ignoring the side eye I was receiving from the people waiting in line.

"Oh, you know, the usual. Fist fights, throwing people out. It's quiet so far tonight, though."

"Hope it stays that way so you won't need my services again," I said, bumping my shoulder against his massive arm.

"Could be, but I gotta say I wouldn't mind seeing you get all lawyer-y with a tight dress on again." He patted my head as if I were a five-year-old child, which made me smile despite my sour mood.

"Say that again and I'll snitch on you to the wife," I said, laughing and walking away with a wave over my shoulder.

Once inside, I smiled at the familiar surroundings, feeling at home in what had become my favorite dancing spot in New York City. It was a chic club with modern leather couches, sleek surfaces, and mirrors placed everywhere, but it was the music that did it for me. Oasis was a reggaeton club, and they always hired DJs with the sickest mixes who knew how to hype up a crowd.

I spotted my girls at the bar and danced my way to them, letting the club energy flow through me.

"Cassie! You're here!" Amelia shouted over the music, moving to make room at the bar. Daisy and Rina quickly embraced me before ordering a round of shots.

"We thought you weren't coming tonight," Rina said against my ear, scanning me up and down.

"So did I." I gave her a tight smile, not bothering to hide how I was actually feeling from Rina. She always seemed to know anyway.

I rarely went out with the girls after a trial since celebrating with my fellow lawyers was good networking. But no one on my team would be celebrating tonight.

"Want to tell me what's going on? You look about ready to jump out of your own skin."

I sighed, and leaned closer to her ear. "Stressful day at court, shitty client that I can't get off my mind. His face actually invaded my brain while I was getting off."

"Is he hot?" Rina said.

"Not one bit. Middle-aged, puffy, red faced-man." I shuddered at the memory. I definitely needed a palate cleanser before I ever got horny again.

"That's unfortunate," Rina said, trying to contain her laughter.

I hated Rina's all-seeing eye, but I had learned to accept that to her I was an open book. We'd been friends since someone farted during yoga, and we burst out laughing instead of pretending it didn't happen like everyone else.

We'd switched yoga studios in the six years since then, but the friendship remained.

The bartender lined up the shots in front of us, ending the conversation. Before he could get away, I ordered myself a gin and tonic and another round of shots for good measure.

"Someone's looking to party!" Daisy whisper-shouted into my ear. Her hand lingered on my lower back, one side of her body pressed firmly against mine.

"I don't want to think tonight," I said, enjoying the feel of my friend's body against my own. Daisy's hand traveled up and down my back, following the curve of my spine until she reached my ass.

Maybe this time Daisy would do a little more than tease me. And maybe that was exactly what I needed—a few externally sourced orgasms to wash the week's stress away.

Preferably without Maxwell's face popping into my mind and scarring me for life.

The bartender lined up the second round of shots, and we downed them. The tequila burned a delicious path down my throat, distracting me from my thoughts almost immediately.

Gin and tonic in hand, I followed Daisy onto the dance floor. We danced together, feeling the music and allowing it to dictate our movements. Daisy put on a show in front of me, shaking her ass to the beat as she grinded against me. I held her firmly at the waist with my free hand, exploring her soft curves as we moved together.

Daisy was hot, fit with a nice, round ass and small perky boobs that meant she rarely bothered with a bra. She always wore the loudest outfits, like the fuzzy, lime green cropped top and matching skirt she had on tonight, but somehow she made it work.

She turned to face me, wrapping her arms around my neck as her sky-blue eyes sparkled with mischief. We'd always tease each other while out drinking, but never really acted on it. Her pouty lips looked soft and tempting, and I wondered what she'd taste like.

Unfortunately for me, this time was no different. As soon as Rina and Amelia joined us, Daisy let go of me.

Maybe some other time, somewhere more private.

The four of us danced in a circle, moving our hips to the beat of the music, arms up in the air. A couple of guys approached, but a quick glance was enough to know that they were not my type. Daisy went off to the side with one of them. A small pang of jealousy filled my chest, but I quickly smothered it.

Tonight was about letting go of stress, not adding to it.

I set my now empty glass down, happy to dance without worrying about spilling my drink. I moved my hips slowly, my hands running up and down my body in a sensuous motion.

The small hairs on the back of my neck stood, and a familiar feeling of being observed froze the blood in my veins. I looked around the club, searching for a particular face in the crowd, relieved when I didn't find it.

Instead, I spotted a tall man watching me intently from the other side of the bar. The club was too dark for me to discern his features properly, but our eyes met for a split second, and he raised his glass before taking a long sip of his drink.

A flush of excitement crept up my chest to my cheeks. I wasn't shy, and being watched was turning me on. Since I knew his eyes were on me, I decided to give him something to look at.

I just hoped he was worth the effort.

Maybe he could be my palate cleanser, I thought.

Losing myself in the beat, I moved my body to the latin music booming out of the speakers. Amelia sang the lyrics next to me, shaking her butt against Rina's.

Emboldened by the stranger's gaze, I kept dancing, letting my hands roam all over my hips, stomach, neck. I squeezed my breasts, feeling my hard nipples through the thin material of my dress.

It felt liberating to dance like this, to let go of all my worries.

The possibility that I was driving this stranger crazy was a big bonus. I put on a show for him, shaking my ass. My little black dress rode dangerously up my thighs.

And he was still looking.

His gaze warmed my skin, but I needed to get closer and see if there was actually any potential there. I didn't want to waste my sexy moves on another Maxwell.

When the next song came on, I spotted an empty table and leaned against it, gathering my hair above my head to cool myself a little. I didn't have to turn towards the mysterious man to know he was still watching me.

I felt his eyes on me. The intensity of his gaze sent delicious shivers down my spine. I waited patiently for the flashing lights to hit the stranger so I could catch a glimpse of him.

Finally, the blue lights flickered across his frame. He was tall and muscular, definitely no Maxwell. For the moment, that was all I needed to know.

I danced with the girls for a couple more songs, shaking my ass and moving my hips to the beat. My hands traveled all over my slick skin as I danced, aiming to tease the stranger from a distance.

"I'm going to get a drink," I shouted in Rina's ear.

I danced my way through the crowd, quickly approaching the bar. As in most aspects of life, there was no point trying to bulldoze through a crowd of people to get where you wanted to go. It was much easier to go with the flow, moving and changing direction as needed.

As I leaned against the bar waiting for my turn to order, I felt a presence behind me. I knew he would come. I had been expecting him, but electricity still coursed through my veins at the sound of his deep, velvety voice against my ear.

"What's your poison?" the man asked, his solid body brushing against my back.

I turned around, positive this was the man who had been watching me dance. He was definitely hot, dark brown hair cut short at the sides and a little longer on top, with muscles that matched the dangerous energy emanating from him.

He cocked a hip against the bar, his dark eyes shamelessly roaming my body.

But there was something more, a presence to him, an aura that spoke of delicious things to come.

"You," I answered, staring straight into his piercing eyes.

A devious smirk stretched his lips, and heat pooled low in my belly in response. "That can be arranged."

I appreciated his response to my forwardness.

The bartender interrupted us, all of her attention on the man standing beside me. I couldn't blame her. He was truly breathtaking.

The stranger kept his attention on me, which definitely stroked my ego.

"Gin and tonic, please," I said, turning to face her.

"Dalmore neat, please," he added, his eyes still on me. His large hand landed on my lower back as he pulled me a little closer. There was no hesitation. He wanted to touch me and he did.

It was a very promising start.

While he handed the bartender his black card, I took my time checking him out. He wore black suit pants that hugged his muscular thighs and lean hips. He'd rolled the sleeves of his light blue shirt up to his elbows, revealing muscular forearms and a silver Zenith watch.

It was clear he was wealthy, and not the typical flashy Wall Street guy that usually came to Oasis. He had the quiet self-assurance of a person who knew exactly what and who he was.

Not that I was complaining. I loved a confident man, especially when he could back it up, which was still to be determined.

The stranger focused his eyes back on me, his gaze lingering on my lips for a second before he leaned down. "I'm James," he whispered in my ear, wrapping his hands around one of mine in a firm handshake.

Deciding to play the game, I turned and pushed my boobs against his solid chest. "Nice to meet you, James," I purred, making sure that my lips brushed against the shell of his ear.

James leaned back to take me in, one eyebrow raised in question. He must have been expecting my name.

It was much easier to live for tonight if tomorrow never really came.

As long as he didn't know my name, we could remain two strangers who met at Oasis and had a good time together. Then tomorrow we could move on with our real lives with only the memory of what we shared.

No expectations. No disappointments.

His grip on my waist tightened. "Were you dancing just for me?" he whispered in my ear. His warm breath on my neck sent a wave of pleasure down my spine.

I nodded, feeling his thumb graze my hip bone. "Did you enjoy it?" His touch was already doing crazy things to my body. I just wanted him to go further, to touch me where it ached.

James's eyes darkened in response, a cocky smirk appearing on his lips. "Enjoy is not exactly how I'd put it." He grasped my hips and pulled me towards him, pressing his rock hard cock against my belly.

The bartender handed us our drinks, and James lifted his glass to meet mine, his eyes never leaving my own. "To you, Jane Doe."

I watched, mesmerized, as he tipped the glass against his lips, his throat working as he swallowed the contents in one go.

Refusing to be outmatched, I lifted my glass. "To tonight," I said and downed my drink too, enjoying the satisfaction I saw in his eyes. Then I grabbed his hand and headed towards the dance floor, ready for the fun to begin.

CHAPTER THREE

W e stood toe to toe, his hands gripping my hips as we swayed to the beat.

I was a little impressed because the stranger had rhythm—no awkward side-to-side step in sight. Instead, his hips mirrored mine, his hard cock brushing against my stomach with each movement.

In my experience, a man who could dance could fuck, so at least things were looking up for tonight.

I spotted my friends behind him, and the three of them gave me thumbs up. My lips stretched into a smile at their silliness, but it quickly faded when I glanced up and saw the stranger's dark gaze focused on my lips.

James pulled me closer to him, wedging one muscular thigh between my legs. I felt my heart beat down there as I shamelessly grinded against his leg. His hand landed on my ass, guiding my movements.

He nibbled my earlobe, his hot breath sending a jolt of electricity down my spine. "If I check right now, will I find you ready for me?"

I wrapped my hands around his neck, running my nails across his nape. "I don't know. I guess you'll have to check."

James squeezed my ass, and his hand moved a little lower. I bit my lip, adrenaline coursing through my veins as his fingers trailed along the hem of my dress. Shivers ran down my spine when he finally slipped his hand beneath my dress, cupping my pussy from behind.

Jesus.

I gasped against his neck, and pressed myself closer to his solid body. Eager to tease him, I ran my teeth over his neck, inhaling his delicious scent. He smelled like a mix of clean clothes and whatever cologne he was wearing, despite the fact we were surrounded by sweaty bodies.

James growled in my ear, his fingers finding my center over my thin lace thong. "Fuck, you are wet."

I bit his earlobe, then ran my tongue down his neck. "I know."

James pulled me impossibly closer, our bodies melding together as we danced. He wrapped my long hair in his fist, pulling my head back, his searing gaze focused on my lips. I smiled, then trapped his bottom lip between my teeth. He growled again, the sound making my pussy quiver.

A probing finger pressed against my slit over my thong, driving me crazy. Then he plunged his tongue in my mouth in a sizzling kiss. I saw stars. He tasted like whiskey, and each flick of his tongue against mine made me want more.

It dawned on me that we were at Oasis, in the middle of the dance floor, surrounded by people, and in a very compromising position. But I couldn't care less. I felt wild and completely in tune with this stranger.

We kissed, everything else fading as our hands touched whatever they could in a passionate frenzy. I wanted to climb him, or better yet have him climb me, invade my personal space inside and out, and crush me with his weight.

Everyone else faded.

His large cock strained against his pants, begging to be released. I longed for it, to feel him drive deep inside of me. I wanted him to make me forget this terrible day, to make me forget everything.

He gripped my hips tighter, pushing his bulge into my stomach. "If you keep this up I might have to fuck you right here."

I bit my lower lip in anticipation, reaching down to trace his throbbing head with my fingertips. "I'm okay with that," I whispered back.

James must have read my mind, because he quickly disentangled us and led me to an empty hallway. He pressed me against the wall, his larger frame holding me firmly in place and completely shielding me from curious looks. At five-eight, I wasn't exactly short, but he still managed to dwarf me. The bastard leaned down to nibble my ear, and I was a goner, shamelessly rubbing my throbbing pussy against his thigh.

"What's your name?" he asked, his voice rougher than I'd expected.

I sucked on his neck in response, probably leaving a mark. Then I traced his length with my fingers, squeezing his head over the soft fabric of his pants. He thrust into my hand, while his own hand caressed my ass.

I lifted one leg to give him better access, and he didn't hesitate to cup my pussy from behind. His long finger traced my slit before he nudged my panties to the side and he wasted no time pushing it inside of me.

The music flowed through the speakers, the bass causing the wall behind me to vibrate. James, the cheeky bastard, pumped his finger in time with the music, the steady rhythm driving me wild. He traced my lips with his tongue before consuming me with a kiss while I clawed at his back, blind with pleasure.

His other hand traveled from my hips to my full breasts, his thumb brushing against my nipple piercing. He pulled back, one eyebrow raised in question. "I didn't notice this before."

I couldn't answer because he chose that moment to switch things up. His finger slipped out of me and coated my pussy in my juices. He circled my clit, still following the rhythm of the reggaeton music bleeding from the speakers.

He was driving me crazy. I pulled him back to me, kissing him wildly. I fisted his shirt when he pinched my nipple, annoyed that I couldn't touch more of him. He pushed two fingers inside of me and pressed down on my clit with his thumb, making me see stars.

My head lolled back against the wall as I panted, but James gave me no reprieve. His fingers curled inside of me, finding my G-spot.

All I could do was hang on to his broad shoulders as this hunk of a man fingered me to climax.

This wasn't my first rodeo, but doing this in public only added to the thrill.

My legs started shaking, and if it wasn't for his hard body pressed firmly against mine, I was sure I'd crumble to the floor.

James kept teasing my pierced nipple, softly brushing it with his thumb, squeezing the hard peak until my pussy pulsed around his fingers. "Come for me, gorgeous," he whispered. He nibbled on my neck, his tongue darting out to lick the sensitive spot behind my ear.

I gripped his ass, lost in pleasure as my walls closed in around his fingers, warmth spreading all over my body until I couldn't take it anymore. I came all over his hand, biting down on his neck to smother my moans.

"Good girl," he growled, his thumb still softly massaging my clit, his fingers still pumping slowly inside of me.

I wished it was his dick instead. It felt surreal that this man I had never met before got me to orgasm in a dark corner of Oasis using only his fingers.

James removed his fingers from my pussy and licked them clean, staring right at me. "I'm not done with you yet," he said as he sucked on my juices.

I smiled at the sight, biting down on my lip as naughty idea after naughty idea sparked in my mind.

I had chosen my palate cleanser well and I wasn't done with him either.

CHAPTER FOUR

James held me in his arms until my orgasm faded and my legs stopped trembling. I needed a drink to cool off, but his erection pressing against my thigh was more tempting. Besides, I couldn't leave him hanging like that.

I grabbed his hand, intending to pull him towards the storage room, but he surprised me by bringing my fingers to his lips and gently kissing my knuckles. Our eyes met, both filled with lust, but I thought I saw something else in there. As if he was slightly confused, yet also amused.

For a second, it felt like he *saw* me, a feeling I didn't quite like. I didn't need to be seen, I needed to be fucked. Hard.

I ignored his tender gesture and gave in to my more primal and immediate desires. With his hand still firmly in mine, I led us to the storage room I'd found by accident last year. Luckily, it was both unlocked and unoccupied.

The moment the door closed behind us, James pushed my body against it, his massive body completely drowning me. He bent down, his lips exploring my neck as his hands came to rest firmly on my ass.

I was lost in sensation, enjoying every bit of pleasure he extracted from my body. But I wasn't content just being on the receiving end. I palmed his massive dick through his pants, squeezing his hard length. His sharp intake of breath made me want to please him more, to tease him until he couldn't take it anymore.

But there was no time for that. We were both too horny and desperate for release to draw this out any longer. Or at least, I was.

Eagerly, I undid his button and zipper, pulling his cock out of his boxers before pushing them down. I smiled to myself at the sight before me, pleased with his dick. It was thick and veiny, and a drop of pre-cum escaped from the head as I slowly worked my hand up and down his shaft.

"Like what you see?"

"I'm not disappointed yet," I teased, biting my lip.

"If you were mine I'd punish you for that," he growled before digging his teeth into the sensitive skin at the base of my throat.

A moan escaped my lips in response, and I squeezed his shaft a little tighter.

With a featherlight touch, James trailed his fingers across my shoulders and lowered the straps of my dress, exposing my large breasts. "Gorgeous," he murmured almost to himself.

Goosebumps rose all over my skin as his breath fanned my pierced nipple, my back arching as my body demanded more. I moaned as he played with my nipple with his tongue, nibbling it with his teeth, sucking it into his mouth. It felt like there was a line connecting my boobs to my center, each lick sending delicious jolts of pleasure straight to my clit.

James groaned against my skin as I tightened my grip and stroked his cock faster. His reaction to my touch made me even hornier. I'd been wet before, but now I could feel my arousal dripping down my thighs.

He continued his exploration, moving from one breast to the other until I needed his dick inside of me, like *yesterday*. I needed to come again. He was teasing me into insanity but it wasn't enough. I wanted more.

Lost in pleasure, I could no longer concentrate on pumping his cock. I caressed the engorged head, spreading pre-cum over the sensitive spot just below it. His fingers trailed down my body, slipping under my dress to pull down my thong. He stepped back a fraction and bent down to drag the fabric down my legs. Once I stepped out of my panties, he sniffed them before shoving them in his pocket.

Fuck, that was hot.

"Condom," I said firmly, as he pushed to his feet. Men always thought they could get away with going raw if they said they didn't have a condom, that they didn't think they were going to be lucky enough to find a girl to fuck.

I was too busy a woman to have to deal with venereal diseases, or worse, an unwanted pregnancy. I liked to be careful, despite the fact that I was on birth control.

The thought of wrapping my lips around his thick shaft made my mouth water, but I'd never do that to some random stranger I'd met at Oasis. Despite how much I wanted to, it wasn't worth the risk.

To my surprise, James immediately pulled a condom from his pocket. I smiled as I watched him roll it over his considerable length, eager to feel his thick cock stretching me out.

Once he was sheathed, he grabbed my ass and lifted me onto a table so my pussy was level with his dick. He teased me, rubbing his length all over my swollen lips, hitting my clit with his head over and over until I couldn't take it any longer.

I reached for his thick, hard cock and placed it at my entry, making my intentions clear. He complied, slowly pushing his dick inside of me until I could feel his heavy balls hitting my ass.

I closed my eyes in pure bliss, relishing in the feeling of fullness that only a good dick can give.

"Look at me," he said when he was fully inside of me.

I opened my eyes to find him watching me intently, his dark brown eyes burning with desire. He started pumping slowly, squeezing my breasts and pinching my pierced nipple in time with his thrusts.

Reaching for him, I unbuttoned his blue shirt, curious to see more of him, eager to feel his warm skin against my fingers. Finally, I pushed his shirt off his shoulders, revealing his glorious chest.

"Wow," I gasped, feeling like a complete dork at my reaction. A smattering of dark hair covered his muscular chest, and I reached forward to trace his pecs before drawing him closer to suck one round nipple into my mouth.

The sight of his abs contracting with each thrust drove me wild. I licked his chest, then wrapped my lips around his nipple again, nibbling and sucking on the hard peak. He groaned, which only spurred me on more.

I wanted to give him as much pleasure as I was receiving.

Wrapping my legs around him, I pulled him even closer. Our lips met in a passionate kiss, our tongues dancing together in perfect harmony. I couldn't remember the last time I'd been kissed with so much intensity, so much passion. But everything about this stranger seemed to be intense.

He cupped my face, softly caressing my jawline. I sucked his thumb into my mouth, and licked it as if it were his dick.

He growled. "Damn it, woman, you're driving me crazy."

I grinned at his comment, then continued playing with his finger, swirling my tongue around it before sucking it into my mouth until he lost his rhythm. He pushed his finger down, testing my gag reflex, but I kept at it while staring into his eyes.

James was beyond attractive, his hard jaw tense, his lips parted as he struggled to catch his breath. But it was his eyes that fascinated me, the expression in them unguarded, filled with lust. It turned me on even more knowing how much this striking stranger wanted me.

Scratching a path down his back, I grabbed his ass, digging my nails into the hard muscle. He groaned and started pumping into me faster, harder. He had to hold me in place to keep me from slipping off the table, his fingers digging almost painfully into my hips.

In one move, he pulled out, picked me up, set me on my feet, turned me around, and entered me again from behind. My body folded itself onto the table from the intensity of pleasure this new angle afforded. The surface beneath me was a little sticky but I didn't care.

I held on to the edge of the table as he pounded into me mercilessly, each powerful thrust sending me into a frenzy of pleasure. He grabbed my ass, squeezing it in his hand, then he parted my cheeks, his fingers coming dangerously close to….

I was too far gone to protest when he started messaging *that* hole. Instead, I relished the feeling of his finger caressing the puckered hole. I enjoyed it even more when he slowly pushed his thumb in. In this moment in time, my body was his, and he was skillfully extracting every bit of pleasure from it.

"Oh God," I whispered as I took a deep, ragged breath. It felt too good.

James slapped my ass and growled, "Not God. James."

I smiled and wanted to roll my eyes at his words, and if it were any other guy, I would. But James's cockiness and confidence were backed up by his skills. "James," I moaned instead.

He let out a guttural cry as his name passed my lips, and I squeezed my inner muscles in response. It was frustrating not to be able to see or touch him, but I felt every little movement he made, enjoyed every touch, every caress. And every moan and growl I elicited out of him only made me want him more.

"Tell me your name," he said in a rough tone, his free hand gripping my hip so hard I was sure I'd have a bruise in the morning.

I heard him but pretended not to. I was close, so close.

"Tell me your name," he repeated. Wrapping my long hair around his fist, he pulled me towards him, arching my back until our faces were inches apart. He was demanding a response, staring me down until I caved, but I was an experienced negotiator. He couldn't intimidate me into replying.

"I like the anonymity," I said in between pants.

James's eyes glazed over as he took in my flushed face, his breath coming out in short pants. "Fuck, you're gorgeous," he grunted. "I want your name on my lips when I empty myself inside of you."

Something deep inside me, maybe that primitive urge to have a man shoot his cum inside my pussy, made me want to cave. To tell him my name, to have him yell it as he came undone.

But I was too stubborn to listen to it. I liked one night stands, and had no desire to see him beyond tonight. There was no need for him to know my name.

James stared me down, his breath heavy as he thrust at a punishing pace. My pussy spasmed around his cock, my body tensing in preparation for sweet release.

"I won't let you come unless you tell me your name," he growled.

I was so close to pure bliss, it was hard to form coherent sentences. When I still didn't reply, he slowed down and the orgasm I'd been chasing slipped through my fingertips. But if this was the game he wanted to play, I'd gladly play it.

CHAPTER FIVE

James's presence overwhelmed all my senses. My ears were trained on his ragged breaths, eager to hear his small grunts and groans and the filthy things escaping his sculpted lips. Around us a faint smell of alcohol lingered in the air, but my focus was on the rich sandalwood and amber hints of his cologne. He had his cock deep inside me, his thumb in my ass, and his left hand holding me firmly at the waist. And it still wasn't enough.

I wanted more, so much more.

He slowly removed his thumb from my asshole and said, "I'll play with this hole some other time."

His sentence brought me back to the present. This jerk was refusing me an orgasm just to get my name, and now he had the audacity to imply we would hook up again? That would never happen.

"You should make the best of the here and now," I said, rocking my hips.

He started moving agonizingly slowly, his left hand snaking around me to tease my clit. "I intend to, trust me, but first I need your name."

I was so close, my body begging for release, but there was no way I could come at this pace, and he knew it. My hips moved to meet his cock in a desperate attempt to make him move faster, harder. But he resisted.

"Please, James," I begged, my legs trembling under me.

James caressed my back, running his fingers over my spine. I arched to meet his touch, and he bent over me, scattering wet kisses across my shoulders, nibbling and sucking on my neck. I undulated my hips to increase the friction, biting down on my own arm, desperate for climax.

He drew tight circles over my sensitive bud, increasing the pressure. Once more I felt my orgasm coming, my walls vibrating against his dick. James let go of my clit and stopped touching me altogether except for his dick.

Then he pulled almost all the way out before slamming back into me.

"James!" I screamed. This was torture.

He pulled out again only to roughly slam into me, his heavy balls slapping against my pussy. I thought he must be desperate to come too, but he kept doing the same thing. Over and over.

"Your name."

I whimpered, but gave no reply.

The bastard chuckled, the sound making me quiver. He knew how eager I was to come and he was playing his hand like a pro. That turned me on even more, if that was possible.

This time, when he drew back he pulled out all the way. I looked back in question but the bastard just smirked at me before fisting his cock and slowly pumping while he watched me.

My eyes widened at the sight of his hand wrapped around his magnificent cock. This man was too hot to resist, but I still had a little fight in me. I reached down to tease my clit, his dark eyes following my every movement.

He immediately moved my hand away, using his own hand to rub my clit. "Tonight your pleasure is mine."

"Then give it to me." There was an undeniable challenge in my voice, one that I knew he'd take.

Placing his dick back at my entry, he spread my juices all over my asshole, lubricating the puckered hole. I raised an eyebrow in question. As much as I would like a good ass pounding, I needed prep time to fully enjoy it.

James spread my asshole open with his thumb before pushing it in. I gasped at the sensation as he fucked my ass with his thumb and rubbed the heel of his left hand oh so slowly against my clit.

"Some other time, I'm gonna fuck your ass so hard you'll feel me for a week. But for now, I want your pussy."

With that, he pushed back inside of me to the hilt. All I could do was whimper when he started pounding into me again, but this time he didn't hold me in place.

My knuckles turned white as I struggled to hold on to the table. "Oh God!" I yelled, as my inner walls contracted around his cock.

"Name," he whispered in between heavy breaths.

When I refused to reply again, he pinched my clit, making me see stars. My legs gave out for a second before I recovered, but I still didn't cave.

"I'm not letting you come until I have your name, gorgeous. I can do this all night."

I whimpered, biting down on my lip so hard I tasted blood. I knew he was bluffing. No man could keep this up all night. I squeezed my inner muscles around him to tell him just that.

"Fuck," he growled, his fingers pressing down on my clit. "I can tell you're close." His voice cut through the haze like glass. "Give me your name and I won't stop. I want to feel you come all over my dick."

My body started shaking, my walls squeezing him tight.

"Cassandra," I finally relented, holding on to the table for dear life.

"Cassandra," he whispered, as if he were savoring the name in his mouth. "Is that your real name?"

"Yes," I moaned.

"Yes, it's your real name, or yes, as in, 'yes, keep doing what you're doing?'"

"Both," I answered, a chuckle escaping my lips. I couldn't believe I was laughing while this stranger denied me orgasms in a club storage room. It was exactly what I needed but never expected to happen. No random guy had ever made me feel this good.

True to his word, James kept his pace at first, but he soon lost control as he drove deeper inside of me.

It was pure bliss to feel him shudder with pleasure, to know that I did that to him. My walls closed around him, squeezing his cock as liquid fire filled my veins.

James wrapped my hair around his fist, pulling my face towards him as he folded himself over me. "Come on my cock, Cassandra."

My legs gave out from under me, and he had to remove his thumb from my ass to hold me up. Heat spread all over my body, burning my insides as I came almost on command. I closed my eyes, but James pulled on my hair.

"Eyes on me," he said roughly as I exploded around him.

My vision blurred but I obeyed, watching him watch me as wave after wave of pleasure took over my body. He held me in place, one finger still lazily grazing over my clit as he pounded into me.

He didn't last long after that, and I couldn't blame him. A loud groan escaped his lips as his thrusts became more erratic, his fingers digging into my hips. I felt him tense and shudder behind me, before he lifted my hips and buried himself deeper.

"Cassandra," he whispered over and over as he emptied himself deep inside of me.

He stayed inside me for a moment while he recovered, both of us panting and unable to move. Eventually he pulled out, the feeling of his dick sliding out of me making me whimper. James carefully removed the condom and placed it on an empty table next to us.

Then, he picked me up and sat me on the table facing him. I didn't think I could walk.

"Are you okay?" he asked, running his hands up and down my thighs.

"Yes," I whispered, looking up at him. This stranger who had just fucked me into telling him my name looked so beautiful I had to blink twice. I took in his large frame, tousled hair, strong jaw, full lips swollen from our kisses… and those eyes. His eyes were glazed over, still looking at me with pure lust, but there was something else. Something that scared me to my core.

James placed himself between my legs and kissed me gently, his lips barely brushing against mine. I planted my hand on his muscular chest, feeling his heart beat wildly against my palm.

"I don't have anything to clean you up," he said, cupping my jaw.

His words snapped me out of whatever post-mind-blowing-orgasm daze I was under.

"That's okay, I'll take care of it in the bathroom."

James nodded, gathering the bunched up material of my dress that sat at my waist. He pulled the straps over my arms, adjusting them at my shoulders. Then he grabbed my underwear from his pocket and helped me put them back on, his eyes roaming over my pussy.

Before we could leave the room, he pressed me against the door. We kissed, and it felt like I could kiss him forever, every day of my life, and never get sick of his taste.

I shook it off and pulled him away to open the door.

Music still played loudly while a mass of people danced the night away. It was almost jarring for the world outside the door to have remained the same while I felt like my own world had forever been altered.

Ridiculous. It's just a hookup.

I pointed towards the restroom, and James followed close behind me. In the bathroom, I locked myself in a stall and took my time peeing and cleaning up, waiting for my traitorous heart to come back to its senses.

I half hoped that when I came out James would be gone, but I doubted it. He was too intense. Too into me, especially for a random hookup. The bathroom had two entries, so I exited through the other one and quickly made my way out of the club.

James was truly the perfect palate cleanser. I hadn't thought about Maxwell and my shattered career at all. But his perfection hinged on the shortness of our encounter, and seeing him again might break the spell. That was the magic of one night stands—no complications.

CHAPTER SIX

I t only took a five-minute conversation with Monty to confirm that I had lost the case. It had taken him two weeks to track Maxwell's international transactions, and although he wasn't done digging, what he'd found was enough to put the nail in the coffin.

I hung up feeling dejected. My first high-profile case would be a bust. This would add at least a couple of years to my goal of becoming partner. I swiveled my chair to face the lonely window, trying to catch a glimpse of blue sky past the gray buildings. But it was no use. Someday I'd have a big office with a panoramic view of the city.

Since that day was not today, there was nothing to do except go back to work. I lowered my head and dove into it, reviewing a settlement agreement for an insider trading case. A few hours later, Olivia, the legal assistant I shared with two other associates, called and announced my next appointment was here. I checked my calendar—James Walton, seven DUIs.

I sighed. Just another run-of-the-mill case.

I stood to open the door to let him in, but the moment the door swung open, I froze. James. It had been two weeks and I had almost completely forgotten his existence. Almost, but not quite. The guy from the club had been starring in my solo times ever since that night. And now he was standing right outside my office, casually chatting with a very flustered Olivia.

Hot red anger took over my entire body. It took everything I had not to call security and have him thrown out of the building. This could not be a coincidence. Out of all the lawyers in New York, he wouldn't just randomly walk into my office.

"Mr. Walton," I said in my most professional voice, offering him my hand. He took it in his big warm hand, and a strange feeling traveled from my palm to my core. *This is not the time to be turned on*, I reminded myself. "If you'll follow me, please."

I led him into my office, shutting the door the minute he was inside. The last thing I needed was my personal and professional life mixing. I took my time sitting behind my desk, noting James didn't wait for an invitation to sit down.

"Mr. Walton, what can I do for you today?"

"I think that after what happened the last time we saw each other, we can be on a first name basis. Please, call me James." He nonchalantly crossed his ankle over the top of his knee, as if his presence in my office was completely normal and expected. "It's nice to officially meet you, Cassandra."

My name rolled off his tongue in a way that almost felt like a caress.

"All right then, James," I started. "Now that we're through with pleasantries, why are you really here? I assume it has nothing to do with DUIs." I closed the bogus file and placed it neatly on my desk.

"You assume correctly. It took me two weeks to find you. There are a surprisingly high number of Cassandras in New York, did you know? But now that I have you in front of me, it was all worth it." He flashed me a mischievous smile, and his long fingers coming to rest on his muscular thigh almost distracted me.

"I'm not sure it *was* worth it, Mr. Walton. I really don't have time for this, so let's cut to the chase. What do you want?"

"You."

I laughed, incredulous. He didn't seem to find it funny, though, his piercing eyes never leaving my face. "I'm afraid I'm not on the table, Mr. Walton."

"James," he repeated, his jaw clenching. "Let me ask you this, did you enjoy yourself at Oasis that night?" I opened my mouth to speak, but he cut me off before I could get a word out. "And don't lie, your body betrays you."

I narrowed my eyes at him, anger getting the best of me. This intrusion in my place of work was unacceptable. The only thing I wanted right now was to get rid of him. "I always enjoy myself at Oasis, regardless of your presence."

James Walton stared at me for what seemed like forever, waiting for me to cave and say whatever it was that he wanted to hear. But I wouldn't be so easily swayed, even if the smell of his cologne and his intense stare were making me all hot and bothered.

Eventually, he was the one to cave. I had to fight to prevent a satisfied smile from taking over as he spoke.

"Cards on the table. I want you. Since that night, I haven't been able to stop thinking about you and how it felt to be inside of you. I went out of my way to find you because fantasizing about you wasn't enough, so now here I am."

I was flattered, but not enough to overlook how creepy his behavior was. "You do know that this is stalking, right?"

He uncrossed his legs and leaned forward, staring straight into my eyes. "I don't care. I know what I want and I want you."

"And if I said I didn't want you?"

"Then you'd be lying."

The truth behind his statement gave me pause.

This man was strikingly handsome, but that seemed like a mere bonus on top of his skills in the bedroom, or storage room more precisely. It wasn't often that I hooked up with a guy who could make me come the first time we had sex. Usually, it took a bit of coaching and gentle instruction.

It would be nice to be with someone who knew what they were doing. That night at the club it had become very clear that we had a lot of sexual chemistry, and judging by the way my body was responding to his presence right now, that chemistry was still around.

"Are you in the habit of stalking all the women you hook up with?"

A slow smirk crept over his face, his dark eyes twinkling with amusement. "Only the unforgettable ones."

I stared at him, wondering if he was trying flattery to win me over. But there was something about him, the way his gaze seemed completely unguarded, that made me believe him. "I don't want a relationship," I finally said, not breaking eye contact.

"We can work around that." His satisfied smirk almost made me double back, but I pressed on with negotiations.

"What exactly are you proposing?"

"Friends with benefits, with an option for a relationship down the road if we feel like it."

"I just said I don't want a relationship."

"I heard you. I just wanted to make my intentions clear. I want you. I've thought about you nonstop since that night at the club. Maybe friends with benefits won't work, but maybe it will. And maybe you'll see how good we are together and change your mind."

"And if I don't? Am I going to be filing a restraining order in the near future?"

James laughed heartily at that, but I kept my expression serious despite how infectious his laughter was.

When he realized I was serious, he gave me a puzzled look. "No. I want you, and I want you to give me a chance. But if it doesn't work, if you truly don't want me, I won't bother you anymore. I'll have to stick to jerking off to you in the shower. I'm sure you'll leave me with some glorious memories to refer back to, maybe some naughty pictures."

I smiled despite my resolution not to give in. I had no idea if he was being honest, but if he was, I certainly liked his direct approach.

"How did you find me?" I finally asked. The question had been burning on my tongue since I'd first seen him outside my office, chatting up my secretary. He hesitated, which put me on my guard once more. "This won't work at all if you're not honest with me."

"I saw you on the news," he admitted. "Imagine my surprise when the woman I'd been jerking to just popped up on my TV. I nearly choked on my coffee when I saw you."

"That didn't take a lot of effort," I said, remembering he said he 'went out of his way.' A chance glance at a screen hardly seemed like hard work.

His lips quirked into a smirk. "I saw you, but I didn't catch your name or the case you were working on. Then, when my mind kept drifting to you, I caved and hired a PI to find you."

My hackles were definitely raised. I knew how private investigators worked. They rarely stopped digging until they found some dirt. "I'm assuming you have a little manila folder with my name on it. What else did you uncover?"

He cocked his head to one side, assessing me with curiosity. "That's an interesting question, Miss Leigh. Have you got anything to hide?"

"The way I see it, Mr. Walton, everyone has something to hide."

"There's no manila folder. I found out where you worked and stopped there. I'd rather get to know you myself than read some summary of your life." He stared at me some more, but I said nothing. "Do we have a deal?"

"Yes," I said, still on my guard but somewhat satisfied with his explanation. "Friends with benefits, but don't try to blur the lines." I reached out my hand for him to shake. James quickly enveloped my small hand in his, that pesky electric current traveling all the way to my core once more.

Then he surprised me by pulling me to a standing position and tugging me forward, bending my body over the desk. "A kiss to seal the deal would be more appropriate, don't you think?"

I licked my lips in anticipation before leaning closer to him. James stood, and our lips met over my desk. He bit my bottom lip, tracing it with his tongue before plunging it inside my mouth.

James held my face, his fingers delicately tracing my jaw, my cheekbones. The soft touch took me by surprise, but it was in no way unwelcome. My body immediately responded, warmth spreading all over my skin.

This gave me an idea—a naughty idea that I was sure he would appreciate.

I pulled back, amused at the disappointed look on his face. When I made my way to the door, James took it as his cue to leave, but froze in his steps when he saw me turning the lock. There was no mistaking the lust in his eyes, and I very much intended to capitalize on that.

"I still have fifteen minutes before my next meeting," I said, my voice coming out breathier than I intended. I leaned against the door and scanned him up and down, biting down on my lip. "Do you think you can deliver?"

James's smile lit up his entire face. He stalked toward me like a starved predator, and I was his very willing prey, ready to be devoured. "I'm always up for a challenge, gorgeous."

Pressing me up against the door, James pushed his hard body against mine, his hands firmly on my waist. I could feel every hard muscle that I knew was underneath his designer shirt, and I couldn't wait to see it in proper lighting.

He kissed me once more, but this was different. He'd been holding back before, but now he explored my mouth like the expert he was. A moan escaped me, and I had to remind myself that I was at work.

I pressed my palms against his chest, making my way to his shoulders to remove his suit jacket. He got the hint and shrugged out of it, his lips never leaving my own. Time was of the essence, so I palmed his crotch, satisfied to find him hard and ready for me.

James started kissing down my jaw, sucking the sensitive skin of my neck. I closed my eyes and leaned my head back against the door, giving him full access. His hands traveled towards my breasts, and I had to suppress a groan as he squeezed them. He expertly undid the first two buttons of my blouse, pushing the material aside to expose my lacy black bra.

He groaned when he saw it, his head immediately coming down between my full breasts. His tongue traveled a slow path along the seam of my bra, up to my shoulder, his teeth grazing my skin as he pulled the strap down. He pulled my bra down, revealing my pierced nipple, his tongue darting out to flick it.

I had to rub my legs together to control myself while he played with my nipple, my breaths coming in short pants.

Finally, he pushed my skirt up and cupped my pussy, the heel of his large hand putting delicious pressure against my throbbing clit.

"One more thing. This…," he said, his voice gravelly with

desire. "For as long as we're doing this, this pussy is mine and mine only. I don't like to share."

"That's too much of a commitment, James," I managed to say.

We stared into each other's eyes for a beat, both unwilling to back down.

But James had more pressing matters in mind. He got on his knees in front of me and slowly kissed a path up my leg. Then, he bunched my pencil skirt up around my hips as he nibbled at the sensitive skin of my inner thigh.

My pussy throbbed in anticipation. I couldn't take it anymore. I needed more. "I said fifteen minutes, James. I really don't have all day."

He smirked at my impatience but delivered anyway. Hooking his thumbs into my panties, he pulled them down my legs. I stepped out of them before leaning against the door again, needing it to support my weight.

James blew on my sensitive skin, making my pussy quiver. He lifted one of my legs onto his shoulder, his hand coming up to grip my ass. The cheeky bastard gave me one final smirk before sucking my clit into his mouth. Stars immediately clouded my vision at the intense pleasure.

He released my clit to give me a long lick, and I had to suppress a groan as he sampled me with his hot mouth. "You're so wet, and it's all for me." He sounded so proud of himself that my first instinct was to disagree with him somehow, but I didn't get a chance.

James's tongue flicked my clit over and over until all I could do was dig my fingernails into his shoulder while my other hand gripped his hair to keep him exactly where he was. My whole body felt like it was on fire, my pussy quivering against his mouth while my heart beat a mile a minute.

Heat gathered in my center as my body tensed, my orgasm fast approaching. James kept his pace, flicking my clit over and over, driving me insane. I put my hand in my mouth to smother my moans at the exact moment James pushed two fingers inside of me.

He flicked his fingers until he found my G-spot. My legs nearly gave out under me when he did. This was exactly why I had decided to give him a chance. It was rare to find a man who knew what he was doing down there, and James definitely knew his way around.

The combination of his fingers inside me and his warm mouth on my clit sent me over the edge, wave after wave of pleasure hitting me with force. I bit my hand to stop myself from moaning out loud, my entire body trembling as James kept licking my clit. I tried to push him away, overwhelmed with pleasure, but he kept his lips on me, softly licking the sensitive bud until my orgasm faded away.

Finally, he emerged from between my legs, his full lips glistening with my arousal. He slowly removed his fingers from my pussy and brought them to his mouth, cleaning them with his tongue. My legs buckled at the sight of this extremely hot man kneeling at my feet, his eyes filled with pure lust.

"Challenge completed," he said, a dazzling smirk on his cum covered lips. He lowered my leg, put my panties back in place, and adjusted my skirt before he stood again. I watched, mesmerized, as he buttoned my blouse with trembling fingers.

"Not completed yet," I said. My voice sounded foreign to my ears, all breathy and hoarse. I grabbed his very hard cock over his pants, but he quickly pushed my hand away.

"This was about you. Tonight we can make it about me, and then you again." He kissed me before I could protest. "And again." I tasted myself on his lips, and the thought of where his mouth had been had pleasure coiling tightly in my core.

I pressed my legs together to control myself, my brain finally catching on to his words. "I can't tonight, I'm busy."

He shook his head, and when he spoke, his voice held a tone of finality. "Tonight."

"I have a busy week. Friday night is the best I can do."

"Tonight." He nibbled on my ear, maybe trying to distract me or use his expert tongue to convince me to change my mind. But as good as he was, I wouldn't budge on this.

"This isn't a negotiation, you know."

James took a step back, his eyes traveling over my face. "I know. I'll pick you up at seven tonight."

I pushed him back, walked around him, and leaned forward to

grab his jacket from the floor. "I am busy tonight, and every other night until Friday. Take it or leave it."

"And," he said, taking the jacket from my hands, "I will pick you up tonight, at seven."

Another thought occurred to me. "Pick me up where? You don't even know where I live."

He flashed me a devious smirk. "Don't underestimate me, gorgeous."

I stared at him dumbfounded, unsure if he was joking or not. "Should I circle back to our talk about stalking?"

"No need, but I *will* see you tonight."

I narrowed my eyes at him, unable to resist smiling at the cocky smirk plastered on his face. "You can come over tonight, but I guarantee you I will not be there. You're welcome to wait outside until I decide to come home, though." I made my way to the door and unlocked it. He watched me with an incredulous look on his face. "Your fifteen minutes are up. I'll see you on Friday." I pushed the door open to stop him from arguing any further.

James paused at the door, giving me a curious look. He clearly wasn't used to hearing the word no. I was more than glad to give him the opportunity to practice managing his disappointment.

He seemed to know when the battle was lost, though. "Friday, seven p.m." He leaned down and planted a kiss on my cheek.

Olivia stared at him with stars in her eyes as he walked by. She almost melted on the spot when he smiled at her and wished her a good day. "New client?" she asked, curiosity burning in her eyes.

"More like an old acquaintance," I explained. She clearly didn't believe me, but I escaped back into my office before she had the chance to say anything else.

Now that he was gone, and my brain was once more in control of my body, the familiar waves of panic seeped into my veins.

He found me. He'd hired a PI and easily found me.

I knew that my job would eventually put me in the spotlight if I was successful. But that was a risk I had been willing to take. I had been careful throughout college, avoiding having my picture taken, not having any social media presence....

It had been seven years since I last saw Andrew. Maybe I had become too careless, too comfortable in my new life.

Stop, I told myself. There was no point in panicking.

My office was too small. It became harder to breathe, my lungs too big for my chest. Sweat gathered on my brow, and my hands started to shake.

I needed to regain control. To calm down.

Breathe, I told myself. *Just breathe.*

Sitting on my chair, I closed my eyes and focused on my breath until the familiar waves of panic subsided. But a part of me wondered whether I had just made a huge mistake.

CHAPTER SEVEN

It took me a moment to recover after James left my office, not only because of my close call with a panic attack, but because I could still feel my pussy throbbing as I waved in my next appointment.

By lunch time my body could no longer feel him, but I still couldn't keep him out of my mind.

I stared absentmindedly at the door where he had eaten me out like an open buffet, daydreaming about Friday and all the possibilities.

Gathering my wits, I grabbed my purse, eager to go out in the fresh air. Since this was New York, the air wasn't that fresh when I stepped outside, but the hustle and bustle of the City filled me with a different kind of energy.

Lost in thought, I let my steps carry me towards El Gato. There were millions of people living in the City, which was the reason I'd chosen to move here in the first place. It was easier to disappear among the masses, or so I had thought.

My mind was still wandering as I pushed the restaurant door open. A cheery hostess greeted me at the door. "I have a reservation under Catarina Machado, please," I told her. She checked her screen before guiding me towards a table.

Rina was still not here, which was unusual since she was always on time, but I took the opportunity to gather my thoughts.

The memory of his warm hands on my body sent shivers up my spine, but I couldn't just ignore the fact he had found me. Alarm bells were ringing loudly in my head, and I needed Rina's perspective to know if I should give him a chance or file a restraining order.

I spotted Rina in a white tailored pantsuit, her brown hair tied in a low chignon. She plopped down on the chair across from me, a little short-winded. "Hey, sorry I'm late, my meeting ran long. I'm freaking starving! Did you order?"

"No, I just got here."

Her presence was enough to bring a bright smile to my lips, despite all that was on my mind. Rina was always bursting with energy, ready to help anyone who might need her, and right now, I needed her. I waited until the waiter came and took our order, and then launched into the events of this morning.

"So, remember that storage room guy from the club a couple of weeks ago?"

"The guy who edged you for your name? Of course I remember, what about him?"

"He showed up at my office this morning."

She opened her mouth in shock. "Shut up! What did he want?"

"More of what he had a taste of at the club, I suppose," I said with a smile.

Rina burst out laughing. "You must have given him a wild ride for him to come crawling back."

"It was wild," I agreed. "And let's just say that what we did in my office this morning would be frowned upon by the partners if they found out."

Her eyes widened. "You had sex in your office?"

"We didn't have sex. He went down on me, and the bastard made me come in under fifteen minutes."

"Fifteen?" she echoed, an impressed look on her face.

"*Under* fifteen."

"Damn, I'm jealous. The last guy I had sex with couldn't find my clit if there were arrows pointed at it. So, when are you seeing him again?"

And that was the crux of the matter, the reason I was dying to have Rina's input. I needed to know if I was being paranoid, or if my hackles were justifiably raised.

"Friday, he's picking me up at seven. But here's the thing—"

"Oh, here we go," Rina interrupted. "Please tell me what's wrong with the extremely hot guy who made you come in your office this morning." She sat back in her seat, arms crossed in front of her chest, waiting for me to speak, her expression daring me to go on.

"He hired a PI to find me. He knows where I work, where I live. Isn't that a red flag?" I watched as my best friend pondered my words for a second, but before she could reply, I added, "Rina, he only knew my first name, and yet he found all this information about me. He found *me. Easily.*"

Rina frowned, her eyes narrowing with concern. "That is a little creepy." Just as I was about to do a little victory dance over being right, she continued, "But it doesn't necessarily mean *he* is a creep. At the very least, he admitted to hiring a PI to find you. That's one point in his favor. What does your gut say?"

I shrugged, sinking back in my chair. "My gut is too overwhelmed by my hormones to be reliable. I don't know what kind of game he's playing."

"Maybe he was impressed by your sexual prowess, maybe your pussy is so good that it ruined all other pussy for him, maybe he couldn't get you out of his head so he had to find you."

"Please. A guy like him can have all the women he wants. I'm not that special."

"Maybe he likes you."

I burst out laughing but stopped when I noticed that Rina didn't find it very funny.

"Why is it so ridiculous to you that a guy might like you? You're intelligent, educated, independent, beautiful, funny…. You check all the boxes."

"But he doesn't know all of that. I mean, other than the beautiful part, because that's really obvious," I joked, flipping my hair, but Rina still wasn't biting.

"And he never will. No man ever will unless you give them a

chance. I know you've had issues trusting men after that dickbag, but not every guy is Andrew," she said, grabbing my hand across the table to soften the blow. To this day, the mention of Andrew still left me a little breathless, made me feel a little powerless.

It was true, I had trust issues. It had taken me a long time to recover from Andrew's abuse, and even longer to be able to be physically intimate with a man. Emotional intimacy required being vulnerable, and even after seven years I was still not ready for that.

"So you think I should give this a go?" I asked.

"The way I see it, you found yourself a hot man who knows how to make you come and who seems to want to make you come, so why not? But you have to trust your instincts. If at any point you feel like something is off, get out, call me, and I'll come and kick his ass."

"Will do," I agreed, a smile tugging at my lips.

The waiter came with our food, placing a delicious salmon and goat cheese bagel in front of me. We both dug in, talking about how things were going at work. Rina launched into a hilarious story about the ad pitches an all-male team had come up with for a tampon commercial, and soon our lunch hour was over.

Outside the restaurant, Rina turned to me, her dark blue eyes shining in the early August sun. "I know that after everything with Andrew, letting a man in can be scary, but not every man is an asshole." She wrapped her arms around me, pulling me in for a tight hug. "Just give him a chance. Maybe he'll surprise you."

I nodded into her hair in response. "I will."

"And don't be in your head so much. Just go with the flow and have fun."

I smiled at her and waved goodbye, feeling lighter. That was the Rina effect. No matter how much I was agonizing over shit, five minutes with her and I felt like I was walking on a cloud. Making my way back to the office, I felt more confident in my decision to enjoy myself with James.

The work week flew by, and fortunately, things got too hectic to allow me to overthink too much. When Friday arrived, I was more excited than anything else.

I mean, if the past was any indication, I was at least bound for a couple of mind blowing orgasms tonight.

On Friday after work, I stood in front of my overflowing closet, waiting for something to magically catch my eye. It wasn't easy to get ready when you had no idea where you were going.

I would've gone with a little black dress, but that's what I had been wearing the night we met at Oasis and I didn't want to repeat an outfit. A flash of color caught my attention, a tight red dress that went down to my knees. I took it out of the closet and the outfit came together in my mind.

By the time I heard the doorbell ring, at exactly seven p.m., I was ready to rock his world. The dress didn't have any cleavage, it didn't show much skin at all, but it left nothing to the imagination as it hugged and accentuated every curve of my body. My trusted Louboutins carried me to the door, where I answered the intercom.

A deep voice came through. "This is James."

"Be right down," I said, grabbing my clutch from the table.

In the elevator, I was surprised to find myself feeling nervous, an unwelcome feeling settling in the pit of my stomach.

Butterflies.

Now that was unusual.

There was no reason to be nervous. Still, I stared at my reflection in the mirrored doors, looking for anything out of place. I had kept my hair loose, the long waves shining in the elevator's fluorescent lights, reaching all the way to my lower back. My makeup was simple, in neutral tones to balance out the bold red of the dress.

"You look fine," I told myself, rolling my shoulders back and raising my chin. "In fact, you look fucking hot." Like a complete dork, I winked at myself in the mirror for an extra boost of confidence before stepping out of the elevator.

When I opened the door to my building, I was greeted by the sight of James leaning casually against the side of a black sports car. In that moment I was glad to be wearing my skin tight red dress, because James Walton looked like he belonged on a billboard.

He was clad in black trousers, black suit jacket, black shoes, and a bold patterned green shirt. It took me aback for a second since it was such a change from everything that I had seen him wear so far, but of course he looked delicious.

Once he saw me, his eyes roamed up and down my body,

shamelessly checking me out, his intense gaze sending a wave of awareness all over me. *All over.*

James met me halfway up the steps to my apartment building, a dazzling smile on his lips as he offered me his hand.

"Hi," he said. "You look phenomenal."

I felt a blush coming on to my cheeks, the compliment pulling at my heartstrings.

"Thank you. You don't look too bad yourself. Although I have to say I wasn't expecting the shirt." I traced the pattern on the shirt, using the opportunity to feel him up a little.

"There's a dress code where we're going. This is my poor attempt at meeting it."

"Wait, there's a dress code? Should I change?" I looked down at my dress, already thinking of different options.

"The dress is perfect," he said, opening the door for me. "You're perfect. I don't know if I want to fuck you in that dress or take it off to enjoy what's underneath."

"How about both?" I suggested, staring up at him.

He took a deep breath, his fingers squeezing my waist as he helped me in. "You're playing with fire, gorgeous, but either way, you're keeping the shoes."

The way he said it, shutting the car door to punctuate his words, made my toes curl. I bit my lower lip in anticipation, shamelessly ogling as James got into the driver's seat and pulled out into traffic. "You know you don't have to take me out on a date. I'm good with just the fucking."

A muscle in his jaw twitched. He sat up straighter, tension emanating from his body. "I will show you a good time in and out of the bedroom, trust me."

Trust—now there was a small word that carried a lot of meaning.

James placed his hand on my thigh, and even through the fabric of my dress, the heat radiating from his palm caused those pesky butterflies to dance in my stomach.

"I was curious to see your apartment. Why didn't you let me up?"

"Why were you curious?"

"Because I want to get to know you." I stared at him, my brows drawing together, so he continued. "Your office was pleasant, but very impersonal. I'm just curious about where you live, what your personal space looks like."

"Admittance to my apartment is a privilege you haven't earned," I said, half joking, half serious. I couldn't remember the last time I'd let a man inside.

He chuckled, the sound reverberating from his chest. "I'll earn that privilege soon enough."

"Where are we going?" I asked, deliberately changing the subject.

"You'll see." His mischievous smile only increased my curiosity, but I chose not to question him because I suspected that was exactly what he wanted.

We drove in companionable silence for a while. Soft rock music filled the silence, but I could barely register it, distracted by his fingers drawing patterns on my bare knee. He was touching my fucking knee and my insides were melting. It was ridiculous to be so sexually attracted to a man that his mere touch on my knee was enough to drive me wild.

Well, not just his touch. His sharp jaw, deep brown eyes, and intoxicating smell played a huge part, too. Even the way he drove, effortlessly navigating through the heavy traffic, was a turn on.

"This is a nice car," I said, taking in the leather interior. "Although you might consider upgrading to something with a radio from this century."

"Thank you. It's a '69 Mustang Boss 429 Fastback, which I can tell by your blank stare means nothing to you."

"No, sorry. The only thing I know about cars is how to drive them."

"It was my grandfather's car. He left it to me when he died. I thought about changing the radio but couldn't bring myself to change a classic."

Fuck! Of course, I had to make a joke about his dead grandpa's car. "I'm sorry, I didn't mean it as an insult."

"No need for apologies." His hand traveled up to my thigh again, his long fingers pressing into my flesh. "Cassettes are not ideal when you're trying to listen to anything from the last twenty years. I inherited my grandfather's collection as well, but the options are very limited."

"Hence the seventies rock?"

A smile broke across his face, so dazzling that I almost had to look away. "Yes, my grandfather was surprisingly into rock for how conservative he was."

"He just had good taste," I said, grinning at him.

James pulled the car over, and a valet appeared as if out of thin air to grab his key. Before I could open the door myself, James had walked around the car and opened it for me. I took the hand he offered and let him help me out of his car, appreciating his gentleman-like behavior.

"Thank you." I looked around me to see where we were headed, but there was no obvious place in sight. "Where are we going exactly?" I repeated my question from earlier.

"This way," he said, placing his hand on my lower back to guide me.

We walked a few steps before he steered me towards a dark alley. I looked at the darkness ahead of me, my legs refusing to take me any further.

"Trust me," James said, repeating that small, heavy phrase.

"You're basically a stranger, leading me down a dark alley. What girl in their right mind would just go with it?"

He gave me a puzzled look, as if he wasn't used to being questioned. Then, after a fraction of a second, his expression changed, a small smile lifting the corner of his mouth.

James positioned himself behind me, his hard chest pressed against my back, making it hard for me to focus on his words.

"See the blue lamp at the end of the alley?" he asked, pointing towards the darkness. "There are steps beneath it that lead to the club. It's a secret location."

"It doesn't seem like a smart business model for a club to be so hard to find," I said matter-of-factly, trying to pretend that his hard body pressed against mine didn't affect me at all.

"That's exactly what I told my friend," he chuckled, the sound traveling all the way to my core. "Come on," he said, offering me his hand.

I gingerly placed my hand on top of his, electricity coursing through my body at the contact. Holding James's hand was already doing strange things to my body. I couldn't wait to see what he could do in an actual bedroom.

CHAPTER EIGHT

I followed him into the darkness until we reached the blue light bulb that, just as he'd promised, hung over a set of steps. We walked down the steps and James knocked twice on the imposing metal door at the bottom. I half expected someone to show up behind a little sliding window to ask him for a password, but the door swung open almost immediately after he knocked.

Maybe he belonged to a secret serial killer society that lured innocent young women to their deaths. I smiled wryly at the thought —I might be young but I sure wasn't innocent. Besides, even if he had some nefarious plan in mind, I was sharing my location with the girls via my phone, and Rina could track me through my smart-watch. And they knew exactly who I was with.

My hand still firmly in his, James walked through the door. It opened into a narrow hallway lit by sporadic, intricate sconces. Again, I was getting more 'evil lair' vibes than 'secret club,' but it was a bit too late to run away.

Finally, the narrow hallway opened to a wider room. The walls were painted a deep shade of burgundy. To my right, velvet purple couches were pushed against the wall, and to the left an attractive woman sat inside an old movie ticket booth.

At the end of the room stood a large set of double doors, the wood carved in intricate designs, muffled music seeping from the other side. The woman stood to leave the booth, revealing a sexy maid outfit, complete with duster.

I was too intrigued now to even think of turning back.

"Mr. Walton," she greeted, pawing his chest with her long acrylic nails before kissing his cheek. James remained quiet, barely reacting to the familiar greeting. Then she swung those heavy doors open, revealing the chaos contained inside.

Everywhere I looked there were colors—reds, oranges, yellows, purples. A waitress walked by me wearing nothing except fishnets, panties, and nipple tassels, her heels higher than I would've ever dared while carrying a tray. Still, she walked around effortlessly, chatting with customers while she served them drinks.

A massive bar dominated one side of the club, with tall tables and discreet booths scattered across from it. I started walking forward, pulled in by the chaotic energy of the place.

James placed his hand firmly on my lower back as we passed by scantily dressed men and women dancing in cages, contortionists performing in small alcoves, and patrons dancing in various states of undress.

I was fascinated, and a little overdressed.

"What is this place?" I turned towards James to find him watching me carefully, gauging my reaction to our surroundings.

"My friend had this idea for an anything-goes burlesque club," James explained. "This is his brainchild, Euphoria."

We went up a short set of stairs leading to a raised restaurant area that faced a stage below. James pointed to one of the upholstered diner booths and I slid in. He sat right beside me, his muscular thigh pressed against me.

The server came to get our order wearing nothing but a Tarzan-like loincloth made of leather. James didn't bother looking at the menu. He ordered a bottle of wine while I chose a cocktail named Daddy's Good Girl.

The waiter turned to leave, and I shamelessly ogled his toned butt while fanning myself with the menu. "I wish I had known about this place sooner."

"Don't get any ideas. I'm still the only dick you're having

tonight, or in the foreseeable future," James whispered in my ear, his warm breath against my neck causing shivers to run down my spine.

His sudden possessiveness took me aback, not necessarily for itself but for how thrilling I found it. "The night is still young," I joked, but James didn't seem to find any humor in it.

"The things I want to do to that mouth of yours." He traced my lips with his thumb, and I playfully bit it, satisfied by the dark glimmer in his eyes.

"Right, about that," I said, my hand coming down to rest over his crotch. "If you want this inside my mouth, you're going to have to get tested."

He stared at me in shock for a second, his eyebrows knitting together as he processed my words. "You do know that I've already eaten *you* out?"

"That was your choice. I don't remember forcing your head down there."

"But you do remember holding me there, right?" He thrust his pelvis into my hand, pushing his hard cock against my palm.

"Either way," I said, clearing my throat, "I'm clean." I pulled out my phone, opened the file with my test results, and handed it to him.

James scanned my phone for a few seconds before handing it back. "So right after we fucked at Oasis you went to get tested?" He gave me a curious look, his head tilted to one side as he examined me.

"That was a coincidence. I get tested every couple of months just in case. But back to the point, if you want my lips wrapped around your dick I need to see some test results."

"I'm assuming my word isn't enough?" I shook my head. "Someday it will be," I thought I heard him say, but the waiter distracted me, not only with our drinks, but with his glistening, semi-naked body brushing against my arm.

The waiter quickly sat my drink down, then did the whole wine tasting thing with James, whose throat worked as he swallowed, an oddly sensual sight.

"Are you ready to order?" the waiter asked, his glistening abs right in front of my face.

"Hmmm…." I hesitated, perusing the menu. "What would you recommend? I'm starving." I bit my lip, focusing my entire attention on the waiter, feeling James's body tense beside me. He was far too easy to tease.

"The Rising Cock is a popular choice, as is the Golden Shower."

"The Rising Cock sounds delicious. Is it spicy?" I asked, playfully batting my eyelashes.

"No, ma'am, but the chef can add some heat if that's what you like."

"Oh I do love some spice, but unfortunately not on my food." I winked, and a cute blush spread over his cheeks at my words.

"I'll have the steak, thank you," James said sharply, his muscles so taut they might snap.

"Of course, Mr. Walton." The waiter immediately sobered and rushed away.

Once he was completely out of sight, I angled my body towards James, taking in his thunderous expression. "The poor waiter. You scared him to death."

"I don't seem to scare you, though."

"Do you want to scare me?"

"No, but it would be really nice if you didn't flirt with the staff, or anyone for that matter."

I leaned over and trapped his bottom lip between my teeth. "I'll try my best," I whispered against his mouth, batting my lashes and planting a sweet smile on my face as I leaned back. "How come everyone here knows your name, anyway?" I asked, making a show of wrapping my lips around the straw and hollowing my cheeks as I took a long sip of my cocktail.

"I'm a regular," he explained after a beat, his eyes focused on my lips.

"I see. So, is this like a sex club?"

His eyes shot up to mine, widening a little. "Is that something you would be into?"

"It depends on the company," I said vaguely.

"It's not a sex club, but it's a good place to vet women."

"How so?"

"Well," he said, planting his hand on my thigh. "If I brought a woman here and she freaked out, then I'd know we're not sexually compatible. I like adventurous women."

"Ah, so this is a date and a test." I glance up at him, giving him my best doe-eyed look. "Do I pass?"

He cupped my jaw and ran his thumb over my cheekbone. "You let me put my thumb in your ass the first night we met, Cassandra. I'd say you passed with flying colors."

My pulse quickened at his words, a low heat settling in my core. "Maybe tonight I could stick my thumb up *your* ass."

James let out a sharp breath as he stared at me, a blush creeping over his cheeks. "I'm up for that."

I grinned at him, biting down on my lip. "This is going to be fun," I said, brushing my hand over his crotch. The thought of fucking his ass sent a thrill through me.

After my relationship with Andrew, it had taken a long time to heal. But eventually I had started exploring my sexuality—boys, girls…. I found I didn't really care. I learned that sex could be fun and truly enjoyable, not just a chore, something to tick off my to-do list before I went to bed.

The waiter came back with our order, and James's body immediately tensed next to me.

"One Rising Cock for the lovely lady," the waiter said playfully.

I winked at him. "Thank you, this looks delicious!" I stared down at my plate, noting the way the chicken thigh bone jutted out between two perfectly cylindrical dollops of mashed potatoes. It was so childish, but I absolutely loved it.

The poor guy had barely set James's plate down on the table when James barked out a thank you, effectively dismissing him.

Just as we were about to start eating, the lights lowered and the stage lit up. A fabulous drag queen came out, dressed as Dolly Parton in her famous blonde wig, and began singing.

"My friend Daisy would really love this place," I said, mostly to break the tension. I was about to elaborate when a handsome blond man approached our table. He was wearing a silk purple robe, open over a pair of black boxers, his washboard abs visible for all to admire.

"James! You have better looking company every time I see you.

Please introduce me to your lovely friend." The words rolled smoothly off his tongue in a refined British accent, clear green eyes sparkling with mischief. He took a seat across from me, making himself at home at our table, despite James's harsh stare.

"Cassandra Leigh," I said, reaching out to shake his hand. I could spot a player a mile away, so it didn't surprise me at all when the man kissed my hand. A low growl came from the other handsome man sitting next to me, so I thought I'd have a little more fun teasing him.

"Elias Coulson, at your service," the newcomer said, still holding my hand. "So, what brings a woman like you to a place like this with this crabby bastard?"

"To be honest, I didn't know I was coming here at all. I was sort of kidnapped," I joked.

"Really? Well, in that case I might just have to throw you over my shoulder and rescue you out of this place." Elias poured himself a glass of wine, lifting it in James's direction before he took a long sip.

I chuckled at the mental image his offer painted. "I might have to take you up on that."

"Eli, that's enough," James interrupted. "Elias is an old friend. He owns this club. Oasis too," he added for my benefit.

"Wow! I was just telling James before that it was a terrible idea to have a club at a secret location, but this place has proven me wrong. It would be too much for some people if it was all out there in the open."

"But it's not too much for you?" Elias asked, one eyebrow raised.

"On the contrary, I'm fascinated."

"Wonderful," he said, clapping his hands. He waved a waitress over, this one wearing a full body leather cat costume. He whispered something in her ear and she scurried off to do his bidding.

"Is it membership only?" I asked, taking a bite out of my chicken.

"Yes. I would love to have an open door policy, but as you said, some people are not very comfortable with lads dancing in cages and ladies wearing nothing but body paint."

"Body paint?" I asked, intrigued by the idea of walking around naked in plain sight. "That's an art in itself, isn't it? I mean, it must be hard to do it on your own body."

"It depends on the design. We often have a professional come in, but if it's simple sometimes I do it, or they paint each other."

"I see," I said, smiling. "I would actually love to try it once. Sounds like a lot of fun to just walk around naked. It's like a secret that only those looking close enough would see."

"Anytime you want, my brush is yours. But I believe if we tease James any longer, his head will explode." He patted his friend's arm affectionately.

James not so casually put his arm around me, his hand resting firmly on my shoulder.

Elias laughed. "No need to stake your claim, mate. I've got my hands full for tonight."

"I'm sorry to disappoint, Elias, but you're not my type." Objectively, Elias was very attractive, and he seemed like a genuinely fun guy with his super outgoing personality, but I was more into the dark and brooding type, like the man sitting next to me.

Elias dramatically put a hand over his heart. "You wound me, but I can accept that James here got to you first. Still, even if you say I'm not your type, call me when you drop this one. I might change your mind."

James placed a hand on his friend's forearm, a threat if I'd ever seen one. He didn't need to speak. The tension in his jaw and the hard look he shot Elias were enough to send the message. The situation was getting a little too tense for me, so I tried a different approach to lighten the mood.

"So, Elias, you and James seem to be good friends. You must have some dirt on him. He seems too perfect to be real." I whispered the last part, as if James wasn't right next to me.

Elias leaned forward, his green eyes darting from James to me. "I fear Jamie has more dirt on me, so I'm afraid I can't spill the beans."

"How bad could it actually be?" I asked, and the two men exchanged a look.

Elias laughed. "Some of it was barely legal and I wouldn't want to taint the image you have of my friend."

"I'm a criminal defence attorney," I said. "I doubt anything you did could shock me."

"Nice try," James said, pulling me even closer to him.

I pouted but still got no answer. James's eyes lingered on my lips for a second before he placed his hand on my thigh, the contact sending my pulse into a frenzy.

The waitress came back with another bottle of wine and fresh glasses. "James here has terrible taste in wine," Elias said, pouring me a drink. "Try this one, darling."

"I honestly wouldn't know the difference, but I do like white better," I said, taking a sip.

Something passed between the two men, the kind of unspoken conversation that only old friends are capable of.

"All right, all right. I'll leave you two alone." Elias lifted his hands up in surrender and got up to leave. But before he did, he approached and kissed my cheek, dropping his card on my lap in the process.

I thought I heard another growl from beside me, but it was smothered by applause as Dolly Parton finished her first song.

Elias whispered in my ear, "You're welcome here anytime. I'll put you on the VIP list." He winked and walked away, and I thought it was very smart of him, because when I turned toward James, the thunderous expression on his face almost sent me running, too.

Still, I enjoyed teasing him.

"You could have told me you don't like red wine. I would've ordered something different." He ran his fingers up and down my arm, goosebumps breaking out all over my skin.

"I don't mind red wine, I just prefer white."

"Noted. And body paint?"

"Yes," I said in a cheery tone. "Can you imagine it? It would be so much fun."

"I can, but I don't like the idea as much as you and Elias seem to." He took a bite of his food before adding, "And by the way, you and Elias? Never happening."

"That's not really for you to decide," I immediately retorted. This wasn't an argument I was having. Teasing aside, James had no right to say who I did or didn't fuck.

James took a deep breath, tension emanating from his rock hard body. "I swear to God, woman, if you keep defying me I'm going to bend you over my knee here and now."

I smiled, biting my lip at the image his words painted. I doubted anyone here would mind.

James shook his head, a small smile playing on his lips. "You seem to like that idea too much. I'm going to have to find another punishment for you."

The thought of him punishing me was exhilarating. I wanted to tease him some more, so I asked, "Where did you and Elias meet?"

"Boarding school, why?"

I bit my lip suggestively. "I heard that sometimes, naughty things go on at boarding schools."

"It was a boys only school."

"Exactly. I thought maybe you and Elias were already… well acquainted. And if that were the case, maybe he'd be interested in having a little fun with both of us."

"Cassandra." The warning in his voice sent a shiver down my spine. "What exactly are you suggesting?"

"The two of you, doing unspeakable things to my body…." I fanned myself for effect, taking immense pleasure in teasing this territorial male.

"You're treading in dangerous waters, gorgeous."

"And what are you going to do about it?"

"I'm taking you home."

"Wait, what about the bill?" I got no answer as James basically dragged me out of the club. By the time I realized what was happening, I was sitting comfortably inside his Mustang, speeding towards his place.

CHAPTER NINE

I already knew he had money. If his clothes, car, and knowledge of secret burlesque clubs weren't enough indication of his wealth, he had that *something* about him that only rich people do. It was in his attitude, in the way he walked into my office and every other room as if he owned the place.

Even so, when he pulled up to a skyscraper on the Upper East Side, I was a bit taken aback. When we entered the elevator and he had to type a code on a screen to press the penthouse button, I knew I was in way over my head, at least financially.

I did well at my job, made enough money that I could afford the mortgage on my cozy one-bedroom apartment in Brooklyn, buy the occasional designer shoe or dress, especially if I found it in a second-hand shop.

This was a different level of wealth, though, one I had only seen in a handful of clients at Feldman & Sullivan.

"So, you're rich rich, huh?" I said, bumping my shoulder against his biceps.

"Rich rich?" he repeated, his eyebrows knitting together.

"Yes, so rich that saying it once isn't enough. Like, diving-in-a-pile-of-gold rich."

He laughed, actually *laughed* at me. "I guess I'm rich rich, then, although I've never tried diving into gold. I can only imagine the pain. But I thought you knew."

"I knew you had money, but not penthouse-on-the-Upper-East-Side money."

"Does it change anything?" He said it casually, but his smile dimmed, his shoulders tensed.

"Not a thing," I answered honestly. "But nineties music videos gave me this idea, more like a fantasy, and it hasn't become an option until now." I turned to face him, pushing him towards the elevator wall with my hands on his chest.

He wrapped his hands around my waist, pulling my body flush against his. "And what is this fantasy of yours?"

I licked a path from his chiseled jaw to his ear, wrapping my lips over his earlobe.

"Imagine a gigantic bed with black silk sheets and thousands of bills scattered on top of it. I'm wearing sexy lingerie and a ridiculous amount of jewelry—diamonds, emeralds and pearls. You come in looking all ripped in black boxers, silk robe, and heavy gold chains...."

"That can be arranged," he said, an amused grin on his lips.

The elevator doors slid silently open, and James walked me backwards towards his apartment. The moment we were inside, he grabbed the hem of my dress and lifted it above my head.

"I thought you wanted to fuck me with the dress on."

He smirked, brown eyes darkening as he took me in. "Changed my mind, but we are keeping the shoes."

I took a step back, his stare searing my skin as I gingerly removed my thong, then unhooked my bra, letting it fall to the floor. Moonlight poured in from the floor-to-ceiling windows, casting shadows over his sharp features. I resisted the urge to cover myself, my cheeks burning as James stood in front of me, fully dressed, dark eyes roaming hungrily over my naked body.

Time seemed to slow as James stalked towards me, pure lust burning in his eyes. He cupped my face with one hand, brushing over my cheekbones, my jaw line, then finally my lips.

"You are breathtaking," he said in a husky voice.

I smiled at the compliment, any shadow of embarrassment gone from my mind. Wrapping my hands around the back of his neck, I pulled him for a kiss. Our tongues danced together as his hands roamed hungrily over my bare skin. He squeezed my ass, bringing our bodies impossibly closer.

James used his grip on my ass to lift me up, and I wrapped my legs around his waist. He carried me past the foyer into an open area before veering left. The lights turned on automatically, revealing a spacious gourmet kitchen with two separate islands, white marble countertops, and what I assumed were top-of-the-line stainless steel appliances. *Amelia would sell a kidney for a kitchen like this*, I thought.

He lifted me onto the counter and spread my legs wide open, the cold marble causing goosebumps to rise all over my body. James wasted no time burying his head between my legs, tasting my arousal with a long lick. I let out a shuddering breath, and he looked up at me, eyes dark with desire, his lips shining with my arousal. "I've been waiting to do that all night."

With a wicked grin, he lowered himself once more between my thighs.

It took him no time to find my clit. James tapped the sensitive bud with the flat of his tongue until I was squirming, ready to explode. I was almost embarrassed to come so fast, but the man had a magical tongue, and he knew how to use it.

The counter was cold beneath my bare skin, but my body was on fire. My muscles tensed, and my lips quivered against his hot mouth. Then he stopped what he was doing, purposely delaying my orgasm.

James circled my clit with the tip of his tongue, the sharp pleasure sending electricity all over my body. My toes curled, my thighs pressing against his head, my body begging for release. And then he changed direction, new sensations erupting in my core at the same time that my orgasm slipped away.

"Please," I begged, propping myself up with one elbow. The sight of James eating me out like I was his favorite meal would be engraved in my mind until the end of times. I moaned when he sucked my clit into his mouth, my hips shooting forward, begging for more. But his warm hands landed roughly on top of my thighs to hold me down, making it harder for me to squirm.

I grabbed a fistful of his hair to hold him in place as I felt warmth pooling at my core. "If you stop one more time, I swear to God," I threatened in between ragged breaths.

James looked up at me from between my legs, his eyes dark with pure lust, and slowly licked his lips. "Don't rush me. This is the best meal of my life."

With a cocky smirk on his face, James spread my legs wide open and licked me from slit to clit while I lay there, completely speechless. Then he pulled back and pushed one long finger inside of me, his eyes fixed on my entrance as he thrust in and out.

I refused to be embarrassed as he stared at my pussy swallowing his finger under the bright kitchen lights. It was impossible to feel self-conscious when James was looking at me with so much awe, his sculpted lips parted as he drove in and out of me. My palm landed with a loud smack on the solid marble as he curled his finger inside me. I wondered how I got so lucky as to find a man who not only knew what he was doing down there, but clearly enjoyed it.

James spread my lips open with one hand and leaned back in, his tongue circling my clit with just the right amount of pressure at the same time that he pushed another finger inside me.

I gasped in pleasure, my back arching up involuntarily. "Fuck, that's so good."

Heat spread all over my trembling body, my heart beating wildly in my chest. I grabbed James's forearm, digging my nails into his warm flesh. He groaned between my legs, the sound sending me over the edge.

"Please don't stop. Please," I moaned.

The pressure built to a tipping point, my entire body tensing until finally James let me come. I closed my eyes as my limbs trembled, my pussy quivering against his tongue as wave after wave of pleasure consumed me.

He kept licking me up and down, his tongue barely touching me as his fingers pumped slowly in and out of me. I pulled his hair to make him stop, the orgasm already too intense, but he kept going until the last of the pleasure faded.

James emerged from between my legs with a cheeky smile on his face. "Good?"

"Shut up," I said, covering my face with my arms as I recovered.

James grabbed me by the shoulders and pulled me up to a sitting position, his face inches from mine. "I want to know what you like." He ran his fingers across my jaw, brushed his thumb over my cheekbones. "What makes you scream. How hard you can take it." He cupped my face. "I want to feel your asshole pulsing around my cock as I make you come, over and over again."

My breath hitched in my chest at his promise. At a loss for words, I did the next best thing. I pulled him towards me and tasted myself on his lips, wrapping my legs around his waist and pressing my heavy breasts against his chest.

I hated that he was still fully dressed. I needed to touch him, to feel his skin beneath my fingers.

One by one, I undid the buttons on his shirt to reveal the muscled chest beneath. James rocked his hips against my core, his hard cock doing delicious things to my body even while still covered by his pants.

He pushed his hands under my thighs, moving up until he reached my ass. Then he lifted me from the counter into his arms, his lips never leaving mine. My heels clattered to the ground one by one, but he didn't stop.

He carried me up the stairs to his bedroom and tossed me on the bed. I giggled for a second as I bounced on the mattress, but the sight of James's hungry eyes as he looked me up and down had it dying in my throat.

I bit my lower lip as I watched him pull his belt out of the loops, then undo his button and fly, his gaze focused on my breasts. Smiling, I palmed my breasts and played with my nipple piercing with one hand, while the other made its way down between my thighs. He growled low in his throat in response, so I opened my legs wider to tease him some more.

Finally, he pushed his pants and his boxer briefs down his legs, his hard cock springing free. I had been dying to see him in good lighting, and now he stood in all his naked glory before my lustful eyes. He was even more impressive than I remembered, his penis long and thick…. I couldn't wait to have him inside me.

He fisted his cock roughly in his hand, pumping twice before he slipped on a condom. I was pretty sure I could make myself come just watching him touch himself.

James hovered over me on the bed, his throbbing head teasing my entrance as he licked a path up the column my neck.

I hooked my heels around his waist and used my weight to flip us over so I could be on top. Then I reached down to place him at my entrance before slowly lowering myself, taking him inside me inch by inch.

"Jesus," I gasped, feeling his hard cock stretch my walls. I arched my back and closed my eyes as he filled me, a rush of pure bliss traveling all the way to my fingertips. Planting my hands on his chest, I took a moment to adjust once he was fully inside me, my entire body shuddering with pleasure, my breath coming in hard pants.

"You're going to have to move soon, gorgeous," James said in a strained voice. I looked down to find him staring at my face, his jaw tight, six-pack on full display as he tried not to move.

I smiled down at him and undulated my hips just a little. He groaned, his fingers digging into my thighs. "You like that?" I asked, repeating the slight movement.

"Yes," James moaned low in his throat, his fingers squeezing my hips. "Do it again."

Biting down on my lip, I complied, but this time I didn't stop. It felt too good to stop. I circled my hips, pleasure coiling tightly in my core as I grinded against him. Then I really started to move, circling my hips, riding him fast and hard, my boobs bouncing up and down. His hands came up to cup them, his thumb grazing over my nipple before he pinched it.

He made me lose my rhythm, so I planted my feet on the mattress, leaned back, and placed my hands on his shins as I rode him. A guttural growl filled the room as I switched positions, and knowing that I did that to him was satisfying on a whole different level.

Sweat gathered at my temples, the wet slapping sound of our bodies connecting filling my ears. James held my hip with one hand, fingers digging into my skin with bruising force. Then his thumb found my clit and pressed down, and I rode him wildly, stars clouding my vision.

"That's it. Ride me harder, gorgeous," James growled.

I obeyed. His thick cock hit the right spot inside me. The pressure of his thumb on my clit became too much. My body started trembling uncontrollably. I dug my fingernails into his shins, my hips moving erratically as I chased my climax.

"Oh God. Oh God," I moaned over and over.

"That's it, gorgeous. Come all over my dick," James said, his gravelly tone traveling straight to my clit. I felt my walls closing around his cock, then all at once I came again. My hips jerked back and forth as my pussy quivered with pleasure.

"James," I moaned, closing my eyes. His thumb was still circling my clit, and the only thing I could focus on was the intense pleasure blinding me to reality.

James sat up and pulled me towards him, swallowing my moans with a kiss. I wrapped my hands around his neck, frantically feeling the hard ridges of his back as he slowly rocked me back and forth on his dick.

I felt my own cum leaking down his shaft, between my asscheeks. James must have felt it too, because he reached down and spread it all over my asshole. "I still want to play with this hole," he whispered against my lips.

Laughing, I buried my face in his neck, nibbling at the sensitive skin. "I think you might be able to handle me," I said, shocked to hear the words leave my mouth.

Suddenly, he flipped me over, effortlessly pinning both my hands above my head with one hand. "Let's see if you can handle *me*." His husky voice traveled all the way down my spine, making me shiver with anticipation.

He reached over to open his night stand drawer and pulled out a few butt plugs. The thought of James using those same toys on a dozen random women made me tense. It might be irrational. Toys could be washed, sanitized, but I still didn't like that idea.

"I'm not a fan of using previously worn toys," I said, ready to argue my point. But James simply put them away without a word.

James spread my legs wide open, his heated stare traveling down my body until he focused on my bare pussy. He watched as he pushed his throbbing head in and out of me, before something flipped inside of him and he slammed his cock in to the hilt.

"You've had your fun. Now it's my turn." He leaned down to kiss me as he thrust slowly inside of me. I groaned, my hips automatically lifting to take in more of him. He moved one of my legs to rest on his shoulder, and I lifted the other. His eyes darkened, and he moved his body forward, pushing my feet toward the headboard.

"Yoga," I said before he could ask. He smirked and started pounding roughly into me. My body was folded like a pretzel. His massive cock, deep inside of me at this angle, was bordering on painful. I loved every second of it.

Somehow James still had the presence of mind to play with my nipples, pinching and rolling them between his fingers. All I could do was take it since my hands were still pinned over my head.

James finally let my hands go, only to push a long finger inside my asshole. I gasped, my entire body trembling with pleasure. Wrapping one hand around his neck, I tightened my grasp to choke him a little. His eyes widened a fraction before he smirked, a groan escaping his full lips.

He planted one foot on the bed, bending his knee to drive even deeper inside my eager pussy. My vision blurred as his hand came down to press on my clit. I moaned his name over and over, probably louder than I would have in my own apartment, but I doubted James's neighbors could hear me.

My orgasm hit me with an intensity I wasn't expecting. I was pretty sure I blacked out for a minute. Red hot fire spread through my body as my pussy spasmed over and over, my asshole pulsing around James's finger. I choked him a little harder, wrapping my other hand around his biceps, nails digging into his skin.

James kept going as a fireworks show exploded inside my body. "Cassandra," he growled, his thrusts becoming erratic, more desperate.

I could barely focus on anything, but there was nothing hotter than watching James as he lost control inside of me, his neck veins popping out, his eyelids half-closed. He came with a groan, whispering my name in between ragged breaths.

Then he buried his head in my neck as he tried to catch his breath, his body still shaking. He lowered my legs, but stayed inside of me for a few minutes while we both recovered.

"I want to say something," he whispered into my neck, "but I don't have the words."

I chuckled, running my hands up and down his back.

He got up to dispose of the condom and came back from the bathroom with a warm wet towel. He spread my legs open and cleaned between them with a gentleness I wasn't expecting. No one had ever done that for me before.

It made me feel all sorts of ways, and I didn't like that very much.

"I have to pee," I announced, scrambling off the bed in the direction of the en-suite bathroom. I closed the door behind me and did my business, then stood in front of the double vanity to take in my freshly fucked look.

My hair was a tangled mess, and there were black smudges of makeup under my eyes. But my cheeks were flushed, my lips were swollen, and my eyes looked glossy with the post orgasm haze.

And he had cleaned me.

I took a few calming breaths before opening the door, fully intending to tell him this was fun but I should go home.

But James was leaning against the headboard of the king sized bed, still fully naked with his phone in hand. I had been too preoccupied before to actually notice my surroundings. The wide room was sparsely furnished with a bench at the foot of the bed, matching nightstands, and a meridian chaise lounge facing the glass wall. Paintings dotted the walls, but the real star was the view, the East River glimmering in the distance.

He patted the spot next to him, a lazy smile on his face. My body moved forward, as if he was tugging at an invisible rope that pulled me to him.

Meanwhile my mind was screaming at me to stop. To leave.

Mind-blowing orgasm or not, I didn't do sleepovers.

I sat next to James, and he tucked me into his body, nuzzling my hair.

"Everything okay?"

"Yes, I feel thoroughly fucked," I said, jutting my chin towards the glass wall. "Can the neighbors see us?"

He chuckled, his hand snaking around my waist. "No, I'd never let anyone see you naked. It's smart glass, I can control the opacity," he explained. "Now let's do some shopping." He was browsing a sex toys website on his phone, but I froze when I saw the prices.

"I really don't need a three thousand-dollar butt plug, James. And why does it come with matching cuff-links? Why is it gold?"

"So when I make you go out in public with me, wearing a butt plug, we can be matching. Here," he said, handing me his phone, "pick whatever you want."

"We'd only be matching if you were wearing a butt plug too. And I don't need any toys, I have a bunch at home."

"Yes, but you don't want to use the ones I have here, and I very much want to fuck your ass."

We spent a long time looking at toys, while I tried not to balk at the figure at the bottom of the page, which in turn made us horny again, so we went for round two. Hours later, I lay quietly in James's arms, listening to his breath get deeper and deeper. It almost lulled me to sleep, but I absolutely did not do sleepovers.

I carefully removed his arm from my waist. He grumbled for a second but thankfully didn't wake up. Then I quietly slipped out of bed.

Before I left his bedroom I couldn't resist the urge to take a peek at his sleeping form. James's wide frame occupied almost the entire bed, his muscular chest moving softly with each breath. He was truly a sight to behold, even in his sleep.

I almost regretted leaving. But still, I made my way downstairs, found my dress and shoes but couldn't find my panties. Then I ordered a car and made my way down, strutting shamelessly past the concierge. Soon, I was in the backseat of a Volvo, at four a.m., with no panties on.

CHAPTER TEN

The next morning, I woke up to my phone vibrating underneath my pillow. I struggled to open my eyes to see the screen; it was six a.m. and the number wasn't one I had saved. Thinking it might be work related, I sat up in bed and answered in my most professional voice.

"Hello, this is Cassandra Leigh."

"Did you really sneak out of my place last night?" He sounded angry.

I groaned. "Fuck, James. It's six a.m."

"That's exactly what I wanted to do, fuck. You, specifically. But I just woke up to a cold, empty bed. Why did you leave?"

"I don't do sleepovers." Silence greeted me on the other end. It lasted so long I wondered if he had hung up.

"And here I was, hoping to have breakfast in bed," he finally said, humor coating his words.

That angered me. I wasn't his maid or cook or whatever. And it was too early. "I'm sure you can allocate some resources to have someone serve your breakfast in bed. It just won't be me."

"You misunderstood me." His velvet smooth voice caressed my ears, almost causing the anger to fade away. "I meant to have *you* for breakfast."

"Oh." I sat in shocked silence for a second. The smallest part of me, so small you'd need a microscope to see it, almost regretted leaving his bed.

"Now tell me, gorgeous, what am I supposed to do with my hard cock?"

"I'm sure you can think of something. You have two hands. Bye James," I said, hanging up.

I didn't want to encourage him into thinking that he could have access to me whenever he wanted. My schedule was insane as it was. I didn't have the time or the will to make him come before I had my morning coffee.

Plus, it bothered me how easily he rendered me speechless.

Unfortunately for me, once I was awake, I could never go back to sleep. I turned on the news while I made coffee and changed, then left it on in the background while I jumped on the elliptical.

The lack of sleep would get to me eventually, but not today. Once I was done working out, I quickly showered and got ready for work. I saw James had messaged me, but I didn't bother checking until I was on the subway.

James: I can't believe you hung up on me.
James: Look what I found *attached photo*

My eyes widened at the image that flashed on my screen. I glanced around me to make sure no one could see my screen before I looked again. I couldn't believe my eyes.

James had sent me a picture of his handsome face, my underwear pressed to his nose. He had his eyes closed, but his expression was pure sin, that ridiculously sexy smirk plastered on his face. My cheeks felt hot, and I couldn't help the smile that took over my face, but I still left him on read.

I checked my work emails, but my mind kept coming back to James. His name flashed across my screen again. I ignored it for all of two seconds before curiosity took over.

James: I can't wait to bury my face in your pussy again.

Getting tested this morning so you can reciprocate. Loved
the choking, btw. We should talk about safe words.

A smile tugged at my lips as I scanned the text. I couldn't wait to wrap my lips around his cock. My fingers hovered over the screen, my willpower to ignore him gradually fading. Safe words were important, so at least that part warranted an answer.

Me: Good. I can't wait for you to come all over my face.
Let's keep it simple: green, orange, red.
James: I'm going into a meeting and you're making me
hard…

A giggle escaped me at the thought of James walking into a room full of suits with a tent in his pants. I ignored his text despite the fact it had made me laugh. I really wasn't the type of girl to spend the day texting my new fuck buddy, even if the texts were more dirty than sweet.

When I finally got into work, I locked myself in my office and refused all distractions. I wanted to finish by noon so I could stop at the shelter. Before I knew it, it was two p.m., and I still wasn't done. The Maxwell case was really going to be the death of me, or of my career. I'd spent all morning trying to find a precedent, something, anything that could get Maxwell out of going to jail. But New York law didn't play around with embezzlement cases, at least not when the money was allegedly found in the accused's daughter's bank account.

Coffee. That's what I needed to be able to push through for a couple more hours. I left my office, rolling my shoulders and stretching my arms above my head to ease some of the tension.

"Olivia," I said, surprised to find her here on a Saturday. "What are you doing here?"

"Hey, Cassie. Mr. Sullivan fired his secretary so the rest of us have been covering her position. I'm honestly drowning in work." She spun in her chair and grabbed a beautiful flower arrangement. "Someone sent you these. I knew you were in your office but I didn't want to bother you."

"That's okay, thank you." I took the flowers from her hand, searching for a card. I didn't recognize most of them except the violets, my mom's favorite. Growing up, I remembered her saying she loved them because they were just as colorful and beautiful as a rose, but they were wild and could survive many storms.

I finally found the card. It simply read: *See you soon.*

James really didn't have to send me flowers, but he couldn't have picked better. It occurred to me that he probably didn't even pick this bouquet—that his assistant or someone else had. It diminished the joy I felt when I first saw them, which was exactly the reminder I needed.

He was only a friend with benefits. I didn't need or want to be wooed.

Shaking it off, I turned to Olivia, who had already returned to her work. We had been working together for almost two years, and I couldn't have asked for a better legal assistant.

"I'm getting some decent coffee from around the corner. Can I get you anything?"

She looked up from her computer with a huge smile on her face. "Do I need to answer that?"

I chuckled. Olivia and I shared a great love of coffee. It had developed out of necessity, but by this point it had become part of who we were. "I'll be right back."

While I was in line for coffee, I checked my messages. Nothing from James which was oddly disappointing, but the group chat with the girls had over fifteen unread messages.

Daisy: Oasis tonight?
Amelia: Yes, please! Ready to kill my boss over here.

I caught up on the drama with Amelia's boss, who apparently thought it was completely fine to have his waitresses work eighteen-hour shifts with no breaks.

Me: Pre-drinks at my place?
Amelia: Yes!
Rina: Be there at 7.

Daisy: Hell yeah!

The thought of spending the evening with my friends put a permanent smile on my face. I walked back to the office with two double espresso almond lattes in hand, ready to take on the Maxwell case once more.

Time flew by and before I knew it, it was four p.m. I called it a day and quickly traded my stilettos for flats before heading to the Little Haven Shelter. I had been volunteering there since college and other than my friends, the work I did there was the only thing that brought me happiness.

"Oh, pretty flowers. Who's the lucky fella?" Sheila asked as I walked into her office.

"Oh, this guy I met a couple weeks ago, insanely hot."

"He sent you flowers, so he must be nice too."

"I guess," I said dismissively, unwilling to discuss my sex life with Sheila. "Did you hear back from Jackie?"

"Yes, I did." Sheila moved some files around. "Here it is, Carl and Lexie's attendance sheet."

I quickly scanned the documents. "Good, they haven't missed school that much. This will play in our favor. Character witnesses?"

Sheila shook her head. "Unfortunately no. She cut ties with her own family years ago, no friends to speak off, and the teachers at the school don't know her enough on a personal level to be effective."

"How about the other moms? Don't they have play dates with the kids or that sort of thing?"

"No one that she could reach out to. You know how it goes, he completely isolated her from everyone."

"Damn it, ok. I'll try to think of something, but her husband is going to have his work buddies testify to what a wonderful dad he is. We should at least have one person speak highly of Jackie. Someone who could say that she goes to all the kids' meetings, doctor's appointments, soccer games. We need the judge to see her as a responsible, involved parent."

"I'll ask again, maybe there's someone we overlooked." Sheila looked over some papers while I scribbled notes on Jackie's case file. "Miranda came in yesterday. Boyfriend violated the restraining order, beat her black and blue. We took her to the hospital and called the cops, filed a report, the usual."

"How bad was it this time?" One look from Sheila was answer enough. "I'll try to push for a felony charge this time. If we're lucky, he'll go in for a couple of years."

We talked over a dozen more cases before I finally left. If I had the resources at the shelter that I had at work, it would be ten thousand times easier to do my job. Sheila was the only lawyer on payroll at the shelter. The rest of us were volunteers, which meant that our clients had to run around from place to place, gathering paperwork and being run down by the system.

It made every case last forever, which was time that these women did not have. I called the DA in charge of Miranda's case to at least make sure her boyfriend couldn't get out on bail. Then I used the rest of my commute to go over some of the cases Sheila had handed over to me.

By the time I made it home it was almost seven p.m., and my stomach reminded me that I had been running on yogurt and coffee alone. I typed a message on our group chat.

Me: Take out?
Amelia: Got food covered.
Me: My savior.

Once that was taken care of, I padded towards the kitchen to put James's flowers in a vase. Feeling a little naughty, I took off my work clothes and snapped a picture of a single violet between my breasts. It wasn't exactly graphic since I covered my nipples with my arm to pull the girls up, and obviously my face wasn't visible, but it was just enough.

I opened the thread to send James the photo, and my skin tingled with excitement when I saw he'd sent me his test results. All clean. Smiling, I sent the picture with a casual 'thanks' message. He replied immediately.

James: Shouldn't I be the one thanking you?

Me: I think there are more interesting things you could do
with your mouth than speak.

I put on some music and hopped in the shower, feeling giddy
with excitement. I couldn't remember the last time I'd had fun
texting a guy.

CHAPTER ELEVEN

At exactly seven p.m., Rina rang my doorbell. I rushed naked out of the bathroom to buzz her in, leaving the upstairs door unlocked for her so I could finish my shower. Before I went back into the bathroom, I spotted the flowers on my kitchen counter and had an idea.

I grabbed a handful of them and locked myself in the bathroom again, then I placed them right over my pussy and snapped a picture of my midsection in the mirror. It looked scorching hot with the water dripping down my stomach and the bunch of flowers covering my crotch. I pressed send and hopped back into the shower.

When I was done, I had another picture from James. It had been taken from underneath a table with several pairs of feet visible in the background. But the star of the shot was the outline of James's very hard cock straining against his pants.

James: You're killing me here.

Knowing he was hard for me in a meeting full of people only made this more fun, so I turned around in the mirror and took a good pic of my ass, grinning as I sent it. I wrapped myself in a towel and left the bathroom to find Rina making cocktails in my kitchen.

"Who's got you smiling like that?"

"James. He's in a meeting and I'm sending him nudes." I scrolled through my phone to show her the one with the flowers covering my vagina.

Rina gave an approving nod, sliding a drink toward me. "Poor guy, he's going to have some blue balls if you don't take care of it later."

I took a generous sip, which I registered as a mistake the moment it hit my empty stomach. "He's going to have to find somebody else to do it. I'm not seeing him tonight."

"Why not? This morning you said he literally made you see stars."

"Yeah, I know. But I can't hook up with the same guy two nights in a row. Besides, I'm going out with you guys tonight"

"I almost forgot about your commitment issues."

"I don't have commitment issues," I countered. "Men are just too much work. I like my life the way it is." We both looked towards the door when the buzzer went off.

"Wait, let's save this argument for when the girls are here." Rina went to buzz them in while I went to my room to grab a robe.

I took the opportunity to peek at my phone, because there was no way I would be texting James in front of Rina again. She saw way too much into everything.

James: I'm going to get back at you for this, gorgeous. This is strike two.
Me: Really? What did you have in mind?

I waited for a second, but when he didn't reply right away, I thought I might give him some ideas.

Me: You could bend me over that table. Bet those guys wouldn't mind the show.
James: I'm in physical pain right now.
Me: Spank me?
Me: Choke me?
James: Turning off my phone. My balls hurt.

Me: Want me to kiss it better?

Me: Or lick it better?

The little icon below his name turned red, telling me he was offline. I couldn't help but chuckle. Poor guy must really be struggling. I slipped on my robe, a thong, and went to join the girls. Daisy and Amelia walked in together, one with a bag full of food containers and the other carrying two duffel bags.

"Did you rob a bank?" I asked Daisy, pointing towards the duffel bags.

"Better, I raided the closet at work." The huge smile on her face said it all. She opened the duffels and dumped a bunch of clothes on my couch. "But food before dresses. No permanent stains on them, please. They need to be back by Tuesday."

"These are all very short, and sparkly," Rina said, picking a little black dress that was a hundred percent sequins. "You know we're not teenagers anymore, right?"

"Thank God for that," Amelia said from the kitchen.

I gravitated towards her since she was the one with the goods. She piled her curly hair on top of her head and scrubbed her hands clean before spreading finger food all over the counter. It was way too much, but if I could keep the leftovers, I wasn't about to complain Amelia was a fantastic chef.

Daisy turned towards Rina, pressing a bright pink dress with feather ruffles against her petite frame. "I know we're not teens anymore, but there's nothing wrong with wearing fun clothes. Maybe if you'd let yourself have some fun you'd get lucky."

"Rina doesn't need luck to get laid, she just needs to loosen her corset a bit." I gave her a cheeky smile while she shot me a dirty look. "But I agree, there's no such thing as being too old to dress up in sparkly clothes."

"Speaking of hooking up," Rina started, staring straight at me. I really didn't like where this was going, "do you guys think Cassie has commitment issues?"

"Yes," Amelia and Daisy said at the same time.

"I rest my case," Rina said, performing a dramatic bow.

"Objection!" I yelled from the kitchen. "I do not have commitment issues and we don't bow in court."

We all sat around my kitchen counter to eat Amelia's food, cocktails sitting in front of us. Amelia pointed to Rina's concoction with a doubtful look. "What is this anyway?"

"Don't start," Rina said, raising a finger to stop Amelia. "It's watermelon and vodka, a classic."

"Sorry, I just didn't want a repeat of the Bloody Mary fiasco."

"Jesus, you fuck up one cocktail once and you never hear the end of it."

"You did give us all diarrhea," Daisy chimed in. We all laughed at the memory, although it hadn't been very pleasant at the time. Four girls, one bathroom. It wasn't pretty.

"What about the time you invented that cocktail? What was it called again?" I asked.

"Death in a Glass," Amelia said, a snort escaping her.

"You really fucked us over with that one. Absinthe and tequila do not belong together," I teased.

Rina rolled her eyes. "Coming back to Cassie's commitment issues. James seems to be very into her. He—"

"I don't want to see him two days in a row and *that* makes me afraid of commitments? Are men who wait two days to call after sex also afraid of commitment?" Rina tried to cut in, but I wasn't done. "Are you judging me for keeping things casual, the same way a man does?"

"Don't try to make this some feminist agenda thing. You told me you didn't want to see him two days in a row because you don't want him getting any ideas. But I think you're actually afraid because *you* are getting ideas—commitment-like ideas."

I almost snorted watermelon cocktail out of my nose at the absurdity of Rina's comment. My friends, however, didn't find it funny at all. Judging by their expressions, they actually agreed with her.

"I know things with Andrew weren't easy, and it didn't end well, but that doesn't mean James will hurt you if you give him a chance." Amelia's sweet voice echoed Rina's words from the other day.

"Whatever," I said, hiding behind my cocktail glass. "Come on, tonight's supposed to be fun."

"Well, my sister just got engaged." Amelia dropped the bomb out of nowhere, and I couldn't have been more grateful for the turn in the conversation.

"Wait, what?" Daisy asked. "Isn't your sister like eighteen?"

"Nineteen. She's one year away from completing her Associate's Degree, so they are planning to get married as soon as that's done. Then they'll move into his place together and probably start popping out babies…. My parents couldn't be happier." Amelia finished her drink in one long gulp.

"And I'm assuming we're not happy about it?" Rina narrowed her eyes, trying to read Amelia's expression.

"Something about being twenty-eight and single?" I offered gently. "You know you're not the only one, right?" I looked around the table of happy, mostly functional twenty-something single women.

Amelia sighed. "Sabrina found someone so young. I'm happy for her, really, I am. It's just, I thought I would have my turn before my baby sister got hers."

Daisy stood to hug Amelia. "Sooner than you think you'll have your bakery, and there you will meet your prince charming. We promise, even if we have to drag him to you. But in the meantime, you know over fifty percent of marriages end in divorce, yeah?"

Laughter filled the room once more, but the sound of the buzzer interrupted our giggles. Rina went to answer, since she was closer to the door. "Expecting anyone else?"

"Nope," I said in between bites. Amelia and I had almost become roommates, but she'd decided to live at home to save money. The selfish part of me wished we had moved in together, because her food was irresistible. Meanwhile I barely used my kitchen.

"Well, speak of the devil…," said Rina, smirking as she joined us.

"What devil?" Daisy asked.

Rina shot me a pointed look, biting her lip to stop her smile from taking over.

"No," I said, realization dawning on me. "It's not possible. He cannot be here right now."

The mother of all blushes spread across my cheeks, something my friends found hilarious and were quick to point out. I hastily stood and shook the crumbs off my robe in a pointless attempt at trying to make myself look presentable.

The fact I wasn't wearing clothes wasn't even the issue. My hair was still wet and pasted to my skull like a cow had fixed it there with its tongue. I wasn't wearing any makeup, which wouldn't be so bad if my hair at least looked decent.

I hastily flipped my head upside down, shaking my hair out to make it look presentable. Then I shot Rina a death glare for buzzing him up without warning.

CHAPTER TWELVE

James must not have expected to find four women in my apartment, because he froze at the door, his eyes drifting over the mess of clothes, food, and booze. Having him over at all was not in my plans, but for it to happen while my apartment looked like an after party had exploded within it was not ideal. In any case, I refused to be embarrassed since he had come uninvited.

"Ladies, I'm sorry for interrupting," he finally said, his smoothness sending shivers down my spine. "I need to borrow Cassandra for a second." Without further comment, he strode confidently toward me, and when I still didn't move—mostly because I didn't really know where to go—he lifted me easily and swung me over his shoulder like a sack of sad potatoes.

"She's all yours," Rina said, like the traitor she was.

I heard Amelia and Daisy giggle before my bedroom door slammed shut.

"Now, what am I going to do with you?"

"I thought you were at a meeting."

"I was, but someone kept teasing me so I had to come take care of it."

He slid me down his front, my entire body flush against his. I was still naked underneath my robe, and my nipples instantly hardened against his solid chest. Loud music started playing in the living room, and James's lips twitched. "It seems like your friends are giving us some privacy."

We stood toe to toe, his hands firmly on my waist. Then they started moving up, thumbs brushing the sides of my boobs. My body betrayed me, my breaths coming out in short pants as his touch continued to explore my body. He caressed my face, his fingers brushing my nose, my cheekbones, following the outline of my lips....

I licked my lips in anticipation. "So, now that you have me here, what are you going to do with me?"

James released a long breath, an evil smirk on his lips. He didn't say a word; he didn't have to. The bastard picked me up again, but this time he quickly sat me down across his knees, ass up, of course. He let my head rest on the bed while my legs dangled off his lap, putting me completely at his mercy.

I couldn't complain. I loved a man who took initiative. The anticipation alone made my pussy throb.

"I've been very forgiving lately," he said, lifting the bottom of my robe. His hand trailed slowly up my thigh, and the tip of his finger had barely touched my ass when a whimper escaped me. He chuckled, his body vibrating with laughter, which made my situation even worse. James had barely touched me, and I was already wet.

He hooked his finger into my underwear, lifting my hips to slide them down my legs. "You flirt with the waiter, and my friend." James closed my legs together, his hand running up my thigh. "You sneak out of my place." I felt his warm palm land softly on my ass, rubbing circles on my cheek, kneading my flesh. "Make me jerk off to memories again."

The image his words conjured up in my brain had me squeezing my legs together, desperate for more. I could clearly picture James standing under his rainfall showerhead, one hand on the wall for support as he stroked his thick cock, grunting as he reached climax. Lusting after this man would be my downfall.

"That's three strikes." James's hand landed on my ass with force this time. I felt a shot of sweet pain race up my spine, the sensation only increasing when he started rubbing and kneading my ass again.

"Then you drive me crazy at a meeting, when I'm far away from you and can't touch you. This behavior is unacceptable. You need to be taught a lesson." James wrapped my hair around his fist, forcing me to look at him. "I'm going to spank you six more times, then I'm not letting you come. Understood?"

I nodded weakly, his words already pushing me over the edge. It didn't help that I could feel his hard cock pressed against my stomach. James delivered another smack without warning. All I could do was whimper into my arm.

"One," he counted as he rubbed the spot he had just hit. He continued the same torture, spanking me, then rubbing the spot in a circular motion.

My ass was on fire, a fire that spread throughout my entire body and gathered in my core. Each time his hand smacked against my ass, the vibrations spread to my quivering pussy. By number four, I could feel my arousal dripping down my thighs.

"Five," James's gravelly voice counted out, except this time he didn't start rubbing my butt right away. Instead, I felt him spread my cheeks apart. He pushed two long fingers inside me for a second, and I gasped, my muscles clenching around him. But the bastard removed them way too quickly. "You have the prettiest pussy."

Out of nowhere, he delivered the final blow. A sharp sting ignited on my asscheek before warmth took over. My entire body trembled with pleasure at the delicious combination of pain and pleasure. James rubbed my sore ass for a few seconds, not going anywhere near where I wanted him, before he picked me up again and set me down on the bed.

I shifted to my side to watch him as he adjusted his hard cock in his pants. His cheeks were flushed, full lips parted as he panted slightly. I couldn't in good consciousness let him leave like that.

"Do you have any lotion?" he asked, looking around my room. I pointed towards the dresser. He grabbed a tube and sat down next to me on the bed; then he put some lotion in his palm, rubbing it between his hands to warm it before he applied it on my ass. "I think this is the hottest thing I've ever seen. Your ass is all red with my handprint on it." He cupped my pussy for a second. "You're so wet. I almost want to go back on my punishment."

"You could easily do that." I spread my legs open to give him a better view. "I bet it would only take you two minutes."

"I bet I could make you come in one. But that will not happen. I still need my reward."

"Isn't spanking me reward enough?"

"Oh no, I think I deserve more." James stood up and undid his belt, pulling it aggressively out of the loops. It made me wish he'd use that belt on me, but those thoughts quickly evaporated as James undid his button, then his zipper. He lowered his pants, his hard cock straining against the black fabric of his boxers.

I licked my lips in anticipation as he freed his cock, showing me just how hard he was. How ready he was for me.

Standing up, I pushed James down on the bed, then turned towards my dresser for a hair tie. James watched my every movement as I secured my hair in a ponytail and dropped to my knees. I wrapped my lips around his head, taking him inch by inch until his balls hit my chin. I held his gaze as I slowly worked my way back down his dick. When I reached his head again, I flicked my tongue over the sensitive spot below his head.

James grabbed my ponytail, wrapping my long hair around his fist. "Fuck," he groaned.

I let him out of my mouth with a loud pop. "I've been dreaming about sucking your dick since I first saw it at Oasis." I sucked on his head while I worked him up and down with one hand, randomly flicking that sensitive spot with my tongue. Each time I did, his hips shot forward, pushing his cock deeper into my mouth. I was loving every second of it.

"Cassandra," he said in a hoarse whisper. With my hand still working his thick cock up and down, I licked a path up one side of his dick until I reached his balls. I started by running my tongue against them to see if he liked it, then I sucked one heavy ball into my mouth, caressing it with my tongue. "Cassie, fuck," he groaned, fisting my sheets in his hand.

I released his ball from my mouth and planted a wet kiss on his inner thigh. Then I licked my way up his veiny cock again, wrapping my mouth around his throbbing head, the salty taste of his pre-cum invading my tongue. James's piercing eyes were locked on mine as I pulled his cock down my throat. I could tell he was losing control by the way his hips were moving, pushing his hard length deeper and deeper.

He was so big, tears stung my eyes, saliva dripping down my chin as I tried to take all of him inside my mouth.

James needed release, and I was more than happy to give it to him.

I started bobbing my head up and down, working my tongue around his cock while I pumped him with one hand. Reaching down, I massaged his balls with my free hand. In seconds, I felt his body tense, his muscles locking in place in preparation for release.

"I'm coming," he warned, but I didn't let up. Hot spurts of cum slid down my throat as he emptied himself in my mouth. I swallowed as much as I could, some of it dripping down my chin as I continued to suck him off. Once I was done milking him, I licked him clean, paying extra attention to the sensitive spot under his head.

James suddenly sat up and pulled me towards the bed with trembling hands. He lay down with his head against my breasts, his pants still around his ankles. "I just need a minute," he said. "That was the best blowjob I've ever had."

"You're welcome," I joked, running my fingernails across his scalp. He seemed to like that, as he nestled himself more between my boobs, his large frame trembling slightly.

We stayed like that for a moment, a completely satisfied James sprawled on top of me, his cum still on my chin. "Am I hurting you?" he eventually asked, looking up at me. "How's your ass?"

"A little sore, but in a good way. You should send me flowers more often if it leads to this."

He propped himself up with his elbow, raising his eyebrows in question. "I didn't send you flowers." He must have seen the confusion on my face. "Were you sending me nudes using flowers some other guy sent you?"

"I thought they were from you," I said, my mind going a mile a minute, trying to figure out who could've sent them.

"Poor guy. He'll never get a thank you like I did."

"Who's to say he hasn't already?"

James hovered over me, running his nose up my neck all the way to my ear. "We have an agreement, or did you forget?" His voice sent chills down my spine. He opened my robe, revealing my naked breasts.

"Maybe he had me before you, dum dum."

"Dum dum?" he asked, his tongue circling my nipple.

"You have a way of stripping me of my words." I pushed him off me, knowing full well that he had allowed me to. "I have to get ready. The girls are probably dying of curiosity."

He stood, and I watched as he carefully pulled up his boxers, then his pants. "So you really don't know who sent you those flowers?"

"No idea. I really thought they were from you."

"I guess you have a secret admirer."

"And you owe me an orgasm," I said in an attempt to change the subject.

"It wouldn't be a punishment if I made it up to you, now would it?" He winked before throwing the door open, his expression imme-diately sobering.

I guess I wasn't the only one who could switch masks like a chameleon. For a second, I wondered if he was the real James Walton when he was with me, but it didn't really matter. I was only interested in sex.

My friends clapped as we walked out of the room, which made me want to wring their necks.

"Ladies, she's all yours," James said, a devilish smirk on his face.

Politeness returned to me, and I introduced them. "James, these are my friends, Catarina, Daisy, and Amelia."

"Would you like a drink, or something to eat?" Amelia offered.

"Thank you, but I should probably get back to my meeting. It was lovely to meet you."

I walked him to the door, my stupid face probably beet red, an uneasy feeling swirling around my stomach.

"Behave tonight?" James asked, kissing me chastely on the cheek.

"Can't make any promises when the punishment feels so good," I answered, biting my lip.

He shook his head and disappeared down the hallway. I stood there for a second too long with my hand pressed against my hammering heart before I shook it off and went back inside.

CHAPTER THIRTEEN

The next day I stayed in bed until noon to catch up on some much needed sleep. After James had left, the girls and I had a great time at Oasis, but my body was definitely feeling the effects of the copious amounts of alcohol we'd consumed.

By the time I checked my phone, I had three missed calls—one from Monty, one from James, and one from a private number. I returned Monty's call first, and we arranged to meet at a park near my house.

I spotted Monty's hunched figure sitting on a bench, a flock of birds surrounding him. "Good morning," I said, handing him a hot cup of coffee.

Monty looked me over, his bushy eyebrows drawing together. "Good afternoon," he countered, the corner of his lips lifting into a crooked smile. "Bad news, kid. Your client is guilty and sloppy. There's money scattered all over the globe. Maxwell transferred assets to everyone he could think of, including his ex-wife."

"What's the history between the two?"

"The usual. Maxwell wanted a younger wife, so he ditched Elinor for a girl his daughter's age. Elinor kept her cool, stayed friendly with Maxwell over the years. As far as I can tell, she knew some of her ex-husband's business ventures were off the book."

Once more, I almost admired Elinor. Her husband had replaced her with a younger girl, and she had waited almost a decade for revenge. "And the prosecution?"

"They've barely scratched the surface." Monty threw a bunch of seeds in front of us, birds fighting for their share of the feast. "I gotta say, kid, Maxwell must have some deep pockets and some powerful friends. It's the only way I can explain away this shitty FBI investigation. I can go deeper, but it might bite us in the ass."

I sipped my coffee, nodding in agreement. "Elinor's testimony isn't enough to convict, but if they find the accounts… we'll have to settle out of court and be done with it. I won't be the one to poke at the hornet's nest by dragging out the trial."

"Wise choice," Monty said as he stood. "Anything else you need?"

I shook my head. "Thanks, Monty. I'll be in touch."

Monty dumped the entire bag of seeds on the ground, and after watching the birds go at it for a few seconds, left without another word. I'd already known Maxwell was guilty, but I had no idea how deep this went. The system itself was corrupt, not just my client. If my job at Feldman & Sullivan's hadn't shown me that, my work at the shelter certainly did.

I was nothing but a cog in the machine that ensured the rich and powerful stayed that way, despite their crimes. Meanwhile, the women at the shelter went bankrupt trying to keep themselves and their children safe.

The urge to move was overwhelming, so I went for a walk to clear my head. I spotted a coffee cart and got myself another coffee. The only way out of this I could see was to settle out of court and pretend I didn't know that this went deeper than William Maxwell. I had always known the system was broken, that as a criminal defense attorney I would defend guilty people more often than not. I just had to deal with it.

I reminded myself that I was a lawyer, not an ethics professor. My duty was to the client. Disclosing the information Monty had given me would be malpractice. Pushing those thoughts out of my mind, I returned James's call. Maybe we could meet and he'd distract me at least long enough for the tightness in my chest to dissipate.

"Hi, gorgeous," he answered, his deep voice automatically bringing a smile to my lips. "How was your night?"

"Fun. I drank too much, though," I confessed.

"I heard. Elias saw you," he explained before I could ask. "He said you were having a good time with your friends and wanted me to ask you for the brunette's number."

"Amelia or Rina? Either way, they are not into casual sex."

"That will break his heart, but I'll let him know. But I actually called to let you know I'm leaving town for a few days."

I frowned, my stomach clenching in something akin to disappointment. He didn't have to let me know, and I hated that I was glad he did. "Anywhere cool?"

"Chicago. I'm going to a few events and I'm taking an old friend with me to fill the seat. I wanted to let you know first in case you saw any pictures in the press and got the wrong idea."

I tossed my empty cup into the trash before heading back to my apartment. "You didn't have to tell me, but thanks, I guess."

James let out an exasperated sigh. "Listen, you keep evading the question and I'm too tired to play the game right now. Would you really be fine with it if I fucked other women?"

"I wouldn't be fine with it," I answered honestly. "But only because I really like sucking your dick and I wouldn't be able to do that if you fucked other people."

The sound of his deep laughter sent a shiver down my spine. Even over the phone James managed to have an effect on my body. It was infuriating. "It's settled then. We're exclusive."

That word felt too heavy, too constricting. But it wasn't like I had time to hunt for another fuck buddy. And I also knew that James's skills in the bedroom were worth the commitment. "Fine," I finally said.

"Don't sound too happy about it," he said, amusement coating his words. "I have to go. My flight is boarding. But be a good girl for me, and when I get back I promise to make you scream until you beg me to stop."

His words conjured images in my brain that had me pressing my thighs together. "Bye, James." I hung up before he noticed the effect had on me, but I couldn't help the goofy smile that took over my face.

It wasn't too difficult to keep my promise to James. The Maxwell case and my work at the shelter kept me so busy I barely had time to make it to yoga with the girls. And every night, when my head hit the pillow, I was out like a light.

James texted every day, and I replied sporadically, the word 'exclusive' still sitting heavily in my chest. I didn't want a relationship, and I didn't have time for one. Although I would never admit it out loud, I knew Rina was right. I had commitment and trust issues, but given my past, it felt justified.

Pushing James out of my mind, I concentrated on returning phone calls and scheduling depositions. We had a meeting with Maxwell later, so my team and I booked the conference room to go over the details. I couldn't wait to put this mess behind me. Hopefully, the partners' memory was short and they would soon assign me another big case. Another chance to prove myself.

Daisy sent a link in the group chat, and I absentmindedly opened it to reveal a picture of James in a tux, with a beautiful, statuesque blonde on his arm. The woman was model thin, and for a second, my insecurities got the best of me. I was more on the curvy side, and my stomach definitely wasn't flat. The girls and I did yoga for stress relief, and the elliptical in my apartment had the same purpose. Moving my body felt good, but I hadn't worked out to lose weight since Andrew.

Daisy: Isn't that James?
Me: Yep. He told me he'd be taking an old friend to some
event in Chicago.

He didn't tell me that his old friend was drop dead gorgeous, though, or that he'd have his arm around her in pictures. Not that it mattered.

Amelia: Old friend? Did he say how close they were?

Me: Guys, it doesn't really matter.

Daisy: You're hotter. His loss.

Rina: Don't make it seem more than what it is. He told her he'd be taking a friend to an event. That's what the picture shows.

Amelia: Exactly. It's not like his tongue is down her throat.

Me: Either way, I don't care. Have to get back to work.

Telling the girls I had agreed to exclusivity was not an option. They would make it a big deal, when in reality it was simply convenient. I put my phone away and opened my laptop to work, and then spent a solid twenty minutes staring blankly at my screen. James was meant to be a distraction, a fuck buddy to help me blow off some steam. He wasn't supposed to occupy this much mental space.

Frustrated, I joined Stacy and Peter in the conference room and we worked on the Maxwell case together. We went over the district attorney's offer and, although we'd still negotiate, we were confident that settling out of court was the best option for our client.

Hours later, my team and I sat in silence, the air around us heavy as we waited for Maxwell. We busied ourselves leafing through the case files until our client walked in with Mr. Sullivan. Seeing Maxwell at all was annoying to me, but having him walk in with a partner raised all my hackles.

The man had stolen millions from naïve old people. He didn't deserve any special treatment in my book. Pleasantries were exchanged, and then I had to endure Maxwell's complaints about his belongings being seized.

"It was my favorite painting, a Manet. Now every time I walk past the hallway, it feels wrong, like part of me is missing." Maxwell whined about how hard it was to live in an empty mansion and drive his own car until Olivia brought him his coffee. "Thanks, sweeetheart," he said, eyeing her up and down.

I could feel my blood boiling, but I schooled my features into a neutral mask. My team and I explained the current state of the case, and the district attorney's offer, but the words didn't seem to reach my client until I said, "Mr. Maxwell, we need to settle."

He released a long breath, as if my statement actually caused him physical pain. "I was afraid you'd say that."

"The evidence is too overwhelming," I continued. "We can't establish reasonable doubt when the money was found in your daughter's account."

"What are we looking at? Community service? A fine?"

I gulped at my client's audacity. He had embezzled millions in funds and thought he could get away with community service. It was truly laughable. "There will be a large fine. And probably some prison time."

He stood and started pacing around the room, his puffy face becoming visibly redder. "Prison? What do you mean, prison?" He turned toward Mr. Sullivan, narrowing his cold eyes. "I'm paying you hundreds of thousands of dollars. Is this the best you've got? I thought you said she was a shark."

I ignored the slight, because seeing him suffer made me a little giddy. "I made an offer to the district attorney. We're looking at five years." At his horrified look, I quickly added, "Good behavior would get you out in three."

"Five years?" he shouted. "I can't go to jail for five years. It would destroy my life." He paced back and forth, huffing and puffing about it all being unfair. "This is ridiculous. Unacceptable. You better fix this. I'm not going to jail."

He pointed a sausage finger at my face, which made me want to break it in half, but I had to keep my cool.

Peter and Stacy looked at him with dumbfounded expressions, momentarily speechless. I was used to my entitled clients, but Maxwell seemed to live in a completely different reality. One where you lied to your lawyer and poorly hid your embezzled money, but still got off scot free.

"How about a trial with a jury? We could appeal to their emotions or whatever," Maxwell suggested.

Before I could respond to his madness, Mr. Sullivan took over. "We could, but that isn't ideal." He walked over to Maxwell and put his hand on his shoulder. "Putting it bluntly, William, a New York jury would have little sympathy for a man accused of embezzling millions in retirement funds. Unfortunately, this is a case we will not win. The best course of action here is to settle and hope that the district attorney accepts our offer."

After Mr. Sullivan spoke, Maxwell was calm enough to go over the details of the offer we'd prepared for the district attorney. But honestly, if I was prosecuting this case, I would send his ass to jail, not only because he was guilty but to punish him for invading my mind during my solo sexy time.

The meeting lasted another hour. By the time we were done, I needed a drink, despite the fact it was still eleven a.m. and I was at work. Maxwell was an exhausting person.

"Can I see you privately?" Mr. Sullivan said, before I could escape.

"Of course." I smiled and followed him into his office. He had a dreamy view of New York through his floor-to-ceiling windows, something I envied and aspired to, but the room felt stuffy. The old furniture and the ugliest green couch I had ever seen, combined with the stale air inside, had me itching to crack open a window.

"Drink?" he asked, walking towards his liquor shelf.

"No, thank you," I said, despite how much I needed one. "So, you're taking over my case?"

"That is what I like about you, straight to the point." He turned his back to me to pour himself a drink, and I patiently waited for him to continue. "But your direct approach doesn't always work with our clients. Maxwell is a sensitive man, and he finds you a little abrasive."

I sat on the awful green couch, simmering in quiet indignation, wondering how this would affect my career. I fought the urge to defend myself. This wasn't a hill I was willing to die on.

Mr. Sullivan sat next to me, angling his body towards me. "Listen, it's nothing personal. The district attorney is a personal friend. I'll talk him into accepting the five years, though I'll owe him. I need to make sure the firm doesn't suffer." His hand landed on my shoulder in what he must have meant as a comforting gesture, but it made me feel yucky. "I'm sure you understand, the firm's reputation is on the line. You and your team should have found the money first, so we could make it disappear. Now it's too late."

Make it disappear? That was highly illegal and not something I would be a part of, but I couldn't say that. "Do you mind if I take that drink now?" I asked as I pushed to my feet, uninterested in the drink but eager to get his hand off me. "So I'm being benched because my client is an idiot?"

"All of our clients are idiots, Cassandra. That's why they pay us the big bucks—so we can get them out of trouble when they do stupid things." He came to stand behind me as I poured myself a drink, placing his hand on my shoulder again. "I know you're upset, but I'm not benching you. I'm just taking over as primary lawyer."

He was definitely standing too close to me now, so I pivoted and started pacing the room to avoid being touched again. "I still want you there," he continued, "especially when it comes to dealing with the press. You have a special way with words and can deflect like no other. Plus, you look good on camera. That's always a bonus." He winked before walking over to his desk and opening some random file, dismissing me without a word.

I downed the remainder of my whiskey before I left his office, feeling dejected, angry, and like I needed a shower. I had never had anyone step in and take over any of my cases before, and to have it happen on such a high-profile case would definitely hinder my career. Feeling like I was drowning in failure, I switched out my heels in favor of my flats and went home to drown my sorrows in alcohol.

Hours later, I was in my sweatpants sipping vodka when my phone started vibrating on my coffee table. James's name flashed across the screen, giving me an idea of something else I could do to take the edge off.

"James," I answered in my most sultry voice.

"Cassandra." The way he said my name made my heart beat a little faster. "Did you miss me?"

"Wait, you were gone? I didn't notice." I got up to pour myself another glass, but the moment I stood, all the alcohol decided to kick in all at once and I nearly fell over my coffee table. Luckily, I landed back on the couch with a humph. Laughter escaped my throat at my own clumsiness, and it was at this exact moment that I realized I was truly drunk.

"Are you okay?" James asked.

"Yep, tripped. Also, might be a little tipsy." I put the call on speaker so I could use both hands just in case I lost my balance again.

I heard some commotion in the background, someone calling his name, then a door closing. "What's the occasion?"

"No occasion, just my boss being an asshole and the death of my career." I was being a little dramatic, but alcohol did that to me.

"Hmm, I see." He sounded distracted, and I heard voices in the background once more.

"You sound busy, though. We can talk some other time. I don't want to keep you."

"I'm yours for as long as you'll have me." Fucking hell, I knew he meant the call, but his words caused my drunk brain to short circuit. I couldn't form any words. "Are you there?"

I cleared my throat. "Yep, here. Just getting another drink."

"Do you want some company? I can pick you up at eight."

"Honestly, I don't feel like going out. I'd rather sit here drowning my feelings towards my boss in vodka."

"Your feelings towards your boss?" he asked tersely.

"God, you are so territorial." I couldn't help the laughter that escaped me. Just the thought of having romantic feelings towards my boss sent me into a hysterical fit of giggles. "I have some intense feelings towards my boss right now, but fortunately for you and your possessive nature, none of them make me want to tear his clothes off. His head? Sure. But not his clothes."

James's deep chuckle had me biting my lip. "Speaking of my possessive nature, were you a good girl while I was gone?" The way he said 'good girl' made me wish he was here, so I could actually do something to earn it, like wrap my lips around his throbbing cock.

The sudden urge to see him caused me to panic, and as if on cue, I heard someone in the background call his name. "You sound really busy, James. Talk tomorrow?"

"Cassandra—" he started.

"Bye, see you tomorrow." I hung up on him, a huge smile on my face, knowing that I had evaded his question and that it would drive him crazy. I took way too much pleasure in teasing him.

With my vodka Red Bull in hand, I walked back to my spot on the couch to continue watching trash TV. There was nothing like a few drinks and a few episodes of Geordie Shore to get my mind off things. Their accents alone made me crack up.

The memory of James's voice lingered in my mind, making me want to see him. I looked around my apartment, taking in the dishes in the sink, the clothes strewn here and there…. I didn't have the energy to clean up now and going out was out of the question. James and my greedy vagina would have to wait until tomorrow.

CHAPTER FOURTEEN

Three episodes of Geordie Shore later, the sound of the doorbell almost made me jump out of my skin. I wasn't expecting anyone and judging by the way the world spun when I stood up, I wasn't very fit for company at the moment.

"Yes?" I spoke into the intercom.

"It's James, let me in."

James. No. Not James. James could not be here right now.

"Why?" I said, then had to repeat it because I hadn't pressed the button.

"I got you something. Let me in."

"Fiiine." I buzzed him in, unlocked and unchained my door, then considered my next move. I took in the surrounding mess, shame nudging at the back of my head at once more letting him see my apartment in its natural state. But he was the one intruding on me again, so if he had a problem with how untidy my place was, he could just clean it himself.

James knocked, and I opened the door for him.

He walked in, looking fine as ever in a black sweater, black pants, and white sneakers. "I don't think I can handle how hot you look right now." My brain to mouth filter was clearly not functioning because I carried on speaking. "Why are you here, James?" I whined. "Look at me, I'm a mess and you come in here looking like you belong on Forbes's hottest billionaire list, which you probably are on."

I frowned, wondering if my last sentence even made sense, but James's hand on the back of my head made me forget I had spoken at all.

"I will take that as an odd compliment. And you look perfect." He swooped down and planted a kiss on my forehead before pulling me in for a tight hug. It felt good being in his arms, pressed against his hard body…. I buried my head in his neck, closed my eyes, and let his already familiar smell comfort me. "Did you just sniff me?" he asked, still holding me in his arms, his chest shaking with laughter.

Quick, think of something.

"What? No!" I stepped away from him, the bag he was carrying rustling against my leg. "I was smelling the food you brought. Chinese?" *Good save*, I thought to myself. Even intoxicated, I could improvise like the best of them. The partners should appreciate my skills more.

"Close, Indian," James answered. He toed off his snickers, walked over to my kitchen as if he had been here a thousand times before, and started taking containers out of the bag. "Plates?" When I didn't answer or move from my spot by the door, he started opening random cabinets.

By the time I made it to the kitchen, still trying to figure out why I felt butterflies in my stomach seeing James so comfortable in my place, he had already set the table. "I'm not hungry, James."

He looked over at my sink where a half empty bottle of vodka sat abandoned. "If you eat, I'll join you in the drinking. It's been a long day. I could use a few drinks." He pulled out a bottle of fine whiskey from his bag, and a beautiful bear-shaped bottle of Belvedere vodka.

Of course, that's what my brain zeroed in on. "That is the cutest bottle I've ever seen. Can I keep it?" I gave him my best puppy look. His returning smile made my drunk heart skip a beat.

He sat down, tapping the seat beside him as an invitation to sit. "If you eat, it's all yours."

"You drive a hard bargain, Mr. Walton." I sat on the stool next to him, taking in all the food he had brought.

"This one's spicy." He grabbed the container and placed it beside him. "All the rest should be safe for you to eat."

He remembered I didn't like spicy food.

I had told the waiter at Euphoria and he remembered.

It was a stupid thing to cause my heart to flutter, so I blamed it on the alcohol.

I sniffed a few containers to disguise the half panicked, half lovesick look on my face, but a huge smile broke out when I smelled chicken mango. "This is my favorite, thank you."

"You're welcome. Now eat up." James must have been hungry because he devoured his food while I sat there staring at him, marveling at the way his throat worked with each swallow.

I finally took a bite out of the chicken, relishing the explosion of sweet and salty flavor on my tongue. "Hmmm," I moaned, "this is really good."

"Please don't moan. I haven't seen you in a week and you're too intoxicated to consent."

"I feel like I'm always horny for you. It's a bit annoying actually," my drunk mouth spilled out. My head felt too heavy, so I leaned into James and rested my head on his shoulder.

He chuckled. "Is that a fact?"

I closed my eyes for a second. His clothes smelled so good and his sweater was so soft and comfortable. "Yeah, you always look so hot. But it's more than that. My brain just can't quite put it into words right now."

"And I'm assuming once you're sober you'll completely deny this conversation ever happened, right?"

"I wouldn't say deny, just deflect." I propped myself up to take a few more bites of chicken, terrified of where our conversation was going, even in my drunken stupor.

James must have sensed my unease because for once, he was the one to change the subject. "I really like your place, it's very cozy."

"Thanks," I said in between bites, "I know it's smaller than your penthouse. You must feel like you're slumming it."

He gave me a hard look, his sharp jaw clenching. "Does the difference in our income bother you?"

"Not really."

"But you think I care that you have less money?"

"I just meant that compared to what you're used to, coming down to Brooklyn to eat takeout in my tiny one-bedroom apartment—"

He pressed a finger against my lips to stop me from talking, something I didn't appreciate at all. "I'm not going to let you finish that sentence. I like you, and I enjoy spending time with you. We could be on a yacht eating caviar or out camping eating food from a can and I wouldn't give a shit as long as you were there. So don't ever think I'm 'slumming it.'"

Fuck.

I had trouble breathing after his little speech, so I stared directly at my plate with wide eyes until I recovered. "So, how was your trip?"

James gave me an incredulous look before shaking his head. I felt he was disappointed with my response, but hearing the words 'I like you' from his sculpted lips had sent me into a panic.

There was nothing wrong with him liking me. For all intents and purposes, it made complete sense since we were friends with benefits. You wouldn't want to hang around a person you didn't like.

"Terrible. You really haven't Googled me, have you?"

"No, although Daisy sent me a picture of you with your friend."

James angled his body toward mine, a dazzling smirk on his lips. "You never answered my question. Were you a good girl while I was away?"

"Were you a good boy while you were away?" I countered, resting a hand on his muscular thigh. He definitely didn't skip leg day.

He chuckled, that stupid smile of his making my heart leap in my chest. "Yes. I told you, she's just a friend. It's a terrible social faux pas to fail to fill a seat at a charity event, even when you pay for it. Otherwise, I would have gone alone. Next time, I'll just take you with me. Now, stop evading my question. Did you behave or do I have to bend you over my knee again?"

The way he said it had me closing my legs and pressing my thighs together. "Yes, for your information, I've been a very good girl. But honestly, I don't have time to go out looking for another man. As Rina put it, when you have a unicorn, you don't go out looking for anything else."

"Wait, am I the unicorn in this scenario?" he asked. I nodded, collecting our plates and pushing to my feet to load them into the dishwasher. "I don't know if I'm supposed to be insulted or flattered."

"Flattered, definitely. A unicorn is a man who is good looking, kind, respectful, and can make you come with just his fingers in the middle of a club. It's a rare creature. Sure you sometimes run into a stallion that appears to be a unicorn, but most men are donkeys." James looked utterly confused by my explanation, so I pressed on in simpler terms. "Unicorn good, donkey bad."

"Thanks, I think I got it now," he said sarcastically, but he looked so cute when he was confused, all I wanted was to reach over and ruffle his hair. So I did, because I could.

I realized I could touch him whenever I wanted, a privilege that I had failed to take advantage of before. He watched me patiently as I stood on tiptoe to ruffle his hair, then he picked me up and set me on the counter.

He cupped my face in his large hands while his piercing eyes traced my lips. I couldn't wait for him to kiss me, so I pulled him towards me. The moment our lips met, I was lost in sensation. James quickly took over the kiss, his tongue eliciting all kinds of funny feelings in my heart.

"I missed your lips," he whispered.

I'd only known James for a few weeks. We'd only been on one official date, but somehow having him in my apartment didn't make me uncomfortable.

That was scary. I pushed him away from me and jumped off the counter. "So," I said, clearing my throat. "Why was the trip terrible?"

James ran his hands through his hair, making me want to do the same. "When I took over Walton Corporation, I invested in a biotech company. It was my decision to branch out since we mostly

invest in real estate. Now this company is being fined for safety viola-
tions, among other things. It caused our stocks to crash, so I had to
fly down to do some damage control."

"That sounds really bad."

"It is. I don't know enough about biotechnology, so I hired a
team to oversee new, safer procedures. But we still lost a lot of
money."

I pulled a bottle of tequila from my liquor cabinet and fetched
some lime. James immediately got my drift, and started cutting up
some lime wedges, since he said I couldn't be trusted with a knife. I
rolled my eyes at him, even though I knew he was probably right.
With my luck, I'd chop a finger off and have to spend the night at
the ER.

"What is it that this company does exactly? Can you make back
the money you lost?"

We drank one shot and I poured a second.

James brightened, his steady gaze focused on me. "We're devel-
oping biofertilizers to replace chemical fertilizers. I can't go into
details because I honestly don't fully understand the science, but
microbes can stimulate crop growth, and it's better for the environment. We partnered with a Belgian biotech company to research
and develop. I just hope this setback doesn't delay our work."

I clinked my glass against his. "To microbes."

James grinned at me before he downed his shot. "And the
money's not the issue. My father wasn't too happy with my decision
to diversify, so now that I'm failing, he can barely resist rubbing
it in."

Somewhere in my drunken brain, his words fully registered. I
placed one hand on his forearm, squeezing reassuringly, and said,
"One setback is not a failure. Especially when it seems like you're
doing what you can to fix it."

A small smile crept over James's face, his eyes crinkling at the
corners. It made him look even more handsome.

"Thank you," he said. "Now let's drink and forget about our
troubles."

After three shots each, I figured that was enough. James fixed a
vodka Red Bull for me—from the bear shaped bottle—and a

whiskey for him. We sat down on my couch, his warm body right next to mine.

His gaze zeroed in on the framed picture by the TV. "Are those your parents?" he asked, pushing to his feet to grab the frame and get a better look.

I swallowed the lump in my throat. "Yes."

"Your mom is beautiful. You look exactly like her."

"Thank you," I said casually, before quickly changing the subject. "What do you want to watch?"

James placed the picture beside the TV and slumped beside me. "What were you watching before?"

His hand landed on my thigh, and even through the thick material of my sweatpants, his touch was making me all hot and bothered. "Something I pretend not to enjoy but secretly do—British reality TV."

"Okay, then let's watch that."

I gave him a puzzled look, but he seemed serious, so I put it on. We spent the next hour making fun of their accents, laughing together. James said Elias could probably do their accent, which led to him telling me a story about how they'd tricked some British girls into thinking they were French because Elias was fantastic at imitating accents.

"Wait, so you both speak French?"

"*Oui*," he said, his dark eyes focused on me. "*Tu es la plus belle femme que j'ai jamais vu.*"

I blinked, trapping my lower lip between my teeth. "I have no idea what you just said, but that was really hot."

James cupped my face, his thumb caressing my cheek. "You're the most beautiful woman I've ever seen. That's what I said."

I froze for a second, then I straddled his lap, our lips crashing together in a passionate kiss. After that, Geordie Shore was completely forgotten. We made out like teenagers, pawing at each other, our lips only parting when we needed to take a breath.

"As much as I'd love to ravish you," he whispered against my lips, "we're both too intoxicated to consent."

I pressed my forehead against his, trying to pretend his decency didn't affect me.

Making out made us thirsty, so I fixed us another drink while James told me about his work and the Walton Corporation.

"I'm stepping into big shoes," he said, leaning against my kitchen counter. "My father, my grandfather, and his father before him were successful in growing the company. They took risks, but it paid off in the end. What if I make the wrong choices? I don't know what I would do if the company failed under my leadership."

"That's a lot of pressure." I handed him his whiskey and trailed my fingers over his forearm, trying to soothe him. "You're doing the best you can, James. At the end of the day, it's all we can do. But for what it's worth, I think it's smart to invest in biotech. Plus, in the long term you're helping the environment, which I find awesome."

He wrapped his arm around my waist and pulled me to him, brushing his lips against my forehead. "You think I'm awesome?"

I smiled, pulling back a little to narrow my eyes at him. "That's not what I said, but you're not too bad."

James chuckled, and I pretended it didn't make me giddy.

"I told you all about my shitty day. Now it's your turn. Why were you upset with your boss?"

Disentangling myself from him, I rummaged the fridge for more RedBull. "I lost my first high-profile case. And now my boss is taking over as primary attorney as we try to settle out of court."

"Settling a case is not the same as losing. Often it's better to settle than drag it out in court, you know that."

"Yes, but this was my chance to prove myself. I want to make partner."

"You're young, gorgeous, you have time to build your career."

I nodded, then switched the subject. Talking about it just made me feel like a failure.

Sometime later, we were back on the couch. James put on a movie that we barely watched, since we couldn't stop talking. I was getting sleepy, so I lay down on the couch and rested my head on his lap.

"Can I tell you something?"

"Anything," James said, his deep voice soothing my jumbled brain.

"I hate my job. All I do is make sure that rich white men keep their privilege. No offence, but you guys suck. And I just clean up after you and make sure you don't go to jail. Preppy white boy driving drunk? Case dismissed. Frat boys get into a fistfight? Daddy calls me to fix it. Caught with drugs? Here comes your lady in shining gavel, except I don't have a gavel because I'm not a judge and gavels are not shiny, but you get the point."

"Why do you do it then?"

"Money." I felt his whole body tensing under me, so I added, "Relax, I don't want *your* money, just the money I can earn. And I earn the most at my job."

"If money wasn't an issue, and you didn't have to work, what would you do?" James threaded his long fingers through my hair, making me even more sleepy.

"Oh no, I refuse to engage in those fantasies. There is no scenario where money isn't an issue. Maybe if I won the lottery, but even then I'm sure it'd be an issue, with taxes and all that."

"Indulge me. What would you do?"

"I'd work at the shelter where I volunteer."

"That's it? No trips to exclusive resorts in the Bahamas or shopping sprees in Paris?"

I laughed. "A week at the beach sounds fun, but I couldn't do that my whole life. I'm not really built for a life of inactivity. Work keeps the thoughts at bay."

"What thoughts?"

I closed my eyes and pretended I didn't hear him, letting his fingers running through my hair lull me to sleep.

Later that night, I woke up fully dressed in my bed. It was still dark out, and as my eyes adjusted to the dim room, I noticed a glass of water sitting on my nightstand next to some painkillers. *James.* I sat up and drained the water, grateful that he was so thoughtful. My mouth still felt like I had swallowed sand, so I begrudgingly got up to get more water. When I stepped into the kitchen, I saw a large body curled up on my couch, feet dangling from the edge.

James.

I walked over to him and crouched next to his sleeping form, my head spinning with every move I made. My memories were fuzzy, but I remembered enjoying his company. He must have carried me to bed when I fell asleep.

"Hey, wake up," I said, reaching out to touch his face. He had a bit of stubble growing, and I liked the scratchy feeling against my palm. A dirty part of me thought I would also like this feeling somewhere else, but I pushed that aside for the moment.

James slowly opened his eyes. "Hi," he whispered.

My palm was still against his cheek. He brought it over to his lips to kiss it.

"What are you doing here?" I asked.

He blinked and sat up, rubbing his face. "I'm sorry. I was too drunk to drive, and I didn't think I should leave you alone."

"No, silly. I meant, what are you doing on the couch? You barely fit here." He blinked, and I realized he had been respecting my no sleepover rule. "Come to bed. You're too big for the couch."

A small smile flashed across his lips. He stood and followed me into the bedroom. I never slept with pants on, so I quickly removed my sweatpants and slipped into bed. James stripped down to his boxers, and I wished my head wasn't pounding painfully against my skull so I could take full advantage of it.

He slipped into bed next to me and wrapped his arm around me. I hadn't actually slept with anyone since Andrew, but I pushed that thought aside the moment it popped into my head. It felt weird to think about my ex as I was getting in bed with James.

"Goodnight, gorgeous," James whispered. He planted a kiss on top of my head, and I felt his muscular body settle against mine. I let myself relax, the sound of his soft breaths lulling me to sleep. Before I knew it, I was out.

CHAPTER FIFTEEN

The next morning, before I even opened my eyes, I regretted the amount of alcohol I'd consumed the night before. It didn't escape my notice that this was the second weekend in a row that I'd gotten blackout drunk. That was out of the ordinary. I couldn't even remember half of what had happened last night.

But I remembered falling asleep next to James.

I reached over, but the bed was empty and cold. A large amount of alcohol had been consumed, but that wouldn't make me hallucinate. James had been here, and he'd left. I covered my face with my blanket, trying to go back to sleep, but I couldn't ignore the tightness in my chest. Waking up alone after cuddling for hours felt like shit.

James was giving me a dose of my own medicine. I guess I couldn't blame him.

I groggily got up to use the bathroom, each step vibrating through my body and causing my head to pound. Water, that's what I needed. I drank from the tap, taking in my sorry appearance in the mirror. Of course he'd left. Who would want to spend time with this unstable mess?

Once I was done feeling sorry for myself, I made my way to the kitchen for a proper glass of water. Suddenly the front door swung open. I stumbled back and nearly choked on my water, the movement causing my stomach to twist and turn.

"Jesus, James! What the hell are you doing here? I thought you left!" I pressed a hand to my heart to calm its wild beating and to stop the nausea my sudden movements had caused.

James sauntered over to me, a mischievous smirk plastered on his face. "I'm not the sneaking out type," he joked.

"Ha ha." I didn't even have enough energy for a witty comeback. Meanwhile, Mr. Walton looked perfectly fresh. Not even a wrinkle on his clothes. "How is it possible that you look hot as always, and I look like a garbage truck ran me over?" I leaned my forehead against the cool granite counter. It soothed my headache, but the position made me want to barf. Tough choices today.

"That bad?" James asked. I groaned in response, unwilling to form actual sentences. "Lucky for you, I'm here." He slid a coffee cup towards me, as well as a smoothie and several takeout containers.

"Are we expecting company?" I managed to croak out, wrapping my hands around the coffee cup.

He started opening the containers, revealing bagels, bacon, scrambled eggs, avocado toast with fried eggs on top, and an assortment of pastries. "I didn't really know your go-to hangover cure, so I got us some options."

The sight of it all and the mix of smells made my stomach turn. Still, I grabbed the coffee and a cream cheese bagel from the counter, while James started in on the bacon.

"How are you not hungover?" I asked as I watched him scarf down his food. "Seriously, is there some secret to it?"

James cocked his head, a mocking smile playing on his lips. "Us rich boys are used to partying. Doesn't really affect us."

My eyes widened as flashbacks from last night invaded my brain. "Oh no! What did I say?"

"Don't worry about it, you're a hilarious drunk. I thoroughly enjoyed myself last night. But there's no secret. I just stopped drinking after you climbed on the counter and hit your head on the ceiling. I figured we needed at least one responsible adult around."

"Oh god, I guess that explains the headache." I rubbed my

head, feeling a tender spot right at the top of my skull. James placed a bottle of Tylenol in front of me. "You're a lifesaver." I immediately took two pills, gulping them down with my water.

"I'm afraid my services come at a cost."

I almost groaned, but I feared the consequences, so I kept it in. "What do you have in mind?"

"I'm attending a party later. I'd like you to come with me."

"What kind of party?"

"That will be a surprise."

"But I need to know what to wear."

He hesitated for a moment, seemingly searching for the right words. "It's a cocktail party. Outdoors. That's all I'm telling you."

I shrugged, lacking the energy to interrogate him further. "I guess I owe you."

"That's the enthusiasm I like to see," he joked. James finished his food, while my bagel remained untouched in front of me. "I'm late for a meeting. But I'll pick you up at four?"

I nodded, the movement causing my vision to blur.

James kissed my cheek, his soft lips warming my skin. "Try to eat something, okay?"

I nodded again, and he was gone.

The moment the door shut behind him I got a little choked up, my heart feeling a little too tight in my chest. I wasn't used to men treating me this way, especially after sex was already on the table. In my experience, and it might be a little sad to admit, men were only nice until they got what they wanted, and that was usually sex. Yet we'd hung out all night with nothing sexual happening between us, other than making out.

James said his services came at a cost, and the idea of this being an exchange soothed me a little.

After finishing my coffee, I crawled back into bed, the pounding in my head making me question my life choices. I was used to drinking. In my world, relationships were built around a glass of whiskey. The odds of being a successful lawyer increased exponentially when you had good connections, and the most effective way to achieve that was to attend parties and go to every after work event, all of which centered around alcohol.

I remembered confessing to James that I didn't really like my job, and I had meant it. But being financially independent was important to me. I couldn't have the lifestyle I wanted if I worked at the shelter.

Hours later, I rolled out of bed feeling much better. My appetite had returned, so I devoured the food James brought. I still couldn't believe that he'd spent the night and brought me breakfast the next morning, and we hadn't even had sex.

I shook it off, pushed thoughts of James aside, and focused on work. Marie, the director at the shelter, had asked me to spearhead the clothing drive this year. I wanted to include professional outfits as well, so the women who came to us had something to wear for job interviews. They often had nothing but the clothes on their backs, and I thought it was important they have not only warm clothes come winter, but an opportunity to reclaim their lives.

Rina was lending me her marketing skills to devise a little campaign to attract more donors, and with a bit of luck, the people we reached would donate money as well. I called her to go over the details, which gave me an idea.

It was great if the women had proper clothes to attend job interviews, but it meant nothing if they didn't have the skills required to sell themselves. I pitched the idea to Rina, and she immediately volunteered to teach a how-to-nail-a-job-interview class, which I appreciated since I really didn't have the time.

We stayed on the phone for a long time, and I didn't once mention James, or what happened last night. Rina would read too much into it. *I* was reading too much into it.

I had to keep things casual.

CHAPTER SIXTEEN

As soon as I stopped working, random scenes from last night invaded my thoughts. James had been respectful, thoughtful, and I was a mess over it. I loved that he'd joined me for drinks and trash TV. That he'd left a glass of water on my nightstand and slept on the couch.

We'd had a fun night without sex.

It was easy being with him, simple. I hated that. It lulled me into a sense of comfort and lowered my guard.

I put on some music to drown out those thoughts while I cleaned, the mess from yesterday my primary focus. Once that was done, I started scrubbing my bathroom tiles until the faint sound of my doorbell interrupted me. "Hello?"

"Delivery for Miss Cassandra Leigh," said a female voice over the intercom.

I hadn't ordered anything, but maybe whoever had sent me flowers at work on Saturday had sent something else. "Third floor." I buzzed the delivery woman in, but didn't open my apartment door. Through the peephole, I saw an elegant woman and a man in a suit rolling a massive metal trunk towards my apartment.

The entire situation was bizarre. I was fairly certain delivery men didn't wear suits. I pulled the door open to a crack. "What company do you work for?" I asked the man from the safety of my apartment, the chain still secure.

"I'm Paul Revello, Mr. Walton's driver. Although today I'm here to assist Miss Adams," he explained, gesturing toward the woman.

James, of course. I opened the door to let them in, still confused about the metal trunk. "What exactly did James send?" I asked.

"Clothes for the event this evening," the woman explained, offering me her hand to shake. "I'm Deborah Adams, Mr. Walton's stylist. He asked me to assist you today."

"I see." I paused for a minute, somewhat offended that James didn't think I could dress myself for a cocktail party. If I did fail to dress appropriately, James would be the culprit, since he refused to tell me where we were going.

"You don't seem to be ready to get dressed," Deborah said, eyeing me up and down.

"Of course not. I still have five hours until James gets here. That's plenty of time, isn't it?"

Deborah gave me a look that showed it wasn't. "How about I unzip a few options while you take a shower, and then we can work from there?"

I wanted to roll my eyes at the woman, but I couldn't exactly try on dresses in my current state.

"Can I get you something before I leave? Coffee, tea, some tequila for putting up with James?" I offered, facing his driver when I said the last part.

He chuckled. "He's really not that difficult. But if you don't mind, we'll just help ourselves to some coffee."

"Of course, kitchen is over there," I said, pointing them in the right direction even though my apartment had an open floor plan and the kitchen was clearly visible. "Make yourselves at home."

I turned toward my bedroom, wondering how this had become my life. A personal stylist. Sent over to dress me. I didn't know if I should be thrilled or offended.

Me: Do I really need help to get dressed?

James: Need? No. You always look perfect. But I sprung this

event on you last minute. I wanted to make sure you didn't stress over what to wear. Is that ok?

Is that ok? Of course it was ok. It was very considerate of him and I really should appreciate his thoughtfulness, but panic crawled through my veins.

Me: Yes, thank you. Have to go shower, see you later :)
James: Don't overthink it. See you, gorgeous ;)

I threw my phone on the bed, grabbed my robe, and headed for the bathroom to shower. *Don't overthink it.* Ha! As if that were possible. The fact that he knew me well enough to know that I would overthink this whole situation was making me overthink everything even more.

After my shower, I joined Deborah and Paul in the living room. Deborah had opened the massive metal trunk to reveal a dozen hanging dress bags. She'd already hung two dresses on the back of my front door.

"I will leave you to it," Paul announced. Turning to Deborah, he added, "Call me when you're ready to go and I'll come pick you up."

Once he left, I tried to probe Deborah about the party, but she quickly dismissed me. "Nice try, but Mr. Walton gave us explicit instructions to tell you nothing. What are your thoughts on this one?" She showed more dresses while I tried not to balk at the tags. Valentino, Balenciaga, Armani, Dior…. Each of the dresses probably cost more than my rent. I could never afford any of this. Maybe old collections, second hand if I got very lucky.

An unwelcome feeling invaded my chest, making it harder to breathe for a second. After all our talk of money last night, I didn't know what to make of him spending so much on me. I reminded myself that this probably didn't even make a dent in James's bank account.

I tried on a few dresses that I thought looked fantastic on me, but Deborah disagreed. "It's too bad we don't really have time for alterations. The Saint Laurent looks fantastic on you, but it's too long. I wish Mr. Walton had given me a little more time."

My brows drew together, a million questions buzzing through my mind. "How often do you do this kind of work for Mr. Walton?"

"I pick everything he wears. I have been his stylist for over five years," she said. "People like him don't really shop. I guess they'd rather be making money instead."

"No, I mean, how often does he send you around to dress his dates?"

"What?" She laughed. "Never."

My gut said she was lying, but I was standing in my underwear in my living room in front of a strange woman. I felt oddly vulnerable, too much to press until she told me the truth. I raised my arms, and she pulled another dress over my head. Apparently, you couldn't just lower these dresses and step into them like a regular person.

Deborah walked around me, adjusting the dress before she let me see it in the mirror. "I think this is the one," she said, turning me to face my reflection.

I couldn't agree more.

The emerald green satin was tight at the top, the cut of the cleavage accentuating the swell of my breasts. It cinched at the waist, then flowed down in an A-line skirt that stopped at my ankles. A slit on one side showed just enough leg.

"It fits you like a glove! Do you like it?"

"I love it," I whispered, running my fingertips over the soft material.

Deborah clapped twice before turning back to her trunk. "Now we just need shoes, a clutch, and I'm thinking earrings? Maybe some rings? A bracelet?" She walked over to me with a handful of shoe bags cradled against her chest.

Again, I tried to ignore the designer brand names, but shoes were my weakness. I tried on a few pairs before we settled on strappy Jimmy Choo sandals. But I drew the line when Deborah presented me with black velvet jewelry boxes and I saw the very real, very large diamonds inside.

"I think the dress and the shoes are enough," I said, a note of finality in my tone. Deborah seemed to understand, but tried to convince me to at least look at the purses. After some back and forth, I relented, because I really couldn't wear a Versace dress and Jimmy Choo sandals while carrying the Vitton Louise purse I got in Times Square.

Hours later, I was just putting the finishing touches on my makeup when the doorbell rang. I ran to the door to buzz James in, unlocked and unlatched it, then dashed to the bathroom to put on my small diamond earrings.

Less than a minute later, I heard the door close behind him. "Cassandra?"

"Just a minute!" I yelled from the bathroom.

"Do you mind if I pour myself a drink? It's been a long day."

"Help yourself! I'm almost done!" Since he didn't seem to be in a rush, I took my time applying my lipstick.

"I see I'm not the only one who works on the weekends," he said.

I peaked out of the bathroom door to see what he meant, but my mind went blank when I saw him standing in my living room in a black tuxedo, his unruly hair swept back, casually sipping his whiskey. Heat spread all over my body, my cheeks burning as my heart beat wildly against my chest.

James looked straight out of a James Bond movie, except I didn't know if he was the hero or the dashing villain. And either way, I didn't care.

My eyes drifted to the pile of files on my coffee table. "Oh, that," I croaked out, my body frozen in place. "It's not really work."

"It looks like work to me," he said, before he looked up and saw me by the door. His eyes slowly roamed up my body until they met mine. "Damn," he whispered, stalking towards me and gently lifting my chin with his finger. "Will you be mad if I fuck up your makeup?"

I smiled. "I can always reapply." The words were barely out of my mouth before his lips were on mine, devouring me with a kiss that made me stand on tip-toes, pressing my body as close to his as humanly possible. I ran my fingers through the little hairs on his nape, nails scratching softly over his scalp. James growled against my lips in response, one hand traveling up my body to wrap around my throat.

James held my hip with one hand, pulling me towards him until suddenly, his lips were gone. He leaned his forehead against mine, both of us breathing hard. "As much as I want this, and I clearly do," he paused to rub his very hard cock against my stomach, "we have a party to attend." His hand flexed around my throat, squeezing once before he let go.

It took me a moment to recover. I stood there with my eyes closed, softly rubbing James's solid chest until I felt like I could move again. "Just give me a moment to fix my makeup."

A soft smile took over James's face, somehow making him even more handsome. He kissed the corner of my lips before clearing his throat and stepping away. I walked back to the bathroom in a daze. The effect this man had on me was both thrilling and terrifying.

I quickly fixed my makeup, spritzed some perfume, and joined James in the living room with a wet wipe in hand.

He was sitting casually on the couch with his phone in hand, in a tux, his lipstick stained lips leaving a ring at the rim of his glass. He looked like he belonged here, which made tears prickle at my eyes. I swallowed hard to get it together.

"So, is this for work or for the shelter?" he asked, pointing at the files.

"Those are for the shelter. I was just going over some cases."

"That's a big pile."

Walking around the couch, I pried the glass out of his hand and plopped myself down on his lap. Eye contact at this stage would've been too much, so I focused on his lips instead, which wasn't exactly a safe choice. I wiped them clean of lipstick, completely ignoring the way his hands were squeezing my waist and how it made my pussy throb. "All done," I whispered.

"We really should go." His hand didn't seem to agree because it made its way down to squeeze my ass. I tried to comply and get up, but he held me in place and whispered in my ear. "Just give me a moment."

My stupid heart skipped a beat as he leaned his head against the side of my neck and planted soft kisses on the sensitive skin. Goosebumps spread all over my body. "You're not helping."

James chuckled against my neck and I felt it all the way to my core. He stood without moving me off his lap, holding my whole body flush against his as he set me down.

"Come on," he said, offering me his hand. We made our way to the elevator and James held me in front of him, facing the mirrored doors. "Fuck, you're breathtaking."

Half of me wanted to snort at the compliment, but the way his eyes burned with lust as he took in my reflection in the mirror…. The weaker part of me was compelled to believe him.

We looked good together. James was perfection in his fitted black tuxedo, the hunger in his eyes only making him hotter. I noticed his pocket square was the same color and material as my dress. Deborah really had an eye for detail.

Meanwhile, I looked flushed, my eyes shining, reflecting the same hunger back at James. The dress was fantastic, my hair flowed in soft waves past my shoulders, and my makeup looked great. But I couldn't fabricate the expression on my face, or the butterflies playing in my stomach.

That was all James. And it scared the living shit out of me.

CHAPTER SEVENTEEN

A black town car was parked in front of my building. Paul stood next to it. The moment he saw us, he opened the back door. "Miss Leigh," he said.

"Paul, lovely to see you again."

The driver offered me a half bow, which nearly sent me into a fit of giggles. It felt like I had stepped into an alternate universe where stylists came to my place to dress me in fine clothes and drivers bowed to me. Not to mention the hunk of a guy in a black tux whose bedroom skills had me weak in the knees and who brought me breakfast when I was hungover.

It was all too good to be true, but I decided to enjoy it until the other shoe dropped, since that would happen regardless.

"Where exactly are we going?" I asked once Paul started driving out of the city.

"A party in North Greenwich." James pulled out a bottle of white wine and poured two glasses. "We're going to need this to survive it."

I gladly took the glass, accepting a world where being chauffeured around while sipping wine was normal. "You need to give me more details than that."

James got comfortable in his seat, scooting over to lessen the distance between us. "It's a party. There will be food, lots of alcohol, and people. People I do business with, people who want to do business with me. It will be mostly networking."

"That sounds like work to me." I repeated his words from earlier, trying to keep my cool as he pressed his index finger to the outside of my wrist as if to feel my pulse. My treacherous heart decided to skip a beat. I took a long sip of wine, knowing that it wouldn't help my situation, but at least it was something to do with my hands.

"That's where you come in, and Elias."

"Oh! Good to know Elias will be there to keep me company when you get too busy with work," I teased, smirking at him.

"Gorgeous, I will castrate Elias if he gets anywhere near you."

"Do you think if I tell Elias that he'll think of it as a challenge and finally seduce me?"

James's callused palm landed on my exposed thigh, warmth pooling in my core at the contact. "You're playing with fire, Barbie Girl."

I had intended to tease him for longer, but his words stopped me in my tracks. Memories of last night trickled into my brain, a flash of me belting nineties hits into a wooden spoon. Not one to back down, I continued, "That's a great idea. Elias and I could role-play as Barbie and Ken. I could be beach Barbie since I already have a pink bikini. All I need is a blonde wig."

James flashed me a dazzling smile as he got dangerously close to me, his lips inches from mine. "Do you remember doing the voices? You scared me a little when you sang the guy's part. It was actually better than the high pitched squeaky voice you did for the girl." He crossed one ankle over his knee, reaching inside his tux for his phone. "At least last night gave me some entertaining stories to spark some conversation today. And there are also the videos...."

I wrapped my hand around his biceps, my fingers digging into the hard muscle. "Hey, that song is a jam and I stand by it! But you win. No more teasing you about Elias tonight."

His satisfied smirk almost made me double back. I didn't know if he looked hotter in his possessive state or after winning an argument. I took a long sip of wine to gather myself, but it had the opposite effect as James's dark gaze lingered on my lips.

"What's your favorite color?" he asked, catching me completely off guard.

"Why do you want to know?"

"Because," he said, angling his body towards me, "I want to get to know you better, and since you rarely volunteer any information unless you're intoxicated, I'm asking." He stared at me with his piercing brown eyes, causing those damn butterflies to have a rave. "Let's play twenty-one questions."

I finally snapped out of my daze. "Aren't we a little old for that?"

"Hmm, I don't know. Is singing 'Barbie Girl' at the top of your lungs while drunk on vodka more appropriate for our age?"

"Touché." I poked him in the chest with my index finger. James caught my hand and brought it to his mouth, placing a kiss on my knuckles. "If you never mention the embarrassing things I did last night, and delete whatever videos you have, I'll play your game," I said, clearing my throat when my voice came out weaker than I intended.

"A lot happened last night, and lucky for me, I was sober as a judge, so I remember everything. I can promise not to tell any embarrassing stories at the party today, but I am keeping the videos. I loved seeing you so carefree."

"You were not sober," I said with a laugh, ignoring that last bit. "And you'd be surprised at the amount of liquor judges can hold down. But fine, I'll play." Despite his teasing, I knew that James would never reveal embarrassing things about me. It was eerie how much I'd grown to trust him in such a short time.

"So, what's your favorite color?" He repeated the question, curling one strand of my hair around his long finger.

"Really? Out of all the questions you could ask, that's what you want to know?" James gave me an impatient look, urging me to answer. "Fine, it's red." A slow smile spread over his lips at my words, and he nodded slowly, as if registering the information. I needed some leverage in case he had any more stories from last night in his memory bank, so I asked, "What is the most embarrassing thing that's ever happened to you?"

He gave me a pointed look that told me he knew exactly what I was doing, yet he still answered me. "I can't believe I'm about to tell you this, but here goes. When I was in middle school, I had a major crush on this girl. Her name was Victoria. Our parents were friends, still are actually, so she came over to my house with them. This was my opportunity. I got all dressed up to impress her, even asked the gardener to cut some of my mom's flowers so I could give them to her."

"That's very cute," I teased, pinching his cheek just like grandmas do.

He grabbed my hand and bit my finger, and it honestly felt like he had just bitten my clit. I drew in a sharp breath, trying to focus on his words as he continued. "Well, she came to our house. I was so nervous that before I could say hello, I threw up all over her pretty pink dress."

Laughter bubbled in my belly at the picture he painted. "Oh no," I said, patting his arm in comfort. "What happened next?"

"She told everyone at school, and they teased me until I left for boarding school."

"I'm sorry, kids can be brutal. But I bet Victoria would regret mocking you if she saw you now."

James cupped my face with one hand, his deep brown eyes locked on mine. "I think I'm better off with you," he said, his words sending my heart into a frenzy. Something passed through his eyes, but for the sake of my sanity, I refused to analyze it.

Probably sensing my discomfort, James brushed his lips against my forehead before he drew back to refill our glasses. "Now that you've got some cannon fodder, your turn. Have you ever been in love?"

I almost spit out my wine. "What kind of question is that? You can't go from my favorite color to that."

"Of course I can," he said, the ghost of a smirk on his lips.

We stared at each other, curiosity burning in his eyes. I didn't want to have this conversation with James. But the more I refused to answer, the more interesting the subject would seem to him. "Yes, I have been in love. My turn—"

"Not so fast, you have to give me a little more." James's hand landed on my thigh again, his thumb drawing lazy circles on the delicate skin. I knew he was trying to distract me, and judging by the fog clouding my brain, his tactic was working.

"It's your fault for asking me a yes or no question. They don't require elaboration."

He rolled his eyes. "Yes, counselor, but please, humor me."

I searched for the right words to be truthful without revealing too much. Maybe I should just lie, make up some story, but that felt wrong somehow.

The smirk slowly faded from James's lips, his sharp gaze scrutinizing my face. "I surmise it didn't end well."

I couldn't take his stare anymore, so I glanced down to remove some imaginary lint from his tux. "These things seldom do, in my personal and professional experience."

"Was he stupid enough to cheat or something?"

"Or something," I answered honestly before quickly adding, "What is the most outrageous rich boy thing you've ever done?"

James wasn't stupid. He knew I was evading the question, but something in my expression must have made him back off. "Rich boy thing?"

"Yes, things ordinary people like me couldn't even conceive of. Like crashing a million dollar yacht."

"Gorgeous, you are the furthest thing from ordinary, but I get your point."

The stupid butterflies fluttered wildly in my belly at his compliment, but I quickly wrote it off as an empty stomach. I hoped the food was good wherever we were going.

"I guess the wildest thing I've done wasn't even my idea, it was actually Eli's."

"That's a shocker."

"For our twenty-first birthday, we pulled money together to buy a small island. We were both born in September, so we wanted to celebrate together. We invited everyone, chartered planes and yachts to bring people over. Let's just say it got pretty wild since Elias did most of the planning—drugs, drinks, dancers, DJs. You name it, we had it. It was one week of non-stop partying. I stopped drinking for a year after that just to recover."

"That sounds like the best twenty-first birthday ever." Something he said clicked in my mind. "Wait, you said your birthday was in September. When exactly?" It was September second, so chances were I hadn't missed it yet.

"The twenty-sixth," he said. "We should go to the island sometime. I'm sure Elias wouldn't mind planning another epic party. God knows he has even more experience now. Or we could go just the two of us. I'm sure we'd be able to entertain ourselves."

"You guys still own the island?"

"We do. It's about ten miles off the coast of Mozambique. Elias still goes there to decompress occasionally. I wish I could go more, but my job is a bit less flexible." He took my hand in his, the tip of his index finger lightly tracing the lines on my palm, causing goosebumps to erupt all over my body. "If I had the right company, I might be persuaded to take time off."

"It's incredible that you *own* an island!" I blurted out, my breaths coming out in short pants. "I mean, how do you even amass that kind of wealth?"

James's brows drew together as he explained. "We're pretty much old New York money. My great-great-grandfather made money in real estate. Since then we've grown a lot, expanded into different areas including tech to keep up with the times. We have a few hotels here and there, et cetera."

I chuckled, raising my brows in question. "Did you really just say et cetera?"

"Yes, I've actually never had to explain where our wealth comes from to anyone before. Our family name is pretty well known." James's finger traced a line from my palm to my shoulder. He swept my hair away, then brushed his knuckles over my collarbone, his hand traveling around my neck to grab my nape.

"Now I feel a little ignorant," I confessed, my cheeks burning. Considering my line of work, I really should have heard of the Waltons. "I might have to do some heavy research when I get home." His gaze landed on my lips as I spoke, and his fingers massaging the back of my head had me suppressing a groan.

"It's actually refreshing. You treat me like I'm normal. I don't have to worry about being Mr. Walton." He shrugged. "When I'm with you, I can be just James."

The look in his eyes was so earnest, so vulnerable, I had to avert my gaze. Taking a sip of my wine, I focused on my hand to buy myself some time to recover.

"I think it's your turn to ask a question," I finally said, clearing my throat.

James released a disappointed sigh. "I think I'll save it for later. But first I have something for you." He reached into his coat pocket and pulled out a simple black box.

The lack of brand stamped on the box did nothing to diminish my anxiety. Hell, if the box had been smaller, I'm pretty sure I would've jumped out the window.

He opened it to reveal a stunning necklace, delicate leaf-shaped diamonds sparkling even in the dim light of the car. But it was the emerald at its center that caught my attention.

This was too much.

"James," I tried, placing my hand softly on top of his to close the box. "I can't. This is too much."

James smiled, shaking his head slightly. "Miss Adams said you refused all jewelry. I don't think I've ever met a woman who'd say no to diamonds." His brows knitted together as he examined my face with those piercing eyes.

Not for the first time, I felt *seen*—something I didn't care for very much. But I still refused to look away. I needed James to understand that I was serious.

Scooting over, James unbuckled my seat belt and gestured with his fingers for me to turn around. Before I could protest, he pressed his index finger against my lips. "Humor me," he said.

The air felt thick. James's gaze never strayed from mine, and for once, I didn't want to look away. Instead, I wanted to drown in his eyes. He was too handsome, too intense. *Too good for me.* My heart was very much in danger of being a fool once more.

In a trance, I felt my body move to face the window. James gathered my hair in one hand, sweeping it over my shoulder. Then he ran a finger down my spine, a soft moan escaping my lips.

I could feel the satisfied smirk on his face even though I couldn't see it, but I was helpless against his touch. James placed the necklace around my neck and fastened it. It sat heavily against my collarbone, the emerald resting just between the swell of my breasts.

When I finally turned around, James looked at me with pure, unmistakable hunger. But there was something else shining in his eyes, something like awe. My stupid heart beat a mile a minute, feeling too big for my chest.

James adjusted the necklace, his fingers brushing against my skin. "It's a gift. It's not polite to refuse a gift." His voice was thick, hoarse. The sound of it made me want to forget all about this party and Paul in the front seat and just jump his bones.

Laughter bubbled in my chest, not because the moment was funny, but because it was intense and intimate, and it made me want to run. "That's the worst argument I've ever heard."

"That's because there shouldn't be an argument at all. You don't argue when someone is giving you a gift." James took his phone out of his pocket, then pointed it at me.

"What are you doing?"

"I want to remember this moment." He licked his lip while he snapped pictures of me, so it wasn't within my power to protest.

My heart raced as I smiled for the picture. Despite the anxiety that came with it, a little voice inside my head told me to trust James. But that little voice didn't know how quickly things evolved. Feelings were messy, complicated, and I could feel them burgeoning in my foolish heart.

CHAPTER EIGHTEEN

The late afternoon sun still shone brightly as the car slowed to a halt, bringing both of us back to reality. The two hour trip had flown by in James's presence. I looked out the window just in time to catch a wrought-iron W in the center of the gate before it slowly opened.

James's sinful smile faded from his face, his jaw hardened, and his shoulders stiffened. It seemed as if he was preparing for battle, and I realized that this was Mr. Walton, not James.

"Anything I should know before we go in? You look a little tense. It's making me nervous."

He took my hand in his, his long finger drawing circles on my palm. "Just stay with me?" He gave me the sweetest look, making it impossible for me to say no.

We drove for a minute or two on a path lined with trees. It opened to reveal a large fountain opposite a white stone mansion. The building itself was imposing, but a variety of trees, bushes, and flowers surrounding it softened the harsh architecture. This type of wealth was on another level than what I was used to, but I swallowed my insecurities and kept my mouth shut, the diamonds and emerald heavy on my chest.

Paul stopped the car in front of the steps that led up to the house. A young man dressed in an suit opened my door and offered his hand to help me out. James materialized beside me and offered me his arm like the perfect gentleman. We walked up the stairs in complete silence, tension emanating from him.

An older man stood beside the door, dressed in an impeccable dark gray suit. He bowed slightly when we approached and said, "Mr. Walton, welcome home."

My eyes widened at his words, apprehension clouding my thoughts. I raised one eyebrow, silently demanding an explanation, but James ignored me.

James smiled and clasped the man's hand in a familiar gesture. "Reggie, it's good to see you. This is Cassandra Leigh, my date." His eyes shone with mirth as I tried to maintain my composure. Reggie kissed my hand in a gallant gesture, while I murmured a polite greeting. Once that was done, James clasped the man on the shoulder and whispered, "How's it looking in there?"

"It's a splendid party, sir. Everyone seems in good spirits, no major drama yet." Reggie reached into his pocket for an envelope. "I know you said no gifts, sir, but Mrs. Hill will starve me if I don't give you this. Happy birthday, sir. It's not much, but the entire staff pitched in."

Happy birthday? I stared daggers in James's direction, but the cheeky bastard didn't even dare look in my direction.

"Thank you, Reggie." James opened the envelope, took a second to read it, then released my arm to hug the older man. "I'll stop by the kitchen to thank Mrs. Hill in person later."

The butler nodded, an affectionate smile on his face. Whatever their relationship was, it was clear that James was very dear to him.

James placed a hand on my lower back and ushered me forward. We crossed the foyer as I tried not to gawk at the double marble staircase or the massive crystal chandelier hanging from the tall ceiling.

"Birthday? *Home?*" I whisper shouted, not bothering to conceal my anger.

James shot me a sheepish look. "Would you have come if you knew?" He looked down at me with the expression of a person who knew what they had done and didn't regret it, that stupid sexy smirk making an unwelcome appearance. I wanted to be mad at him, but I couldn't find it in me. "It's just a party. My parents love an opportunity to organize an event, especially now that my father's retired."

I stopped walking, words tumbling out of my mouth as alarm bells rang in my head. "Your parents? I can't meet your parents. Are you crazy?"

He stopped in front of me and placed his hands on my shoulders, gazing down at me as an amused smile played on his lips. "Why not? They're just people."

"I know they're just people, James, but they are your *parents*. I don't do parents." Meeting the parents implied commitment, steadiness…. Things I didn't want at all.

James's hands traveled down my arms to settle on my waist, his face inches from mine. "Hence why I didn't tell you," he said, before winking and placing a sweet kiss on my forehead.

I knew he was trying to distract me, and I didn't like it, especially because it worked. Still in a daze, I followed as he guided me to a set of double doors leading to a garden. The faint sounds of a string quartet, glasses clinking, and the murmurs of conversation reached my ears, reminding me exactly where I was.

If only I could get away with murder, James would be my first victim. *Second, actually.*

Right when I was about to tell him, nay, *order* him to have Paul take me home immediately, a young woman with pin straight raven hair and striking gray eyes approached us.

"Jamie! You're here!" The woman launched into his arms, and James immediately let go of me to hug her. "Happy birthday," she said, pressing her lips to his cheek.

"Liz, this is my date, Cassandra Leigh. And this is Elisabeth, my sister." James unnecessarily emphasized the word sister, as if I cared. I wasn't the jealous type, and we were fuck buddies, something I needed to remind him of as soon as I got a chance.

"Nice to meet you," Elisabeth said, walking over to kiss my cheek.

I plastered a smile on my face, too polite to show how much I didn't want to be here. "Likewise."

"Good luck out there," she whispered to James, before disappearing behind us.

"She's going to hide in the kitchen," James explained.

"Can I hide there too?"

"Oh no. You get to stay right beside me, glued to my arm all night."

I rolled my eyes. This man was infuriating. I wanted to say more, to argue my point. But I didn't want to cause a scene.

We made our way to the garden where the party was taking place, and for all the grandeur of the house, I enjoyed the garden infinitely more. The lawn was perfectly manicured, but it was the wild variety of flowers, green plants, bushes, and tall trees that caught my eye. It didn't look perfectly arranged like everything else. It was as if nature had been left alone to do its thing, and I couldn't help the pang in my chest at the thought that my mom would have loved it.

There was a paved area to the left where tables had been set up across from a bar. As much as I wanted a drink to steady myself, I didn't want a repeat of last night. We followed a winding path to where a temporary wooden deck had been set up to accommodate a string quartet. A handful of couples danced while the other guests gathered in small groups around tall tables scattered around the garden.

We made little progress before a middle-aged man stopped us. "Happy birthday, my boy," the man said, patting James on the back. James thanked him and introduced me, but the man barely acknowledged my existence with a nod before launching into a discussion about stocks.

James indulged him until he spotted someone in the crowd that caught his attention. People tried to engage him in conversation as we waded through the garden, but he pushed forward with determination.

"Mother," he said, placing his hand on her shoulder.

The woman immediately turned around and threw her arms around him, burying her face in his chest. "Happy birthday, darling," she said, pulling him down to place a kiss on his cheek. "I can't believe you're already thirty-three!" She saw me standing behind him and gave me a curious look.

"Thank you," he said, before placing his hand on the small of my back and pulling me forward in an act of complete cruelty. "Mom, this is Cassandra Leigh."

"It's lovely to meet you, Mrs. Walton," I said, offering her my hand. James's mom was a tall, elegant woman, probably in her late fifties.

She offered me a kind smile as we shook hands. "Please, call me Barbara." As she spoke, an older version of James wrapped an arm around her shoulders, except his eyes were a stunning gray, like James's sister. "This is George Walton, my husband."

I smiled politely, trying to disguise how awkward I felt. "It's very nice to meet you, Mr. Walton."

"Likewise," he said, shaking my hand. His gaze lingered on the necklace sitting on my chest before he eyed me up and down suspiciously. Mr. Walton senior turned to James and started talking about some properties, completely ignoring my existence, which wasn't exactly the height of good breeding.

We were soon joined by other men who wanted to chime in on their conversation.

The newcomers barely wished James a happy birthday before jumping into a discussion on the stock market without sparing me a glance. I was relishing being ignored when Barbara wrapped her soft hand around my arm.

"Come with me, darling. Let's leave the men to their business talk."

If there had been a polite way to refuse her, I would've gone for it, but my mind went blank as I followed her around the garden. She introduced me to a few people who were milling around, talking in small groups, then led me to a table. We sat on the high stools, and stayed silent for a few minutes, watching the crowd.

"James hates celebrating his birthday. I was surprised when he called this morning to say he was bringing a date," Barbara said, her shrewd eyes examining my every move.

I smiled politely, not really knowing what to say. "It was a last-minute invitation. I hope it wasn't an inconvenience."

"Of course not, dear. James hasn't brought a girl home in many years. We're happy to have you."

I wasn't entirely convinced she meant it, but I brushed it off. "This is a beautiful garden."

Barbara cocked her head to one side, a familiar gesture that took me a second to place. James did the same when he was curious. "Do you garden?"

I laughed. "Not at all. I probably wouldn't know a weed from a flower." My mom would have bristled at my confession, but it was the truth. She'd spent hours caring for our little garden, and as much as she'd tried to teach me, I still couldn't keep a cactus alive.

"It's a lot of work. I spent hours designing this garden, trying to save plants that didn't take, and stopping others from growing where I thought they shouldn't." Barbara was looking off into the distance, and I followed her gaze to find that she was staring at James. "It took me a long time to come to terms with the fact that I couldn't control nature. The moment I let go was when it all clicked together."

As if on cue, James's gaze found mine, the edge of a smile playing on his lips. When I looked back at Barbara, I found her staring at me, a soft expression on her face.

"Nature will find her own way," she said, placing a hand lightly on my arm. "We just have to let her."

Before I could conjure up a response, a gentleman came to ask Barbara to dance. He whisked her off, and I sat there, wondering what the hell she meant with all of that.

A waiter passed by me with a tray of wine, and I snatched a glass, abandoning my plan not to drink. James was now surrounded by three women who seemed to be vying for his attention. He stood there, his back ramrod straight, sharp jaw clenched.

"Cassandra," a man said in a familiar British accent. I looked up to find Elias staring down at me, a devilish spark in his eyes. He promptly took my hand and kissed it before taking a seat. "I didn't expect to see you here."

"I didn't expect to be here," I said honestly. My eyes were drawn to James despite my best efforts. One of the women had her hand around his forearm, her body brushing against his with every move she made.

Elias followed my gaze, then released a loud chuckle. "James might need your help to get away from those three."

"He can wait a little longer," I said, turning away from James to face Elias. "I didn't even know it was his birthday."

Elias's green eyes sparkled with mirth. "He hates these parties. There isn't a single person here except for his family, me, and maybe you, that actually cares about him. But they will pretend to."

I ignored the bit about caring for James. "And you're not throwing him an epic party this year? James told me about the island."

"I tried to, but he refused. He said he'd rather spend his Friday night with a certain someone." Elias watched me closely as he said this, and I could feel my cheeks warming. "Now, you'd better go rescue your man before Leticia's claws are permanently engraved on his arm."

He's not my man, I wanted to say, but I stood and made my way over to James.

With a cheery smile on my face, I approached the group. "Jamie! I've been looking all over for you," I cooed, wrapping an arm around his waist.

"Ladies," James said, wrapping his arm around my shoulders. "This is Cassandra Leigh. Cassie, this is Amanda, Jessica, and Leticia Livingston."

"Wow, are you all related?" I asked, genuinely curious. The three of them were handsome, with flawless blonde hair and lithe silhouettes, but that was where the resemblance stopped, unless you counted the way they were all looking me up and down, assessing me and clearly finding me not good enough for their precious Mr. Walton.

"Cassandra Leigh," one of them repeated. I didn't even know which one and I couldn't be bothered to find out. "I don't think I've ever heard of you. Who's your family?"

"Oh, you're right. You've never heard of me or my family." The three gave me a quizzical look, but I refused to elaborate. "Jamie,

I'm starving," I said in a sultry voice, looking up at him from under my lashes.

James fought a smile as he turned to them. "Ladies, if you'll excuse me, I have to go feed my girl." The look on their faces was priceless, almost enough to make me forget James had just called me his girl, but not quite. "Jamie?" he whispered as we stepped away from them.

"I wanted them to think we were close," I murmured back.

A thoroughly amused smile flashed on his lips, and his shoulders shook with contained laughter. "Mom and Lizzie are the only people who call me Jamie, so I guess it works. But please don't ever moan it. I think I'd go soft."

"Noted," I said, chuckling softly.

We tried to make our way to where I assumed food was, but we kept getting stopped by his guests. I stayed dutifully by his side, listening to one boring conversation after another. My only comfort was James's hand planted firmly on my lower back, and his familiar scent tickling my nostrils.

After what felt like hours of mind numbing conversation, nature called and I excused myself to use the restroom. Once I stepped inside the mansion, I realized I should have asked James for directions. This wasn't exactly the type of establishment to have a little sign on the wall pointing towards the nearest restroom. Despite its size, it wasn't an establishment at all. It was a house. Where real people lived.

I was walking back to the main hall to see if I could find someone to point me in the right direction when I saw James's father. He marched towards me, his steps echoing around the empty corridor.

"Miss Leigh," he said, "how curious to find you wandering around my house." The accusation was clear in his tone as he stared down at me, his lips pressed into a flat line. Although I wasn't really sure what he was accusing me of.

James's father or not, I wasn't about to let this man intimidate me. I straightened my spine and lifted my chin before speaking in a clear tone. "I was looking for the restroom. Maybe you could point me in the right direction."

He narrowed his eyes, his jaw clenching, but when he spoke his tone was neutral, polite. "Of course. Follow me, please." He started down the hallway before I had a chance to say anything else.

We walked in silence to the bathroom. Once there, he threw the door open, and I gladly disappeared inside. Given his father's blatant dislike of me, I wondered what James saw in me.

I did my business and took my time washing my hands. This evening was turning out to be significantly more intense than what I'd signed up for when James and I first started seeing each other. I wanted casual sex, no feelings, no drama. Although the sex was mind-blowing, I wondered if it was worth all this commotion.

When I opened the door, I had to mask my surprise at seeing James's father leaning casually against the wall with his hands in his pockets.

"Wouldn't want you getting lost on your way back to the party," he explained, a corner of his lips lifting into a sneer.

I didn't miss the meaning behind his words, and I was done playing games with the man. "Don't worry, my purse isn't big enough to hide anything of value." I lifted my tiny clutch that barely fit my phone, lipstick, and house keys.

Mr. Walton's eyes narrowed, his nostrils flaring as he took a step toward me. "Cassandra, wasn't it?"

I nodded.

"James said you were a lawyer. I didn't know lawyers made enough money to buy diamond necklaces."

Judging by the diamonds on the necklace, I'd estimate the price at around half a million dollars. "I'm a criminal defense attorney, and you're right. I make good money, but not nearly enough to afford anything like this."

He looked me up and down with disdain, his hard gaze focusing on the diamond necklace. "James is a good man, but he trusts people a little too easily. A pretty face comes along and he doesn't care how much comes out of his bank account to keep it."

The accusation was clear this time. This man was calling me a gold digger to my face. I almost wanted to laugh.

"That's very insulting to James. Do you really think your son is that stupid?"

"Sometimes a man doesn't think with his head."

I released a frustrated sigh. "Look, you've clearly made up your mind about me. You think I'm after his money and there isn't much I can say to change your mind. But I'll say this: your son has better sense than to fall for a gold digger, and I'm more interested in what's between his legs than I am about the contents of his bank account." I took in his shocked expression with satisfaction. "And the necklace was a loan so I could better fit in here," I said, gesturing around with my arms. "It goes back to James the moment I'm out of here. Now, if you'll excuse me, your son must be wondering where I am."

I turned to leave, but Mr. Walton grabbed my arm to stop me. Panic flared in my chest. This was a big house with plenty of secluded corners where bad things could happen. Fear crawled over my skin as blood rushed in my ears. I didn't care who he was—violent men came from all backgrounds. Still, I raised my chin and stared at his hand gripping my forearm with undisguised disgust. Right as I was opening my mouth to demand he let me go, a familiar voice came from behind me.

"What is going on here?"

CHAPTER NINETEEN

Mr. Walton removed his hand from my arm as if it burned him, his expression thunderous as he stared James down. "Your lady friend and I were just having a little chat."

James's arm snaked around my waist, pulling me to his side as he raised his chin. Something unspeakable passed between the two. I couldn't see James's face, but his father's cold eyes narrowed dangerously, his hands closing into tight fists.

Right, time to put an end to this.

I turned to stand in front of James, placing a hand on his chest to force him to look at me. It worked. His gaze lowered to mine, sending a wave of awareness washing over me.

"We should get back to the party," I said sweetly. His father made a displeased sound behind me, but I ignored him.

"What were you two talking about?" James asked me, his eyes never leaving mine.

"Your father was just asking what kind of law I practiced." The lie flew smoothly from my lips, but James didn't really seem to believe me. "Come on, I'm really thirsty." I grabbed his hand and forced him to follow, very aware of the fact that I couldn't actually physically force him unless he'd let me.

"I don't like it when you lie to me," he said the moment his father was out of earshot.

"Well, I don't like it when you lie by omission and bring me to meet your parents without any advance warning. Especially when you admit you knew I wouldn't come if you'd told me."

James stopped in his tracks. "I know. I'm sorry."

His words completely disarmed me. I was ready to argue. To remind him that we'd agreed not to blur the lines. That by forcing me to meet his parents, he wasn't respecting the boundaries we had established together.

"It's no excuse," he continued, "but it's my birthday. I'd rather spend it with you than with most of these people." He tucked my hair behind my ear, then cupped my jaw. "What did he say to you?"

He was calmer now, the anger completely gone.

"It doesn't really matter what he said. I'm not bothered by him."

"But I am. You're mine. He doesn't get to be anything but nice to you."

I smiled, refusing to acknowledge his words—*you're mine*—despite the shiver that ran down my spine. "Not everyone will like me, Jamie, and that's completely fine by me."

Something passed through his eyes—something that scared me to the core—but he said nothing. He just pulled me closer and ravished me with a kiss. I had only called him Jamie to ease the tension, since I thought he'd be amused. But the intensity of the kiss and the way his gaze burrowed into my soul.... It spelled trouble for my guarded heart.

After James had calmed down and wiped my lipstick from his lips, we returned to the party.

The rest of the evening was agonizingly slow. James and I flitted from one insipid conversation to another, Elias's dry humor and stolen moments as we swayed to the music our only respite. It was well past midnight when we finally ducked into the car, the silence within music to my ears. I slipped off my sandals, wiggling my freed toes on the soft car mat.

"Do your feet hurt?" James asked, pulling my feet to his lap. I moaned when his cool fingers pressed against my aching soles, immediately relieving some of the soreness.

"I love heels, but they always hurt after a few hours." I settled back into my seat while James rubbed my feet. No man had ever done this for me, unless I paid him to.

James nodded and continued the massage, his gaze unfocused. Throughout the rest of the party, he had been charming and had freely engaged in conversation with anyone who approached, but I could tell he was tired.

I left him to his thoughts as we drove on in comfortable silence. It had been a long night. Meeting James's family had never been in my plans, and especially not without warning.

"I really don't appreciate being ambushed like this, James," I said, needing to make my boundaries clear. "A party is not the same as your *birthday* party, at your *parents'* house."

James released a deep sigh, his fingers still working their magic. "I'm sorry. The truth is, I was dreading this party. I loved hanging out with you yesterday, so I thought if you were with me, it would be more palatable. It won't happen again."

I nodded, satisfied with his response, but he wasn't done. "I'm sorry for my father's behavior. Will you tell me what he actually said to you?"

"He expressed some concern over the disparity in our incomes," I said, measuring my words.

Unsurprisingly, James seemed to grasp exactly what his father had truly said. He stopped rubbing my feet for a second, his jaw clenching dangerously. "I see. I'll deal with him. He'll never disrespect you again. That's a promise."

Judging by his tone, he was deadly serious. But I didn't want to cause a rift in the family. At the end of the day, I truly didn't care what Mr. Walton Senior thought of me. "He was just trying to protect you, James. I'm assuming you've had a girlfriend or two whose motivations were a little dubious."

James released a low chuckle, but there was no humor in it. He set my feet down to pour himself a drink, silently offering me one. I shook my head, remembering my recent excessive drinking. So many lawyers used alcohol to cope with the stress. I didn't want it to become a problem.

"Back in college, I dated a girl named Camilla for two years.

Everything was great, I was going to propose. Then she told me she was pregnant. It was a bit shocking since I always wore a condom, but I believed it was mine. Accidents happen. My family wasn't so trusting. They wanted a paternity test to confirm."

He took a long, fortifying sip as he recollected. "She seemed a little offended, but didn't protest. A few days later, Elias came to me. They'd become friends, so Camilla thought Elias would help her come up with a plan to dupe me. She had cheated on me multiple times. And now she was worried that when the paternity test came out and the truth was revealed, her family would cut her off. They would never approve of a child conceived out of wedlock, especially when the real father didn't come from money."

I rolled my eyes, annoyed at this girl's family. "Jesus, was this in the fifties?"

"It might as well have been," James said, offering me a small smile. I wrapped one hand around his arm, nestling into his side as he continued his story. "There are strict rules in my world, especially for women. I don't agree with any of it, but her family was traditional."

"What was her plan?"

"The general idea was to fake the paternity test. She was hoping Elias would help finalize the plan. Maybe throw money at some doctor to forge the results."

"But Elias came straight to you," I said.

James nodded. "Elias and I are like brothers. She must have been truly desperate to go to him."

I put myself in her shoes for a second—pregnant and on the verge of being cut off from her family and the money that came with it. "What happened to her?"

"Well, we broke up and I kept the pregnancy to myself. Eventually her parents found out, and when she confessed it wasn't mine and the father had no money, they cut her off. She had the baby and married the father. Her late grandmother had set up a trust fund for her, but she wouldn't have access until she turned twenty-five, so times were hard." James drained his drink before setting down his glass. His hand landed on my thigh, immediately waking my sleepy body. "I found her a place to stay and arranged a job for the father. The last I heard, she was living happily in California."

I stared up at him, eyebrows raised in confusion. This woman cheated on him and tried to convince his best friend to dupe him into believing he was the father of her child. "Why did you help her?"

"She cheated, but I still cared for her. I didn't want her or the baby to suffer." James caressed my bare thigh, drawing random patterns on the skin as I stared at him, completely dumbfounded. He must have been done talking about it though, because he asked, "Do you get along well with your family?"

I froze, an uncomfortable heaviness settling in my chest. "No. I mean, not anymore." I had to swallow the lump in my throat before I could get the next words out. "They died in a car accident."

James pulled me in for a tight hug, and I had to fight the tears clouding my vision. No matter how many years passed, I'd never stop mourning the loss of my parents. "I never really know what to say in these situations," James murmured.

I buried my face in his neck, a small smile on my lips. "There isn't a class in boarding school on how to respond to your sex friend sharing about her dead parents?" I tried to joke, but judging by his tense muscles, he didn't find any humor in it. "It's been a long time, James. I don't know if there is anything to say."

"How old were you?"

I settled back into my seat, James's hand wrapped firmly around mine. "Sixteen."

"What happened after? Did you go into foster care?"

"No, I was lucky. My neighbors were good friends with my parents. They let me stay with them until I finished high school and left for college. Honestly, it wasn't so bad. They were really great. Other than not having parents anymore, my life didn't change that much."

The corner of his lips lifted into a crooked smile. "For some odd reason, I don't believe you. But I'm not going to force you to talk about it."

I nodded absentmindedly, the tightness in my chest refusing to dissipate. The necklace still weighed heavily around my neck, which reminded me of something. "Can you unclasp this?" I asked as I turned around.

James's cool fingers brushed against my skin as he unclasped the necklace, a tingling sensation traveling all the way down my spine. I carefully placed the necklace in its box and handed it to him. "Will you keep it for me?"

James eyed me suspiciously, one eyebrow raised. "It's a gift."

"I know. But I live in Brooklyn, and this is worth more than my building."

He pondered my words before he said, "I will keep it safe, but it's yours. I want that to be clear."

"Yes, sir," I joked, but the blaze in his eyes had me crossing my legs and pressing my thighs together. "By the way, I never did wish you a happy birthday." I reached up to caress his jaw, tracing a line to his lips. His eyes darkened as his tongue darted out to flick the pad of my finger before he playfully bit it. A jolt of electricity traveled straight to my core as my breath became heavier.

Moving closer, I nibbled playfully on his bottom lip in between teasing licks. James cupped my face, taking control as he dipped his tongue in my mouth. He tasted like whiskey and sin, a heady combination that made me forget everything but here and now. His hand traveled up my waist to squeeze my breast, warmth spreading like wild fire everywhere he touched.

I quickly undid my seatbelt and climbed on his lap, desperate for more. My hands roamed his broad chest, reveling in the warmth radiating from his skin, even covered by his shirt. James slipped his hands under my dress to palm my ass, and I rocked my hips back and forth to rub my crotch against his hard cock.

James's lips left mine to trail burning kisses down my throat, leaving me completely breathless. Remembering Paul in the driver's seat, I wrapped my hands around his throat and squeezed a little to get his attention.

"Happy birthday," I murmured against his lips.

James chuckled, then rested his forehead against mine, our labored breaths mixing together. "Thank you for coming tonight."

I settled back in my seat, my eyelids heavy with sleep. Leaning against his shoulder, I let my eyes close and drifted into sleep. I woke sometime later to James gently coaxing me awake.

"Hey, gorgeous. We're back in the city," he whispered as he rubbed my shoulder. "As much as I want to spend the night buried inside of you, I need sleep. Come home with me?"

We'd already spent last night together, just sleeping. Two nights in a row was definitely out of the question, even if it included sex. "I'm exhausted, and I need to be at the shelter early tomorrow. I should go to bed."

James nodded and a half an hour later the car pulled over in front of my place. He slowly disentangled our bodies. I was glad he didn't insist, since he'd probably be able to change my mind. I was finding it harder and harder to resist this man.

Ever the perfect gentleman, James walked me upstairs to my door, kissed me goodnight on the cheek, and left. I closed my door and stood there for a second. He kissed my fucking cheek and I had the goofiest grin on my face.

I didn't like how that made me feel. I didn't like it at all.

I needed to snap myself out of it, and I had the perfect idea how.

CHAPTER TWENTY

Over the course of the next couple of days, the idea floating in my mind quickly turned into solid plans. Daisy and I went shopping to prepare for it, her excitement nearly matching my own. I teased James about a surprise on Friday, but refused to see him during the week, something he wasn't too happy about.

I needed to put some distance between us after last weekend and I was also drowning in paperwork. It wasn't explicit, but I felt like the partners were punishing me for botching the Maxwell case. Dozens of trivial cases landed on my desk daily, and I was struggling to keep up with the ridiculous amount of work. At least my billable hours were through the roof, a small silver lining as my dream of becoming partner before turning thirty-five seemed more and more unreachable.

In between boring cases, I ordered a present for James. The fact he had spent the eve of his birthday dealing with my drunk ass made me feel a little guilty, so I figured a gift would make up for it. My little surprise with Daisy would compensate for the lack of sex that weekend and make it clear that we were friends with benefits. Nothing more.

By the time Friday rolled around, I was ready to let my hair down. James had dinner plans, so he was coming over after. I texted him a sneak-peek of my lingerie, bouncing from foot to foot as I selected toys for the night. An hour before he was supposed to come, Daisy arrived. A thrill went through me when I saw her standing there, her blue eyes alive with excitement.

I had been day-dreaming about this for a whole week, and now it was finally happening.

We had a glass of wine while we changed into the matching sets we purchased—red for me, black for her—and then we discussed boundaries and safe words. Green, orange, red—the same words James and I used.

Daisy disappeared inside my bedroom when we heard the doorbell, her giggles echoing in my ear as I buzzed James in. Butterflies danced in my stomach at the thought of seeing him. We'd been texting and talking on the phone all week, but I missed the flesh and bones James, even if I would never admit it out loud.

My breath caught in my chest at the sight of him clad in dark blue pants and a white shirt. It was so simple, yet so effective. He should give Deborah a raise.

"Hi, gorgeous," he said, wrapping his arms around me as he brushed a kiss against my hair.

I buried my face in his neck, letting his scent wash over me. It scared me how good it felt to be in his arms, how familiar everything about James had become in such a short time.

He gathered my long hair in his hand and pulled my head back, swooping down for a toe-curling kiss. I wrapped my hands around his shoulders, standing on tiptoes to press our bodies closer. His hand landed on my ass, but before things could escalate, I pushed against his chest.

The giddy smile on my face got bigger when I saw the hunger in his eyes. "Would you like a drink?"

He nodded and followed me to the kitchen, his hand never leaving my body. "What's the surprise?"

I poured him a drink and walked over to the couch. James pulled me to sit on his lap and I didn't protest. "I felt bad you had a shitty birthday," I said, planting my palm on his chest. "First because you had to put up with drunk me, second because your birthday party was a business event, so I had an idea."

James nuzzled my neck, his grip on my hip making me lose my train of thought.

"I thought my friend could join us tonight."

He froze. "Your friend?"

"Yes, Daisy," I said. He eyed me suspiciously, one eyebrow raised. "Consider it a birthday treat." I licked a path up his neck to his ear, taking his lobe between my teeth. "If you don't like the idea, she'll leave."

Right on cue, Daisy stepped out of my bedroom, wearing nothing but black lingerie. "Hi," she said, eyeing James with appreciation.

James's grip on my hips tightened. He tugged on my hair until I faced him, a question clear on his face. I beckoned Daisy forward with my finger, seductively biting my lip as James's cock stirred under me.

"You remember Daisy? You've met briefly." I patted the spot next to us, and she took a seat.

"It's nice to see you again," he said, his gaze focused on her face.

We had a little chat about boundaries, and I showed James Daisy's test results. I had offered to pay for her STD screening since this was my idea in the first place. Once that was settled I climbed off his lap and pulled my friend to her feet, turning around so she could unzip my dress. Daisy's hands drifted up my back and over my shoulders to slip the dress off. It fell into a pool at my feet, revealing the matching lingerie set in red. We thought it would be fun to coordinate outfits.

James smiled as he took us in, taking a long sip of his whiskey, leaning back to enjoy the view. Facing Daisy, I gently grabbed her chin, my mouth one inch from hers. We both giggled as our lips met, my curious tongue darting out to taste her. She opened her soft lips for me, warmth spreading all over my body as our kiss deepened. Our tongues explored, teasing each other, all nervousness gone.

I couldn't resist letting my hands roam her back, making my way down her slender body to land on her firm, round ass. We had been circling around each other for years. Now that it was finally happening, I planned to take full advantage of it.

James grabbed my arms and pulled me back into his lap. "I'm getting jealous," he growled, possessively consuming me with a kiss. He held the back of my neck to deepen the kiss, the whiskey on his tongue and his own taste an intoxicating blend. "Are you sure about this?" he whispered in my ear, low enough that Daisy couldn't hear.

"Yes," I whispered back as I nibbled his earlobe. Daisy sat next to James, and I suddenly felt the need for a drink. "I'm getting us drinks," I announced, disentangling myself from his arms.

The moment I stood to leave, Daisy straddled James's lap. He looked straight at me, silently asking for approval he didn't need. I nodded and winked before heading towards the kitchen, leaving the pair alone to get better acquainted.

If I wanted to, I could see what the two were doing from the kitchen, but I focused on making the drinks instead to give them some privacy. I poured three shots of good tequila, a whiskey for James, and two gin and tonics for Daisy and me.

I walked back into the living room with a little tray of drinks in hand to find Daisy sucking on James's neck. The moment I stepped into view, his gaze was on me. Goosebumps broke out all over my skin as his piercing brown eyes looked me up and down. He made me feel hot, desired, and I wanted to reciprocate.

Setting the tray down on the coffee table, I handed James his shot. His fingers brushed against mine, sending sparks between us. Daisy sat next to him, and I handed her a shot, too. She was flushed, her hard nipples pushing against the thin fabric of her lacy bra, begging to be sucked.

James pulled me to his lap again, holding me firmly at the waist to keep me there. His fingers dug into my skin when I reached for my shot. "To James!" I said, raising my glass.

"To James," Daisy echoed, downing her shot.

"Why don't you sit back and enjoy your treat," I suggested, lifting myself off his lap. I offered Daisy my hand to help her up, and she gladly took it. I sat her down on the coffee table right in front of James, kneeling in front of her so he could have the best view.

Daisy held the back of my head to pull me in for a long kiss, our tongues exploring each other's mouths with passion. I kissed my way down her throat, past her collarbone, to her perky tits. Wrapping my lips around one hard nipple, I licked and sucked, gratified by the soft moans she released.

She pressed my face against her breasts, holding me there, but I had more interesting places to go. I pulled back and spread her legs open, exposing her slick lips through the crotchless panties we were both wearing. James groaned behind me, but I ignored him, focusing completely on Daisy and her wet pussy.

"Is this all for me?" I asked, lightly running my fingers over her lips.

"Yes," she groaned, pushing her hips forward to increase friction.

I positioned myself, pushing my hips into the air so James could see my pussy too. Daisy squirmed as I blew on her clit, her pale skin flushed. Part of me wanted to tease her longer, but we'd been doing that for years, so I ran my tongue from her slit to her clit, finally tasting her.

"Cassie," she moaned, grabbing a fistful of my hair to keep me there. She didn't have to, though. I wasn't planning on going anywhere until I felt her come all over my mouth. Using the flat of my tongue, I circled her clit over and over at the same speed, feeling her quiver against my lips.

When I felt she was close, I changed the pace. It wouldn't be any fun having her come in the first few minutes. I licked her up and down, her hips jolting forward as her pleasure increased. I squeezed her thighs to keep her legs open as I fucked her with my tongue, her intoxicating scent driving me wild.

"Fuck, Cassie, please," she whispered between ragged breaths.

I felt James move behind me, so I looked back at him, my lips slick with Daisy's juices. "No touching yet," I said when I saw he meant to join us.

James obediently sat back, and I dove into Daisy's pussy, eating her out like she was my favorite dessert. Her hips bucked wildly, an orgasm fast approaching. I kept my pace but increased pressure on her clit, driving her over the edge.

Daisy came on my lips, her thighs squeezing my head as her whole body tensed, then shook all over. I lapped her up slowly until her orgasm started to fade, then I emerged from between her legs with a huge smile on my face.

She leaned forward and spread her cum all over my lips. "Babe, we should've done that years ago," she said, bringing her fingers to her mouth.

James cleared his throat behind us, his hard cock straining against his pants. He obviously needed attention.

"Don't you think he's a little overdressed?" I asked Daisy as I stood.

"We should help him with that," she answered as she licked her soft lips.

I straddled James, his hands promptly moving to my ass. Daisy sat next to us, sipping her drink while I unbuttoned his shirt. James's fingers roamed down past my asshole to my dripping wet pussy. I felt him probing my slit, running his fingers over it until finally he pushed them in.

I gasped, arching my back so he could go in deeper. James sucked on my neck as I finished unbuttoning his shirt. He was making me lose focus, so I sprang to my feet, immediately feeling the loss of his fingers inside me.

Letting Daisy take over, I watched from my spot on the couch as she unbuckled his belt, then undid the button and unzipped his fly. I took a long sip of my drink as she pulled James's pants down to reveal the full outline of his rock hard cock beneath black boxers.

My chest felt oddly tight at the sight of Daisy kneeling in front of James, running her long fingernails over the outline of his dick. Finally, she pulled the elastic down and his dick sprang free in all its glory. She gasped when she first saw it, and I couldn't blame her. I felt strangely proud of James's magnificent cock.

James placed his hand on my bare thigh, squeezing my flesh as Daisy worked him slowly up and down. "Fuck, babe," Daisy said. "You said he was big, but I had no idea you meant *this* big." She looked at his cock with curiosity, her brows drawing together in question. "I wonder if he'll fit."

Daisy lowered her head, licking around James's engorged head like a lollypop. James groaned, his fingers digging into my skin almost painfully. I pushed his hand away and sat on the coffee table, where Daisy had been before. Then I opened my legs exactly as she had, giving him a full view of my bare pussy.

I caressed my body while Daisy sucked James off, running my hands over my full breasts. A sharp jolt of pleasure ignited my clit when I pinched my pierced nipple between two fingers. Eagerness took over as I cupped my pussy with my other hand, pushing two fingers in and curling them to find my G-spot.

James watched me with laser eyed focus as he held Daisy's head, keeping her where she was. I touched myself while James watched, feeling beyond attractive as his dark eyes glazed over. Releasing my nipple, I brushed my hands over the smooth fabric of my lingerie until I reached my clit.

The combination of my fingers inside me while I played with my clit was bound to be fatal. James seemed distracted by my little peep show, his hips jerking violently as he fucked Daisy's mouth with abandon. She couldn't fit all of him, but she took him like a champ, working her hand up and down his shaft while she sucked on his head.

My body tensed on the coffee table. I threw my head back, unable to control myself as an orgasm pooled in my core.

"Look at me," James ordered. Daisy and I both looked up, but my heart skipped a beat when I saw he was looking straight at me, eyes dark with desire.

My walls closed around my fingers as my pussy spasmed. James's name escaped my lips as I came, his gaze traveling down to watch my quivering pussy.

"I'm coming," he announced for Daisy's benefit, and she pulled away. His movements became more erratic until, with a jerk, he came all over her lingerie clad boobs. She worked her hand up and down his shaft, milking him until the end.

The sounds of our combined heavy breathing filled the room as we slowly returned to reality. A smile tugged on my lips as I took in James's satiated expression and Daisy's chest, sticky with cum.

"That was really hot," I said, still panting slightly as I joined James on the couch. Daisy sat on my lap, her arm over my shoulders as we all took a moment to recover.

"We should move this to the bedroom," Daisy said. I agreed, but I wanted to finish my drink and get a refill before.

James ran the back of his hand over my lingerie covered breasts. "You're both overdressed."

"You can fix that," I teased. "Why don't you take care of Daisy while I go get us a refill?"

Daisy stood to one side, finishing up her drink while I bent over the table to place the empty glasses on the tray. James smacked my ass playfully before bending over me and whispering in my ear, "I can't wait to see what else you have in store for tonight."

I turned around in his arms and seductively bit his lip. "I think you'll have a good time." Grabbing the tray and Daisy's glass, I returned to the kitchen and poured everyone a drink and a shot of tequila like before. As I walked back into the living room, James was slowly undressing Daisy, and that tight feeling in my chest made another appearance.

Ignoring it, I joined the pair and handed each of them a shot.

"To James," I repeated the same line from before.

"To an unforgettable night," James said, his voice husky with desire.

We downed our shots, and I instructed James to finish undressing Daisy. I'd seen her naked before. We weren't exactly the type of girls who were embarrassed to be in the nude around our friends. But seeing James peel off her lingerie, his hands roaming all over her toned body…. I needed to open a window because it was truly getting hot in here.

"Now you're the one who's overdressed," James said once he'd finished removing Daisy's clothes. I had to fan myself with one hand at the sight of the two of them walking towards me.

Daisy positioned herself behind me, threading her fingers through my hair before she pushed it aside to unclasp my bra. Once she was done, James slipped the thin straps past my shoulders, my breasts bouncing free once he pushed the flimsy material down.

I bit my lip, purring as he squeezed my breasts in his skilled hands.

Behind me, Daisy continued pulling my lingerie down until it fell to the floor. I stepped out of it, then turned towards her. "Let's go," I said, pointing to my room with my chin.

Daisy disappeared into the bedroom, but James put a hand on my arm to stop me from leaving. "Are you sure you want to do this?"

I frowned. "I am, but you don't have to do it if you don't want to. No judgment." My hand landed on his broad chest, and his heart beat wildly beneath my palm. "Daisy will leave, and we can still have fun."

"I want to. But I'm afraid you'll regret it tomorrow." The look he gave me was exactly why I'd thought of a threesome in the first place. It was becoming more and more clear that there was a chance James felt something for me, something other than lust.

It made me uncomfortable.

I needed him to understand that this was all about sex.

"I won't regret it," I said firmly, giving him an open smile. James nodded and brought his fingertips up to my lips, softly caressing them before he grabbed the back of my head and pulled me in for a rough kiss.

Even after we parted and made our way to my bedroom, I could still feel his lips on mine, could still taste him on my tongue. His touch was seared into my skin, and I had the distinct feeling that even after our agreement ended, I'd remember it.

Daisy was on her stomach in the middle of my bed, propped up on her elbows. She'd turned on the music and lit the candles we'd set up earlier, the soft light casting shadows over her curves. Once she heard us come in, she turned to face us, a seductive smile playing on her pink lips.

"It took you guys a while," she said, gesturing towards the toys I'd left on the bed. "I almost started by myself."

"I think James could use a little attention," I told Daisy, gesturing towards his hardening cock. She promptly stood from the bed and kneeled in front of him, taking him in her mouth without preamble. I loved the fact he had such a short refractory period and was oddly proud to see him hard again.

I walked over to the toys, looking over my stash to see what I wanted to use on Daisy. Grabbing a huge black dildo, I sat on the edge of my bed in front of the two. James's eyes never left me as I poured a healthy amount of lube over the dildo, working it in my hands like I would with the real thing.

"Daisy, do you think you can take this?"

She narrowed her eyes as I pointed the dildo at her and cocked her head to one side. "Yes. I need something to stretch me out before I can take James."

James was clearly letting us take the lead here, since he was more domineering when it was just the two of us. I liked that letting me take control didn't seem to threaten him. Instead, the way he was looking at me like he wanted to devour me told me he actually enjoyed the switch in dynamics.

"Lie down on your back," I whispered in his ear. He happily obliged. Daisy wrapped her lips around his throbbing cock again, but this time she straddled him in reverse cowgirl.

I positioned myself over James's head, facing Daisy, fully intending to hover over him so he could breathe. But James had other things in mind. The second my pussy was directly over his head, he pulled me down to fully sit on his face.

He sucked my clit into his mouth, holding me in place with one hand while he pushed two fingers inside of me.

"Oh God," I called out, grabbing Daisy's ass and squeezing her flesh. Her pussy was dripping wet, pink lips swollen. I couldn't resist her. I started caressing her while James ate me out. The gagging noises Daisy made while she sucked James off almost made me want to switch positions. Almost, but not quite.

I grabbed the black dildo and slowly pushed it inside Daisy. She arched her back in pleasure, giving me an even better view of her glistening pussy swallowing the dildo.

"That's so hot," I whispered to myself as I pushed the toy in and out of her, stretching her tight walls.

James's expert tongue increased pressure on my clit, and his fingers found my G-spot. Stars clouded my vision as I rode him wildly, my hips jerking back and forth as he tried to hold me in place with one hand.

My ears were ringing. I could barely hear the music in the background over the sounds we were making. James blew on my clit, and I lost all control. I held on to Daisy, my fingernails digging into her ass as I thrust the dildo in and out of her, her hips moving to meet me.

James groaned against my lips as my pussy quivered, my orgasm fast approaching. I leaned forward and kissed Daisy's back, raking my fingernails over her soft flesh as pleasure coiled tightly in my core. James's fingers pressed against my G-spot as his tongue brushed over and over against my swollen clit.

It was overwhelmingly delicious. My moans filled the room as warmth spread all over my skin, my toes digging into the mattress. Wave after wave of pleasure rocked my body, sending me into a frenzy. James's fingers slid out of me so he could hold my hips, his magical tongue still working my clit until I couldn't take it anymore.

I tapped his hands and lifted myself off him, landing in a puddle of limbs at his side. The satisfied smirk on his cum covered lips made me smile, but I also wanted to wipe it off his face. Daisy was still working his cock, the dildo sitting idly inside of her.

James took over for me while I recovered, but he was far less gentle. I watched as he pounded Daisy with the dildo, his hand sneaking around to tease her clit. He was too in control. I wanted him wild.

Moving down the bed, I massaged his balls as Daisy licked his head. James planted his feet on the bed to give me better access, and I reached for the lube. I coated his asshole in lube as I massaged his balls, then stroked his puckered hole before slowly pushing a finger in.

His hips jerked up as his inner walls gradually relaxed around my finger. "Fuck, Cassie. Don't stop," James grunted.

A thrill went through me at his words, so I slowly pumped in and out of him, eager to please. Daisy was having a hard time maintaining a steady rhythm as her own orgasm built. I swallowed her moans with a kiss, making my way down her body to suck on her nipple.

James and I both focused on Daisy, and she completely let go of his cock.

"Cassie, please," she moaned. Her pale skin was flushed pink, eyes glossy, making her look even more beautiful.

"That's it, come for me," James whispered. I nibbled on her

nipple before sucking it into my mouth. Her hips jerked, her entire body trembling with pleasure. Daisy buried her face in my neck as she came, before rolling over to lie next to James.

James gave me a cocky smile and tried to pull me to him, but I stopped him. He watched me intently as I slid my finger out of his asshole and grabbed a butt plug. I coated the plug and his asshole in lube, my eyes lifting to watch his face as I pushed it in.

His lips parted in a gasp, but once it was safely in, he pulled me to him. "I can't believe you're fucking my ass before I fuck yours."

I giggled at his words. "The night is still young."

He growled and pulled me in for a long kiss that made me want his dick inside me. I grabbed a condom and rolled it on his throbbing cock before straddling him. But James was impatient. He drove his thick cock inside me all at once, fucking me from below. All I could do was hold on.

Daisy recovered and started playing with my breasts, her little pink tongue darting out to lick my nipples. Her soft hand moved down my body to tease my clit. I was so sensitive it bordered on painful, but Daisy's touch was gentle.

Between James pounding into me and Daisy teasing my breasts and clit, it didn't take long for another orgasm to hit me with force. James didn't stop. He kept going as my walls closed around him, his movements becoming more erratic until he exploded inside of me.

After that, we all needed a moment to recover. We took a water break, then went right back to fucking until the early morning hours. A little past three, James and Daisy collapsed on the bed on either side of me, their breaths becoming deeper as they fell asleep.

I lay there, staring at my ceiling, feeling things I shouldn't be, and hating myself a little for it.

CHAPTER TWENTY-ONE

I lay quiet in James's arms, waiting patiently in bed until I was sure that both he and Daisy were sound asleep. For whatever reason, I couldn't shake this nagging feeling that something was wrong.

Once I was sure they were out, I slid down the bed and stood by the door. James and Daisy were sleeping on my bed, naked. I hated seeing her there next to him. But I had no reason to feel this way. This wasn't my first threesome, and last night had been fun. Everything had gone exactly as planned, yet this odd tightness in my chest persisted.

It was probably because the two of them were still here, in my apartment. I enjoyed having my space, especially after a threesome. I just needed some peace and quiet to clear my head.

I took the empty glasses from the living room and loaded them into the dishwasher, then folded James's clothes neatly on the couch.

The matching lingerie sets Daisy and I had worn still lay discarded on the floor. I stared at them for a second, pushing away memories of James peeling the clothes off Daisy's body. He had seemed enthusiastic, which made sense—Daisy was hot. But I wondered what he'd think of her in the light of day.

Daisy came from a similar background to his. Her family was

also old money. Although she no longer had contact with them, the two were bound to have more in common than me and James. Not that it mattered, I reminded myself.

It was none of my business.

I felt too jittery to rest. The apartment was as clean as it was going to get at five a.m., so I opened my laptop and started designing a poster for the clothing drive I was organizing for the shelter.

A while later, my bedroom door creaked open, and James emerged in all his naked glory. My heart did a little somersault at the sight, skipping a beat or two like the traitorous bastard it was.

I had followed my heart once, and it had landed me in the hospital. I didn't think I could do it again.

"You also sneak out of your own bed?" James said, his sleepy voice playing with my heartstrings.

Ignoring how much I wanted to jump into his arms, I answered in a monotone. "It was a bit crowded."

James sat next to me on the couch, still buck naked, his muscular thigh pressing against mine. "Everything okay?"

I nodded while I selected a template for the poster.

"Do you want to put that down? Tell me what's eating at you?"

"There's nothing wrong. I just couldn't sleep, so might as well get some work done."

He pried the laptop out of my hand and placed it on the coffee table, forcing me to face him. "Do you regret last night?"

"No," I said immediately. "It was very fun. We should do it again sometime. Maybe with another guy this time." I spoke fast, way too fast for a regular person.

"That's never happening. I'm not sharing you."

"That's bold of you to say when my friend is still asleep in my bed." It was an unfair thing to say, given that last night had been entirely my idea. But I couldn't shake this uncomfortable feeling in my gut, gnawing at my insides.

"Turns out I'm reluctant to share you, even with other women. Last night was mind blowing. Watching the two of you together, the two of you on top of me... was phenomenal. But I'd rather have you all to myself."

I had no reason not to believe him, but a part of me couldn't conceive of a man not wanting a threesome. "Are you saying that if I surprise you with another threesome, you won't go for it?"

He paused for a second, rubbing the back of his head. "It depends on the context. A surprise threeway for our tenth anniversary? Absolutely yes. But next week? I'd have to pass."

"Two hot girls willing to have sex with you and you'd pass?"

"I told you, I'm reluctant to share you. I'm only interested in fucking *this* hot girl." He nibbled on my neck, stopping the words that were forming in my mouth. "Can I ask you something?"

"You can ask."

"What is your sexual orientation? Either way, I'm not judging, but you were very enthusiastic last night. I just need to know if I have to be jealous of the other fifty percent of the population as well."

I laughed softly, not wanting to disturb the early morning stillness. "I like men, and I like women. Some women, not all women. Some men, not all men."

James nodded as he pulled me closer. "You're something else, you know that?" 'Something else' seemed like the exact phrase to describe me, but unfortunately I didn't think James and I meant it in the same way. "What were you working on?"

Grabbing the laptop, I showed him the poster. "We're organizing a clothing drive for the shelter I volunteer at."

"Do you need any help? I'm sure I could find you some donors."

The rational part of me wanted to say yes, the more the merrier. But accepting help from James felt wrong, so I quickly changed the subject. "I'm starving. Sex is good cardio. I think I'll have an indulgent breakfast today."

"What did you have in mind?"

"I'm not sure. None of my usual places are open at this hour."

James stood, his muscular butt at eye level. I couldn't help myself. I sank my teeth into the hard muscle, just hard enough to leave an imprint. He jerked away from me in surprise, then gave me a bewildered look when he realized what had just happened.

"Sorry, I couldn't resist," I explained, biting my lip to contain my laughter.

He turned to face me, a playful grin on his lips. "I'm getting dressed before you think of biting anything else."

I watched his muscles relax and contract as he pulled on his clothes, fanning myself for effect, but I was only half-joking.

Once dressed, James walked the short distance to my kitchen, opening cabinets and inspecting the contents of my fridge.

"What are you doing?"

"Making you breakfast," he said as if it was obvious.

James Walton rendered me speechless yet again. I couldn't remember the last time a guy had cooked me breakfast or anything else for that matter. Andrew's face flashed across my eyes, but in the six years we had been together, I couldn't think of him doing more than passing me a box of cereal.

With a jolt, I leaped off the couch, not wanting Andrew on my mind. I tried to help James, but he physically stopped me by picking me up and placing me on my kitchen stool. He told me to just drink my coffee while he took care of breakfast, so I sat and watched as James fucking Walton moved around my kitchen with ease, that quiet confidence radiating off of him.

It should have been jarring to me to have a man take over my space and tell me what to do. But it wasn't, and that was a problem. For years I'd kept my relationships casual, not allowing anyone past the fortress I had built around my heart. But I could feel James chipping at it with his thoughtfulness and sweet gestures. Not to mention his skills in the bedroom. And I wasn't sure how to feel about it.

"I didn't know billionaires could cook," I said, pointing at the perfect pancakes stacked on a plate. "I thought you always had your meals delivered or just magically appear on your plate when you're hungry."

He laughed, the sound filling my kitchen. "When I moved back here for college, I got my first apartment. It was living alone for the first time, and it was college, so I mostly ate out or got take out. But even in New York that got boring after a while. When I started working for Dad, I hired a chef, but I hated it, so I eventually asked that chef to teach me his ways. Then I fired him."

"Oh yes, the old teach a man to cook and you'll be out of a job adage," I said, as I poured syrup on top of my pancakes.

"Hilarious," he admonished. "He's the head chef at one of Elias's restaurants." He flipped a pancake in the air before sliding it onto the growing stack. "Living alone made me realize how I was never truly alone before. My parents worked long hours, but there were always people in the house. Cooks, gardeners, Reggie, cleaning staff, and, of course, my sister. Then at boarding school, I had a roommate. Once I had my own place, I got used to being by myself. Actually, I enjoyed it a lot. Too much to have a chef, or anyone else, working long hours in my space, so I had to learn."

I almost moaned when I took my first bite, the fluffy sugary pancake the perfect indulgence after an intense night.

James chuckled as he dug into his own pancakes. "Now I'm glad I did, because watching you eat my food with such gusto gives me immense pleasure."

"Don't flatter yourself. The immense pleasure from last night made me really hungry this morning."

"Well, I'm taking credit for at least sixty percent of that immense pleasure, so I will flatter myself."

We ate breakfast, the conversation flowing easily between us. When I stood to clear the dishes, James unceremoniously picked me up again and dropped me on the couch. "What are you doing? You cooked, so I should do the dishes," I protested.

"I don't consider the cooking to be done until I've finished cleaning the kitchen." He raised one finger to silence me when he saw I was about to speak, anger finally rising inside me at being manhandled. "And I knew you'd argue, and I'm running on very little sleep and I have to go into work soon, so it's just easier to put you away." He winked, then turned his back on me to focus on the dishes.

This man was going to be the death of me. It was infuriating, but at the same time, I appreciated his gesture. I wanted to bash him over the head with the frying pan, but I also wanted to drop to my knees in front of him. One man wasn't allowed to make me feel this many emotions all at once.

Settling on calming myself down, I opened my laptop and worked to the sounds of James cleaning up after making me breakfast. The words danced across my vision, and I didn't even try to make sense of them. I just needed to look busy. My focus was too scattered to actually get any work done.

Judging by the noise, James should be almost done. My legs unfolded from under me of their own account, and in seconds I was standing behind him, wrapping my arms around his large frame simply because I could. And because I wanted to. And life was too short to deprive yourself of small joys.

"Thank you for breakfast, and for cleaning up," I said, my face pressed against his back. He turned around in my arms, and I pressed my face against his chest, inhaling his now familiar scent.

"You really shouldn't sniff me," he said, chuckling. "I haven't showered yet."

I looked up at him from beneath my lashes. "I don't mind. Makes me feel like a cavewoman."

His shoulders shook with laughter, the sound echoing all the way to my heart. James picked me up again and settled me down on the clean counter.

"You really need to stop picking me up," I said, scowling. "I'm not a doll."

"No, but that pout makes me want to fuck you like one." He dragged his teeth over my bottom lip, but we both froze when we heard a noise coming from my bedroom. "I was hoping to leave before your friend woke up."

"I seem to recall you giving me a hard time when I snuck out of your place while you slept."

"This is a completely different situation. I'm not interested in seeing her naked again." He brushed his lips against mine. It was barely anything, a hint of a kiss that left me wanting more, but it still made my heart race.

James rested his forehead against mine, his eyes closed, heart hammering against my palm. "I can't really think right now," he admitted, a small smile forming on his lips, "but I'll call you later."

I nodded, even though it wasn't a question.

Walking him to the door felt wrong somehow. James wrapped me in his arms, warmth radiating from his body and seeping into my skin. He kissed my forehead, and he was gone.

I closed the door, smiling like a lovestruck teenager, the idea that maybe this could actually work flitting briefly in my mind before I squashed it.

Daisy's voice pulled me out of my reverie, my smile crumbling away. "Morning, Cassie. Coffee?"

"In the pot," I said curtly. I felt a perverse sense of joy when I noticed James hadn't made any extra pancakes for Daisy. *His pancakes are just for me.*

I watched as she trekked across the living room towards the kitchen clad in my bathrobe. I wanted to scream at her for wearing something of mine without asking first.

"Damn babe, that guy? So hot. I was kind of hoping he'd still be around in the morning for another round. But I guess you can't expect a guy to stick around the next day."

I saw red for a second. "He has a life, you know," I snapped, unable to stop myself. She didn't know James. It was really unfair to talk about him like that. He was a decent man. He made me pancakes.

Daisy shot me a puzzled look. "Babe, are you ok?"

I turned away to grab a hair tie and busied myself with piling my hair on top of my head. "Yeah, sorry," I lied. "I didn't get much sleep after last night. I think I just need a nap."

It was thinly veiled, but I still hoped she'd take the hint and leave so I could finally process by myself.

Daisy narrowed her eyes. "I should get going too. I have a shoot this afternoon I still need to prep for." She abandoned her coffee and went to the bedroom to get dressed while I dried dishes that didn't need drying and put them away. Before she left, Daisy placed her hand on my shoulder. "Are you sure you're ok?"

I smiled, although I could tell it didn't reach my eyes. "Nothing that a few hours of sleep can't fix."

The moment Daisy left, I went into my room and ripped the sheets off the bed. *Better, much better.* After a long shower, I crawled into my fresh sheets, actually hoping that sleep would fix whatever was wrong with my heart that made me hate my friend.

CHAPTER TWENTY-TWO

It had been months since I'd had such a tedious workday. I went from meeting to meeting, answered emails, and made phone calls, all of it completely on autopilot. The minutes ticked by. Every task took double the time it usually did.

I did all the things I was supposed to do, but it didn't *feel* like I actually got anything done.

I had no shiny new case to throw myself into, just the same old boring DUIs. I groaned as I opened yet another uninteresting file, hoping against hope that the next client had done something awful to land on my desk. It was bad for humanity, but great for my sanity.

I couldn't get the image of James fucking Daisy out of my mind. The little noises she made when he was fully seated inside her…. It had been so hot in the moment. But in retrospect I just wanted to claw the bitch's eyes out of her skull so she'd never see James's face again.

And I hated myself for it.

Daisy was my friend. Hoes before bros, always.

But this particular bro seemed to be an exception to the rule.

And I hated that too.

"Cassandra?" Olivia's voice coming from the speakerphone

pulled me out of my head and my circular arguments. "There's a delivery for you."

"I'll be right out," I said into the phone. Pushing thoughts of James and Daisy living happily ever after together out of my head, I left my office to get the package. A delivery man was chatting with Olivia, a square box sitting on the counter between them.

I took the package back to the privacy of my office, leaving the two to chat in peace. A small smile tugged at my lips as I opened it to reveal a box of chocolates. *James.* Those damned butterflies fluttered wildly in my stomach as I searched for the card, eager to read his note.

But when I pulled it out, my smile crumbled. There was no signature, just like the flowers, but this time the note read: *Can't wait to see you.*

On impulse, I threw the box of chocolates in the trash and saved the unsigned card in my drawer. Dread crawled up my spine as I wondered who this person could be.

Andrew came to mind, but it made no sense at all.

I didn't have any connection to that brand of chocolate. They weren't my favorite, and neither were the flowers that I had received.

The Maxwell case was still making headlines, and I knew that we'd received some hate mail, but that was par for the course. This felt different, personal. *Can't wait to see you.* I shuddered as the full meaning of those words registered.

Shit. Grabbing my phone, I tapped on Monty's name.

"This is Monty."

"Hi. This is Cassie, are you busy?"

"Always," he said with a gravelly chuckle. "What can I do for you, kid?"

I hesitated, wondering exactly how to frame my concerns without revealing my past with Andrew. "A few days ago I received flowers and today a box of chocolates. There was no signature on the cards. The first one read, 'See you soon', the second, 'Can't wait to see you.' Maybe I'm overreacting, but I have a gut feeling about this. Can you look into it?"

"Were the flowers and chocolate delivered at your home or the office?"

"The office." I heard papers rustling in the background, and I could almost picture Monty scribbling notes.

"Anything else I need to know? Jilted exes? Disgruntled clients? Enemies?"

"None that come to mind," I said, even as Andrew's name floated in the back of my head. "But I'm a criminal defense attorney, I'm sure I pissed someone off at some point."

He let out a deep chuckle, and said, "Send me a list of anyone you think might be unhappy, and I'll see what I can find. Meantime, keep your eyes open, and if anything out of the ordinary happens, give me a call."

"Will do. Thanks, Monty."

"No problem, kid. I'll let you know if I find anything. Take care." With that, he hung up, leaving me alone with my thoughts.

My computer made a sound indicating that I had a meeting in ten minutes. I just hoped it would occupy my brain enough that I'd completely forget about James, James and Daisy together, and the mystery of the flowers and now chocolate.

Unfortunately, it didn't.

After another meeting that could've been an email, I pulled the stacks of files from the shelter out of my messenger bag. The partners knew I volunteered at the shelter, and had even been kind enough to help me out a few times in my first year here. I was definitely not supposed to be working on it on company time, but fuck it.

I started going over the cases one by one, making notes and phone calls as needed. When four p.m. rolled around, my head was still buried in the briefs, and I would've carried on if Daisy's name flashing across my screen hadn't gotten my attention. I didn't want to talk to her, so I read the messages as they popped up on my smartwatch without opening the chat.

Daisy: Dinner at my place? I have news!
Rina: I can be there at 7 p.m.
Amelia: Can't. Double shift tonight.

Daisy: That's okay. I'll call you with the news after your
shift?
Amelia: Yes, please!
Daisy: @Cassie can you make it?
Me: Yes.

The thought of seeing Daisy made my stomach churn, but I
was a firm believer in ripping off the proverbial Band-Aid. I'd
have to see her eventually and there was no better time than the
present.

I left the office, stopped by my apartment to change and grab
my yoga mat, then I went to a class at our regular yoga studio. It
usually calmed me, 'usually' being the operative word. But by the
time I got on the subway to head to Daisy's place, my mind was still
reeling.

My phone rang, and I had to physically stop myself from smiling
when I saw James's name.

"Hi," I answered, keeping my tone neutral.

"Hi, gorgeous. I'm sorry I didn't call you earlier. I've been in
meetings all day."

"That's alright. I was at work all day too."

"What are you doing tonight?"

"I'm on my way to Daisy's. She has some news to share." I hesitated for a second before adding, "But after I'm free."

"Great. Send me the address and I'll pick you up."

"I have to go home first to shower. I just got out of a yoga class."
That was a valid reason for wanting to go home first and had
nothing to do with me not wanting James to have Daisy's address. It
dawned on me that Daisy might be more James's type. I remembered the picture she sent me when he was away, the 'old friend' he
took to that charity event. She looked more like Daisy than me,
without a doubt.

"You can shower at my place."

"And meet up with you all gross and sweaty?"

"Yes," he said, laughter coating his words. "Let those
pheromones drive me even crazier."

His gravelly voice made me all warm and gooey inside. I hated it. My cheeks burned, and despite my attempts to stifle it, my lips stretched into a stupid grin. *Jesus, I'm a lost cause.*

"I'll text you the address." I ended the call before I said something embarrassing.

By the time I made it to Daisy's, I was fashionably late, and it was very much on purpose. The thought of being alone with her irked me. Rina should be on time, but I still timed it so I'd be twenty minutes late, just in case.

The moment I walked through the door of Daisy's bright loft, she squealed with excitement and handed me a glass of champagne. Rina was sitting on the couch, so I plopped myself next to her.

"So," Rina started, "tell us the news."

"I got a call this afternoon. I met this guy when I was doing a shoot for a second-hand shop in Chelsea. Anyway, his friend is friends with some woman who owns an art gallery, and they asked if I'd like to do a show."

"Shut up!" Rina exclaimed, shooting up to hug Daisy.

"Congratulations, Daisy," I said, not moving from my spot on the couch.

"Thank you." She beamed, her blue eyes sparkling.

"I mean, it's great news, but I wouldn't get too excited. It's not like it's guaranteed your stuff will sell." I could feel the energy in the room shifting and Daisy visibly deflating. But she needed the reality check. She floated through life without a plan or clear direction, her perpetually optimistic outlook carrying her through the tough times.

"But it's still great visibility, even if you don't sell." Rina gave me a pointed look, but I couldn't help myself.

"What work are you going to show? I can't imagine many people being interested in your regular photography." It might sound mean, but Daisy took any job she could find, which meant that she was photographing weddings, gender reveals, baptisms.... It wasn't necessarily the type of work you'd show at an art exhibit.

Daisy plopped down on the mustard yellow chair across from me, the excitement gone from her face. "I know. They're interested in my fashion photography because that's what they've seen. I think I have some suitable pieces, but I'll definitely have to create some new shots."

"I can help you go over what you already have, and come up with new ideas," Rina offered.

Daisy's cheeks turned a cute shade of pink, her smile returning as she turned to Rina. "Really? It's going to be hard to have everything ready on time since the show is in three weeks, but I think it will be worth it."

"Of course, it will. Anything that gets your name out there."

The doorbell rang and Daisy rushed to get the food she'd ordered. As soon as she was gone, Rina elbowed me painfully in the ribs. "What's wrong with you? Our friend just got great news and you're raining hard on her parade."

"She's so optimistic. I don't want her to get her hopes up only to be crushed by reality."

Rina gave me a suspicious look, but luckily for me, Daisy returned with the food before she could say anything else. We sat around the coffee table to eat, and I remained mostly quiet.

I didn't need Rina to point it out to know that I was being mean. My concerns were genuine, and Daisy had a tendency to get carried away, to dream too big, but who was I to crush her?

The conversation flowed around me as Daisy and Rina discussed possible shoots. Daisy wanted to shoot in black and white, which I thought was silly for fashion since you wouldn't be able to see what color the clothes were—a point I couldn't stop myself from making. But she insisted the way the fabric moved and the feel of it would be better captured in black and white.

"I know I probably won't make a lot of money, but maybe this will lead to more fashion shoots. If it means I don't have to do another dog birthday party, then I'm happy."

I didn't stay long after that, and I didn't know if it was because being around Daisy was making me irrationally angry or because I was looking forward to seeing James again. Both options were concerning.

When I walked out of Daisy's apartment, it almost felt like I was having déjà vu. James was leaning against his Mustang just like he had on our first date, except this time he was wearing sweatpants and a simple black hoodie.

He looked delicious. James in a suit or tux was hot, but casual

James had me wet before I'd even walked down the steps. And judging by the way his eyes roamed up and down my body with unmistakable hunger, he felt the same way about me in my yoga gear.

"Cassandra," he said, a dazzling smile stretching his lips.

His smile was infectious, and I couldn't help returning it. "James," I greeted back. He pulled me into his arms for a tight hug, and despite my tendency to overthink, my worries faded to the background.

Without another word, he opened the door for me, his hand barely brushing against my back. It was enough to send my body into a confused frenzy. His touch did something to me I couldn't explain.

"I've never seen you dressed so casual," I commented as he pulled out onto the road. The same seventies rock as before bled from the stereo, and I wondered if he'd like the gift I'd ordered for his birthday. I had spent hours on it. It would be disappointing if he hated it.

He smirked. "I came straight from hockey practice. Now we both need a shower."

"I didn't know you played hockey."

James's hand rested on my thigh as he drove, that quiet confidence radiating off of him. "I guess it never came up. Elias and I played at school, then college. When I took over the company, I started a corporate team, and Elias conned his way in. Now we do a little tournament every year."

"Elias conned his way in?"

"In theory, you have to work for Walton Corporation to be a part of the team, but Elias found a loophole. He's a skillful player, so I let it slide."

"I've never actually been to a hockey game. That's the one on ice, right?"

He laughed, squeezing my leg. "That's right. I'll take you to a game once the season starts, or you could come to watch practice."

"Watching a bunch of hot guys hit each other with sticks? Sign me up, please," I joked.

He shook his head. "So, what was Daisy's news?"

I didn't want to talk about Daisy, least of all with James. "She's doing an art exhibit in a couple of weeks."

"That's a great opportunity for her."

His words echoed Rina's, and I silently agreed. Even James was being more supportive of my friend than I was. I felt even more like an asshole.

James parked in his building's underground car park, and we made our way to the elevator. His tongue darted over his sculpted lips as his eyes roamed my body, a fire burning in them.

"Did you really walk around the city wearing this?"

"What's wrong with my outfit?"

"These pants are like a second skin, but I'm not complaining," he said, his hand traveling over the curve of my ass.

"I was wondering if you'd lost your possessive edge. My comment about the hot hockey players got nothing."

"That's because I trust you. Now that you've agreed to be exclusive, I trust you to keep your word."

I rolled my eyes. "That's no fun. I enjoy teasing you."

"I know."

The elevator doors slid open and James swooped me up and threw me over his shoulder. "Let's shower so we can use all those toys we ordered."

"You know I *can* walk, right?"

He slapped my ass playfully as he walked up the stairs. "I know, but this is more fun."

CHAPTER TWENTY-THREE

James set me down in his bathroom suite and wasted no time peeling off my clothes. He released my hair from its ponytail and, in a few movements, had us both naked under the water jets.

I did nothing but watch as warm water flowed down his chiseled body, past his hardening cock. James grabbed a shampoo bottle and applied a generous amount to my hair, his dexterous fingers massaging my skull as he lathered my hair. Washing it was a pain in the ass since it was so long, but James didn't seem to mind.

"Close your eyes," he said, his voice coming out hoarse with desire. He positioned me under the water and rinsed the shampoo out of my hair before applying conditioner to my ends. This definitely wasn't the first time he had washed a woman's hair, a thought that didn't give me any pleasure.

Once he was done, he moved on to my body. His touch was light, airy. Judging by his hard cock brushing against my belly, he was as turned on as I was. Yet, his touch wasn't sexual. James washed me with care, his touch almost reverent as he kneeled in front of me to wash my pussy.

Tears prickled at my eyes. It was ridiculous, but I had never been treated this way before. With all of the men and women I'd been with since Andrew, touch had been strictly sexual. And Andrew.... Well, when I was sick he made me sleep on the couch so I wouldn't wake him with my coughing.

James's hands glided over my wet skin as the water rinsed away the suds. When he was done washing me, I wanted to reciprocate, but he grabbed my wrist to stop me.

"You don't have to," he said, bringing my knuckles to his lips.

"I want to."

An almost shy smile appeared on his lips, and he let go of my wrist. I reached for the shampoo with trembling fingers, my heart hammering in my chest. I had never washed a man before. This was a level of intimacy I never allowed, and it made me nervous.

But as James bent down to help me reach his hair, I felt an overwhelming urge to take care of him. I shampooed his hair, the soft strands gliding over my fingers as I rinsed, then applied conditioner and let it sit while I scrubbed his body.

He chuckled and moved away as I ran the loofa over his armpits. "That tickles," he said, lowering his arms.

I smiled up at him, trying to disguise the enormity of this moment and how much it was affecting me. "Noted," I said, purposefully tickling him some more and giggling when he squirmed away. "Turn around."

James obliged, and I marveled at his muscular asscheeks before parting them to wash him thoroughly. Maybe this was routine for him, but washing him, touching him like this.... He was tearing down my walls without even knowing it.

Once I was done washing his ass, I turned my attention to his legs, his feet. Then I slid my hands up his thighs, and after coating my hands in shower gel, I started washing his cock and balls. I swallowed hard, my gaze focused on his hard length as I finished rinsing the suds and started slowly stroking.

"I'm not going to last long if you touch me right now."

"That's okay," I said, dropping to my knees. "You'll last longer later."

With that, I wrapped my lips around his throbbing head, tasting the water that dripped down his body. James widened his stance, his muscles tensing as I ran my hands up his thighs. I wrapped one hand around his thick cock, working him up and down as I teased the sensitive area around his head with my tongue.

James groaned, his breath coming out in short pants. "That's it. Faster," he growled.

I obeyed, moving my hand more quickly up and down his shaft, my tongue swirling around his head. I flattened my palm over his abs, feeling his muscles relax and contract as I sucked him off.

"Cassandra," he breathed.

My free hand glided down his muscular body to cup his balls. He released a satisfied growl as I massaged him, his hips jerking back and forth, shoving his dick deeper into my throat. As his movements became more erratic, I released his heavy balls, my fingers trailing up to caress his asshole.

James shuddered, throwing his head back as his palm smacked against the wall. "Fuck, Cassie. Don't stop."

I smiled around his cock, flicking my tongue over the sensitive spot under his head just as I pushed a finger in his asshole. Once I found the fleshy bulb inside, I tapped the pad of my finger against it over and over, changing the rhythm and the pressure until James released a guttural groan.

"I'm coming," he said, his entire body shivering with pleasure.

Just as the words slipped from his lips, hot spurts of cum shot into my mouth. I moved my head back as I stroked him with one hand, aiming for my mouth, my finger still pressing down on his prostate. James's body trembled as he climaxed, his hand in a tight fist against the wall, eyes closed, muscles relaxing and contracting as he struggled to breathe.

He was beautiful.

The sight of him set my blood on fire, and knowing that I did this, that I elicited those groans and guttural growls…. Pleasure coiled tightly in my core, but there was something else, something I wasn't willing to name yet.

James's cum dripped down my chin to my chest, coating my breasts. I slipped my finger out of his ass to caress his thigh, the hard muscle still shivering as pleasure coursed through his body. When I looked up, James was gazing at me through heavy-lidded eyes, a fire burning in his deep brown gaze.

I offered him a smile before I wrapped my lips around his sensitive cock again, licking him clean. He groaned, hooking his hand under my armpit to pull me up.

He pressed me against his chest, holding me tight under the water stream. "I love your mouth on my cock," he whispered in between ragged breaths.

"I want to run my tongue over every inch of you."

James growled in response. Grabbing my ass, he lifted me up to his height, smashing his lips against mine. I wrapped my legs around his waist, holding on to his wide shoulders as every swirl of his tongue against mine stoked the fire blazing in my veins.

His dick grew hard against my pussy, my body begging to be filled by him. But James set me down and put some distance between us. "I have better plans for tonight," he explained.

James scrubbed his body clean once more under my heated gaze before he washed his cum off my body. He lingered on my breasts, his palm brushing against my hard nipples. My body might have been clean but my mind was anything but.

The moment I stepped out of the shower, he wrapped me in a fluffy warm towel, handing me a second one for my hair. "I don't know how you wrap it around your head," he admitted.

He was still buck naked, water droplets traveling down his muscular body, past the hairs on his solid chest, down the ridges of his abs, to his now semi-hard cock.

And instead of focusing on this exceptional specimen, I was thinking about how adorable he looked when he admitted he didn't know something.

I need to get my priorities straight.

James took his time patting my body dry, then he gently unwrapped my hair before combing it and blow drying it, which took forever. But again, he didn't seem to be bothered by it. "I love your hair, it's so soft," he said as he twisted the strands into a braid. Once he was done, he gave it a tug. "It's also the perfect leash."

The thought of James using my hair as a leash made my pussy throb.

I wanted to ask where he'd learned to do braids, but after the threesome and my strange bout of possessiveness, it was better not to know. His past was none of my business, just like my history was none of his.

We made our way to his bedroom hand-in-hand, and I felt an odd mixture of shyness and excitement when I saw the black box on the settee at the foot of his bed. I flipped the lid under James's heated stare and took out a gold vibrating dildo.

James came up behind me and placed his hands on my hips, his chin resting on my shoulder. "Is that what you want to play with tonight?"

"Whatever you want. I'm all yours." The words had come out easily and it wasn't until I said them that I considered their double meaning. But with James's growing erection pressed against my butt, I knew now was not the time for clarification.

"I like the sound of that," he whispered, and a cascade of tingles traveled down my spine as his hot breath tickled my ear. A flush crept up my chest when he grabbed my braid and pulled me back towards the side of the bed before roughly throwing me down on the soft sheets. He grabbed my legs and flipped me over to lay on my stomach, and his hand came down hard, connecting with my ass with a loud smack.

I gasped, warmth spreading from my asscheeks to my throbbing pussy.

"I want to fuck you so hard that even if you refuse to see me for another week, you'll still feel my cock inside of you with each step you take." James slapped my ass again, then I felt his lips on my sensitive skin—the contrast between his stinging palm and warm lips exquisite. His tongue dipped to where my asscheeks and thighs met. I'd never thought of that spot as an erogenous zone, but his warm mouth had me fisting the sheets. "And I'll start by fucking your ass. Do you want that?"

I nodded, breathless and needy beneath him, but that wasn't enough for him. "I need a verbal answer, Cassandra."

"Yes. I want you to fuck me so hard I can't walk."

James released a guttural growl in response, his fingers digging into my hips as he dragged me towards him and dropped to his knees. His fingers teased my slit before I felt his teeth sink into my inner thigh. "Fuck, Cassie. You're so wet for me." I didn't have time to reply. James pulled me further towards the edge of the bed, and then his tongue brushed over my clit.

Pleasure coursed through my veins as he assaulted my clit with quick flicks of his tongue, and my hands fisted the sheets as he sucked the sensitive bud in his mouth. I was so turned on, so fucking horny, that it took him only a few minutes to have me coming on his tongue.

While my orgasm ripped through me, James lavished soft kisses on my inner thighs that sent tingles all over my skin. I scored my fingers through his hair, grabbing a fistful and pulling him to me for a kiss. He swallowed my moans, and I relished in the exquisite feeling of his muscular body flush against mine. My hands explored the broad expanse of his shoulders, the ridges and dips as his muscles relaxed and contracted, while our tongues tangled together.

Being with James was pure ecstasy. A world of sensations I could easily get lost in. And I found myself fearing it less and less.

"Get on all fours for me, gorgeous," he said, sounding husky and breathless.

I quickly obeyed, getting into position with trembling limbs as James reached for the box. He kneeled on the bed behind me, and I lowered my upper body at the same time I lifted my hips up in the air.

"Good girl." His gravelly voice sent a jolt of electricity straight to my clit, and I wiggled my hips in response. He slapped my ass, the sharp sting soothed by his warm palm gently rubbing the sore spot in a circular motion. Then started massaging my asscheeks with both hands.

I groaned into the mattress as he squeezed my ass, his deft fingers edging closer and closer to my asshole. Finally, he spread my asscheeks open, and I felt his tongue circling my puckered hole. A shiver went up my spine, and muscles I didn't know I had relaxed as my focus narrowed to each stroke of his tongue.

He ate ass with the same enthusiasm with which he ate pussy. I was writhing on his sheets and moaning his name like a sacred prayer, but I needed more.

"Fuck, I love your ass," he said, lifting his head as he squeezed it in both hands.

"Are you going to fuck it or just tease me?"

He slapped my ass again, harder this time, and the shockwave of pleasure plain traveled all the way to my fingertips. "Patience, gorgeous."

A groan escaped me as he slathered lube all over my asshole, a thrill of anticipation rushing through me. Then I felt his probing fingers pushing in. I gasped at the sensation but pushed my hips back for more.

"You're eager, aren't you? Don't worry. I'll give you more." With those words, he oh-so-slowly pushed his thick cock into my pussy until he was all the way in. I gasped as he filled me and just when I thought he would start moving, I felt him push something cold inside my asshole.

"Oh God," I moaned.

"You like that?"

When I didn't reply, he pulled on my braid to make me look at him. "Do you like that?" he repeated in between heavy breaths.

"Yes," I whispered. A smirk overtook his face, and then he pressed a button and the butt plug started vibrating inside me. My eyes widened at the sudden onslaught of pleasure. I already felt so full, and adding the vibration made it even more intense.

James started moving, and all I could do was take it. His hands dug into my hips as he slowly thrust in and out of me. He was being gentle, too gentle. I wanted more.

"Harder," I moaned, not recognizing my own voice.

James's hand came down on my ass hard, sending vibrations all over my body. "You're not the boss here. If I want to fuck you slowly, I will. Understood?"

I made a noncommittal sound, and James's hand landed on my ass again. "Don't make me repeat myself," he warned.

"Yes," I moaned. But my hips moved to meet his cock of their own accord, and there was nothing I could do to stop it. James's hand moved under me to tease my clit, and I couldn't take it anymore.

I was so deliciously full. Hot red lava flowed through my veins and gathered in my core. My orgasm ripped through me like fireworks, exploding all over my body and leaving me in a quivering mess on the bed.

But James didn't stop. He flipped me on my back, pulled the butt plug out, and replaced it with his hard cock. I gasped, my back arching off the bed as he slowly inched inside my asshole until he was fully seated. Struggling to catch my breath, I held on to his biceps, digging my fingernails into his muscles so hard I left little moon-shaped marks behind.

"Fuck, James," I whimpered.

He bent down to kiss me, his lips barely brushing against mine. "Can you take it?"

I nodded against his lips, unable to form words. He cupped my face, his tongue darting inside my mouth. I kissed him back as he slowly started to move, his other hand coming up to tease my pierced nipple.

We kissed as he thrust in and out of my ass until I got used to the sensation, then he leaned back and grabbed the vibrating dildo I had been holding before. I watched with wide eyes as he slowly pushed it in my pussy, my breath hitching at the overwhelming fullness.

"Look at me," James growled once the vibrator was fully in. "You look so beautiful with your mouth open like that." He pushed his thumb inside my mouth and I instinctively sucked on it.

James growled, then roughly pushed both my legs together, placing them on his right shoulder. This made the dildo fit even tighter against my walls, the pressure exquisite but so intense I whimpered. With what I would qualify as an evil smirk, he pressed a button and the vibrating dildo came to life inside of me.

"James," I moaned, along with some incoherent babble. The moment he started moving, my eyes rolled back in my head. I bit down hard on my lip until I tasted blood. James ran his thumb across my lips to stop me, then surprised me by wrapping his hands around my throat.

My hand moved up his arm, fingers blindly gripping his forearm.

Out of nowhere, my body started shaking uncontrollably. My pussy convulsed around the vibrator as James continued pounding into me. I struggled to catch my breath with his hand still wrapped around my throat. It felt like a pleasure bomb had gone off all over my body, every nerve ending alive with a fire I had never experienced before.

My moans filled the room but I could barely hear myself over the blood rushing in my ears.

"That's it," James said, his voice thick with lust. "Come for me, gorgeous."

"James, please," I begged, although I had no idea what I was begging for.

"I'm almost there, gorgeous. Hold on just a little longer for me."

Pleasure coursed through my veins, thick and heavy, as the dildo kept vibrating inside me, and James continued pounding into my ass even as it pulsed around him. I wanted to close my eyes, but I couldn't stop looking at James.

The way his abs trembled with each thrust, his skin glistening with sweat and those full lips parted as he panted…. It was a work of art. Then his gaze met mine, and the sinful expression in his eyes stole all the air from my lungs.

James's muscles tightened as he neared his climax, and he moved faster and faster until he stilled. "Cassandra," he groaned, as he emptied himself inside of me.

I almost wept with relief when he turned the vibrator off, my pussy still spasming from my never-ending orgasm. It was intense. So deliciously intense.

James carefully pulled out and removed the condom, tossing it on the floor. I felt oddly empty, but that emptiness was soon replaced by James pulling me into his arms and cradling me against his chest, his strong arms wrapped tightly around my trembling body. We were both sweaty and covered in lube, but he didn't seem to care as he pressed feather-light kisses all over my face.

"How are you feeling?"

"Like Jell-O," I said, smiling into his neck.

He chuckled. "When I first saw you at the club I had no idea it would be this… intense between us. I'm glad I found you."

"I'm glad you found me too," I said, only a little surprised I actually meant it.

James stared at me through half-lidded eyes, his beautiful face still flushed from our tumbling. I traced his cheekbones, my fingers smoothing the small lines between his brows. He closed his eyes, a content expression on his face. The moment was so intimate, it pulled at my heartstrings in an almost painful way.

I moved to straddle his lap, teasing his full lips with my tongue, nibbling at his lower lip. His tongue darted into my mouth and his hands moved to my hips. Soon his cock grew under me, I reached for a condom, ready for round two.

James sucked on the sensitive skin right below my ear. "I'm fucking you slowly, now. Can't have you too sore for tomorrow."

Later, once we'd both finished, he carried me to the bathroom and we showered again.

"Will you stay?" James asked. When I didn't reply, he shook his head a little, then disappeared into his walk-in closet.

I sat on the edge of the bed, wrapped in a fluffy towel, wondering what the disappointed look on his face meant. Wondering why I had this sinking feeling in my chest. Wondering why the little voice in my head wanted me to stay.

He emerged from his closet wearing jeans and a simple t-shirt and handed me a pair of sweatpants and a t-shirt. "Come on. I'll take you home."

I promptly slipped the clothes on, ignoring the odd feeling in my chest. "You don't have to do that. I can just order a car." I stood on shaky legs to grab my phone, but James stopped me.

"I'd rather take you home myself," he said firmly.

On the ride home he seemed relaxed, not at all angry that I didn't want to stay the night. We made plans for the following day, and I wondered if his birthday gift had arrived yet. He parked on the curb in front of my building, walked me upstairs to my door, then kissed me on the forehead and wished me goodnight.

No pressure to stay at his place. No anger about driving me home.

I had never had my boundaries so easily respected and it rattled me. But maybe this was all just an act. Andrew was perfect in the beginning, and look at how that turned out. I wouldn't let myself fall for that again.

CHAPTER TWENTY-FOUR

Whenever we could, the girls and I met up for Sunday brunch. The four of us had busy schedules, but we prioritized our friendship, making it a point to see each other at least once a week. On this particular Sunday, Daisy completely monopolized the conversation. She went on and on about the exhibit, and since I didn't want to chime in with something negative, I didn't say anything at all.

When Daisy passed a tablet around the table to show her pictures, I sat there sipping my mimosa, dreading my turn. Amelia gushed about each photo, finding details to admire. But when she handed me the tablet, the words just flew out of my mouth.

"Are you serious? These are so basic. They look like they belong on some influencer's social media feed, not an art gallery." It was the truth, but as I watched Daisy's shoulders sag and the spark leave her eye, guilt gnawed at my insides. Maybe if I hadn't been so bent out of shape over the threesome, I could've found a kinder way to phrase it.

Rina shot me a look, but when I gave her the tablet and her eyes widened slightly, I could tell she agreed with me.

"It's just the general idea," Daisy said, her pale cheeks turning pink.

"Well, there's room for improvement," I said earnestly.

"And plenty of time to improve," Rina said as she glared at me. "I think we need to start with a theme and go from there."

Daisy nodded as Rina returned the tablet, her muscles stiff as she swiped through her photos. With a forced smile, she excused herself to use the bathroom and Amelia followed. Now that we were alone, I knew I wouldn't be able to avoid Rina's scrutiny.

"Why are you being such a bitch to Daisy?"

I rolled my eyes, schooling my features to mask my uneasiness. "I'm not being a bitch. The pictures suck. Shouldn't her friends be honest with her?"

"Honesty without compassion is just cruelty, Cassie. Now spill, before they come back." Rina gave me a look that told me she wouldn't let this go.

"Fine," I said, releasing a deep sigh. "James, Daisy, and I had a threesome the other night. I guess it's been bothering me a little."

Rina narrowed her eyes at me. "You're jealous."

"That's ridiculous."

"Is it? You are many things, Cassie, but mean is not one of them. And it would explain your obvious animosity toward Daisy."

I took a bite of my food, refusing to look at Rina as I chewed.

"How are things with James?"

"Fine. Casual. We're going out this afternoon." Last night hadn't felt casual, but I wasn't about to admit that to Rina. She'd see way too much into it, especially if I told her he'd driven me home after I declined to stay over.

"So you're not mad at James, just Daisy. Interesting," she said, her inquisitive eyes fixed on me.

Before Rina could say anything else, Daisy and Amelia returned. I bristled at the sight of Daisy in her stupid, puffy yellow dress. Rina's eyes were trained on me, and as I glanced at her, she mouthed, "*Jealous.*"

Jealous. Even thinking the word made my breath hitch a little. Jealousy implied feelings, and if I admitted to being jealous....

A little voice inside of me asked if it would be so wrong to catch feelings for James. Sexually we were compatible, that much was clear. And we were both busy, both invested in our careers, so we had similarities there. He seemed nice, respected my boundaries, and brought me food and comfort when I was drunk and angry. Not to mention he was insanely attractive, and his laugh made butterflies dance in my belly.

The girls focused on Daisy's predicament while I tortured myself with thoughts of James and commitment and jealousy. Eventually, we said our goodbyes, and Rina fell into step next to me as I turned to leave.

"You deserve to be happy," she said out of nowhere. I gave her a puzzled look, but she continued. "Ever since we met, you've been fighting to rebuild your life. You worked through law school, landed an excellent job, got promotions…. I've seen you struggle and I've seen you thrive. But the smile on your face the day James came to your place? That was different."

I swallowed the lump in my throat, my eyes burning. "And your point?"

Rina stopped walking by the subway entrance, her no-nonsense tone giving me pause. "My point is there's more to life than working. I'm proud of you for reaching your goals, but your job doesn't make you happy. If James makes you happy, then I wish you'd give him a real chance."

"And if it ends badly?"

"Then Daisy, Amelia, and I will be there to support you. And if James doesn't make you happy, then maybe some other guy will. Or a different job, another path. But you need to let yourself be happy. You've earned it."

Rina gave me a quick hug, and there was nothing I could do to stop the tears from welling in my eyes. I nodded, then turned to walk home, her words echoing in my mind.

When James's car rolled to a stop in front of my building, I was already sitting on the steps, his present hidden in my purse. I couldn't help the smile that took over my features, and for once, I didn't want to.

Rina's words had stayed with me, and after a couple of hours of sulking, I decided to be a little more open-minded to the possibilities.

James rounded his car and met me on the sidewalk, pulling me in for a tight hug. "You're so eager to see me you couldn't wait upstairs?"

Instead of replying, I buried my face in his neck, letting his clean scent wash over me. James released a quiet chuckle, his chest vibrating underneath his charcoal suit.

"Did you come straight from work?"

"Yes," he replied, leaning back to look at me.

The sun shone on his face, and I realized I'd never noticed the specks of green around his pupils. My heart fluttered in my chest, so I had to look away. Clearing my throat, I said, "I've got something for you."

James leaned back to look at me, surprise clear on his face. Then he smiled, and it took my breath away. "What do you have for me?"

"I'll give it to you in the car," I said, my cheeks warming.

He opened the door, and I slipped in. By the time he took his seat, I'd fished his present from my purse and clasped it on my lap.

A boyish grin appeared on his face, his eyes widening when he saw the package. "You got me a present?"

I nodded and handed it to him. "Yes, open it."

James carefully unwrapped the rectangular box, then gave me a curious look. He flipped the lid open to reveal a dozen cassette tapes compatible with the radio in his car.

"Happy belated birthday." A thousand thoughts rushed through my head as James examined the tapes, taking them out of the box one by one to look at the labels. "I thought you might like to listen to some different music from time to time," I explained.

It was a silly gift. James had the means to replace his car radio or get other tapes if he really wanted to. Maybe he enjoyed listening to the same songs over and over. Maybe it reminded him of his grandpa.

He cocked his head to one side, a small smile stretching his sculpted lips. "How did you find these?"

"I found a guy online who knows how to transfer digital music to tapes. I just sent him the playlists, and he did it."

"You made me all these playlists?"

"I wanted you to have options. But it's okay if you don't like them."

"I love them," he said, flashing me a dazzling smile, "thank you."

I smiled, a little of my anxiety dissipating. James pulled me in for a hug, his grip on my waist sending a tingling sensation all over my skin. It was enough to make me want to climb on his lap and ride him right now, but I controlled myself.

James replaced his grandfather's cassette with one from the box, a goofy smile on his face as Eminem's 'Love You More' started playing. I didn't know if he liked rap, but judging by his reaction, I'd made a good choice.

We sang along as he drove, laughing at how bad we sounded. Eventually, James pulled into an empty parking lot, a large building looming a few feet ahead. We walked into the suspiciously empty ice-skating rink, goosebumps breaking out all over my skin at the difference in temperature.

"You could have told me we were ice-skating. I would've worn something different."

James stepped in front of me, his warm hands traveling up and down my arms. "But then I would've missed how beautiful you look in this dress."

I narrowed my eyes at him, but his lips met mine and whatever I was going to say slipped my mind.

James wrapped his hand in mine and guided us to the locker rooms. He pulled out some clothes from the duffel bag he'd carried inside. "Here, let me help you get warmer."

The look in his eye made me feel pretty warm already, and when he pulled my dress up to reveal the lingerie beneath, that look turned almost feral. James took a deep breath, his hands on my hips, and rested his forehead against mine. "I just wanted to take you ice-skating, but at this rate, we're never going to make it."

I shivered against him, and he must have thought I was cold because he stepped back and pulled a t-shirt over my head. It smelled like him, and so did the sweater and jacket he put on me next.

Then, James Walton kneeled in front of me. His lips brushed against my inner thigh, that one small contact doing more to warm me than the layers of clothing he'd put on me. I ran my fingers through his soft hair, massaging his scalp. He groaned as he held the pants so I could step into them, then stood easily to pull them up my legs.

"Did I really need the padded clothes?" I asked, fingering the extra pads on my knees.

"Yes, I don't want you to get hurt."

The clothes fit me perfectly. In the back of my mind, I knew Miss Adams was responsible for the outfit. But James still had to think of it, to instruct her to buy padded clothing because he worried about me getting hurt. It made my heart swell in my chest. I swallowed the lump in my throat, wondering if this was really real. And how long it would last. No one could be this thoughtful, this perfect.

"Have you ever skated before?"

"On roller skates. But that was twenty years ago."

A devilish smirk slowly crept over his face. "I'll be your teacher."

James patted the bench, and I silently complied. He took my feet in his hand and covered them in thick, comfy socks. "Ms. Adams told me your shoe size, but I got a couple of smaller and larger sizes, just in case. There's nothing more painful than ill-fitting skates."

He had me try on the three different pairs of skates to see which ones fit better, then laced them up for me. Standing in front of me, he removed his suit jacket, steady fingers unbuttoning his shirt to reveal broad shoulders, defined pecs, his abs, and the enticing V that led to paradise.

I ogled him without shame, taking in this mountain of a man who wanted me with an intensity and a softness I'd never experienced before. Rina had been right. I didn't *need* a man, but James made me feel light, airy. Maybe I *wanted* a man.

Someone who understood my crazy hours because they were equally ambitious and hard working. Someone who liked it a little rough in the bedroom and wasn't afraid to experiment. Someone who respected my boundaries, and was so worried about my well-being that they made me wear padded clothes.

Someone who would never hit me.

"Penny for your thoughts," he said as he unbuttoned his pants.

I blinked, pushing those thoughts away. "When did you learn to skate?" Deflection was my mother-tongue, a skill I had learned with Andrew and refined throughout my career as a lawyer. A part of me wished I could just tell him the truth, but would he still want me if he knew how broken I was?

James put on black sweatpants that, to my delight, hugged his ass and did nothing to conceal his boner. "My father taught me as a kid. We have a lake on our property, and when it'd freeze my sister and I would skate there. He'd join when he had the time. When my mom caught us, she got us a coach. I loved hockey, my sister was into figure skating, and Mom was terrified we'd fall and cut ourselves, or each other, with the blades. But she still came to every practice, every game."

I smiled, his words painting an idyllic picture in my head. The familiar pang of loss and grief filled my chest, but I pushed it down. I had similar memories of my own family. My parents had been supportive and had never missed my school events, no matter how boring Dad thought debate tournaments were.

James pulled me to my feet, his hands on my waist to help me keep balance. "My father couldn't come to all the games, but he always made time for the important ones. I know he was an asshole to you, but he's not a bad person."

"He was an asshole to me, but it doesn't mean he *is* an asshole. I'm sure he has to deal with people whose primary concern is money, and he was being protective."

"In my world, the dating pool is very small. We date each other because we know what it's like to have money and have other people covet it. To always wonder if people like you for you, or your family name...." He slipped on a dark gray jersey with the letters WC stamped on the front and the number seven under his name on the back. "He was trying to be protective, but he was also being an elitist asshole. As a man, I have a little more control over my life, and my choices. But if my sister brought home a plumber or even a lawyer, my parents would probably disown her."

"Would you disown her?"

"Never. I want her to make her own choices." He sat next to me and slipped on his skates. "But the pressure to please the family and society is still there."

"And you're defying society to hang out with me," I stated.

James threw me a sideways glance, his jaw set tight. "Is that what we're doing? Hanging out?"

"It's an accurate description."

He shook his head and stood even taller, now that his black skates were on. "Come on," he said, offering me his hand. "Let's hit the ice before I have to spank you again."

"I'm not opposed to it," I said, as we walked to the rink hand in hand.

James put a helmet on my head, and as he was adjusting the straps under my chin said, "You look very cute." He brushed his nose against mine, and I giggled at the intimate gesture.

"Deborah did a good job with the outfit."

"Miss Adams didn't pick this, I did. As much as I trust her fashion sense, she doesn't exactly specialize in sportswear."

"You went to an actual store to get this?"

He raised one eyebrow, his head cocked to one side. "Why does that surprise you?"

"Because Deborah said men like you don't have the time for trivial things like shopping."

"Miss Adams is correct. But for you, I can make time." James stepped on the ice first, then stretched out a hand to help me. "Although I confess I had to ask my assistant to take it to the cleaners."

I shook my head, at a loss for words. I took tentative steps, my legs wobbling as the skates hit the ice. The speakers came to life, and we skated to soft rock music. James patiently showed me his technique, his movements fluid and confident as he glided effortlessly over the ice. I held on to the wall as I tried to skate, swaying back and forth, trying to maintain balance.

After a couple of rounds around the ring, I felt a little steadier on my feet. James hovered nearby, catching me every time I stumbled. "You don't have to babysit me. Go skate. I'll be fine."

"I'm not babysitting you. I'm teaching you."

"I know, but I don't want you to be bored, and your looming professional ice-skater presence is making me self-conscious."

"First, I'm never bored when I'm with you. Second, you shouldn't feel self-conscious. You're doing great. And lastly, I'm not a professional."

I shoved him away, almost falling to my ass as I did, but he lifted his hands in surrender and skated away. He sped over the ice, skating backwards and doing sharp twists and turns. I stopped admiring him to focus on my technique, adjusting my posture as I tried to mimic James.

After a few more rounds, I was ready to let go of the wall. James immediately appeared beside me, ready to catch me if I fell. He corrected my posture and showed me the right technique once more before taking off at lightning speed. My movements gradually became more fluid, and I moved further from the wall as my confidence increased.

When he passed by me again, James did some fancy move and sprayed ice all over me.

"Show off!" I shouted over the music, his boisterous laughter my only reply as he sped away.

James joined me again after a few minutes, the grin on his flushed face making him even more attractive. "Ready to go a little faster?" He skated backward in front of me and held out his hands. I didn't hesitate, and he started skating backward with me in tow as I tried to move my legs faster.

"You're getting the hang of it pretty fast. Stop skating for a bit. Let me take you for a spin."

I did as he said, and soon we were speeding around the ring, the cold air biting at my cheeks. James was in complete control of my movements, and while it was scary at first, I was soon laughing as he went faster and faster.

James did a maneuver to stop on the ice, and I slammed right into him. He laughed as he gripped my hips to stop me, his face more relaxed than I'd ever seen.

"You didn't teach me how to stop," I complained, his laughter filling my ears.

"Good thing I'm rock solid," he said, a smirk on his lips.

I shoved his chest playfully, rolling my eyes at his cockiness. We took a break, and as we made our way off the ice, I asked, "Did you rent out the whole place?"

"Not exactly, since I own it. But I did book it for the afternoon."

It was a bit much to reserve the whole rink for the two of us, but the fact we were alone awakened my naughty side. But as we rounded a corner, I discovered we weren't completely alone, and my dirty mind would have to wait. Outside the rink, a man had shown up with a coffee cart and an assortment of pastries.

James meticulously planned this date, I thought. Rina's words echoed in my mind, forcing me to recognize how much fun I was having.

"Mmmm, coffee," I moaned, as the warm deliciousness made its way down my throat.

James wiggled his eyebrows. "We don't have to keep skating if you want to do *something else.*"

"Something else is definitely on the menu, but I want to learn to go a little faster."

Yesterday, if I'd known my interest in skating would make James light up the way he did, I would have refrained from saying anything. But today, I found myself wanting to please him in a way that wasn't sexual.

James told me about his hockey days as we sipped our coffees, detailing his many injuries. It explained why he was so adamant I wear a helmet and padded clothes. He had his reasons for being protective, but the fact he cared at all if I got hurt made my chest feel tight.

I stood to test my balance and gain a little edge before I said, "Last one on the ice has to be tied up tonight." With that, I raced awkwardly towards the ring, but James easily took over, a smug look on his face.

"I win," he said, smiling victoriously.

I walked onto the ice, skated my way towards him, and placed a hand on his chest. "Just like I'd planned," I said, a cocky smirk on my lips.

His eyes widened a fraction before his lips smashed into mine, his tongue in my mouth sending a jolt of pleasure straight to my clit.

"You're insatiable," he said, pulling back despite me clinging to him. "Come on, you wanted to learn how to skate faster."

I almost fell backwards disentangling myself from him, but he helped me regain my balance, maybe in more ways than he knew.

We skated for a couple of hours, laughing easily together. James taught me how to go faster, and how to stop, which landed me on my ass more times than I could count. But every time I fell, James was there to help me up.

Later that night, he did tie me up, and when we were both too exhausted to do anything else, he drove me home, walked me to my door, and kissed me goodnight.

CHAPTER TWENTY-FIVE

After our ice-skating date, things seemed to shift between James and I. I was giving him—us—a real chance, and although we never openly talked about it, he seemed to know, especially when I agreed to go out during the week.

In the week that followed, we saw each other almost every day. I attended a charity event with him, posing for pictures beside him as the elite wondered about the woman who'd snatched up one of their bachelors. We had dinner dates at fancy restaurants and then we devoured each other at his place or mine. Sometimes we cuddled on the couch afterward to watch a movie. But at the end of the night, James drove me home or left, respecting my boundaries.

There was only one thing weighing heavily on my mind: Daisy. We hadn't spoken since brunch, which was unusual. She was busy with the upcoming exhibit, and my schedule was equally full. I used it as an excuse to avoid her. But guilt gnawed at my insides every time I remembered how mean I had been to her. I needed to apologize.

As I strolled through the supermarket on Sunday, I thought about calling her to see if she was home. But apologies weren't my forte, at least not when they were sincere. It could wait another day, I told myself.

An unknown number flashed across my screen, pulling me out of my reverie.

"Hello," I answered, as I pushed my cart into the produce aisle.

"Hi, is this Cassandra?" The female voice on the other side sounded vaguely familiar, but I couldn't quite place it.

"Yes, this is she. Who is this?"

"This is Elisabeth, James's sister. We met briefly at his party?"

I froze with a bunch of bananas in my hand, effectively losing my ability to speak. "Yes, hi. I remember you. How are you?" I asked, using small talk to get through the initial discomfort.

"Great, thank you. I was talking with James yesterday and he mentioned you were collecting clothes for a charity you volunteer for, and I have clothes. Lots of clothes, actually. I was wondering if you were still accepting donations?"

James talked to his sister about me. I had a million questions, the first one being why? The second, what exactly did he say? But I couldn't ask any of those, so I stifled my curiosity and focused on the potential donations.

"Of course, we always accept donations."

"Great! I'll drop by later today!" She hung up before I had the chance to say anything else.

Later today was a little vague, but I'd planned to spend most of my Sunday afternoon at the shelter going over briefs and sorting through the bags we'd already received. I could easily justify staying until James's sister dropped by.

I finished grocery shopping and dragged my granny cart home to put it all away before heading for the shelter. Elisabeth came in just after five p.m., a suit-clad man following close behind her carrying multiple bags.

"Hi," she said. "Where can I put these?"

"Hi! Right over here." I pointed to an empty spot on the floor. Elisabeth set her bags down and the man behind her did the same. "Thank you! That looks like a lot of clothes. I really appreciate it."

"Oh, anytime. I can probably bring a few more bags if I go over my closet again. Mom saw me carrying these out and said she was going to see what she had too, so you can expect a lot more."

I opened the bags to see what she had brought, and was

surprised at the contents, although I really shouldn't have been. There were a couple of shirts the women at the shelter could probably wear, but most were designer dresses. "Are you sure you want to donate these? They must have been expensive."

She looked a little self-conscious, tucking her glossy raven hair nervously behind one ear. "Yes, I'm sure. Honestly, some dresses still have the tag on, and others don't even fit me anymore."

"Right," I said, trying to phrase it nicely. "I'm not really sure we can accept this…. It's just that the women who will benefit from the clothing drive probably have nowhere to wear designer dresses." Not that the women didn't deserve nice, fancy outfits. But their priorities and ours remained helping them rebuild their lives and feed themselves and their children.

Elisabeth lowered her head, shoulders dropping in disappointment. "Oh, I see."

"Don't get me wrong, this is very generous of you, but we were looking for more practical clothes. Stuff they can wear daily, or to job interviews. I don't mean to be rude, but you could probably sell one of these dresses and have enough money for a year's worth of clothes."

"That's a great idea!" she chimed in, visibly brightening.

"What is?"

"You could sell them. All of them. That way you could use the money for the shelter, to buy new clothes or whatever else you need."

I kicked myself over the fact I wasn't the one who had thought of it. Money was exactly what the shelter needed. "You're right, that's a great idea. But are you sure? These are so expensive, I kind of feel bad accepting them at all."

"Please," she dismissed me with a wave. "Most of it has been sitting in my closet untouched for years. You could have a little fundraiser, like an auction. I bet I can get some of my friends to donate, and if you take men's clothes, I'm sure Dad, James, and especially Elias have stuff they don't wear too."

The wheels immediately started turning in my head. I could get a few volunteers to model the outfits, or just use mannequins to display them. If I could find a location for a good price, I wouldn't mind paying it out of pocket, and for the rest, like music, lighting, and food, I could get help from the girls.

The women from the shelter would probably be more than happy to help too. Maybe they could model as well. It was all coming together in my mind, and I got excited about what it could mean for the shelter if we managed to pull it off.

Legal fees, clothing, food, better facilities…. I just needed Marie's permission.

"If you're sure about it, we'll take them! I love this fundraiser idea. We need money more than we need clothes."

"Great! I have to run, but do you think I could help you with this? I don't have a lot of experience, but—"

"Of course! It was your idea in the first place," I interrupted before she got the chance to get down on herself.

"Thank you," she said, giving me a quick hug. "I'll call you when I have more donations!"

"Thank *you* for bringing these and for the fundraiser idea."

She smiled and sauntered off, the burly man following right behind her.

Meanwhile, I opened up my journal and started scribbling ideas. I knew Oasis was closed on Tuesdays, so maybe if I asked nicely, Elias would let us use the space for a friends-and-family discount.

I wasn't above using James's connections to help the shelter, as long as I wasn't personally benefiting from it.

After brainstorming, I picked up a few bags that had already been sorted and took them down to the laundry room in the basement. I put a load in the wash and grabbed the clothes from the drier to fold upstairs in our makeshift lounge/dining area. A few women sat around watching TV, playing cards, and just casually chatting

"It looks like we're getting more donations this year," Marie said, coming to help fold the clothes. We separated them by size and season while I told her about the fundraiser plans. Luckily, Marie was on board, so we started discussing more practical things, like how the payments would be processed and where we needed to use the money first.

A few residents came to help us fold the laundry. Usually everything at the shelter was first come first served, but we knew most of our residents well enough to determine who needed a winter coat or formal wear for a job interview, so we set certain items aside.

It was generally peaceful at the shelter. All of the women came from abusive relationships or abusive families. The last thing most of them wanted was drama. It warmed my heart to see them welcoming each other and making sure the newcomers had enough to eat, warm clothes, and whatever else they needed.

It made me wish I had experienced that when I was in a similar situation.

We were busy distributing coats when we all started at the sound of the shelter's main door closing. A few seconds later, a man walked in, the surrounding air suddenly heavy as silence took over the room.

"Hello," he said, looking at us with wide eyes. "Is this the Little Haven Shelter?"

This wouldn't be the first time that an abusive partner came here searching for someone, so I gave Marie a knowing look before stepping towards him to shield the women from view. "Yes, it is. Can I help you?"

He was looking down at his feet, not making eye contact with anyone. "I don't know, actually."

I noticed his shirt and jeans were a little frayed, but he looked clean if a little disheveled. He had his hands buried deep in his pockets as he shuffled from foot to foot.

Something was off, but I needed to get him away from the women before questioning him further. I tried to put a hand on his arm to guide him to the office, but he flinched back, so I raised my hands up in front of me so he could see I wouldn't touch him again. "There's an office in the back. We can talk in private."

He slowly nodded and followed behind me as I walked towards the office. I heard Marie following a few steps behind him, but I glanced over my shoulder to make sure she was there.

The man didn't seem aggressive, but I wasn't going to risk being alone with him.

I pointed towards a chair and he gingerly took a seat, giving

Marie a wary glance when she walked in and shut the door behind her.

"I'm Marie, the shelter's director. This is Cassandra," she said, pointing at me. "She volunteers here as a lawyer. Can you tell us your name?"

"Josh," he said while staring at his shoes.

Marie offered him a kind smile. "So Josh, can you tell us why you're here?"

He was silent for a long moment. Marie and I understood that something was wrong, so we gave him space and time until he was ready to share his story. His eyes welled up, and he blinked and rubbed at them roughly to prevent the tears from falling.

"Would you like some coffee?" I offered, standing and making my way to the pot. He nodded weakly, and I made a fresh pot to give him the time he needed to calm down a little. But when I handed him his coffee, his hands were still shaking.

I took a seat across from him and patiently sipped my coffee while Marie did the same. "Take all the time you need," Marie said softly.

"I don't really know what to do, or where to go." He wiped his eyes with his sleeve and took a deep breath. "My girlfriend trashed our place, destroyed all my clothes." He took a sip of his coffee, then kept staring at his cup as the words poured out of him. "She's always been a little aggressive, a slap here, a punch in the arm there. It didn't really bother me at first, but then she started pinching me so hard it left marks. It hurt so I asked her to stop, but she just called me a pussy, talking about how women weren't strong enough to hurt men."

He finally looked up at us to gauge our reaction. He must have seen that we disagreed with that statement, so he carried on. "Then it got worse. Every time we argued, things would get physical."

I raised an eyebrow in question, wondering if he'd hit her too, but he reassured me. "I never touched her like that. I guess I could, you know. I'm stronger than her. But I just never wanted to hurt her. I love her."

The way he said it made me ache for him.

"What made you come here today?" Marie asked.

He let out a deep sigh and looked down at his mug again. "I was supposed to be off work at twelve, but someone didn't show, so I had to cover their shift. It got busy, so I didn't have time to warn her I'd be late. By the time I got home, the entire place was trashed. I was tired from a long day, so I argued with her, asking why she destroyed my shit. I was upset. My console was in pieces on the floor, my clothes were ruined…. I don't have money to replace those things.

"So I yelled at her. She came at me, slapping me and punching me, so I just held her to stop her. But then she kicked me really hard in the balls, so I let her go. Next thing I know, she has a knife pointed at me. She actually tried to stab me."

He stood and lifted his shirt to show us a deep cut on the side of his stomach. His upper body was dotted with small bruises. The cut wasn't too bad, but it definitely needed cleaning. I filed that away for later.

"I got out of there as soon as I could, but I don't really know where to go."

"Have you tried talking about this with your family? Your friends?" Marie asked.

He shook his head, and I understood. It was hard enough for female survivors of physical assault to come forward, but male survivors had an even harder time since society dismissed them under the assumption that if they wanted to, they could defend themselves.

As if it was that simple.

"Josh, I understand that this is a hard time," Marie said, "but we don't take in men. Have you tried any of the male shelters?"

His shoulders dropped, and he nodded. "Yes. I stood in line for two hours and then they announced the shelter was full. I tried others, but the same thing happened. The last one I tried said you guys might be able to help."

"Right," Marie said. "I'm just not sure if the women here would be comfortable having a man around."

If the poor guy had any hope before, now all of it was lost. He physically deflated, sinking further into his chair as he fought to keep the tears from falling.

"I understand," he said, wiping his eyes with the back of his hand.

"But just for tonight, we'll find you a place to stay," I said, completely overstepping Marie's authority. She gave me a pointed look, but I would deal with the consequences later. This guy needed help, and I wasn't about to just let him sleep in the streets. "We can't put you in a room with the rest of the women, but we'll find a solution for tonight. Tomorrow I'll help you apply for housing in a male shelter, okay?"

Tears flowed freely down his face now as he nodded. "Thank you."

Marie stood and placed a hand on the back of his chair. "Come on, let's get you some warm food while we figure out your sleeping arrangements."

"Thank you, thank you," he said, looking at both of us.

Marie and Josh left the office, and I followed them to look for an empty room he could use. I found a storage closet on the second floor. It wasn't large, maybe just enough for a mattress on the floor after I cleaned up a bit.

I got to work making room, placing Christmas and Halloween decorations in the hallway outside. Some of the girls helped me carry the boxes to the basement. When they asked me why I needed the room, I was tempted to lie but told the truth instead.

They were understanding and helped me carry a mattress, blankets, and pillows up to the room. Marie showed Josh to his room, and we helped him get settled before returning to the office.

"I'm sorry for overstepping," I said, "he just seemed so helpless and earnest, I didn't want him to sleep outside tonight."

Marie offered me a soft smile. "I know, Cassie. But this is a women's shelter, he can't stay here."

I nodded, and let out a deep breath. "I'll make some calls in the morning, see if I can find other accommodation."

"Me too. I have a few contacts I can reach out to, we'll figure something out."

We said our goodbyes and I headed to the subway, my brain going over Josh's options as I walked. I wrote a few emails and scheduled them to be sent at eight a.m., so they would be at the top of the person's inbox.

It had been a long day, but when my head hit the pillow that night, I had a warm feeling in my chest knowing that I had at least helped one person.

CHAPTER TWENTY-SIX

A couple of days later, the strain on my relationship with Daisy continued to weigh heavily on me. To me, apologizing was akin to shouting to the world I was jealous, and I didn't want to do that.

But I still owed Daisy an apology.

After work, I made my way to her place. I knew she'd be home since she had said so in our group chat, but I texted her and walked around the block until she answered and told me to head up.

I hesitated in front of her building but eventually gathered enough courage to make my way to her loft. This was a Band-Aid I needed to rip off.

Jealousy wasn't an emotion I was used to feeling, and I didn't like it at all. I especially disliked what it implied about my feelings for James. This went beyond possessiveness—a dull ache invading my chest every time I pictured Daisy and James together.

But whatever feelings I had for James, I refused to let that interfere with my friendship with Daisy.

Hoes before bros. Always.

I walked up the stairs to her building and stopped at her front door. Despite being a lawyer and thriving in arguments, I really hated confrontation in my personal life. I'd rather just let bygones be bygones.

But this feeling festering in my chest wouldn't allow it, so I rang the doorbell.

"Hi, babe," Daisy said as she opened the door. "Come in." She led me to the couch.

Daisy's loft was bathed in light, the large windows and open floor plan allowing the sunlight in. She had converted most of it for her photography business, creating several mini-studios, each uniquely decorated with changeable backgrounds, along with props and dozens of costumes. The only doors in the place led to the bathroom and bedroom. Everything else was set up for her shoots, including the deep blue velvet couch I sat on. She had spent a large chunk of her trust fund in this place, and it showed.

"I was just making tea. Want some?"

"Sure, thanks," I said, thinking that at least I'd have something to do with my hands over this awkward conversation.

She filled the electric kettle and grabbed two mugs from the yellow cupboards. "So, what's up?"

"Well, I've been a bitch to you lately, and I'm here to apologize."

An awkward silence settled over us as the water boiled, making my skin itch.

Daisy frowned as she poured boiling water into the mugs. "Okay." She set the mugs on the coffee table, black tea for me, green tea for her, and joined me on the couch. "Why the bitchy attitude?"

Maybe I needed some rum in my tea, because for the life of me, I couldn't figure out how to delicately broach the subject. But this was my friend. I should be able to say what was on my mind without sweating this much.

I wiped my clammy hands on my jeans, bracing myself. "The other night was very fun, and I don't regret it at all. But when you two fell asleep on my bed, and I lay there thinking… I felt like maybe you were a better match for James."

Daisy's eyes widened, her brows drawing together in confusion. "What are you talking about?"

"You know, you're gorgeous and fashionable and outgoing. You have more experience running in the circles James does—"

"Wait," Daisy said, putting a hand over her mouth to contain her laughter. "You're jealous? Of me?"

I sighed. "It appears so," I reluctantly admitted. "This is all ridiculous, but when you came out of my room that morning, I wanted to shove your head in the garbage, and I hate that I felt that way."

Daisy burst out laughing, her eyes sparkling with mirth. "Babe, James is not into me. It didn't even feel like a threesome. It was more like I was having sex with you while he was also having sex with you. Do you know what I mean?"

I didn't. We'd all had sex with each other in equal measure, but that wasn't what I wanted to focus on. "The point is, I don't want to feel that way about you. You're my friend."

"You're right, you've been shitty, but I forgive you." Daisy took a sip of tea, an amused smile shaping her lips. "I've never seen you get jealous before."

"Well, it sucks."

"I don't know how he is with other women, but that night, I don't think he made eye contact with me once." She placed a hand on my arm reassuringly. "That man was completely engrossed by you. Think about it, he didn't even kiss me on the lips…. I don't think you have anything to worry about, especially not on my end."

"I'm sorry, this is so stupid. I didn't come here to talk about James, but to apologize to you."

"It's not stupid for you to have feelings, babe. But I'm glad you came to talk to me. I love you and I don't want what happened to mess up our friendship."

"It won't," I promised.

"Good." She beamed. "What are you going to do about James?"

I frowned. "What do you mean?"

"He clearly likes you, and as much as you might not want to, you like him too."

I shrugged. "So what?"

"He might not be interested in me, but I'm not the only girl out there. Maybe he'll meet someone who likes him and isn't afraid to show it."

"Well, then James will have a choice to make," I said, even

though the thought caused my heart to physically ache. *Jesus what is wrong with me?* "I'm sorry for being so mean to you. This exhibition is a great opportunity. I should've been more supportive. I'm really proud of you, and I hope the show goes well."

Daisy waved my apology away. "You were rude, but you were also right. I've been rethinking the whole concept to try to be more original, but it feels like everything I come up with has already been done."

"That might be true, but it wasn't done by you. Your vision, your interpretation, your voice is what will make whatever you come up with unique."

Daisy stared blankly at her tea, deep in thought. I let her be, well aware that sometimes she spaced out when she had an idea. After a few minutes, she seemed to snap out of it. "Rina is coming over for dinner, so I can show her what I have. Do you want to stay? I'd like your feedback."

"Of course." I smiled, glad we were on good terms again, even if the animosity had been completely one-sided.

Acknowledging my jealousy and apologizing alleviated the hostile feelings I was having towards my friend. I was thankful I hadn't irreparably damaged our friendship, and that after being honest with her, we could hang out like normal. We worked quietly side by side until Rina joined us, and I enjoyed a peaceful night with my friends.

Now that the business with Daisy was resolved, I asked James to come to her show with me. He immediately agreed, stating he was excited to get to know my friends better. That made me nervous, but I shrugged it off. I guessed part of giving us a chance included meshing our worlds a bit, even if it scared me.

We'd made plans to go out to dinner on Friday before the exhibition, but Daisy ended up needing help setting up, and then I got called into work to bail out a high-profile client. I called James to tell him I couldn't make it to dinner since I was probably only getting home around eight, and that I'd meet him at the gallery. He was understanding of my hectic schedule, which made butterflies dance in my stomach.

The client was intoxicated and had completely trashed his hotel room. Another random case that was nowhere near my specialty. I normally only handled white-collar crime, but since Maxwell, they had assigned any unwanted case to me.

I rounded the corner to my apartment, thinking about approaching the partners about it. To my surprise, James was sitting casually on the steps of my building, clad in a dark blue suit with a white shirt under it. He smiled when he spotted me, slipping his phone into his pocket.

He met me at the bottom of the stairs and slipped my messenger bag off my shoulder before kissing my forehead. "Hey, gorgeous."

"James, what are you doing here? I thought we were meeting at the gallery."

"Have I ever let you *meet me* anywhere?"

I smiled despite how tired I felt, waiting for that familiar sense of unease, but it never came. We walked together up to my apartment, and James just hung out while I got ready. It felt so normal, so natural to have him around. It was a pleasant, but still terrifying feeling.

Once I was ready, I joined him on the couch. "Can I have Elias's number?" I had tried to find a location without relying on James's connections, but the fees were insane, so I had to put my ego aside and accept help.

"Sure," he said, cocking his head to one side. "Can I ask why?"

"I've been trying to find a location for the fundraiser, but everywhere I ask is above our budget. Oasis is closed on Tuesdays, so I thought I'd ask Elias if we could rent the space at a friendly rate."

"Interesting. Did it ever occur to you to ask *me*?"

"No. Not really," I answered honestly.

"Why?" He pinched his nose as he clenched his jaw. "I own hotels. Hotels that have ballrooms and meeting rooms that would be perfect for a charity event."

"I'd just rather not cross that line."

James released a heavy sigh and ran his fingers through his hair, messing up the slicked-back look he was sporting. "So asking Elias is fine, but asking your—" he stopped himself before the words slipped out, then quickly amended, "asking me is crossing a line?"

"Yes," I said firmly. "I'm not sleeping with Elias."

"That's great to hear, but what does that have to do with me helping you?"

"Everything," I said, as I tried to fix his hair. "We should get going."

James propped my chin up with one finger. "Is it because of what my father said?"

I blinked. "No," I said, but James raised one perfectly arched eyebrow, and it was enough. "Yes and no," I amended. "The truth is more complicated."

"And you won't tell me?"

I shook my head, and James released a sigh, but he didn't push me. The truth was that I didn't want to—couldn't—rely on him. If I depended on James to throw this fundraiser, and our relationship ended for whatever reason, then I'd be left high and dry. Depending on people was dangerous. It tied you to them in such a way that severing those ties was more painful than dealing with the conditions and caveats that came with every act of service.

And I never wanted to feel that way again.

By the time we made it to the gallery, at least fifty people were already there. I found Daisy in the crowd talking to an old couple and waited until they'd walked away before I approached.

I pulled her in for a quick hug, a big smile on my face. "Congratulations! This was such a huge turnout."

"Thank you," she said, her eyes shining with happiness. "Rina's social media campaign worked. I've already sold a picture."

"The merit is also yours," James said. "Your photos are wonderful."

James and Daisy started talking about composition and movement in her work, so I tuned them out. I had half-expected to feel jealous, but as the two talked, I felt nothing but relief that my friend and James could easily converse.

He wasn't lying. Daisy's photos, even to my untrained eye, were stunning. I didn't know exactly how she did it, but in each frame, the fabrics came alive, their colors bright and vivid, the materials light and alive with movement. I was glad she'd abandoned the black and white idea. Daisy was bright and colorful, and the pictures reflected her bubbly personality.

I spotted Rina and Amelia in the distance and waved them over. As they approached, I turned to James and said, "You remember Rina and Amelia?"

"Yes, we met briefly." James nodded in their direction, flashing them a dazzling smile.

"It's nice to see you again," Rina said, a knowing smile on her lips.

James and Rina immediately fell into conversation about the social media campaign she'd launched to advertise this show, and what she'd do for the shelter's fundraiser. Daisy asked Amelia and me to eavesdrop on the people looking at her work, so we went to look at the photos.

I loved how easily James seemed to get along with my friends. It made me happy to see them together, just talking. And I hated my treacherous heart for putting ideas in my head. That maybe this could really work. It had me dreaming of a future where we all ate dinner together, bantering and laughing like old friends. Happy.

A shiver went up my spine and I pushed those thoughts away.

Amelia and I walked around the gallery, admiring Daisy's photos but mostly eavesdropping. Nearly everyone around us seemed to have a positive reaction to her work. Some offered critique, but none that was directed toward the artist but, rather, toward specific pictures that simply didn't suit their tastes.

"This is gorgeous," Amelia said.

We stopped in front of a large frame, admiring the juxtaposition of the yellow dress and the deep green forest. Nature was the theme Daisy had settled on, and she had nailed it. In some photos the outfits blended with nature, as if they were part of it. And in others, like this one, the contrasting colors made the clothing stand out. It made me want to be the girl in the dress, running free through the woods. The dress itself was phenomenal, but Daisy had managed to capture the model's essence. Fierce, free, and fearless.

I wanted it on my wall.

A prickling sensation on the back of my neck had me surveilling my surroundings. I turned to look at James, but he was deep in conversation with Rina, Daisy, and some man who'd joined them. The familiar feeling of being watched caused the hairs on my arms to stand. I scanned the crowd but didn't find anyone looking at me.

Amelia stopped a waiter, her voice pulling me back from my thoughts. "I wonder who catered this event. The salmon puffs are the perfect dough to filling ratio."

"Oh, that reminds me. We're organizing a fundraiser for the shelter. Do you think you could cater? The pay wouldn't be great, but we're auctioning designer clothes James's sister donated. Maybe wealthy people will come and fall in love with your food."

A flash of dirty blonde hair behind Amelia caught my attention, blurring everything else. My mouth went dry, the buzzing in my ears drowning out Amelia's words. I looked behind her again but didn't see anyone.

I shrugged it off, struggling to control my quickening breath. "We can discuss the details later," I said, assuming Amelia had agreed to cater. "I haven't even set a date yet."

"Great! I'll come up with a menu. Dios, I can't wait until I have enough money for my bakery."

"How far are you from your goal?" I asked absently.

Amelia sighed in frustration. "Maybe another year? Faster if I can get a better job…."

Whatever else she said was lost to me as a cold shiver ran down my spine, goosebumps breaking out all over my body. I'd learned to trust my instincts long ago. Something was definitely wrong. Again, I looked around me, my blood running cold in my veins as dread took over.

My breath caught in my throat when I saw him, right behind James, Rina, and Daisy. I blinked, hoping my mind was playing tricks on me and that when I opened my eyes, he'd be gone.

But there he was—Andrew.

I stared at him, eyes wide, my heart hammering against my chest. And he stared back, a wicked grin stretching his lips. For a moment I was locked in place, muscles tight, unable to move.

"Cassie, are you okay? You're super pale. Do you want to go out for some air?"

A hand landed on my lower back and I flinched. James looked at me, his eyes lined with concern. "What's wrong?" He looked in the direction I'd been staring, and I blinked, willing my lungs to slowly draw in air.

I hadn't even noticed them move, but James, Rina, Daisy, and Amelia were all surrounding me, worry marring their expressions.

"I'm fine," I said, my voice barely a whisper. "I'm fine. I'll just… I'll be right back." With that, I turned on my heel and headed for the bathroom, tears threatening to spill with each step.

Andrew.

He was here.

I locked myself in a stall, putting my head between my knees as I hyperventilated. *This can't be happening*, I thought over and over again. Maybe it was just someone who looked like him—but that smile. No, Andrew was truly here, and wishful thinking wouldn't solve anything.

You need to calm down. Breathe.

There was nothing I could do about it now, I knew that much. He was taunting me with his presence, just like he had with the flowers and chocolates, I gathered. I wanted to hit myself for not realizing it sooner, but not now, not here. I still had to go out there and support my friend.

I collected myself as best as I could, washed my hands, and wiped off the makeup that had run under my eyes. When I opened the door, James was leaning against the wall, his hands in his pockets.

"Are you alright?"

"Yes," I lied, placing my hand over my stomach. "I think I ate some bad food, though."

James gave me a small smile and pulled me into his arms. "You're shivering. Come on, I'll take you home."

I reveled in the feel of his strong arms around me, already grieving his loss. Leaving was the only thing I wanted to do, but I couldn't do that to Daisy, especially after being such a bitch to her. "No, I don't want to miss Daisy's show."

"I'm sure she'd understand."

I shook my head. "I can stay a little longer."

"Okay, but if you feel worse, we'll go."

James brushed his lips against my forehead, and we made our way back to the party. I didn't see Andrew again, but I could feel him watching me. The hours passed agonizingly slowly, my anxiety rising with each dreadful minute. When James dropped me off, I cut our night short, claiming my stomach hurt.

The second the door closed behind me and I was alone, panic gripped me. I stumbled to the couch and held my head in my hands as intrusive thoughts took over. This was all my fault. I'd been too careless, gotten too comfortable, and he'd found me.

Images of me lying on the cold bathroom tiles, cradling my head with bloody hands, flashed in my mind, and despite my best efforts, I couldn't keep the memories at bay. Broken shards of glass digging into my knees as I cleaned, bits of food scattered all over the floor because I'd forgotten he didn't like parsley.

His cousin's wedding, when he shoved me against a wall and choked me, cruel words flying from his lips as he accused me of flirting with the bartender. We had to leave early that day, because I couldn't hide his fingerprints on my neck. Then he blamed me for missing his cousin's special day and locked me in the bathroom until the next morning.

I remember being grateful he didn't hit me again.

When facing a dangerous situation, there were three choices: fight, flight, or freeze. And every bone in my body told me to run.

I avoided James all weekend, claiming I had caught a stomach bug. He still came over to check on me and bring me soup, and I hid under the blankets like a coward, feeling and looking like shit. At least that was one thing I didn't have to fake.

After a couple of sleepless nights, I knew what I had to do, but that didn't make it any easier. When I went back to work on Monday, I dodged James's texts and calls, hoping he'd get the hint. Avoiding him was a strategic maneuver. I had to end things, and he'd never believe me if it came out of nowhere. Especially since things were good between us.

By the time Thursday rolled around, he'd stopped calling. Part of me was glad, but it hurt that he'd quit on me so easily. A pain I couldn't—wouldn't—allow myself to feel.

I was avoiding the girls too. Rina was too perceptive for her own good, and I didn't want them involved in my mess. The thought of never seeing them again would be heart wrenching if I acknowledged it. The only way I could keep functioning was to shove it all down until I felt nothing at all.

I stared down at my notes after a meeting, but before I walked back into my office, Olivia stopped me. "There's someone here to see you. I told him you were in a meeting, but he said he'd wait in your office."

Fear told me it was Andrew, but Olivia would never let a stranger into my office.

I steeled myself and opened the door. "James, what are you doing here?"

James looked ridiculously handsome in a black suit, black shirt, and black tie. I wondered if he'd chosen this particular outfit for a reason, but I still didn't let my eyes linger.

"You're avoiding me. I figured you couldn't dodge me at work, so here I am."

"Right," I said, shutting the door behind me. I skirted around him, making sure we didn't touch, and took a seat at my desk. A few weeks ago, James had come here to propose an arrangement, and now I knew exactly what to say to end it.

For a second I felt awful for hurting him, but it was better than stringing him along. Then I wondered if I actually had that ability. It wouldn't take long for him to find someone else to fulfill his needs. Perhaps someone more suited to his lifestyle, someone who didn't have a cargo train's worth of luggage.

At least that's what I told myself.

"Could you escort Mrs. Lennox to the meeting room and let her know I'll be right there?" I asked Olivia over the phone. Then I turned to James. "What can I do for you, James?"

He raised one eyebrow, his deep voice making my heart pound against my chest. "You could start by telling me why you're avoiding me."

I made myself look him in the eye. "I'm not avoiding you. I'm very busy. But since you're here, I'd like to take this opportunity to end our agreement."

"No."

"No? That's not an unacceptable answer." Before he could interrupt me, I quickly continued. "Do you remember the first time you were in this office? You agreed to accept my decision when I chose to end our agreement. Will you go back on your word now?"

"Why? I thought things were progressing. That you—"

"I was clear from the beginning when I said I didn't want a relationship, so don't pretend to be surprised by this outcome." I started rearranging papers on my desk to keep my hands occupied. I couldn't face him anymore. I needed a second to recompose myself.

James narrowed his eyes. "I don't believe you. There's something else. Something you're not telling me."

"Listen, I don't think I could be any clearer. I have a client waiting, so I have to go." I stood to leave. James stood too, his tall frame doing dangerous things to my heart.

I thought I saw a flash of hurt in his eyes, but his voice was steady as he said, "I'm not taking no for an answer. Not unless you give me a valid reason."

I released a frustrated breath and glanced at my watch as if this conversation was an inconvenience. "You have feelings for me," I said, looking for confirmation I didn't need in his eyes. "But I don't have feelings for you. I wanted sex. I made it perfectly clear that was all I wanted. You're trying to blur the lines. You even introduced me to your parents without my consent." I paused, the next words I had to say coating my tongue with a bitter taste. "I don't reciprocate your feelings, and it's unfair of me to keep you around. Now, if you'll excuse me, I have a client."

I turned around to leave, but when I sensed James following me, I stopped. "Please don't make me file a restraining order. Goodbye, James." With that, I turned on my heel and left, feeling his gaze on me until I entered the meeting room.

CHAPTER TWENTY-SEVEN

I had no idea how I counseled Mrs. Lennox. It was all a blur to me. When I finally made it back to the privacy of my office, I realized I had been half hoping James would still be there. He wasn't. But it wasn't relief that flooded me in my cold, empty office. Just a familiar terror that engulfed me until I couldn't breathe.

Andrew.

He was back, and now nothing would be the same again.

I felt like the walls were closing in on me, so I hastily gathered my stuff, notified Olivia that I had to leave for an emergency, and hit the pavement. My steps carried me to Central Park, then I walked some more. I got lost in the fall beauty of New York, the city that had helped me disappear among the masses, the place where I got a second chance. The knowledge that I had to leave it all behind sat heavy in my chest.

In my haste to leave I'd forgotten to switch shoes. The balls of my feet burned, and I could already feel blisters forming on my heels, but my stilettos still carried me forward.

I walked and walked, playing out all the possible scenarios, but saw no other choice. I couldn't let Andrew into my life again, so I had to disappear. Rina would never forgive me. She was the sister I never had. But the thought of Andrew standing behind my friends at the art show, the thought of him hurting them… it was too much to bear.

I was leaving to protect them. The girls, James, Rina… none of them needed to have Andrew mess with their lives. I couldn't do that to them.

Eventually, my steps took me to a subway station, which led me to my apartment. I climbed the stairs on my sore feet instead of taking the elevator, relishing the pain. None of this would have happened if I had been more careful about my picture being taken.

At first, I'd been paranoid about it. I'd never let anyone take a picture of me. But once I was out of college and it became clear my chosen career would occasionally put me in the spotlight, I'd relented. I couldn't exactly explain to my bosses why I didn't want to be on camera.

It had been so long, I genuinely thought he'd moved on, forgotten all about me. He'd made no attempt to contact me. There was no reason to believe I was still on his mind.

It was naive of me.

I walked into my apartment, desperate for a shower. After that, I'd sit down and come up with a strategy for leaving. Dropping my purse and shoes by the door, I padded towards the bathroom, but my plans were thwarted when I saw Andrew in my kitchen, casually sipping James's whiskey.

My blood froze in my veins as I stood there, eyeing the distance between me and the door, unsure if I should run. He was in my apartment. Would I make it to the door? And if I didn't, would my running trigger his anger?

I blinked away the tears stinging my eyes and squared my shoulders. The flowers, the chocolate, showing up at the art show, and now this. He was taunting me, and I wouldn't give him the satisfaction of seeing me frightened this time. Letting the anger at seeing Andrew in my space flow through me, I stepped a little closer.

"Andrew," I said in my most measured voice, "what are you doing here?"

"That's a weird way to greet your fiancé," he said, flashing me his most charming smile. He poured me a shot of whiskey and slid it across the counter separating us.

For a second, I saw him as the boy I'd once loved, but that was quickly washed away by the man in front of me. The one invading my home, my safe place. A bitter part of me had hoped he'd aged poorly, but he was still handsome. His sandy brown hair was shorter now, his caramel eyes a little harder, but time had been kind to him.

I took a sip of whiskey to calm my nerves. Despite wanting to put him in his place, I knew that now wasn't the time. I didn't want this situation to escalate. "That was a long time ago," I replied softly. "What brings you here now?"

Andrew reached for my hand on the counter and I flinched away from his touch. "You," he said, his lips stretching into an amused smile that didn't quite reach his eyes. "I thought I'd come after you when you left, but I had to keep up appearances. The boys were quick to insinuate you'd run off with some loser." He took a sip and slammed the glass down on the counter. "You made me look like a fool. That was a nice touch."

"I think you did that to yourself." The words escaped before I could stop them, regret immediately filling my chest when I saw his jaw tense, his hand tightening around the glass.

"Careful," he warned. "I've been very patient. I let you have your little fun for a few years, but I'm back now and you will not disrespect me."

My nails bit into my palms as I forced myself to take a deep breath. "You *let* me have my little fun?" I repeated, incredulous.

"Baby, come on. We got together so young, I think we both needed a break to have some fun, so we could grow. But there was never any question in my mind that you're the one for me." He stalked slowly towards me, hunger flaring in his eyes. "I think it's about time to remind you I'm the only one for you."

I moved sideways, keeping the counter between us, blood rushing in my ears. "You're delusional." How was this going to end? *Time.* I needed time to come up with a strategy to force him out of here.

"I told Mom and Dad I was coming for you, to get you back. You have no idea how excited they are to see you." Andrew strolled towards me, his bloodshot eyes scrutinizing my retreating steps. "You hurt them, you know. When you left. But I explained to them it was a mutual decision, that we were going to take a break."

"How are your parents?" I asked, stalling for time. "It's been so long since I've seen them. I miss them." Maybe I could call one of my neighbors to scare him away. But it was the middle of the workday. Even if I wanted to involve an outsider in my mess, odds were no one was home.

"Mom saw the photos of you and some guy, a millionaire at that." He laughed, the sound grating my ears. "Never pegged you for a gold digger before, but I guess you did mooch off my parents for years. You've just moved up a level now."

"Andrew, I think you should go. It's been a long day and I'm tired. Let's have a drink tomorrow. We can catch up then," I offered.

"Why don't we catch up right now?" he asked as he refilled his drink. "We're already having a drink." He pointed to my glass and took a seat on a stool.

I sat on the opposite stool, keeping the counter between us. "Fine, but one drink. I'm exhausted, and I'm having dinner with a client later, so I still need to get ready." The lie came easily, and right now seemed to be my only option. Andrew might be slightly wary of hurting me too seriously if I was expected somewhere.

He shook his head, his mouth contorting into a dreadful grin. "Dinner with a client? Is that what you call them now?"

I bristled at the insinuation but kept an impassive expression. Andrew had always been the jealous type. Any male that came in my vicinity was a threat. I couldn't let him get to me. "So, what have you been up to?"

"Finally! It's about time you took an interest in someone other than yourself." Andrew lifted his glass, and I reluctantly returned the gesture. "I'm not as rich as your sugar daddy, but I do well for myself. You'll see it when we go back home."

My stomach lurched at his words, and I had to fight hard to maintain my composure. I didn't know if he'd moved back to our hometown or if he meant the apartment in Seattle. Maybe I should've kept tabs on him, tracked his movements, but I wanted to put the past behind me. Forget it ever happened in the first place.

That was a mistake. I knew that now.

"Andrew, your home isn't my home anymore," I said carefully.

"Of course it is, babe. You don't know what's best for you." He stood, and in two movements was on my side of the counter. I jumped off the stool, walking backwards to maintain our distance. "We're meant to be together. There's no one else for you and no one else for me. I promise, if you do what I say, everything will be fine."

"You need to leave now. We'll talk tomorrow," I tried again, infusing every word with finality, but he just sneered.

Andrew grabbed my chin, his crazed eyes staring unblinkingly at me. "We will talk right now."

Tears clouded my vision as I realized that if couldn't de-escalate this situation, he would either rape or kill me; maybe both. His grip on my chin tightened as I tried to back away, his empty stare focusing on my lips.

He inched closer, his foul breath stinging my eyes. "For once, just do what I tell you."

Andrew grabbed me roughly by the back of my head, smashing my body against his before forcing his tongue into my mouth. I bit down hard, a coppery taste coating my tongue. In a flash, the back of his hand made contact with my cheek. Pain spread like wildfire on the left side of my face. I stumbled backwards, landing hard against the counter.

"Why would you do that? Now you've made me angry." He wiped the blood off his mouth with the back of his hand and stalked towards me. I scrambled to get away, but it was too late. Andrew grabbed a fistful of my hair, yanking my head back, and his mouth smashed against mine.

I was bracing myself, trying to find my balance to knee him in the balls, when he pulled away and wrapped his hand around my throat. Andrew pressed down on my trachea as I gasped for air, frantically trying to remove his hand.

"Be a good girl and pour me some whiskey while I get the door," Andrew said, letting me go.

I crumpled to the floor, gasping for air, tears blurring my vision. As the ringing in my ears faded, I started to make sense of Andrew's words. *The door. No.*

Scrambling to my feet, I grabbed a knife from the counter.

Hurting me was one thing, but if it was any of my friends at the door and he dared raise his hand against them... I was fully prepared to use the knife.

I heard Andrew unchain the door, then open it. To my surprise, James's voice reached my ears. "Is Cassandra here?" His tone was careful, controlled, but there was no mistaking the anger beneath it. *No, this can't be happening. James can't be here.*

"No, she isn't," Andrew sneered.

"I'm not leaving until I see her." James's clipped tone left no room for discussion, but Andrew wasn't so easily convinced.

"You won't be seeing her anymore. Not now. Not ever. Understood?" The threat in his words was palpable, but James didn't seem to care because after a few seconds, he barreled around the corner towards me.

I had seen James angry when his dad insulted me, but this was different. His jaw locked in place as his gaze zeroed in on me. His warm eyes turned cold as he scanned my face, then my body. He strode in my direction, but Andrew grabbed his arm to stop him. James shook him off as if he was nothing, not even breaking his stride.

James stopped in front of me, and I flinched back. He placed his hand on my shoulder, his touch featherlight, and asked in a low, rumbling voice, "Did he do this to you?"

I averted my gaze, trying to swallow the lump in my throat, the action causing me to grimace. Part of me was glad he'd come, but I really wished he hadn't seen any of this. He gently lifted my face and I winced in pain at the movement.

Andrew grabbed James by the back of his suit jacket, but he didn't even budge. His eyes fixed on the knife still firmly in my hand, and something changed in him. He was no longer the calm before the storm, but the storm itself.

In one movement, he had his hand wrapped around Andrew's throat. "Call the police."

I must have looked like a deer in headlights. James gave me a questioning look, then suddenly doubled over in pain. Andrew had kicked him in the nuts while he was distracted. I stepped forward with the knife in hand, ready to do whatever it took to stop him.

But James quickly recovered. He punched Andrew with so much force that he crumpled to the floor. "No police?" he asked, confirming what I had tried to convey with my eyes alone. I nodded. A flash of disappointment crossed his eyes before he pulled Andrew to his feet. Andrew, ever the sleazy bastard, grabbed the whiskey bottle and swung it at James's head.

James encircled his wrist, twisting it at an odd angle until the bottle smashed on the floor. This didn't stop Andrew, though. He charged forward, aiming his full rage at James. Unperturbed by the blows Andrew landed, James pulled him close and punched him over and over in the side. It scared me how good he was at fighting. Andrew didn't stand a chance against him, but I didn't want James to get in trouble because of me.

"James," I whispered, his name slicing my throat like glass. He heard me anyway, and with one look in my direction, he simply nodded, grabbed Andrew by the back of his neck, and led him out of my apartment.

My treacherous body shook all over as I stared at the empty doorway. I gasped for air to appease the burning sensation in my lungs, my wobbly legs threatening to give out under me. Now that Andrew was out of sight, I felt the panic I had been fighting take over me, but I couldn't let James see me that way.

I had to pull myself together.

At least until he left. He had seen enough.

Kneeling down, I gathered the broken pieces of the whiskey bottle in my hand, focusing on what I could control. James found me while I was ineffectively blotting the liquid with paper towels.

"Leave that," he said, picking me up from the floor. I still couldn't bear to look him in the eye, too afraid of what I'd see there.

"I'm just cleaning up." It was barely a whisper, my voice as weak and raw as I felt. Andrew must have squeezed too hard and injured my vocal chords again.

James effortlessly picked me up from the floor and set me down on the counter. "Let me take a look at you," he breathed. He forced my chin up, but before our eyes met, I lowered my gaze.

"Hey, look at me," he said. I slowly lifted my eyes, hoping I wouldn't see pity reflected back at me. But when our gazes locked, the cold fury in his eyes had been replaced by something far softer. He brushed his fingers against my swollen lips, and I tried not to wince. "You don't have to talk about any of this if you don't want to, but are you sure you don't want me to call the police?"

I nodded, the lump in my throat too large for words to form.

"Come on, let's get you cleaned up." James carried me to the bathroom like a doll, and for once, I had no objection. He set me down on my bathroom sink, then turned around to fill the tub. "Do you have a first aid kit?"

"Yes, in the cabinet." I moved to get it myself, but James stopped me. He found the kit, grabbed a few things, and started cleaning up my lip wound. It stung, but I barely reacted, completely taken off guard by the fact that James was still here.

He shouldn't be here.

He shouldn't have to see me like this.

"You're pretty good at that," I commented. It hurt to speak, but I pretended it didn't. The silence was too much to bear. I just wanted him gone so I could allow myself to fall apart for a few minutes.

"Thanks," he said, cleaning up my busted lip with surgical precision. "I play hockey, remember? Over the years, you learn how to care for cuts and bruises."

I nodded, taking in the bruise that was forming on his cheek. "I'm sorry you got sucked into this mess."

"This might not be the best time, but are you involved with that man?"

I shook my head. "I haven't seen him in seven years."

"The last time I took a punch to the face, it was from Elias." I looked up at him in surprise at the sudden change of subject, but he continued, "We're both competitive, and when he was made captain over me, I didn't take it very well. I lunged at him and he punched me square in the face. It took two months for my nose to heal, and the coach benched me for three games."

"Why are you telling me this?"

"It came to mind," he said, as he cleaned the dried blood off my lips. "That was the day we became best friends. Elias had been voted captain fair and square, so he didn't hesitate to put me in my place. I liked that about him."

He was trying to distract me, and I was infinitely grateful for it.

The corner of his lip lifted into a small smile. "All right, you're all cleaned up now. Do you want to take a bath while I take care of the kitchen?"

"James, you don't have to do that. I'm fi—"

"I don't have to do anything, Cassandra. I choose to. I want to." He looked me straight in the eyes and it was just too much. "I'll leave you to it, but don't lock the door, ok? I want to check in on you."

I nodded weakly and watched James walk out of my bathroom and close the door behind him. The moment he was gone, I realized his presence had been the only thing holding me together. It was harder to put up a front when there was no one there to witness what happened when the mask slipped off.

Suddenly, being on the sink was too much. I slid to the ground, hugging my knees against my chest.

Andrew.

The events of the evening played in a loop in my mind as I picked apart every little thing that had happened, all the things I should've done to prevent this. I'd been mostly careful, I wasn't on any social media, avoided getting my picture taken… but my job put me in front of the cameras. And my relationship with James had put me in the gossip tabloids. There had been photographers at his birthday party, and the event I attended with him.

It was unfair. So unfair that I had to limit myself, police my life just so I could be safe, and for what? The moment I slipped, he found me. Now that he knew where I was, I'd never be safe again.

A sob escaped me, and I quickly buried my face in my arm before letting it all out. My body hurt all over, and a burning sensation invaded my lungs as I gasped for air in between sobs. Hatred coursed through me, a vicious anger that threatened to destroy everything I'd worked so hard for.

I hated myself.

So much.

I knew what Andrew was and had still let the relationship last for as long as it did. I knew what he was and I had still let him find me.

What if Rina, Amelia, or Daisy had been here? They would've tried to protect me and he would've hurt them, too. And if James wasn't so good at fighting Andrew could've seriously injured him with the whiskey bottle. I couldn't allow that to happen.

I was gasping and sobbing in a puddle of my own self-inflicted misery when James came in to check on me. I didn't even have the energy to be embarrassed.

"Let's get you some air," James said, before bending down and scooping me off the floor. He walked to my small balcony and sat on the sole chair with me on his lap. "Just breathe, I'm right here." He rubbed my back as sob after sob ripped through me. "It will be okay. You're not alone."

It took me longer than I wanted to, but I eventually managed to calm myself down. "You shouldn't be here. You shouldn't have seen any of this. You shouldn't have to see me like this." I said my thoughts aloud, thinking that maybe if he was aware of how damaged I was, he would actually walk away.

"Why not? Because it's not pretty?" he said, making me self-conscious of how I must look right now. "Life is not always pretty, Cassandra. I don't want just the shiny parts of you. I want all of you, even the parts you think aren't worthy of love."

His words hit home in more ways than he knew. And the uncontrollable sobbing that followed was a solid clue into my current state of mind.

Love.

I had loved Andrew with all I had, but it was never enough.

I was never enough.

"It's ok. You're ok. I'm here." James patiently rubbed my back as he whispered comforting words to me over and over. "You're shivering. Are you cold?"

I nodded weakly, my face buried in his solid chest. Despite the cold, I didn't want to leave James's strong arms. His large hand rubbing my back was slowly but surely calming me down. He enveloped me in his arms, bringing his suit jacket around me to keep me warm.

I would let James comfort me, just for tonight. Then tomorrow, I would figure out what to do about Andrew.

Eventually, the sobs subsided and James stood with me cradled firmly in his arms. He carried me to the couch and then disappeared inside the bathroom for a few minutes.

Get it together. He must think you're pathetic. I went to the kitchen to clean up the mess, but James had already done it. Tears welled in my eyes. *I don't deserve him.*

The thought played in a loop in my head, and everything James did only served to prove me right.

The doorbell rang, and I froze, my heart hammering against my chest.

"It's ok," James said, walking towards me. "I ordered food, and some people are coming to fix your door."

I blinked. "What's wrong with my door?"

"I assume you didn't let that man in." He paused, waiting for my answer. When I shook my head, he continued, "There's no sign of forced entry, so maybe he picked the lock?"

"I hadn't thought about it. When I came home, he was here." Everything had happened so fast. I didn't have a chance to process it.

He went to get the door, and I stood in the kitchen, staring blankly at the wall. As far as I knew, Andrew didn't know how to pick locks…. I couldn't make sense of it.

I wasn't hungry, but James was being so kind, so thoughtful, that I forced myself to eat. He'd ordered comfort food, tomato soup and grilled cheese, and we ate in silence as the men behind us replaced the locks and added three deadbolts. Each bite felt like a knife slashing my throat open.

I didn't have the words to thank James for his kindness. Everything felt like too much and I was just exhausted. I skipped the bath in favor of a quick shower, and when I joined him in the living room again, he was getting comfortable on my couch.

"Come on," I whispered, holding out a hand for him. He studied me for a long minute but eventually wrapped his warm hand around my cold one. It was selfish, I knew that, but I didn't want to spend the night alone.

James removed his clothes and slipped under the covers with me. I felt his warmth even through my pajamas. He didn't say anything, didn't press me. He just held me in his arms as I cried myself to sleep.

Hours later, I woke up to find him staring at me, his face marred with concern. Now that I'd had a little rest, I thought he deserved to know, and confessions were always easier in the dead of night.

"When my parents died, Andrew was right there beside me. He held me in his arms while the police officer explained about the car crash." My voice came out weak, barely a whisper, but I had James's full attention. "Andrew's mom, Patricia, rallied the community to raise money for the funeral. She took care of it all. The only thing I had to do was attend. When all of that was over, Bill, Andrew's dad, took care of the insurance, the house, all of it. My parents rented, so I didn't really have a place to go. Bill and Patricia took me in, remodeled the garage into a bedroom for me, helped me sell everything in the house. I wanted to give them that money as payment for letting me stay, but they put it and the insurance money into a savings account and told me to save it for college."

I stared up at the ceiling, the words flowing out of me. "Despite the loss of my parents, those last two years of high school were golden. Andrew became my whole world. It was only later, much later, that I realized how much of a problem that was. We had planned to apply to the same colleges and move in together, and that's exactly what we did."

I took a deep, shaky breath. James brushed his hand up and down my arm, the feeling of his strong hand on my skin giving me warmth and courage to keep speaking.

"The first time he hit me, I actually couldn't believe it. This was Bill and Patricia's kid. There was no way people so kind, so generous, so caring, had raised a son who would hit his girlfriend." I paused again, fighting the tears that threatened to spill over. "He apologized profusely, of course, begged for forgiveness, said it would never happen again. But it did. It always did. And I forgave him each time, because how couldn't I? He was all I had. His family was all I had. Leaving him would mean breaking off my relationship with Bill and Patricia. My friends were his friends first. I would have no one. I didn't want to be alone, so I stayed."

I felt James's body tense beside me, felt his breath get shorter as he listened.

"It wasn't always awful. When he wanted to, he was the perfect boyfriend. The lows were unbearable, but the highs? He knew exactly what to say and do to make me feel loved, happy. But those highs got fewer and farther between. I finally had enough when I was curled into a ball on our kitchen floor. He kicked my head so hard I was barely conscious, but the kicks kept on coming. I guess I passed out at some point because I woke up in bed the next day in the worst pain I had ever experienced in my life. I had no friends, he made sure of that, so I took a taxi to the hospital. My arm was fractured in three places. I had bruised ribs, a concussion…. Laying in that hospital bed, I realized that being alone and losing everyone and everything I had was better than living like this."

Tears flowed freely down my face now, and James wiped them away with his thumb. "When the doctors asked me what happened to me, I told them I was mugged. They weren't fooled, but there wasn't much they could do. Andrew was my emergency contact, so it didn't surprise me when he showed up at the hospital. He sobbed at my feet about how he lost control, how terrible he felt, that he couldn't believe that this had happened to me. As if he didn't have a foot in doing it." I laughed at my stupid joke, but the sound that came out of my mouth sounded more like a cry than anything else.

"I guess part of me already knew that if I didn't leave him, he'd probably end up killing me. I had read enough papers about women in abusive relationships in my psych classes to know that. When I got into NYU Law, I hid the letter from him. He didn't know I had applied for schools far away from Seattle. The doctor came and told us they'd like to keep me for a couple of days to monitor my concussion and my ribs. This was my chance. The next day when Andrew was in class, I checked myself out of the hospital, packed a duffel bag, and got on a Greyhound bus to New York. Andrew controlled my finances, but I had slowly saved a little over four thousand dollars. I spent the last money I had to change my name and rent a room in New York. It was tiny, but it was home. I was safe."

James hadn't said anything as I told him my sob story, but now he asked, "Why no police?"

"Bill and Patricia. They love their son, and they did so much for me. I can't do that to them."

"So it doesn't matter what he does to you, as long as other people don't have to suffer?" He sounded angry, and I let the silence linger until he added, "Come stay with me."

I turned on my side to face him. "I can't do that."

"Why not? He can't enter my building, security is much better than here. You could have your own bedroom if that's what you're worried about. It doesn't have to mean that we're moving in together. It could be temporary until this situation is resolved."

This situation will never be resolved, I thought to myself. If after all these years he had still come for me, I didn't see why he would suddenly just stop now. But James didn't need to know that. He didn't need to know that I already had a plan in mind.

"Can I think about it?"

"Of course." He kissed my hair, the gesture so sweet it made me nauseous with guilt for lying to him. "You're not alone anymore," he whispered as he pulled me gently into his arms.

For now, I allowed myself to take comfort in his arms. I would write him a note. I couldn't leave without at least that, not after everything.

I just hoped he wouldn't try to find me this time.

Cradled in James's arms, I felt safe, protected. But as Andrew had taught me, safety was merely an illusion.

CHAPTER TWENTY-EIGHT

The morning sun wafted in through the window, bathing the room in its warm glow. I had been awake for hours, watching the shadows play on James's beautiful face. In the early morning stillness, reality seemed so far away. If only we could stay here, his hand on my waist, his soft breath fanning my face.

But daylight invited reality in. As the blanket of night faded, the purple bruises marring his strong jaw appeared. I hadn't put them there, I knew that, but I might as well have.

I slipped out of bed, sparing James one last glance. In the bathroom, I took stock of the damage. Small bruises had formed on my neck, but I could easily hide them with a high collar. The cut on my bottom lip could be written off since the swelling had subsided, but there was no amount of concealer to hide the marks on my cheek.

Still, I reached for my makeup bag, the movement igniting a dull pain in my side. Lifting my shirt, I noted the ugly bruise forming over my ribs where I had landed against the counter. I took a deep, shaky breath and applied a layer of concealer on my cheek, focusing on the bruises I couldn't hide.

A soft knock on the door startled me. My foundation clattered against the sink as it slipped from my fingers.

"Are you okay?" James's groggy voice came from behind the door.

"Ye—" I tried, but the single syllable sliced my throat open. I shut my eyes to prevent the tears from falling, reaching blindly for the faucet to take a sip of water. Last night I could still push through the pain to speak, but this morning my throat felt like sandpaper. The water helped a little, but I still couldn't talk which was very inconvenient with James here.

James knocked again, and I moved to open the door. Once I did, his eyes roamed my body before he wrapped his arms around me. "Good morning, gorgeous." He let out a sigh of relief as I buried my face in his neck, inhaling his scent.

"Speaking hurts," I said, the words barely a whisper. His body tensed around me and he drew back to look at me. A flash of anger passed through his eyes, but it was gone in a blink.

"Let's get you some breakfast," he said, guiding me towards the kitchen.

I placed my hands around my throat and shook my head, trying to communicate that food was not an option.

James didn't miss a beat. "Is there anything you can eat that wouldn't hurt?"

The thought of food sliding down my sore throat made me shudder. I shook my head again, and James moved to make coffee. His sleepy face and hair sticking up in all directions did nothing to lessen his attractiveness. But the bruises on his jaw were a sore reminder of last night, and that this would probably be one of our last mornings together.

I opened the fridge and pointed between James and the food. He set the mugs down on the counter and stood in front of me, his brown eyes locked with mine. "Do you want me to stay with you today or would you rather I call your friends? You shouldn't be alone."

My eyes widened, panic flaring at the edges. The girls could never find out and I needed to be alone. I shook my head.

James seemed to understand. "Then I'll have breakfast at the office."

We had coffee in silence, the air around us heavy with unspoken words. It was the first time I felt awkward around James, not that I could blame him for the tension. He should never have witnessed the things he did last night. Now that he knew, he would never look at me the same way.

"I know you said you don't want to involve the police, but what's the plan here?"

I lowered my head, using my hair to partially hide my face. The skeleton of a plan I'd formed in the small hours of the morning weighed me down. I couldn't tell him, not yet, and certainly not face to face.

The silence stretched out between us until James took my hand in his and said, "My offer stands. Please stay with me for a while." He paused, gauging my reaction, but I gave nothing away. Finally, he sighed and propped up my chin, forcing me to look at him. "I need you to be safe."

The emotion in his eyes was too much to bear. I averted my gaze, my face burning with shame. I was a coward. A better person would tell him right now. My lips parted, but the words refused to form.

James offered me a small smile when I'd rather he be angry. "I'll leave you alone for now, but I'll come over later to check in, okay?"

I nodded weakly, and James tipped his head back to look at the ceiling. He muttered something under his breath before disappearing into the bathroom. I sat there, staring blankly at the wall, until I heard the door open.

He slipped on his suit jacket and strode towards me. Even after the events of last night, James radiated that quiet confidence that had drawn me to him in the first place. He enveloped me in a tight hug, my side screaming with pain even as his warmth comforted me.

"Please think about my offer," he said, brushing his lips against my forehead. I offered him a small nod, and he left.

Once he was gone, I refused to let myself feel. I took a few deep breaths and spun into action. For the first time in three years, I called in sick. My broken voice on the phone was enough to convince them of my illness, so I used it to record a voice message to the girls, pulling out from our plans for the weekend.

Their get-well messages broke my heart. Amelia immediately

offered to bring over some comfort food, but I refused, claiming I was contagious. There was no way they would believe me if they saw me. My lies left a bitter taste in my mouth, but I would do anything to protect my friends.

I collapsed on the couch, my limbs heavy. All I wanted was to close my eyes and not exist for a bit, but there was still something I needed to do. I scrolled through my contacts and pressed call. The line rang twice before he picked up.

"Morning, kid," Monty said.

"I need a new identity." It hurt to speak, but saying the words out loud offered a new kind of pain. I had worked so hard to rebuild my life. I never thought I'd have to start all over again. Thankfully, Monty didn't question me. He was silent for a bit, his heavy breathing the only sound between us.

"I see," he finally said. "I was going to call you today about the flowers, and the chocolates, but I'm assuming you've already figured it out." When I didn't reply, he took my silence as confirmation and gave me a list of documents he needed from me, all of which I already had. "After I get the papers, it will take a few days. Anything else I can do for you, kid?"

I wondered how much he knew about my past. Knowing Monty, he'd probably run a background check on me the first time I hired him. "No. Thanks, Monty."

"Anytime, kid. I'm a phone call away if you change your mind."

The line went dead, the enormity of what I was about to do dragging me under. I curled up into a ball and let my eyelids drop, my sore body and frazzled mind welcoming temporary oblivion.

I woke with a start a few hours later to the sound of my doorbell ringing. Fear swelled within me, but I didn't think Andrew would be bold enough to ring. He'd just try to sneak in again, but I reminded myself that James had had my locks replaced and added deadbolts. Even if Andrew had become a master lock picker, he wouldn't be able to pick four locks before I noticed.

Whoever it was, I had no intention of buzzing them in. I didn't want company. Checking my phone, I saw that I'd missed a phone call and two texts from James.

> James: Hey, gorgeous. Just checking in. Do you need anything?
> James: I sent over some food. It should be there around twelve thirty. Please eat.

Groaning, I left my spot on the couch to let the delivery person in. When I tried to tip the guy, he said he had already received a generous tip to ring my doorbell and wait until I answered. *I really don't deserve James.* This thought was confirmed when I opened the bags to find five different soups.

Tears brimmed in my eyes. He truly deserved someone better.

> Me: I'm sorry I didn't reply. I fell asleep. Thank you for the food, I will eat.
> James: Glad you got some rest, gorgeous. Bon appétit.

Despite the knot in my stomach, I opened a container and swallowed a few spoonfuls of creamy pumpkin soup. Food was the last thing on my mind, but since James had gone to the trouble to send it, the least I could do was eat. Now that I had taken a nap, my mind was clearer, and there was still a lot to do before I disappeared.

I swallowed a couple of painkillers, put an ice pack around my throat, and got to work.

The fundraiser and the clothing drive were my top priorities. I would probably leave a few cases open at the firm, but they had the resources to handle it. The shelter was a different story. I had to close all of my cases, or at least leave enough material behind for whoever took over once I was gone.

I was in no mood to talk to people, but I still had to secure a location for the fundraiser. After drinking tea with honey to soothe my sore throat, I bit the bullet and called Elias. "Hi, this is Cassandra Leigh. James gave me your number," I said, ignoring how each word sliced my throat open.

"I've been expecting your call. Are you all right, darling? You sound a little rough."

"Sore throat," I explained. "I volunteer for a women's shelter, and Elisabeth donated a bunch of designer clothes. She gave me the idea to auction them off and keep the money for the shelter."

"So I've heard. But again, what can I do for you?"

I rolled my eyes. "I know Oasis is closed on Tuesdays, so I was wondering if you'd rent us the space."

"I don't think you can afford my rates."

"I was hoping for a friendly discount," I said. Elias howled with laughter, and I felt too empty to even try to argue with him. I waited patiently until he was done, scrolling through my emails until he calmed down. "You *can* just say no. There's no need to laugh at me."

"I'm only laughing at your roundabout way of asking for a favor. I reckon your budget is tiny?"

"Pretty much non-existent," I confessed.

"The space is yours, free of charge. And I'll help you plan this little auction of yours. Do you have a date?"

"No, not yet. But you don't need to help plan the event. Letting us use the space is generous enough."

"I'm better at partying and party planning than you are. Give me a ring when you've got a date, and we'll throw the best charity auction New York's ever seen."

Elias hung up, leaving me staring blankly at the phone. I doubted James had told him anything, but maybe he'd hinted I needed help. In any case, I was glad Elias was willing to plan this. That way when Monty came through, I could leave without worrying the fundraiser would fail.

For the rest of the day, I focused on work. James and the girls checked in a few times, and I replied to their messages, afraid they'd come check on me if I didn't.

Later, when I caught myself thinking about Andrew, I put the briefs aside and started researching. I needed to find a new place to start over, somewhere Andrew would never find me. None of the big cities were appealing to me. I planned to stay out of the limelight, to pick a boring career that wouldn't interest journalists.

This time, I wasn't going to make the same mistakes.

James came over after work, so I had to keep myself together. The moment he walked through the door, he pulled me into his arms, brushing a kiss on top of my head. I wrapped my arms around his waist, pressing my uninjured cheek to his solid chest.

"What have you been up to?" he asked, eyeing the dozens of files scattered on the dining room table.

"No rest for the wicked," I said, attempting a smile.

Dinner was a quiet affair, and afterwards he still had work to do, so we both sat at my table with our laptops. After a couple of hours, James gently forced me to stop, and we watched TV.

He was quiet, never pushing me to talk. I thought his presence would bother me, but I felt at ease as we cuddled on the couch.

It was cruel to keep him around, to let him comfort me when I'd probably be gone by next week. But at the same time, I wanted to spend as much time with James, and my friends, as I could.

When bedtime came, I watched incredulously as James made himself comfortable on the couch. I raised my eyebrows in question, gesturing towards his improvised bed.

"I don't want to leave you alone during the night, so I'll sleep on the couch until the situation is resolved."

"You don't have to stay over. I'm fine."

"I already told you I don't *have* to do anything."

Ignoring the pang in my chest, I led him to my bed, where I fell asleep to the sound of his steady heartbeat. Enveloped by James's familiar scent and soothing presence, I slept soundly despite the turmoil in my life.

Hours later, I awoke with a start, my heart hammering against my chest. Whatever I'd dreamed about had my stomach in knots, but I took comfort in James's warm body curled against mine, his arm draped over my waist.

He grounded me in reality, and my muscles gradually relaxed, my heartbeat slowing to a steady pace. Even asleep, his presence was enough to soothe me. A small smile formed on my lips when I felt something hard poking me. I wiggled my hips to push closer, tingles erupting all over my skin when he growled softly against my ear.

I turned around in his arms to find James still half asleep, the ghost of a smile on his lips. I brushed a finger over his cheekbone, the purple bruise on his jaw a cruel reminder that our time was limited.

"Good morning, gorgeous," he said, pulling me closer as he opened his eyes. As soon as he did, his eyes widened and his cheeks turned an adorable shade of pink. "I'm sorry. He has a mind of his own around you." He reached down to tuck his hard cock into the waistband of his boxers.

"That's okay," I said, my voice as small as I felt. "I'm just surprised you're attracted to me after what you saw the other day."

Anger flashed in his eyes, but he blinked, and it was gone. "I'm always going to be attracted to you. Nothing can change that. But right now, I just want to be here for you. I can't really control the boners, but that doesn't mean I'll act on it."

Guilt gnawed at my insides, but I said nothing.

"What is this?" He lifted my shirt further, revealing the angry purple bruise on my ribs.

"I landed against the counter," I explained, pulling my shirt down.

But James was having none of it. He raised my shirt, his fingertips brushing against my ribs to assess the damage. "Why are you trying to hide this? We need to go to the hospital. Your ribs might be broken."

I pulled the blanket to my chest, putting a stop to his examination. "Broken ribs hurt more than this. Plus, even if I went to the doctor, there's nothing they can do. I don't have any trouble breathing, so there's nothing to do but wait until the pain goes away."

"You're speaking from experience."

It wasn't a question, but I nodded anyway. James's eyes narrowed, his jaw ticking dangerously. "What's the plan here, Cassie? We can't just wait until he comes back. There must be something we can do." James focused on my face, and whatever he saw there didn't please him. He took a few deep breaths, then cupped my face gently in his big hand. "There must be something I can do. Let me help you."

My heart beat wildly in my chest. It was so tempting to allow James in, to rely on him for protection. But I couldn't do that, not when the consequences of his involvement were imprinted on his jaw.

I blinked away the tears and extricated myself from his arms. This was my burden to bear, and I wouldn't drag anyone else down with me.

James didn't comment on my silence. We had coffee together, then he brushed a kiss on my forehead and left for work. It was a lovely ritual, and I wondered how many mornings like this I would have before I watched him leave for the last time.

CHAPTER TWENTY-NINE

I spent the following days in a state of anguished indecision, torn between leaving and staying. My packed bags lurked in a corner of my closet, ready to go as soon as Monty gave me the green light. He was creating a new identity for me, including fake degrees and work references so I could keep practicing. It wasn't exactly legal, but as a criminal defense lawyer, I was used to turning a blind eye.

Money would be tight for a while, but I had an emergency fund I could tap into, so at least I wouldn't have to start from scratch this time around. The moment the papers came through, I'd have to set up a new account and transfer the money. As an exit plan, it wasn't half bad.

The only problem was having the guts to leave. I still remembered that first week in New York. I'd had nothing except the few clothes I'd shoved into my duffel bag and a picture of my parents. But as I wandered the crowded streets searching for a cheap place to spend the night—the cold air biting at my cheeks, my feet sore from walking all day—I had never felt more free.

Now that freedom was being ripped away from me again, the life I had painstakingly built for myself burned to ashes because of my inability to deal with Andrew. I would never know if Amelia opened her bakery, or if Daisy finally saw the success she deserved.

And Rina... she would never forgive me for leaving, and it wouldn't even be fair to ask it of her.

She was my person, and the thought of never hearing her call me out on my bullshit again was too much to bear.

And then there was James. He was kind, generous, and supportive, not to mention insanely hot... and so far, I had seen no red flags. He came over every day, made sure I ate, tried to distract me, and if he could tell something was off, he never said anything.

I wrote them all goodbye letters detailing my reasons for leaving and asking them to never try to find me. I owed them at least that much by way of explanation.

Some of my neighbors had heard about the clothing drive and flooded my apartment with donations. I was glad for the distraction. Anything to get away from my thoughts. The bruises on my face hadn't faded so I still hadn't returned to work. But by Wednesday, I couldn't avoid the girls any longer.

Amelia, Daisy, and Rina came to check on me, and I thanked the makeup gods for making a concealer with enough coverage to hide my bruises. I was so committed to my lies that when they walked through the door, I was bundled up on the couch, tissues scattered all around me.

"Hey, babe," Daisy said as she walked in.

Rina eyed me suspiciously, her inquisitive eyes scrutinizing my features. If I could fool Rina, I'd be off the hook, so I faked a violent cough.

Amelia sat next to me on the couch, placing her cool palm against my forehead. "Honey, you're looking a little thin. Have you been eating?"

I nodded weakly. "It hurts to eat, but James has been feeding me."

"Mamá sent you some homemade syrup," Amelia said, handing me a mason jar. "It should help your sore throat."

I offered her a small smile and thanked her, pushing down the guilt until it was nothing but an empty feeling in the pit of my stomach.

Rina pointed towards the dozens of bags littering the floor. "What's with the bags?"

"Neighbors heard about the clothing drive."

Daisy jumped up and clapped her hands. "If we can't help you get better, at least we can help you with this mess."

"And while you two do that, I'll get started on dinner," Amelia said.

I tried to argue, but the girls got busy emptying bags and sorting through the donations. Whatever Amelia was making smelled delicious, and for the first time in days, my stomach actually grumbled. I sat there, listening to my friends' chatter, my eyes burning with unshed tears, knowing I was going to leave my chosen family behind.

Determined to enjoy my time with them, I sat on a stool close to Amelia. "How's the wedding planning going?"

"Great, actually," Amelia said as she chopped vegetables. "I've never seen two people so in love. They agree on everything. It's maddening."

"Someone's jealous," I teased.

"Honestly, I just hope my sister is making the right decision. They're still in the honeymoon phase and getting married. Mamá is over the moon, though," she said with a shrug.

Daisy's howling laughter had both of us turning to see what was so funny. She was holding up an adult-sized onesie that had photos of presumably the previous owner stamped all over it. We gathered around the onesie, the four of us laughing at the pictures, particularly one where the man wore a very short, very tight wrestling outfit.

"Can I keep it?" Daisy asked. "This is art."

I nodded, my eyes brimming with tears from laughing so much. Rina and Daisy continued sorting through the clothes while I kept Amelia company in the kitchen.

"Do you have any sturdier bags?" Rina asked, coming towards the kitchen. "Daisy just ripped through a bunch instead of untying them."

"Yeah, in my closet." I stood to fetch them, but Rina stopped me.

"It's okay, I'll get it."

She disappeared inside my bedroom, and my heart leaped in my chest, a sick feeling twisting my stomach. *The bags. The letters.* My breath caught in my chest as I turned to stare at the empty doorway with wide eyes, hoping she wouldn't find them. I had stashed my packed bags under a few trash bags of donated clothes so James wouldn't accidentally see them. But now my forethought might come around to bite me in the ass.

"Hey Daisy," Rina shouted from the bedroom, "there are some donated bags in here too. Come give me a hand."

"Those aren't for the shelter! Leave them!" My throat burned as I tried to speak loud enough so Rina would hear me. So she wouldn't find the letters.

"What do you mean?" Rina asked, appearing in the threshold with a trash bag in her hand. "These are clearly donated clothes. Daisy, come help me."

With that, she disappeared inside my room again, and I watched with my heart in my throat as Daisy sauntered merrily after her. I could picture Rina picking up the trash bags filled with clothes, revealing the packed suitcases underneath and a handful of envelopes sticking out in the front pocket. *Fuck.* I swallowed the lump in my throat as I imagined Rina seeing her name scribbled on an envelope. Daisy's name on the next one.

The silence coming from my bedroom became too loud. I glanced towards the door with wary eyes, and Amelia followed my gaze.

"Are you guys okay in there?" Amelia asked while she stirred the soup.

Rina appeared on the threshold, clutching a piece of paper in her hands. "What's this?"

"Rina—" I started, but she quickly cut me off.

"Andrew was here?" she asked, assessing me carefully.

Amelia froze with the wooden spoon in her hand. "What do you mean?"

Rina covered the distance between us in two long steps and wrapped her arms around me, hugging me tight. I winced, and she drew back. "You're not sick, are you?"

"He hit you?" Daisy said as she left my room, her letter clutched against her chest.

I nodded, unable to say it out loud. Everything hurt. I didn't have the energy for this.

Abandoning the soup, Amelia sat on the stool next to mine, taking my hand in hers. "Are you okay? What can we do?"

I shook my head. "I'm fine. There's nothing to do, and I don't want to talk about it now."

Daisy joined us in the kitchen, her big blue eyes shining with unshed tears. "Are you really leaving?"

I nodded again, the concerned look in my friends' faces making it harder to breathe.

Rina took a deep, calming breath, and reached for my hand on the counter. "Listen, no one could ever blame you for leaving Andrew the way you did the first time. But now? You have an amazing support system in place, you're financially stable, you have a solid career, your own apartment…. There's no reason for you to just take off."

"My own apartment? Is this supposed to be my safe place? Because it didn't feel very safe when I came home to find Andrew in my kitchen." I pushed to my feet, putting some distance between me and the girls. "Now that he knows where I am, he'll never give up. I'll always be looking over my shoulder, waiting for the moment he'll strike again. I can't live like that, not anymore."

"So you go to the police, you file a report, you get a restraining order. What you don't do is give up."

A bitter laugh escaped me. "Do you know how many case files I go through each week, how many women file restraining orders only to end up dead or all black and blue in the hospital? If the police can't help all those women, what makes you think they can help me? It's just a piece of paper, Rina. It won't stop him."

"So running is better than fighting?"

"Rina—" Amelia tried to interrupt.

"Who are you? Because you're not my best friend. My best friend is a fighter. She got herself out of a fucked up situation. She fought to rebuild herself, her life, to thrive, not just to survive."

"Oh, please," I said, my voice raw with pain. "Spare me your lectures. You act like you have everything figured out, giving everyone your two cents as if you know better. Well, you don't know better. You have no idea what you're talking about."

"This isn't about me, Cassie."

"You're right. It isn't. It's about me. My choices. My life. You don't get to dictate it."

Amelia stepped closer to me, placing a hand on my shoulder. "I know you're scared, but you're not alone this time around. I'm here. Rina and Daisy are here. We're all willing to help, to fight for you."

This was the reason the plan was to disappear. I was too much of a coward to tell them face to face because I knew they would try to talk me out of leaving. They didn't get it. And I hoped they'd never have to understand abusive relationships. How it breaks you. I didn't want them fighting for me. I wanted my friends to be safe, even if that meant never seeing them again.

I let out a derisive laugh. "You can't even stand up for yourself at work. What makes you think you can face Andrew?"

"Cassie—" Daisy started, but I cut her off, ignoring the tears in her eyes.

"And you? You've never struggled a day in your life. You float through life doing this and that, searching for your 'true calling' or whatever it is. Well, some of us don't have that privilege. Some of us have to fight and sacrifice everything just to survive." I clutched my aching ribs, trying to ease the pain. "Don't pretend like you know what I'm going through. None of you do."

Tears threatened to spill, but I kept them at bay. I was tired of all of this. At this point, starting over felt easier than dealing with the fallout of leaving. I sat quietly on my couch, sinking into the soft pillows. There was no more fight left in me. "I'm tired. You should go."

Rina dropped down next to me on the couch, her dark blue eyes soft and her voice gentle. As if she were talking to a cornered animal. "We're your friends, Cassie. We're not leaving you alone when you need us the most."

"Come stay with me," Amelia said, perching against the couch. "I'd like to see that asshole try to get past my cousins."

Daisy sat in front of me on the coffee table and reached for my hand. "And you're a lawyer now. You know what to do, there's no reason to leave."

"You're right," I said, my throat scratchy and raw. I swallowed hard and drew my hand back. "You're my friends. I've had fun hanging out with you. But that's all you are: friends. I can make new ones. I know what I'm doing. If you're not going to respect that, then get the fuck out of my house and leave me alone."

Rina looked as if I slapped her, her eyes wide and her mouth slightly agape. "Cassie—"

"Get out."

"That's it?" Daisy asked in between soft sobs, pleading eyes trained on me.

I didn't say anything else, my jaw tight, my gaze focused on the wall like a coward. Rina grabbed her purse and left, followed by Daisy.

"The chicken noodle soup will be done in fifteen minutes. I set a timer," Amelia said gently before she followed them out.

I welcomed the pain shooting through my side as I doubled over in hysterical laughter at her parting words, unable to control myself. Of course Amelia would be concerned about the food at a time like this.

Tears ran freely down my face as I sobbed and laughed all at once.

My chest ached as I panted, trying to catch my breath in between sobs. Almost a decade of friendship gone in a blink of an eye, and I had no one to blame but myself.

I let myself feel the pain until Amelia's timer went off, spurring me back to action. Then I wiped the tears away and shoved it all down. I couldn't let myself be guided by my feelings. I'd done that before with Andrew and it had landed me in a hospital bed.

The urge to do something, anything to get my mind off of the last twenty minutes, was too strong to ignore. I turned off the stove and grabbed as many bags as I could carry before making my way to the shelter. I dove into work, trying as hard as I could to forget the girls' hurt expressions.

I was kneeling down on the floor, separating laundry, when a shadow by the door caught my attention.

James was standing there, his jaw tense, a distant look in his eyes.

"You're leaving." It wasn't a question. He already knew.

"How—"

"Daisy called me. She wanted me to change your mind." He stepped into the small office and shut the door behind him. "When you ended things between us, was that the reason? Because you already knew you were leaving?"

I nodded. "I didn't want to string you along."

"So everything that happened in the last few weeks meant nothing to you." He didn't try to disguise the pain in his eyes, and I hated myself for hurting him.

"That's not true, James."

He nodded, but I didn't think he believed me. "I can't do this anymore," he paced around the room, running his hands through his hair. "I care about you, you know that. I'm a patient man. I was willing to wait until you realized that you care about me too. But maybe I was wrong."

"You're not wrong. I do care about you," I admitted, but the hurt expression in his eyes told me it was the wrong thing to say. Too little too late.

"But you're leaving. And you weren't even going to tell me, were you?"

I hung my head in shame, my heart constricting in my chest. "You deserve better than this, James, better than me. I bet you could walk into any club in New York and find a perfect girl who doesn't have all this baggage, all this damage."

James let out a frustrated sigh. "That first night at Oasis, all I wanted to do was fuck you. And once I did, I wanted to keep doing it. It was pure lust. But then you walked out on me, and I couldn't stop thinking about you. I had to find you." He stepped toward me and gently cupped my jaw, his thumb brushing over my cheekbone. "Every little piece of you I uncovered has completely beguiled me. Your sense of humor, your strength, your compassion, your intelligence." He cocked his head to the side, and his lips lifted into a sad smile. "And I especially love the way you melt into my arms when we hug."

I couldn't bear to look at him, to see the emotion in his eyes. But I also couldn't look away. This was all my own doing, and I deserved every bit of pain his words brought.

"I love you, Cassandra, and I don't want to let you go. But if that's what you really want, I won't try to stop you. Whenever you decide to leave, give Paul a call. He'll pick you up and my plane will take you wherever you need to go, that way you won't have to buy a traceable ticket. In the meantime, I've hired a security team to watch over you until you leave, so don't be scared if you see two tall men hanging outside your apartment."

I nodded, my lips trembling as I tried not to cry. He was being so kind. I didn't deserve it.

James wrapped his arms around me, and I hugged his waist, melting into his embrace for the last time. I closed my eyes and took a deep breath, inhaling the familiar sharp notes of his cologne. The tears I'd been holding finally spilled over, trailing a silent path down my cheeks and soaking into his suit jacket.

"I mean it, Cassandra," he whispered into my hair. "Whatever you need. A place to stay, a lawyer, money. Call Paul. I need to make sure you're safe. Even if you're not mine. Even if you never were."

A sob escaped me and James drew back, offering me a sad smile. I wanted to say that I was his. That I would never forget his kindness, how it felt to be in his arms, and all the happy moments we spent together. But I couldn't. It wouldn't be fair.

So I watched in silence as he retreated.

He spared me one last glance before he turned around and left. And I stood there staring at the door for the longest time, feeling my fractured heart shatter into a thousand tiny pieces.

CHAPTER THIRTY

When I got home later that night, I closed the door behind me and stared at my empty apartment. The sweet and spicy smell of Amelia's soup still lingered in the air. Just a few hours ago, this place had been filled with laughter. Now the silence was overwhelming.

No girls. No James.

I was alone.

A vicious sob ripped through me, tearing through my chest before I had a chance to stop it. I stumbled to the couch with shaky legs, struggling to catch my next breath.

Stop it! Get it together. I rubbed furiously at my eyes. But it didn't matter. I couldn't stop the thoughts. Sob after sob shook my body as a sharp pain burned in my chest. I wrapped my arms around myself, rocking back and forth as I gasped, struggling to breathe.

Alone. I was alone again.

I reached for the framed photo of my parents, clutching it against my chest as I wept. Just for a little while, I allowed myself to miss them.

My parents looked so happy in the photo, so full of life. It had been a warm day. Mom wanted to be outdoors, so she put together a picnic and we headed to the lake. We spent hours lazing in the sun, skipping rocks and trying to find tadpoles. It was the perfect summer afternoon.

I had gone off to play somewhere, and when I came back, Mom was making a flower crown. She placed it daintily on top of her head, her long, silky hair flowing in the breeze. Dad turned to her, his eyes shining with adoration as he declared that she was his queen.

That's when I snapped the picture. Two years later, they were dead.

Time had blurred most of my memories, but this one was crystal clear. When I left Andrew, this picture was the only one I had taken. All I had left of my parents were my unreliable memories and this photo. I wished I had one of the three of us.

A few months after they died, Andrew had expressed concern that I wasn't healing. He said it wasn't normal to talk about my parents all the time. So I grieved in silence, and once we left for college, I stopped talking about them altogether.

Andrew and his parents were the only people in my life who knew my parents. It felt silly to talk about them to people who had never met them. Another reason I stayed with Andrew—because as he put it, who would I go to? I had no one.

Cruel words meant to wound, and he never missed his mark.

I wondered what my parents would tell me now. If things would've turned out the way they had with Andrew if they were still alive.

Hopeless musings. I couldn't bring them back.

I couldn't erase my past with Andrew either, but I also didn't know how to move forward.

When I first saw him, my first instinct had been to run, just like before. I was terrified of him. Scared he would hurt my friends. He had a way of making me feel small, powerless.

He made me believe that since my parents were gone, he was the only one who would love me. So I bent over backwards, chipping away at myself to become someone he could continue to love. But it was never enough. I was never enough.

With trembling fingers, I returned the frame to its original place.

It was too much. I couldn't deal with it anymore.

I fished my phone from my pocket and emailed the firm, letting them know I wouldn't be in for the rest of the week. Reality was too much to bear.

Hiding in my room wasn't a permanent solution, but it was all I had the energy for. I crawled into bed and slept.

The morning light brought me out of my slumber, and I couldn't believe I had actually slept through the night. I stared at the empty pillow next to mine, an ache invading my chest as I remembered James's sleepy face.

I'll never see him like that again, I thought as I grabbed the pillow and tossed it across the room.

Releasing a deep sigh, I padded towards the bathroom. I refused to look at myself in the mirror. The combination of bawling for hours and fading bruises was sure to be jarring, and I didn't need to add another layer of self-hatred to the pity party.

Amelia's soup was still on the stove. Sighing, I grabbed the pot and dumped the food my friend had lovingly made for me down the garbage disposal. *Fitting,* I thought as I abandoned the dirty pot in the sink. My stomach felt empty, hollow; just the thought of eating made me nauseous. I stood in front of the coffee maker for a while, completely lost in thought, until I snapped out of it and decided I also didn't want coffee.

I poured a glass of water and collapsed on the couch, staring blankly at the TV. My mind pulled me in a thousand different directions. I felt lost, out of control.

I needed to clear my head.

Jumping off the couch, I grabbed the bear shaped bottle of vodka James had brought over. If I had known then what I knew now, would I have continued our relationship? I wondered if the brief moments of happiness we had shared were worth this pain.

Shaking my head, I focused on the bottle. It was one thing to drink socially, but it was crossing a line to start my day with vodka. I didn't want to use alcohol as a crutch to deal with my feelings, but I also didn't want to deal with them at all.

The cute little bear stared back at me, its previously blank expression growing angrier the more I stared.

Fuck it, I thought. What better time to drink than when your life is falling apart? I had alienated my friends and pushed away a good man who claimed to love me.

A man I might have strong feelings for.

I poured two shots and downed one after the other. The vodka set a fire in my empty stomach, replacing the hollowness that had settled there. Then I poured two more and tossed them back.

Grabbing the bottle and a shot glass, I settled at the dining room table with a notepad. I needed a plan, but I didn't know where to start. Monty's paperwork would come through any day now, so I had to decide. Stay or leave.

I thought leaving was the right thing, but it didn't feel right.

Andrew had started the chain of events that led to the current disaster that was my life, but I was starting to realize that I had caused most of the damage myself. I could have told my friends Andrew was back. I could have told them I was leaving, and why. In my heart, I knew they would have packed my bags and helped me disappear if that was truly what I wanted.

But what *did* I want? Sighing, I poured another shot. The vodka slipped smoothly down my throat, numbing the pain even if only momentarily.

James. It had been so selfish to stretch my time with him, knowing I was leaving.

It was clear he cared about me. He'd told me time and time again, but even if he hadn't, his actions spoke loudly. Padding me up when we went ice skating, cooking for me, always driving me home and walking me to my door, even when it was late and he had work in the morning. He respected my boundaries, massaged my sore feet, and kept me company when I was upset about work.

The memory of water dripping down James's body interrupted my train of thought—my hands scrubbing him clean, the look of pure awe in his eyes as I washed him. I shook my head and downed another shot.

But that was before Andrew. Before James knew how broken and damaged I was. We hadn't had sex after that; I wasn't ready for inti-

248

macy. James clearly enjoyed sex, and I did too. But he deserved to be with someone who didn't go through phases where their demons prevented them from providing it. How long would it be until he resented me? He might love me now, but my baggage would undoubtedly poison our relationship and make him miserable.

James deserved better.

A shudder went through me and I pressed my palms to my eyes, hating the wetness on my face. I tried to clear my head and focus on the blank sheet of paper in front of me, but I couldn't make any progress with my plan. How could I, when I didn't know what I wanted?

It felt like all my life I'd been reacting to Andrew. I moved to New York to get away from him, pierced my nipple because I wanted my body to be mine, and Andrew always wanted my skin to be unmarred. It took some time, but eventually I healed enough and started exploring my sexuality. Most of my partners were interested in my body and nothing else, and when they crossed that line, I was quick to cut them loose.

Until James.

My chest ached at the thought, and I squeezed my eyes shut to prevent the tears from falling. I poured another shot, spilling vodka all over the table, the paper I was supposed to be deciding my future on soaking up the alcohol.

Perfect, I thought as a bitter laugh erupted from my lips. Abandoning the shot glass and my future, I carried the bear-shaped bottle to the couch and drank until I passed out, refusing to think, to hurt anymore.

Unfortunately, pain was something I could only temporarily escape. This time, I could barely avoid it for a couple of hours before it returned with a mocking vengeance. Mixing vodka with an empty stomach wasn't my brightest moment, and I paid the price as I clutched the toilet.

My stomach twisted painfully as I heaved, angry tears dripping down my face. The last time I had been drunk and throwing up, Amelia was there to hold my hair. Now I was alone, and it was all my fault.

I couldn't keep acting like this.

Pushing to my feet, I stripped naked and stepped into the tub. I turned the shower on and sat under the stream, hoping the water would wash away some of the pain.

Andrew had scared me, and my first thought had been to run, just like before.

But I wasn't that girl anymore.

The familiar sound of my doorbell snapped me out of my slumber. I jumped out of bed, hope swelling in my chest at the thought of the girls coming to check on me.

My head spun as I stood, my body automatically doubling over to lean against the bed. I groaned as a stabbing pain exploded on the right side of my skull, blinding me for a second. The doorbell rang again, and I pressed my palm against my forehead as I tried to control the pain.

I stumbled to the intercom. "Yes?"

"Good morning, Miss Leigh. This is Paul Revello, Mr. Walton's driver."

Morning? How long had I slept?

"I have a delivery for you," he continued as I stood, shivering from head to toe.

Gathering myself, I mumbled, "Of course, come on up."

I buzzed him in and looked down at myself. Yesterday, I had hastily slipped on an old, large t-shirt. It was stained with bleach from when Daisy convinced me to dye her hair at home to save money. Her hair had turned an interesting shade of green, and we'd all pooled money together to help pay for a color correction at a nice salon. The memory brought a small smile to my lips, and when I noticed, I had to swallow the tears.

I wasn't exactly in the mental or physical state to receive visitors, but I was burning with curiosity. Maybe James had sent me a note. Or food like before.

Paul knocked on my door, and I let him in. "Good morning, ma'am," he said, eyeing me with concern. He handed me a simple black gift bag, frowning as my trembling fingers grasped the handles.

"Thank you," I said, my voice weak and scratchy.

He bowed his head lightly. "Of course." His eyes zeroed in on my face, and he hesitated before asking, "How are you, ma'am?"

I swallowed. The bruises on my cheek and throat were still visible. I hadn't bothered properly removing my makeup from two days ago, but I doubted it had survived all the crying, vomiting, and a shower. Re-applying it hadn't even crossed my mind. He didn't seem surprised by the bruises, though, so I wondered if James had told him.

"I'm sorry. I must look awful. I have the worst flu." The lie flew from my lips before I registered it. "How are you?"

Paul's frown deepened for a fraction of a second before he schooled his features into neutrality. "I'm doing great, ma'am. Thank you for asking." He turned towards the door, and I took his cue and opened it to let him out.

I clutched the bag tightly in my hands, the uneasy feeling in my chest growing until I couldn't take it anymore and the words spilled from my lips. "How is he?"

It was barely a whisper, but Paul froze in the doorway, a weary expression on his face. "I believe he might also have the flu." Paul shot me a knowing look before bowing his head and disappearing down the hallway.

He's hurting. I couldn't deal with that thought right away, nor could I open the gift bag despite my burning curiosity.

My body felt like it had been through a giant garbage disposal. Everything ached and my head throbbed painfully. Before I did anything else, I needed to take care of myself.

In the kitchen, I took slow sips of water while I munched on a salt cracker. I needed painkillers, but on an empty stomach it would just do more damage, so I forced myself to eat. I only managed two crackers, but at the very least it settled my stomach enough to swallow some ibuprofen.

Clutching the bag to my chest, I sat on the couch to open it. Inside of it was a thin envelope and a familiar black box. Setting the box aside for the moment, I gingerly opened the envelope, trying to keep my hopes in check. This wouldn't be a love letter from James. It couldn't be. But my heart still sank when I realized it was the details of my security team. Names, phone numbers, pictures. I stared at the faces of the four people who'd be watching over me in teams of two, committing them to memory.

I was right. It wasn't a love letter. But was there a better way to show love than to hire an entire security team to protect someone?

My gaze landed on the box and I flipped the lid open, already knowing what I'd find. The green emerald pendant surrounded by leaf-shaped diamonds glimmered even in the dim light of my apartment.

I clutched my chest, my breath choppy and shallow as I pondered the meaning behind James sending the necklace. He was supposed to keep it safe, at least that's what I had asked of him. But I never had any intention of keeping it.

Maybe I could sell it.

I grabbed my phone from my bedroom, ignoring Rina, Amelia, and Daisy's names as I scrolled through the notifications. Despite my cruel words, my friends kept checking on me, but I wasn't ready to face them.

Carefully placing the necklace on my coffee table, I did a reverse image search and froze in shock at the numbers on my screen. The necklace was a vintage Harry Winston, with a retail price close to one million dollars.

Holy shit! I can't keep this.

Why would James give me something so expensive? And why send it to me now?

Maybe he meant for me to sell it. Starting fresh with close to a million dollars in my bank account would be easier. I wouldn't have to worry about money for the rest of my life if I was careful.

But I couldn't do it. I placed the necklace back in the box and hid it behind my rarely used pots in the kitchen. Then I stood there, remembering the time James cooked me breakfast and all the silent mornings we had spent together after Andrew attacked me.

It occurred to me that I had never phrased it like that before, even in my head. I always said or thought something like *Andrew is back*. Never *Andrew attacked me*. Andrew assaulted me. That was a fact, and even after all these years, I couldn't say it out loud.

A shuddering breath went through me, exhaustion seeping into my bones. But I'd had enough of sleeping. I needed to figure out my next move. With a legal pad in hand, I grabbed a water bottle and made my way to my balcony for some fresh air.

The last time I had been here, James was cradling me to his chest, his large hand stroking my back in soothing circles. I cringed at the thought, my cheeks hot with shame over how I had acted that day.

James had seen me in a crisis, unable to control my emotions. And even after seeing what a hot mess I was, he had said those three words. But how long could that last? Reality would soon set in, and dealing with my broken psyche on a daily basis would eventually become a burden.

I had so many conflicting feelings and thoughts; I didn't know how to unravel the chaos my life had turned into.

The truth was, I didn't want to leave. I liked my life. This city had forced me to grow into the woman I was today, and although I was far from perfect, I had to look at my accomplishments objectively. I had graduated law school in the top three percent of my class, even though I barely survived my first year. After interning at Feldman & Sullivan's for the summer, I had received an advanced offer and secured my career two years before graduation.

Professionally, I had done well. And then I'd met Rina and my personal life bloomed. She had forced me out of the house, which led to us meeting Amelia and Daisy. I found friendship and love when I had firmly believed leaving Andrew meant I would be alone for the rest of my life.

But that wasn't true, and now that my thoughts weren't clouded by my fear, I could recognise that. The old adage, *you never know what you have until you lose it*, came to mind. I missed my friends, and I missed James.

Nearly a decade ago, I had lost myself to Andrew, and now that I had painstakingly rebuilt myself, my life… I had to fight for the woman I was and the woman I had become. For the life I had built.

This time I wouldn't let Andrew take it from me.

CHAPTER THIRTY-ONE

The first step was to gather information. It struck me as odd that Andrew found me now, after seven years. Maybe he'd seen me in the press with James like he said, and it had triggered him. But maybe something else had made him want to find me now, and luckily, I knew a man who could find out.

The line rang once before Monty's gravelly voice greeted me. "Hey, kid. Your papers are almost done. I ran into a little speed-bump, but it's all smoothed out now."

"Actually, I won't be needing those anymore."

He laughed, the sound raspy from years of smoking. "Change your mind, did you?"

"I did. I'm sorry for wasting your time. I'll still pay, of course, but I'm calling about something else."

"Don't worry, kid. It was no trouble. What can I do for you?"

"Andrew Laherty, born May 28th 1994 in Hamilton, Ohio. Whatever you can dig up from the last ten years." I paused, searching for the right words. "He had a girlfriend a few years back. Her name was Samantha Decker...."

Monty released a deep sigh, and I could picture him smoothing his thick mustache. "Kid, there's no need to lie. I know."

My first instinct was to play dumb, but there was no point.

When I didn't break the silence, Monty continued, "I do a background check on all my clients, and when I found out Cassandra Leigh had only existed for a few years, I dug a little deeper. Found the hospital records and put two and two together."

"Right," I said, exhaling heavily. "I guess there's no point beating around the bush. He found me and I need to know what pushed him to do it now. Plus, whatever other information I can use against him."

"You putting him behind bars this time around?"

"I don't know," I answered honestly, a flush of shame creeping over my neck.

Monty promised me he would prioritize my request and call me when he had anything juicy. At this point my bill must be exorbitant, but I couldn't dwell on it.

I spent the rest of the weekend puttering around my apartment, burying my head in work and ignoring my phone. At night, I clutched James's pillow to my chest, his lingering scent lulling me to sleep.

Monday eventually came, and I couldn't hide in my apartment anymore. I hadn't been out of the house in days, and as I made my way to work, I kept glancing over my shoulder. Andrew probably wouldn't approach me in public, but I had the distinct feeling I was being watched.

As I walked, my eyes scanned the crowd for the security team James had hired. But either they were excellent at their job or absolutely incompetent, because I couldn't see them anywhere.

I was grateful for the closed space of the subway car, despite the sweaty bodies brushing against me. Standing near a door, I scanned every face in the packed car for familiar caramel eyes and dirty blond hair.

Once I was satisfied Andrew hadn't followed me onto the train, I pulled out my phone to distract myself. The pit in my stomach grew a little deeper as I scrolled through the dozen messages from my friends. They were worried about me, and I had been too focused on my own misery to shoot them a simple reassuring text.

My fingers hovered over James's name. I opened the thread, and reading over our last texts almost brought a smile to my lips. There were no new texts from him, not that I was expecting any. He had told me to call him, but that was contingent on my needing his plane. Not because I missed his cheeky texts. Actually, now that I thought about it, he told me to call Paul, not him. The realization stung, but I'd made my bed, and now there was nothing to do but lie in it.

Welcoming cool air greeted me when I stepped into the office. Olivia was happy to see me, smiling broadly as she updated me on the work I'd missed. I was eager to disappear into my office and focus on something other than my life.

A little after lunch, Mr. Sullivan summoned me. Nothing good could come out of it, but I promptly stood and made my way to his office. My steps were confident, my expression neutral as I steeled myself, ready for anything the day threw at me, or so I thought. I knocked lightly on the door, my clammy hands leaving a mark on the cool metal of the doorknob as I pushed it open.

"Ah, Cassandra! Good news! We've reached a deal with the Maxwell case, so we can finally put this mess behind us." He was standing by his liquor cabinet, pouring whiskey into two crystal glasses, an enormous grin plastered on his face.

When I approached, he handed me a glass, which I politely accepted. After the other day, I wasn't quite ready to drink alcohol again, but I couldn't decline. "That's great news! So what's the damage?" My voice was still a little rough, but at least it didn't hurt as much.

"It was a hard bargain, and I owe Grayson, the DA, for sweeping this under the rug. Officially Maxwell will get five years, but we'll get him out in eighteen months, maybe sooner."

Eighteen months. After stealing millions in retirement funds from innocent, naïve old people, Maxwell would only get a year and a half. It was a joke. The investigation into his embezzlement case had been shady from the beginning, and this was just the cherry on top of the corruption cake.

I couldn't wait to put this case behind me and never have to see Maxwell's face again. "Thank you for cleaning this up," I heard myself say, my features relaxed despite my inner turmoil.

Mr. Sullivan clinked his glass against mine, and I took a tentative sip, fighting the wave of nausea as the sharp smell of alcohol burned my sinuses. "Maxwell wasn't too happy about it. But no matter. We're having a press conference at five, and I need you to share the news. Put a nice spin on it, you know the drill."

He handed me a file, and I leafed through it, skimming the details of the deal with the DA. We went over a couple points, then I left his office, anger rising in me. *"Go to the police, file a restraining order,"* Rina had said. But the justice system was a joke, and as I crafted my speech for later, anticipating the inflammatory questions that might be thrown my way, I realized I was part of the problem.

In a healthy justice system, it was logical to defend people accused of crimes. After all, not every defendant was guilty. But when Monty mentioned the botched investigation, I hadn't asked him to dig deeper. Instead, I'd chosen to stay quiet. I was a fucking hypocrite, raging about injustice in my volunteer work while enabling corruption at my actual job.

Still, I went through with the press conference. It was my job. I stood at the podium in front of dozens of reporters, wondering what kind of person I had become. All I wanted to do was tell the truth.

But this was the reality we lived in. The survivors at the shelter lived in fear of retaliation, knowing the law couldn't help them while people with money and power like Maxwell got away with doing awful things.

And somehow it had become my job to defend them.

No, not *somehow*.

This was a decision I had made all by myself, because helping to protect the rich and powerful was good for my wallet. After Andrew, financial freedom had been important to me, so I chose the career that paid the most, with little concern for morality and ethics.

The press fired question after question after I announced that Maxwell had taken a plea bargain. I fielded their questions, spinning my narrative—that Maxwell had shared valuable intel with the prosecution and had been granted a reduced sentence for his cooperation. That, unfortunately, I couldn't reveal more, since that information pertained to ongoing investigations.

The public wouldn't be too happy, but their outrage would only last until a fresh scandal broke out. Then Maxwell, and whoever else was involved in this, would be all but forgotten. I spent the next twenty minutes giving non-answers to journalists' pertinent questions until Mr. Sullivan finally put an end to the press conference.

"You did good," he said as we walked through the lobby to the elevator, patting me on the back.

I had been playing with the truth for so long in my professional life, I wondered when that had seeped into my personal life. "Thank you," I whispered.

Maybe this job was getting to me, skewing my morals in such a way that I shifted the narrative to justify my actions. Shutting the door to my office, I sat down and took an objective look at my behavior the past few days.

In retrospect, there's no way I would've decided to leave without a word if I hadn't reframed it in my mind as trying to protect my friends and myself from Andrew. I had acted selfishly under the guise of selflessness, all the while convincing myself there were no other options.

Lies. So many lies.

There were other options. I could have gone to my friends for help and support. I could have accepted James's offer to stay with him. Seven years ago, I didn't have a support group, or the knowledge and the resources to take legal action against Andrew.

But I did now. The truth was, I was terrified of allowing myself to be vulnerable, to admit I *needed* someone, like I had needed Andrew. I was scared of relying on my friends, of accepting their help, and that was so unfair to them.

The girls and James were nothing like Andrew.

I put myself in their shoes for a second. If one of the girls was in a similar situation, I would move heaven and earth to help them. I would beg them to stay with me, to press charges even if nothing came out of it. And if they didn't come to me for help, I would wonder what kind of friend I was that they couldn't rely on me in their time of need. They loved me just as much as I loved them. I knew that. But I didn't even give them an opportunity to help me.

My phone rang, bringing me back to reality, so I put a pin in all my personal drama and focused on work.

Hours later, I left work in a daze, my legs carrying me automatically. The hairs on my arms stood, and I scanned my surroundings for any sign of danger. This time, I caught sight of Ivan, the burly bald man who was part of my security team. Relief flooded through me when he offered me a subtle nod before disappearing into the masses again. I kept walking, and despite feeling a little safer, my heart lurched at every mop of dirty blond hair in my periphery.

Ever since my first semester in law school, my goal had been to become a top legal defense attorney and to make partner before thirty-five. Now I couldn't really find it in my heart to care.

Rina said she wanted me to be happy, not just in my romantic relationships, but in my chosen career too. I had thought becoming partner would make me happy, but the past few days had me questioning everything. Had she known I was unhappy before I did?

I froze in front of a hair salon. A sign on the door read *walk-ins welcome*. Without much thought, I pushed the door open.

A tall woman in her mid-forties greeted me with a kind smile. "Hi, how can I help you?"

"I saw you take walk-ins."

"We do! What did you have in mind? If you're looking for a color, it might be better to make an appointment."

"No, I was actually thinking about chopping it all off."

The hairdresser's eyes widened as she rounded the counter. She stood next to me and examined a few hair strands. "Are you sure? Your hair is really healthy."

"I'm sure," I said.

"Well, in that case, I'm open right now. Or you could wait half an hour for one of my colleagues to be free."

It was just hair, but it suddenly felt like the weight of the world on my shoulders, and the urge to chop it all off and be free was overwhelming.

"No, let's do it now," I said, before I lost my nerve.

"All right, if you're sure. I'm Denise. Why don't you follow me to my station?"

"Cassie," I said, following her lead.

We walked further into the salon, and she pointed to a chair. "How much are we cutting off?"

I pointed towards my shoulders.

"That's a good eleven inches, honey," Denise said as she showed me how much hair that was. "Are you sure? Once I cut it off, there's no going back."

I nodded, my hands shaking under the black cape she'd put on me. "Can I donate it?"

"Of course," she said, brightening. "We take donations for Wigs for Kids."

"Cool," I said, my heart hammering against my chest. "Let's do it."

Denise nodded, and split my hair into four sections, tying each off with a hair band. "Are you ready?"

I nodded, swallowing the lump in my throat. Denise's movements were quick and precise as she cut off my hair. With each snip of her shears, the wounds I had buried deep inside split wide open. Grief weighed me down, an old sadness making my heart heavy.

When I first moved to New York, I thought about cutting it, but I loved my hair. As a little girl, I wanted it to be just like my mom's, long and shiny. I had so many fond memories of her brushing it, braiding it, teaching me how to keep it healthy. At the time, it felt like the only thing still attaching me to her, and I wasn't ready to let go just yet.

Andrew loved my hair, too. Especially when he used it to hurt me. One time I had fallen asleep on the couch with the TV on, and that wasn't allowed. So he'd grabbed a fistful of my hair and dragged me all the way to the bedroom. He'd ripped some big chunks out, and I remembered being grateful that at least my hair was thick enough to hide the bald spots.

Denise stopped to hand me a box of tissues and said, "That's okay, sweetie. Let it all out."

I hadn't even realized I was crying. "I'm so sorry," I said, unable to stop the tears flowing down my cheeks.

"Don't worry about it. We all go through it sometimes." She handed me a bottle of water and I gratefully took a sip. "Okay, let's take a little break," she said gently. "We're all done with the big chop, but I need you to be still, otherwise it won't be even, sweetie."

I nodded, taking deep breaths to compose myself. "Do you have a bathroom?" Denise nodded and led me to the restroom. The moment the door shut behind me, whatever shred of composure I had left vanished.

My butt landed heavily on the toilet and I pressed my hand over my mouth to drown out the sobs. Denise's kindness only made me cry harder because it reminded me of the good people in my life. Past and present.

Andrew's parents had taken me in. Bill and Patricia stood at my graduation, clapping and whistling as I made my valedictorian speech. They'd never tried to replace my parents, but they went above and beyond for me. Cutting ties with them had hurt almost as much as losing my real parents.

Yes, I had lost a lot. But I was also fortunate enough to have found Rina, Daisy, and Amelia. I needed to apologize, to beg for their forgiveness.

I didn't want to be broken anymore. I wanted to be someone who was deserving of their friendship, of their love.

Bracing myself, I stood to look in the mirror. My tears had smudged my concealer, revealing the bruises on my cheek. I was sure Denise saw them and I appreciated her discretion. My once long, brown hair now reached just below my shoulders. It was definitely different, but not exactly a grim look. It'd probably be cute once my face wasn't red, splotchy, and swollen.

After splashing cold water on my face, I dried it with toilet paper and reapplied concealer, then foundation. My eyes and nose were still a bit red, but it would do. I made my way back to Denise's station, and she handed me a cup of tea.

"Chamomile," she said, "it will calm your nerves."

I gratefully accepted the mug and murmured a thank you.

Denise gave me some time to drink my tea while she answered the phone. Then she washed my hair and proceeded with the cut. Once she was done, she blow dried it and styled it before turning me towards the mirror.

Tears threatened to spill again as I took in my reflection. Denise had done a fantastic job styling my now barely shoulder length hair into soft waves. It was a drastic change, but a welcome one.

Maybe a public breakdown was what I needed to put things into perspective.

"Thank you, it looks great," I said honestly.

"It really suits you. Whatever you're going through, sometimes a fresh haircut is just what we need to turn a new leaf."

I smiled and gave her a generous tip before I finally made my way home.

Whatever direction my life was going, it wasn't making me happy. But before I tried to figure out what would career-wise, I needed to get my friends back. Whatever else I decided to do, I wouldn't be happy without the people I cared about beside me.

Me: Hi! First of all, I'm okay. Sorry for ignoring your texts and calls. And I am so sorry for how I behaved, the things I said…. I want to apologize in person because that's what the three of you deserve. Please, let me try to explain. Dinner at my place tomorrow?
Amelia: Of course! So glad you're okay!
Daisy: I'll be there.
Me: Thank you!!

My eyes teared up at Amelia's message. She'd always been the more compassionate and empathetic of the four of us, and I could've almost guessed she would've been the first to reply. Daisy's response was less enthusiastic, but at least she was willing to hear me out. But Rina didn't even read the messages.

My chest heaved up and down as I stared anxiously at my phone, waiting for Rina to reply. I had been especially cruel to her, and I would understand if she didn't forgive me. *Maybe she's busy.* I clung to that thought while I went through some briefs for the shelter, but when I returned to my phone a couple of hours later, I still had no notifications.

I waited a while longer before I tried again, trying to focus on work, but the thought of permanently losing my best friend was too much to bear.

The girls were my chosen family. Life wouldn't be the same without them.

My phone vibrated, and I almost jumped out of my seat.

Rina: 8p.m.

Yes! I celebrated internally, and cracked a smile. It was the first genuine smile since I had seen Andrew at the gallery. Tears flooded my vision, but I fought them off and went back to work.

I just hoped they would forgive me.

As I stared at the pages, I couldn't help but think about James. I had been purposefully refusing to think about him all day. It hurt too much. Since the girls were willing to hear me out, I wondered if he would too.

I clutched my phone with trembling fingers, scrolled through my contacts, and hovered over his name. If I called, he would answer because he would think it was an emergency. The last thing I wanted was for James to think something was wrong. I didn't want him to come to me out of a sense of obligation, or because he thought I needed saving.

Releasing a deep sigh, I texted him instead.

Me: Hi. Everything's okay. I'm safe, so don't worry.
Me: I miss you. Can we talk?

I waited with bated breath for his reply, but hours later I drifted off to sleep with my phone clutched in my hand and still no answer from James.

CHAPTER THIRTY-TWO

Sometimes it seemed like the universe was out to get me.

I had planned to be home around six, so I'd have time to shower, clean up a bit, and prepare my apology speech. The idea was to make cocktails and appetizers to lighten the mood. We would drink a little, catch up, and then I would apologize.

But I didn't have time to stop at the supermarket, or to craft a carefully worded apology.

I was stuck at work until seven, spent my commute ordering each of my friends' favorite foods, then barely made it home with enough time to shower and pull some wine out of the fridge before my intercom buzzed.

A couple minutes after I let them up, the doorbell rang. I nervously tucked my shorter hair behind my ear before opening the door to all three of my best friends. The girls stared at me in shock when they saw me, but they didn't say anything.

"Hi, come in," I said awkwardly. Judging by their hard stares, they weren't going to make this easy for me, and they didn't have to. I had screwed up and was ready to deal with the consequences.

None of the girls said a word to me as they walked inside, but at least they took a seat on the couch unprompted. There was only room for three on my couch, so I sat on the coffee table facing them.

I wiped my hands on my pants before glancing up at them. "So, the food will be here soon. Would you guys like some wine?"

"We didn't come here to drink," Daisy said, her eyes hard as she peered at me.

"Right." Maybe I should've had a couple of shots beforehand, because I needed some liquid courage right now. I took a deep breath to steady my frayed nerves, then said, "I'm sorry. When I saw Andrew at Daisy's art show—"

Daisy's head shot up, her face draining of color. "What? He was at my art show?"

I nodded, making a point to look at my friends when my impulse was to avert my gaze.

"Is that why you looked so sick?" Amelia asked, frowning. "Why didn't you tell us?"

"Daisy, Rina, and James were talking, and he was behind them, staring at me. I panicked. I could barely hold it together, but I didn't want to ruin Daisy's night."

Rina nodded thoughtfully. "And later? You had plenty of opportunities to tell us."

I couldn't meet her eyes, so I stared at my hands. "I have no excuse, but I'll tell you everything now. A couple of days after seeing Andrew, I decided to leave. A few days later, I ended things with James. When I came home, Andrew was here, casually having a drink in my kitchen. We fought, he hit me, and if James hadn't come in when he did, I'm not sure what would have happened."

"What happened when James showed up?" Rina asked.

"They fought. James kicked him out, then…." The lump in my throat became too big to swallow and I had to pause to gather myself. "He took care of me," I finished, my brows drawing together. It was the best way to summarize it, but it was still painful to say.

"Why leave though? There are other options."

This time, I lifted my eyes to meet Rina's gaze. "What other options? You know I can't call the cops on him and even if I could, I doubt they would do anything."

Daisy's tone was angry when she said, "You *can* call the police. Why are you still trying to protect him?"

"Not him, his parents. They did so much for me. I can't exactly repay them by putting their son in jail."

Amelia placed her hand on my knee, squeezing it lightly. "Cassie, have you ever thought there might be others? Other women he hurt?"

Rina nodded. "If you won't do it for yourself, do it for them. And for any future woman he might get involved with."

I stared blankly at my hands in my lap, wondering how I could have been so selfish, so clueless. It hadn't even crossed my mind that he might hurt other women. And I should know better.

Daisy let out an impatient huff, crossing her arms over her chest. "You felt trapped, and you decided to run. But why didn't you tell us? Fuck, if that was really your only option, we would have helped you pack."

"I didn't want you involved in all the ugliness. What if he came after you?" A shudder went through me at the thought of Andrew hurting my friends. "I thought I was protecting you by leaving you in the dark."

"But we're your friends," Amelia said, squeezing my knee again. "We're supposed to be there for each other, especially during tough times."

I nodded thoughtfully, wishing I'd had time to prepare the right words to convey my jumbled feelings. "After Andrew, being vulnerable, even in front of you, was impossible. How many times have you seen me cry?"

"Never," Daisy said, her brows drawing together as if she'd just now made that realization.

"When my parents died, I was truly devastated. I didn't think twice about opening up to Andrew. It never occurred to me he would use it against me someday. I was open, vulnerable… I needed him, and he took advantage of that for years." I crossed my arms over my chest, releasing a deep sigh. "Now I'm a closed off asshole who'd rather leave forever than be vulnerable with her friends for more than five minutes." I tried to fight it, but tears started slowly creeping down my cheeks. "You know what the fucked up part is? When James came in that day, I wasn't grateful. I was so embarrassed, so ashamed he saw me like that."

"There's nothing for you to be ashamed about," Rina said firmly.

Dismissing her words, I continued, "I felt like it was my burden to carry, my mess, but I also didn't want you to see this side of me. Deep down, even though objectively I know you care about me, I didn't think you'd still like me as a person if you truly knew how broken I am."

"You're not broken," Rina and Amelia said at the same time.

"I am. I tried to pretend I wasn't, but—"

"No," Rina said, "you are not broken. You're a survivor and the strongest person I know."

Shaking my head, I ran the back of my hands over my cheeks, wiping away the tears. "I worked hard to be strong and now look at me! I'm a fucking mess, crying all the damn time…. I never wanted you to see me like this."

Daisy leaned forward to hold my hand. "You're going through so much right now, it's completely normal to be overwhelmed, to cry."

"We're here to support you," Amelia repeated. "You just have to allow us to be here for you."

I took a few deep, calming breaths. "I'm sorry I lied and planned to leave without a word. And I'm sorry for the things I said. I loved Andrew. I loved him and he destroyed me. It took everything I had to walk away and put myself back together. But it's like he kept some pieces of the puzzle so that I'd never be able to be myself again."

"Maybe you're not the same person you used to be," Rina said, "but that's not necessarily a bad thing. God knows I'm not the same woman I was when I was twenty."

"None of us are," Amelia confirmed.

They all laughed at that, and the sound warmed my heart.

The food arrived and put a pause in our conversation. While I answered the door and paid the delivery man, Daisy and Amelia set the table, and Rina poured us white wine. We settled around the table, silently picking at the food, the air around us still heavy.

"Let's address the elephant in the room," Daisy said, turning to face me. I racked my brain for what it could be after all I'd admitted, my gaze flying from girl to girl to try to figure it out. "Cassie's hair."

The girls burst into laughter as I fingered the short strands. "Is it that bad?"

"If you cut bangs, you'll look just like Dora the Explorer," Daisy said.

"It's not that short," I protested.

Amelia made a show of rubbing her belly, then said in an exaggerated Spanish accent, "Yum, yum, yum. Delicioso!"

Laughter filled the room, and I looked at my friends' smiling faces, wondering how I ever thought I could live without them. "So, does that mean you forgive me?"

"I do," Amelia said, as she reached for my hand across the table.

"We all do," Rina said, while Daisy nodded in agreement. "But you can't keep us in the dark again. You have to trust us."

I nodded, tears brimming in my eyes. "Thank you," I said, sniffing. "Is my hair really that bad?"

"No, we're just teasing you," Amelia said. "I liked the long hair, but this length suits you."

Daisy shot me a questioning look. "Why did you cut it? I mean, you've had it long since I met you."

"I had a little bit of a mental breakdown this week." I laughed, the sound a bit jarring to my ears. "I was walking around, saw a salon, and thought, why not? It was time for a change."

"Alright," Rina said, amusement dancing in her eyes. "Any other changes we need to know about?"

"I think I'm quitting my job."

The girls stared at me in silence. Amelia and Daisy's eyes were wide. Rina gave me a knowing look and asked, "Why?"

"It doesn't make me happy." Admitting it out loud made it real, more tangible. My unhappiness was a problem that needed solving, and now that I was aware of it, I could be more proactive. "I want to do something more with my life. I want to help people."

Rina offered me the biggest smile, her stormy eyes shining. "I'm so proud of you."

I returned her smile, then waved her away before fresh tears spilled over. "But enough about me. What have you guys been up to?"

We caught up while we ate. Daisy's show was over and she'd sold eighty percent of her photos, which was fantastic. She shrugged, disappointment clouding her bright blue eyes. "No other opportunities have come from it, though."

"Yet," Rina amended.

A team manager position had opened at Rina's marketing firm and she had applied. Amelia had started looking for another job, ideally one where her boss wasn't a complete jerk. Four days without my friends and I had missed so much. I couldn't imagine a lifetime without them.

"So, what now?" Rina asked as we cleared the table.

"I don't know," I said honestly. "It was hard to start over, and I'm not letting Andrew force me to give up the life I worked so hard for. He hasn't made contact again, and I don't know if he will. Maybe James scared him off. I've already asked Monty to look into him. I guess we'll see what he can uncover and go from there."

Rina shot me a pointed look. "And you'll press charges?"

Bill and Patricia's faces flashed in my mind, giving me pause. "I'll see what Monty says."

Rina stared at me, one eyebrow raised, and Amelia shook her head slightly.

The silence stretched until Daisy broke it. "Have you talked to James?"

"I did," I answered, while I loaded the dishwasher. "He came to the shelter to confront me and we broke up."

Daisy finally looked up from her glass, her eyes brimming with tears. "I'm so sorry, babe. I thought maybe he could convince you to stay."

I offered her a small smile. "Don't worry about it."

"So he couldn't convince you?"

"He didn't try and I can't blame him. I wouldn't put up with my bullshit either," I said, turning my back on them to wash my hands. "I strung him along, and in the end, he told me he loved me and that he wanted me to be safe, so he hired a security team for me. Who does that?"

"A really good person?" Amelia offered. "Besides, it's not like you purposefully set out to hurt him. He's smart enough to see that."

"Exactly," Rina added. "You've been going through a lot and you made some poor choices. It's understandable. What matters now is how you move forward."

I shrugged as I joined them at the table. "I texted him that I wanted to talk, but he didn't reply."

The girls stared at me expectantly, but I had nothing else to add. Rina's sharp gaze zeroed in on me and she said, "What are you going to do about it? Give up?"

"I want to apologize, because that's the least he deserves. But if he really doesn't want to see me, I guess I can't force him. I don't think he'll forgive me," I said, staring at my untouched wine.

"Why not? We did," Amelia pointed out.

"After the day Andrew broke in, he basically moved in because he wanted to keep me safe. He comforted me, fed me.... Fuck, he took care of me. And during all that time, while he held me as I cried, I knew I was leaving."

"The way he looks at you...," Daisy said, her gaze drifting. "I wish someone looked at me like that." She shrugged, and her pouty lips curved up as she focused on me. "There's no way he won't forgive you."

It was more complicated than that, but I didn't say anything else on the subject and neither did they. We chatted and laughed until it got late. As I watched my friends leave, I couldn't have been more grateful for their forgiveness.

Before Rina left, she gave me a quick hug and whispered, "You should call James again." She leaned back to look me in the eye. "Loving people is scary for a lot of reasons, but it's more painful to lose them without even trying."

Later that night, before I went to bed, my finger hovered over James's contact in my phone. I texted him again, reiterating that everything was fine and I just wanted to talk. Half an hour later, he opened the message and I pressed the call button. It rang once, then went straight to voicemail. I hung up and clutched the phone to my chest, the knowledge that James dodged my call settling uncomfortably in the pit of my stomach.

I couldn't even be mad. But I needed to talk to him. In the end, it didn't matter if he wanted nothing to do with me. He deserved an apology, and I would find a way to reach him.

And then, maybe, I could convince him to give me another chance.

CHAPTER THIRTY-THREE

Over the next few days, I tried to call James a dozen times, hoping he'd answer. I made sure to text him beforehand so he'd know it wasn't urgent. But my texts remained unanswered, and my calls went straight to voicemail. Sometimes I let his familiar deep voice caress my ear as he told me to leave a message, but that final beep at the end never failed to chip away at my hope.

Missing James was messing with my head. I had so much to do, but my thoughts kept drifting back to him.

It took some mulling over, several pros and cons lists, and a pep talk from the girls, but I handed in my resignation letter. The partners were surprised, wondering if I'd received a better offer at a competing firm. When I explained I wanted to shift specialties to domestic violence, Sullivan's reaction surprised me. He offered to connect me with a top lawyer in the field.

I thanked him profusely, and by the time I left his office, I felt ten times lighter. Even though it would mean less money, I was sure of my decision.

After work, I made my way to the shelter. There was still a lot to do for the fundraiser, and I wanted to talk to Marie about possibly hiring me. I walked to the subway, and again, the hairs on the back of my neck stood.

It might be anxiety and paranoia, but since Andrew showed up, I only left my place to work or go to the shelter, despite the security team. In the interest of my newfound openness, I told the girls, and they came to my place to hang out so I wouldn't be anxious.

As I walked, I kept glancing over my shoulder and avoided areas with low foot traffic. I missed going on walks in the park, but it was too open. It made me too vulnerable.

I breathed a sigh of relief once I closed the shelter's door safely behind me. I made my way to the office and found Marie, her nose glued to the screen.

"Hi, Marie. Can we talk?"

She lifted her warm brown eyes to take me in and nodded silently. I saw my name on a sticky note on top of a dozen new files and figured this was the perfect opportunity to ask for a job.

Marie turned to me and offered me a small, sad smile. "You're leaving us, aren't you?"

"What? No." I sat opposite her and mentally reviewed some arguments to convince her to hire me. "The opposite, actually. I'm quitting my job, and I was wondering if you would hire me on full time."

Her eyes widened. "Cassandra, you know how much we value you here. But we can't match your current salary."

I smiled, attempting to reassure her. "I know, that's okay. Pay me whatever you can. I just want to help people."

"Honey, you already do," she said softly. "I know something is going on with you lately and you missed a few updates. That idea you had for a 'How to Succeed in an Interview' class? Nine out of the fourteen women who attended managed to secure a job, and two of them are on the verge of moving to their own apartments."

I grinned at the news, my eyes burning a little. "That's great to hear! Rina is great, isn't she?"

"She is, but it was your idea. We've already received more donations for the clothing drive this year than last year, and if this fundraiser goes well, we won't be struggling to keep a roof over our heads next year."

"It will go well," I said, pulling out my phone to show her

pictures of Oasis. "I've already secured a nice spot, and help from people who know wealthy donors."

"I have no doubt you'll do an amazing job. That's what I've been trying to tell you," Marie said, leaning back in her chair. "Your ideas and all the work you do are making the shelter thrive. Not to mention all the cases you've handled. You've put a lot of abusers behind bars and kept so many families together. I can't pay you what you deserve, but whatever position I can offer you, it's yours."

Tears brimmed in my eyes as I stared at her, dumbfounded. "I'm so sorry," I said, blinking. "I've been so emotional lately. I don't know what's wrong with me."

Marie smiled, kindness and understanding shining in her eyes. "Whatever you're going through, can I help?"

My first instinct was to say no. I didn't need to involve another person in my mess. But Marie had always been so kind to me, and I was trying to be more honest. Plus, helping domestic violence survivors was literally her job. "Not surprisingly, I guess, I have an abusive ex-boyfriend and he made a comeback."

Her smile fell, and she leaned forward, concerned. "What do you need?"

I sighed. "Nothing. I don't actually know what I'm going to do." Taking a deep breath, I gave her the short version.

Once I was done, Marie's lips were set in a straight line, her eyes filled with concern. "You need to press charges," she said. I opened my mouth to say something, but she stopped me. "It doesn't bode well that he found you after seven years, Cassie. I know you have your reasons for not involving the police, but you've seen enough cases to know better."

I looked down at my lap, my cheeks burning with embarrassment. "I know."

Marie grasped my hand in hers. "He's already assaulted you once. What do you think will happen when he finds you again?"

When, not if. Marie was sure he'd come back, and I had a feeling she was right.

"I hired a private investigator to look into it," I said, letting her assume I would use whatever information Monty dug up to build a case against Andrew. It wasn't exactly a lie, but I couldn't explain my irrationality without sharing a lot more than I was willing to.

"Good," she said. "Now about the job. Let me talk to our accountant and I'll come back to you with some numbers."

I nodded and thanked her for everything, and then we got to work. While I sorted through donation bags, Marie updated me on everything I had missed. We discussed potential dates for the fundraiser and where to allocate the funds.

"We received a large donation from the Waltons, so we'll use that to fix the roof."

My breath caught in my lungs. Maybe I had heard her wrong. "The Waltons?"

"Yes, they're old New York money. They donate a lot to charity."

I could feel the blood draining from my face. "When was this?"

She gave me a puzzled look. "A couple of weeks ago. You said Elisabeth Walton was helping with the fundraiser, so I thought it was connected...."

Marie kept talking, but her words fell on deaf ears. Two weeks ago. That was around the time Andrew showed up and I told James everything. I couldn't breathe.

Excusing myself, I escaped to the bathroom to calm down. I needed to talk to James. To apologize, to thank him. Not only for the donation, but for everything he'd done for me.

In a desperate move, I clutched my phone in my hand and called Elias. I needed to talk to him about the fundraiser anyway, but maybe he could help me reach James.

"Cassandra," he drawled in his posh British accent.

"Hi! We finally have a date for the fundraiser if you're still willing to help," I said, skipping pleasantries.

"Of course! My word is a contract."

I paused at that. Maybe since James and I were no longer involved, Elias had no interest in helping. "I know you said you would help, but you don't have to. Honestly, we can find a different space."

"What's the date, Cassandra?" From his tone, I could almost see him roll his eyes.

"I have two potential dates for you, November twenty-second or twenty-nine. Either works perfectly for us, so it's up to you."

"Twenty-nine it is. When can I take a look at the clothes? I need to see what I'm selling."

"Can you meet me at the shelter on Monday? I'll have to see if Elisabeth is available since she wanted to help organize the event."

"I'll text Lizzy. Around five?"

"Perfect," I said, trying to find an opening but running out of time.

"All right, see you then, darling."

"Elias," I said before he could hang up.

The silence stretched between us until finally he said, "Yes?"

"Have you heard from James? I've been trying to call him, but I can't reach him."

Elias's boisterous laughter felt like tiny needles prickling at my heart. "Oh, no, darling. I'm not getting involved. Ciao, Cassie." The line went dead.

I stared at my phone, pondering my next step. For now, I had to put it out of my mind and go back to work. There was a lot to be done, and I didn't want Marie to think I was slacking now that she might hire me.

A few hours later, I called a car service to go home. There was no way I was walking around alone at night, even with James's security watching from a distance. After verifying the driver's identity, I slipped into the car, my shoulders sagging. By the time I locked my door securely behind me, exhaustion weighed me down and all I wanted was to crawl into bed.

But I wanted to crawl into bed with James, not alone. I wanted to feel his arms around me, to bury my face in his neck and inhale his scent.

Ignoring the little voice that told me not to do it, I settled on the couch and entered 'James Walton' in my search engine. The first results were photos of James with beautiful women on his arm at several events, and there I was among them, smiling at the camera.

This was probably the picture Andrew had seen.

My fingers scrolled through the images before I could stop myself, checking for recent pictures. Maybe he'd moved on and that was why I couldn't reach him. I had no right to be jealous, but I breathed a little easier when I saw the most recent photos were with me. I clicked on one, my eyes tearing up at the sight.

It was from his birthday party, but not one of the pictures we had posed for. This one was taken when we were dancing. James had his hand firmly around my waist, our bodies pressed together. We stared into each other's eyes, a playful smirk on his lips while I smiled brightly up at him.

I looked… happy.

For a second, I contemplated walking to his penthouse and camping outside until he showed up. But I still had my pride, and making a scene in front of his building was not in my future. Sighing, I crawled into bed, clutching the pillow that still smelled like him to my chest.

As I stared at the ceiling, surrounded by his scent and haunted by his absence, a desperate idea came to life in my head. Elias and Elisabeth were meeting me at the shelter on Monday. It would be the perfect opportunity for a last-ditch effort.

CHAPTER THIRTY-FOUR

The clock ticked painfully slowly as I pretended to answer emails, my gaze flitting to the shelter's door every few seconds. After over a dozen unanswered messages and calls, the idea I had formulated late at night when I couldn't sleep seemed to be my only choice.

Elias and Elisabeth showed up a little after five, accompanied by two large men. The three men carried bags while Elisabeth sauntered in wearing a gorgeous white wrap dress. It made her raven hair appear even darker.

"Cassandra," Elisabeth greeted in a cheery voice. She kissed my cheek as if we were the best of friends and pointed to the men carrying bags. "I corralled my friends and family into donating. I hope that's okay."

I returned her smile. "Of course. The more the better."

"You won't say that when you see the truck outside," Elias grumbled as he set his bags down.

My eyes widened. "Truck?"

Elisabeth gave me a sheepish look. "Things got a little out of hand. I already had a few bags, but then Mom mentioned it at the club and things escalated from there."

"That's okay. I'm sure Elias here will manage to auction everything off."

Elias shot me a look and was probably about to say something cheeky when Marie walked in. Her brows drew together in confusion as she took in Elias's impeccable suit, Elisabeth in head to toe Chanel, and the two burly men next to them.

"Marie, this is Elisabeth Walton and Elias Coulson." I had already filled her in on their generosity and their roles in putting together the fundraiser. She introduced herself and thanked them repeatedly for their help before her gaze turned to the two burly men.

I shrugged at her questioning look, and Elisabeth was quick to introduce them as Marco and Cameron, her security.

"They're also here to help unload," she added quickly as her cheeks turned pink.

Marie asked some residents to help, and in no time the office floor and the hallway leading to it were covered in bags. Elisabeth, Elias, Marie, and I sat in the crowded space to go over the plans for the auction.

"I've got twenty models, but if necessary I can find more," Elias said. "The DJ is booked. I've got valets and waiting staff lined up." He paused, looking over the checklist on my screen. "We're going to raise a decent amount of money."

I took in Marie's wide eyes, knowing exactly what she was thinking. "Elias, we can't afford to hire valets and servers, or a DJ."

Elias waved a dismissive hand. "It's on me. I told you I'd be planning this for a reason. You need to spend money to make money. Plus, the models are all volunteers, and everyone else works for me."

"Some of my friends are willing to model, too," Elisabeth added.

My eyes burned at their generosity, and I hated that I was still a crying mess. It spoke volumes to James's character that even after I treated him like dirt, his best friend and sister were here, helping me put this event together.

Maybe this meant I had a chance. I just needed to get Elisabeth alone. We spent over an hour planning, and once we were done, I thought I had missed my chance, but then Marie offered to give them a tour of the shelter.

I followed behind them, waiting for an opportunity to get her alone. Finally, she asked if she could use the restroom and I gladly offered to take her. As the rest of the group went on without us, I led James's sister down a side hallway, gathering my nerve and the words I'd need to bring her over to my side. It was time to ask for a favor.

CHAPTER THIRTY-FIVE

The next day, I met up with Elisabeth around eleven, and we made our way to Walton Corporation together. My heart hammered in my chest as we rode the elevator to the top floor, and I actually felt like I was going to throw up. I couldn't remember being this nervous since the first time I went to court.

James's sister must have sensed my nervousness, because she reached out and squeezed my arm reassuringly. Her quiet presence beside me was the only thing keeping me together. If I'd been alone, I would've been hyperventilating.

Each step brought me closer to facing him, to owning up to my mistakes and asking for forgiveness. My fingers tightened around the bag containing the necklace. I didn't know how he'd react to me returning it, but I couldn't keep it. It was ridiculously expensive, and since I would never sell it, keeping it was a liability.

Elisabeth led the way as we exited the elevator. Our steps echoed on the marble floors as we passed the reception area and walked deeper into the building.

We made it to another reception area, where a woman in her early forties greeted us warmly. Elisabeth introduced me and chatted with her for a beat as I stared at the door separating me from James with apprehension. I was so lost in my own thoughts, I didn't even catch her name.

"Is my brother in? We're meeting for lunch," Elisabeth said casually.

The woman smiled and gestured toward the door. "He's expecting you."

Elisabeth knocked lightly on the door, and I heard his deep voice for the first time in over two weeks. Butterflies danced in my stomach in response, and I stood on wobbly knees as she cracked the door open. With an encouraging smile, she nudged me forward, and I squared my shoulders before stepping into his office. No matter how this ended, giving up now was not an option.

The second I crossed the threshold, James's familiar scent tickled my nose, and my heart came to a crashing halt before it started pounding wildly against my chest. He was sitting behind his desk, his face hidden behind two screens. When the door shut behind me, he lifted his head with a smile, but it crumbled when our eyes met. His eyebrows lifted in surprise for a split second before his gaze traveled once up and down my body, as if checking for injuries.

"You grew a beard," I blurted out.

This wasn't exactly what I had planned to open with, but my brain short-circuited. The short beard accentuated his sharp jaw and somehow made his piercing brown eyes even darker. I stared at his beautiful face, trying to catch my breath.

"Cassandra," he said, pushing to his feet with a sense of urgency in his movements. "What are you doing here? Is everything okay?"

I stepped further into his office and offered him a reassuring smile. "Everything's fine. I just wanted to talk to you."

The concern faded from his eyes and was quickly replaced by an icy glare that pinned me in place. He didn't want to see me, that much was clear. When he spoke again, his tone was flat, emotionless. "How did you get in here?"

"Your sister," I murmured, unable to speak up.

James shook his head and returned to his chair. "I'm busy."

He had every right to give me the cold shoulder, and I was prepared for rejection. *You can do this*, I told myself. Lifting my chin, I walked the few steps to his desk and took a seat on the plush white chair across from him, trying to emulate that quiet confidence that always radiated from him. "I know for a fact you're free for the next hour."

He scoffed as he arranged some papers on his desk. "I was free for my sister, not for you."

His words cut like glass, slicing into my wounded heart. I remembered the time he said he'd always make time for me and it made me panic a little. Now that was all I wanted. Time with James.

Taking a deep breath to steel myself, I met his unflinching gaze and said, "I came to apologize. I was awful to you, and you deserve better. I'm sorry."

James stared at me, his expression unreadable. He was usually so open around me, it hurt to see him so closed off. I was sitting right across from him, but the distance between us felt unsurmountable.

"Thank you for the apology. Now, if that's all, I have work to do." He reached for his desk phone and pressed a button. "My assistant will see you out. Call Paul if you need anything."

He was dismissing me. *Shit.* Panic surged through my veins and I twisted over his desk to end the call, leaving James staring at me with his mouth hanging open.

"Cassandra—"

"I'm not done," I said, cutting him off. There was so much I wanted to say, and since this would likely be my only opportunity, I wasn't about to waste it. "You don't want to talk to me. I get it. You don't have to say anything. Just listen. And if at the end you still want nothing to do with me, I promise I'll leave you alone."

James stared at me, a flicker of warmth returning to his eyes. He settled back in his chair and made a 'proceed' gesture with his hand. It wasn't the most encouraging overture, but I pressed on.

"I don't want to make this about Andrew, but it's hard to explain myself without mentioning him. Our relationship wasn't always abusive and violent. He was sweet and caring when he wanted to be." Blood rushed in my ears as I confessed my deepest fears, the words tumbling awkwardly from my lips. "It made me distrust people, question their sincerity, their motives. Abusers don't have it tattooed on their foreheads. I was scared that your niceness, your kindness and generosity, were nothing but a façade."

James remained silent, his gaze boring deep into my soul. Vulnerability wasn't my forte, but I didn't conceal anything. All the turmoil from the last few weeks, my fear and confusion… my pain. My feelings were stamped across my face for him to see.

"I've built these walls around me," I continued, "and refused to let myself develop feelings for anyone, because if I did and they turned out to be like Andrew, how could I survive that again? And what would it say about *me* that these are the partners I choose?"

The words tumbled from my lips in quick succession, as if I was ripping off a Band-Aid. If I let myself think about it, I'd be too mortified to say them out loud. James's expression softened a little, the stiffness in his shoulders decreasing a fraction. My eyes stung, but I fought to keep it together. There was so much I wanted to say, and I couldn't do it through sobs.

I swallowed past the lump in my throat, fighting the tears to get the next words out. "But when Andrew broke into my apartment, you were there for me. I felt so exposed, so vulnerable, and you held me together even as I pushed you away. I should've told you I was leaving, but you made me feel so cherished, so loved and protected. It was selfish, but I wanted to feel that way a little longer, so I strung you along."

James nudged a box of tissues in my direction, his lips set in a thin line. I mouthed a thank you before wiping away the tears. Despite my confessions, he remained completely composed, his posture rigid and his jaw tight.

This ominous feeling twisted in my stomach, and I wondered if I was saying the wrong things. I fiddled with the bag sitting on my lap and licked my parched lips. That little voice in my head told me it was too little, too late. That James didn't want me anymore.

I'd been denying my burgeoning feelings for weeks, afraid of being vulnerable, of being hurt. But sometimes, you just have to do things scared.

"It was unfair of me to keep pushing you away, to keep pretending our connection was nothing but sexual when it's always been more. I was scared. I am still scared," I said, finding his eyes through a hazy cloud of tears. "Since we broke up, I've had to actively force myself not to think about you. Because if I did, I would think about waking up to your face on the pillow next to mine, about morning coffee and easy laughter, and about how when you hug me it feels like everything will be right in the world. And I couldn't let those thoughts in, knowing I'd never see you again."

Finally, James's composure crumbled, and his eyebrows drew into a frown. It wasn't exactly the reaction I was hoping for, but it was better than nothing. Tears flowed freely down my cheeks, and I reached for another tissue to wipe them away before I became a slobbering mess.

I had told myself I was prepared for rejection, that I could handle it.

Lies, so many lies.

When I lifted my head again, James was studying me carefully. I sat up and cleared my throat, trying to put as much meaning behind my words as possible. "I won't let my fears dictate my life anymore, James. Falling for you has been terrifying, but I'm more scared of never telling you how I feel and always wondering if we could've had a future together." Shrugging, I finished awkwardly with, "I had to shoot my shot."

He released a long breath as he roughly threaded his fingers through his hair. "What do you want, Cassandra?"

"You," I said, my voice as small as I felt.

James leaned back in his chair and folded his arms across his chest, his eyes still guarded. "You want me?"

"Yes. I want you," I repeated firmly, hope rising in my chest.

He cocked his head to one side, and my heart skipped a beat when his lips slowly stretched into a small smile. "What are you proposing, exactly?"

Something between a sob and a chuckle escaped my lips as his raspy words brought me back to that first day in my office when I had asked him the exact same question.

Gathering myself, I said, "A boyfriend and girlfriend agreement."

Finally, his lips stretched into a full smile, and hope swelled in my chest. "Boyfriend and girlfriend, huh?"

I let out a shaky breath and repeated, "Yes, boyfriend and girlfriend."

James leaned forward, decreasing the distance between us. "That's an interesting offer, Cassandra. However, before we reach an agreement, there are a few details I'd like to iron out."

He still wants me. My pulse raced as I sat up, noticing for the first time how comfortable the chair was, and squared my shoulders. "What do you have in mind?"

"First, I want you to move in with me. We can circle back once the situation with your ex is resolved, but until then, I want to be sure you're safe."

My lips lifted into a cheeky smirk as a wave of relief washed over me. "Do I get my own bedroom?"

"No," James said firmly, pinning me with a look that left no room for argument. "I want you in my bed, our bed. And every night I want to fall asleep with your soft body pressed against mine, and every morning I want to wake you up with my head between your legs."

"Deal," I said, biting my lip at the mental picture. "I would also love to wake you up with your cock in my mouth."

"You're incorrigible," he said, shaking his head, but he couldn't fight the smile tugging at his lips. "The security team stays."

"Agreed." It was reassuring to know that if Andrew approached me in public, someone would be there to protect me. "Anything else?"

His lips lifted into a dazzling smirk as he offered me his hand to shake. "Should we seal the deal?"

I pushed to my feet and placed my hand in his, reveling in the jolt of electricity traveling from his palm straight to my heart. A wide grin spread across his face as he clasped my hand in his and I pulled him towards me over his desk. "A kiss to seal the deal would be more appropriate, don't you think?"

His gaze dropped to my mouth, and I couldn't wait any longer. I inched forward to brush my lips against his. It was nothing, barely a touch, but I felt it all over my body. A tingling sensation that stole my breath away and filled my veins with liquid fire all at once.

James immediately responded, his lips brushing softly against mine, his tongue coaxing my lips apart, our hands still clasped together. The edge of his desk dug into my thighs as I leaned over it, trying to get closer. I craved his taste, his scent, his touch. I ran my fingers over his jaw, basking in the feel of his short beard against my palm.

A part of me couldn't believe that this was really happening, that James still wanted me. "I've missed you so much," I whispered against his lips. "Can you forgive me?"

He pressed his forehead against mine, our heavy breaths mingling. "Of course, gorgeous."

James pulled back and rounded his desk. I met him halfway and threw myself into his open arms, immediately burying my face into his neck and inhaling deeply. Warmth filled my chest as familiar notes of sandalwood and amber inundated my senses, and a sense of peace washed over me.

Home. He feels like home.

He held me tightly in his arms, one hand around my waist, the other cradling the back of my neck. "Fuck, I missed you."

I clung to him tighter, my fingers digging into his back.

"Every time you called, all I wanted was to run to you, to hold you like this again. But I knew if I heard your voice, if I saw you again…. I couldn't let you in and risk saying goodbye again, Cassie." He took a deep breath and stared deep into my eyes. "So, with that in mind, are you sure about this? About us?"

With a shuddering breath, I stepped back to look at him. The pained expression on his face was too much to bear. I hated that I had put it there. "I'm sure, James. If you'll have me, I'm not going anywhere." I reached up to smooth the tension lines between his brows, my fingers trailing over his cheekbones, his straight nose. "But is this really what *you* want? I have so much baggage and trauma, it's bound to affect our relationship."

"I want all of you, Cassandra. My life, my world, is dull and lifeless without you. I feel like I can take a full breath for the first time in weeks."

"I'm all yours," I said, lost in his deep brown eyes.

Happiness shone unbridled in his gaze as he smiled from ear to ear. He cupped my face with both hands and said, "And I'm yours."

My smile widened as happy tears flowed down my cheeks, and I pressed my palm against his heart, anchoring myself in the moment so I'd never forget it. I slid my hand under his suit jacket and stepped in between his feet, erasing the distance between us.

James cupped the back of neck to pull me even closer, his nose brushing against my cheek as his mouth found mine. I parted my lips, welcoming each stroke of his tongue. His grip on my waist tightened, and he angled my head to the side to deepen the kiss.

The feel of his warm, muscular body pressed against mine was heavenly familiar. I never wanted to let him go, ever again. He angled his head back a little, our breaths mingling together as we paused for air.

"As much as I never want to stop kissing you, we should talk," he said, guiding me towards a couch on the opposite side of his office. "Would you like some water?"

I nodded, and James moved to grab a bottle from a mini-fridge under the bar. His office was incredible, but I had been too preoccupied to notice. Floor-to-ceiling windows gave the room a panoramic view of New York that belonged on postcards. A creamy white couch with a coffee table and two matching armchairs sat on the far side of the room. His desk was to the right, facing the view.

That made me smile. I had been in many fancy offices, and the CEOs usually had their backs to the view. It was a status symbol, used to intimate and show dominance. But James seemed to actually want to admire the view.

James pointed towards the bag I'd abandoned in my chair. "What's that?"

"The necklace," I said. "It's far too expensive to keep in my unused pots, so I thought I'd return it to you."

He grabbed the bag, and we sat side by side on the plushy white couch. He handed me a water bottle, and while I took a long sip, he said, "We'll put it back in the safe when we get home."

My body tingled with excitement at his choice of words. "You feel like home," I said, reaching for his hand. Time seemed to slow as our eyes locked, the adoration shining unguarded in his dark gaze stealing my breath away.

"You scared me," he continued. "After that day, it was like you weren't even there. You put on a smile, but your eyes…." He cupped my face with one hand and I leaned into his touch. "The spark is back now," he continued, as he leaned a little closer, his eyebrows drawing together in concern, "but are you really okay, Cassie?"

I took a deep, shaky breath and leaned against his shoulder. "Honestly, I am not." Admitting it felt wrong. I was so used to pretending everything was fine all the time. "This whole situation with my ex is terrifying. I don't know how long he's been stalking me or what he'll do." I glanced up at him and planted a kiss against his jaw. "But I will be. I already feel much better."

James pressed me a little closer, his hand drawing soothing circles on my back. "What can we do? There must be something."

"I'll file a report and get a protective order, but I want to warn his parents first."

"Okay," he breathed. "And in the meantime, you'll be safe at the penthouse, and security is on high alert. We'll get through this together."

"Thank you," I said, squeezing him tighter. "I don't know if I would've gone to work without the safety net of having security around."

"There's no need to thank me, gorgeous. I'd do anything to keep you safe." He propped my chin up with his thumb and index finger, and I sat up a little when I saw his earnest expression. "You said you were scared I'm putting up a front, and I get it. But I always mean what I say, Cassie, and what you see is what you get. It's not an act."

"I know," I whispered, wishing I could infuse more certainty into my words. The little voice in the back of my head that told me anyone could be an abuser was still there, but I wasn't convinced it was a negative thing.

Maybe instinct wasn't innate, but something that developed with experience. I didn't have enough life experience before Andrew to have that instinct, that gut feeling that told you something's off about a person. But I did now, and not a single bone in my body told me I should be wary of James.

"Come on," he said, offering me his hand. "I'm taking you home."

We walked out of his office hand in hand, the goofy smile on my face refusing to fade. Elisabeth was long gone, and James hastily told his assistant to cancel all his appointments for the day before leading me to his car.

My heart felt too full, and I couldn't stop grinning as James played one of the cassettes I gave him, and we sang along as we drove to his penthouse. I stared at his beautiful profile, that quiet confidence radiating off him.

It was surreal to be here with him, his hand casually squeezing my thigh.

James forgave me. And he still wanted me.

Yes, I thought as we drove on, *some things are truly worth the risk.*

CHAPTER THIRTY-SIX

I t was a quick drive to James's penthouse. He parked and we made our way to the elevator, hand in hand. My heart beat a mile a minute as we rode up to his apartment, the air around us thick with promise. I fiddled with the buttons of my blouse, fighting against the fluttery feeling in my stomach. My palms started getting clammy, and I let go of James's hand before he noticed.

I was surprised at how nervous I felt. This was James. There was no need to be nervous, I knew that, but as we stepped off the elevator, I couldn't shake this feeling in the pit of my stomach.

"Hey," James said, pinning me gently against the wall, "what's going on in that gorgeous head of yours?"

My first instinct was to laugh it off, to change the subject, but I knew I couldn't do that. "I'm nervous," I admitted.

James ran his nose down my cheek, sending a shiver down my spine. "Why?"

I shrugged. "Hooking up was one thing, but this is more. I'm not used to it, I guess."

"It is more," James said, his eyes locked on mine. "I didn't bring you home to pounce on you. You've had a lot of traumatic events in the last few weeks, so sex being off the table is completely normal.

But we don't need to have sex to be intimate. I just want to hold you."

I bit down on my lip. His understanding of my needs was the greatest aphrodisiac of all. My voice was thick with desire as I said, "Pouncing sounds good."

"I know, gorgeous," he said with a chuckle, "but we have all the time in the world. There's no rush. I'm happy just cuddling on the couch with you."

Once more, my heart felt too big for my chest. I grinned at him, letting him see just how happy he made me. "We can cuddle after."

With that, I stood on tiptoes and trapped his bottom lip between my teeth. A growl from deep in his throat escaped his lips, the guttural sound sending a tingle down my spine.

Finally, James captured my lips, his expert tongue against mine spreading warmth all over my body. He wedged a leg between my thighs, pressing his pelvis against mine while his hands moved up my ribcage, his thumbs brushing the sides of my breasts.

When I moaned into his mouth, he pulled back and shot me a cocky grin. "Upstairs?"

"Yes," I panted, clawing at his chest.

James smirked and stepped back to throw me over his shoulder. I let out a delighted squeal, taking advantage of this position to admire his toned butt as he climbed the stairs. He laid me gently on the bed and stood over me, his burning gaze sweeping over my body with unprecedented hunger.

When I walked into his office earlier, I'd been fully prepared for rejection, but I had still planned for victory. Underneath my pencil skirt and turtleneck blouse, I wore a matching white lace bra and thong, paired with a white harness set that criss-crossed all over my body. The top straps wrapped around my shoulders and throat, and the bottom had a garter belt I paired with thigh-high stockings to complete the look.

It had been a while since James had seen me naked, and I couldn't wait to see his reaction. I pushed to my feet and peeled off my blouse, watching him watch me as I revealed the outfit. He stood stock still, dark eyes devouring every inch of skin I uncovered.

Pushing to my feet, I unzipped my pencil skirt and let it fall to the floor, keeping my heels on as I stepped out of it.

James drank me in, his gaze lingering a little too long on the fading bruise on my side. "Does it hurt?"

I frowned. I understood his concern, but that wasn't where I wanted his mind to be as I stood in sexy lingerie in front of him. "Not anymore. The bruises just take a while to disappear."

James stepped forward and brushed the tip of his finger along my ribs, causing goosebumps to spread all over my skin. My chest heaved as he traced the edges of my lacy bra, teasing me, driving me crazy. He wedged a finger under the strap criss-crossing over my chest and snapped it playfully, the stinging sensation traveling straight to my clit.

"You're breathtaking," he said as he unhooked my bra. He slipped the straps over my shoulders and let it fall to the floor before kneeling in front of me. "You have no idea the filthy things I dreamed of doing to you." He hooked his fingers in my thong and slowly dragged it down my legs. "Now you're here and I don't know where to start."

He strode towards the bed and grabbed the simple black jewelry box. I hadn't even noticed he'd brought it with us. Then he stood behind me, his hard cock pressing against my back as he fastened the necklace. Its weight settled on my collarbone, and I brushed my fingers against the emerald, wondering what he was doing.

"Just fulfilling that fantasy of yours," he answered my unvoiced question. "It's not a pile of gold we can dive into, and I'm missing a few gold chains, but like you said, it's ridiculously expensive." His breath brushed against my ear as he spoke, sending a delicious tingling sensation down my spine. "I have some cash I could throw on the bed but that doesn't seem very hygienic."

My shoulders shook with laughter. "I can't believe you remember that," I said, surprised he recalled a silly thing I'd told him the first time I came over. This man was beyond anything I'd ever dreamed of, and I still couldn't believe he was all mine.

He wrapped his arms around me from behind and rested his chin on my shoulder. "I want to make all your dreams come true."

Turning around in his arms, I let out a shaky breath as I reached to caress his cheek. "You're so good to me, words fail me," I said honestly, "but maybe I can show you." My body ached for him, for his touch. But I also needed to touch *him*, to feel his warm, solid chest beneath my trembling palms. I reached to unbutton his shirt, but he wrapped his hand around my wrist to stop me.

"Not yet," he said in a husky tone, bringing my hand up to his lips to brush a kiss over my knuckles. "I want to maintain a semblance of control, and I can't do that if you touch me."

"But I want to touch you. I want you to lose control." My voice was breathy with need, and I didn't care. I wanted James to wrap his hand around my throat, throw me on the bed, and ravage me.

A devilish smirk stretched his lips as he bent to cup my face. "So impatient."

In one movement, he picked me up and dropped me on my back on the soft sheets. My breasts jiggled as I bounced on the mattress, and James growled as his eyes followed the movement. He trailed the glittering diamonds resting against my collarbone with the tips of his fingers before centering the emerald perfectly between the swell of my breasts.

"You're so beautiful, diamonds pale in comparison," he said, his fingers moving up the column of my neck to cup my jaw. My cheeks burned in response, and an amused smile quirked his lips. "Will you also blush when I tell you how many times I fisted my cock to memories of you? Of your sweet little cunt swallowing my cock?"

Breathless, I stared up at him, completely drunk on lust. His words stoked the fire already burning inside of me, making me want him impossibly more. "Do whatever you want to me," I said, my gaze locked on him.

James's eyes darkened, and a low growl slipped from his lips, but to my dismay, he pulled back to remove his suit jacket. He stood over me, a fire burning in his gaze as it raced over every curve of my body, making me press my thighs together.

He had barely touched me and I was already dripping wet.

Once the jacket was off, he rolled up his sleeves as if he was getting ready to work before crawling on top of me. The blue silk tie dangling from his neck brushed against my bare thighs, tickling my sensitive skin.

I reached for him, threading my fingers through his soft hair, guiding his lips to mine. He propped himself up on his elbow, his full lips moving slowly against mine as he cupped my face. It wasn't enough. I wrapped my legs around his hips, pulling his weight down on top of me. James groaned when his hard cock and my pussy aligned and I tried to grind against his hardness.

"Patience, gorgeous," he rumbled against my skin. His hand traveled down my side, brushing over the curve of my breast and hip to cup my ass. He squeezed my flesh, lifting my hips to rub his trouser-clad cock against my bare pussy. I threw my head back, moaning as he hit the right spot.

James trailed kisses down my throat, his beard tickling my soft skin. I couldn't wait to feel it tickling me elsewhere. He traced my collarbone with his tongue, his hand coming back up to massage my breast. His tongue circled my nipple again and again, without actually touching it.

It was torture. Pure, carnal torture.

"James, please," I moaned, tugging his hair to push his face into my breasts.

He responded with a quick flick of his tongue on my taut nipple. My breath hitched at the contact, wetness trickling down my pussy. He placed one leg between my thighs, and my hips jerked up and down as I rubbed my clit against his soft wool pants, my body already desperate for release. He continued his torture, flicking his tongue over one hard nipple over and over, while he massaged my other breast. His touch was light, airy, adoring.

It was too much and not enough.

I wanted James to consume me, to bury himself so deep inside of me I'd feel him for a week. But more importantly, I needed him to want me like before. Before he knew about Andrew.

I brought his hand up to my throat, and James stilled on top of me. "You're being too gentle," I said, chewing on my lip in frustration.

James's fingers flexed once around my throat. "I understand, but I haven't tasted you in a while." He licked around my pierced nipple, pinching the other between his thumb and index finger. "So if I want to worship every inch of your body, and do it slowly," he said, licking a path down my stomach, "I will."

He kneeled on the floor and grabbed me by the back of the knees to pull me towards him. "Open your legs for me, gorgeous."

I spread my legs open, and James groaned. His eyes darkened as he stared at my glistening folds, his breath coming out in short pants. He pressed his thumb against my slit, then dragged it up, spreading my juices all over my center. Then he started oh-so-slowly dragging his thumb up and down, licking his lips as he watched me quiver under his touch.

The sight of him looking at me like that was too much to bear. I needed release, and I needed it now. "James, please," I begged, lifting my hips.

That devilish smirk stretched his lips again, his eyes so dark I could barely see the brown in them. "Lie back and enjoy it like a good girl." He disappeared between my legs, his warm, wet tongue licking a trail of hot lava down my pussy. "Can you do that for me, gorgeous?"

My hips buckled at the pressure of his tongue on my clit, pleasure coiling tightly in my core. "Yes," I moaned.

James hooked his arms under my knees, his palms pressing down on my lower belly. "Fuck, I missed your taste," he said, his tongue lapping at my entrance. He pulled back and watched as he pushed a finger inside me. "I love how wet you get for me."

I gasped when he added a second finger, then blew softly on my clit. Warmth pooled in my core, and I lifted my hips to meet his lips, eager for more. With a wicked grin, James obliged.

He pressed his mouth against my pussy, his beard tickling my labia as he ate me out like this was his last chance, licking and sucking until all I could do was whimper and beg for more. My walls vibrated around his fingers as he pumped in and out, his movements slow and deliberate, the pad of one finger brushing against my G-spot.

I groaned, arching my back as my head lolled back. One of my heels slipped off my foot and clattered on the ground, and I made quick work of shaking the other shoe off. His hand moved up to squeeze my breast, and I gripped his corded forearm, desperate to touch him.

"Please," I begged, unsure what I was begging for but certain James would deliver. I felt him smile against my swollen lips, and then he sucked my clit into his mouth at the same time as he pressed down on my G-spot.

I groaned, fisting the sheets as my thighs trembled around him. I was amazed at how well he knew my body, at the intensity of pleasure he could extract from it. His name rolled off my tongue over and over, the pressure building in my core until I couldn't take it anymore. My muscles tensed, and my pussy quivered against his lips.

He continued his torture, increasing the pressure on my clit and pressing down on my lower belly. A powerful orgasm ripped through me. My inner walls clenched around his fingers. Hot, fiery pleasure coursed through my veins, until all I could do was whimper.

Warmth spread all over my body as wave after wave of pleasure consumed me. I didn't have a coherent thought in my head. All I could focus on was James's tongue brushing against my clit, his fingers pressing against that place inside of me, blinding me with pleasure.

Eventually, James stopped his sweet torture and slowly slid his fingers out of me. I groaned, regretting his absence the second he was gone, but he gathered my trembling body against his and sat back against the headboard. His fingers traced my cheekbones, and I closed my eyes to enjoy the soft caress.

"I never thought I would have you in my arms again," he said, his heart racing wildly beneath my palm.

"Me neither." A month ago, his affection would've sent me running, but now I wrapped an arm around his waist, nuzzling his neck. I was desperate to feel his warm skin beneath my palms. "You're overdressed," I said, sneaking two fingers between his shirt buttons to tug on the little hairs on his chest.

"Before you have your way with me, I want to tell you something, two things actually. Just fight the instinct to run, please."

I could tell from his tone that this was important. My legs were still shaking, but I straddled his lap to face him. "No running," I said firmly, holding his gaze. With shaky fingers, I started undoing his buttons to reveal his glorious chest.

James planted his hand on my hips, snapping one of the straps criss-crossing over my body to get my attention. "I want to fuck you raw," he said, lips still glistening with my juices. He shrugged as I looked at him with wide eyes. "I've never done it, and I want to fill you up with my cum, feel your pussy squeeze my bare dick instead of my fingers. If not today, then some other time."

Swallowing the lump in my throat, I took a fistful of his hair and brought his mouth to mine, tasting myself on his lips. I kissed him with all I had, all the feelings I couldn't verbalize. At a loss for words, I reached down between us and unbuckled his belt.

"Deal," I said, palming him through his pants. I was on birth control and I trusted James. The thought of his bare cock stretching me felt wicked, as if we were about to do something that wasn't allowed. "What's the other thing?"

"I'll tell you later," he said, his voice deep and breathy.

Smiling, I undid his button and fly, then turned around and crawled towards the end of the bed on all fours, giving him a perfect view of my pussy and asshole.

"You'll be the death of me," James growled as I removed his shoes and socks, then pulled his pants down. He helped me by lifting his hips, then shrugged off his shirt.

I kneeled between his feet, biting my lip as I took in his thick, powerful legs, his trademark black boxers struggling to contain his erection. "Only small deaths," I said, as I lowered his boxers and wrapped my hand around his throbbing head.

"Cassie," he breathed.

I tore my gaze away from his gorgeous cock to take in his expression. His deep brown eyes shone with an enticing mixture of lust and adoration. It was the hottest look I'd ever seen, so I held his gaze as I ran the tip of my tongue over my top lip, then gave his head a tentative lick.

James groaned, the sound low in his throat. I did it again, swirling my tongue around him like my favorite lollipop. His dick twitched against my tongue and I opened wide, his hard length sliding down my throat until my chin touched his balls.

His breath was heavy and his voice strained when he said, "Fuck, gorgeous, I'm going to come if you don't stop."

His words reached my lust-drunk brain, and while it was tempting to let him come in my mouth, I wanted to feel him inside of me. I released him with a loud pop and moved to straddle him again.

Our lips met in a feverish kiss, my heart beating a mile a minute as I finally felt his bare skin against mine. I lowered myself until I felt his hard length against my pussy. James sucked in a breath, his fingers digging into my waist.

I held onto his shoulders as I rubbed my pussy over his length, my juices glistening on his hard cock. He was so warm, so hard. It felt so good.

"Jesus, Cassie," he groaned.

I glanced up to find him staring down at us, eyes glazed over, lips parted. He was so handsome, a part of me still couldn't believe I was here. That he forgave me. I undulated my hips, rubbing my pussy over his length and letting his head get closer and closer to my entrance until I couldn't take it anymore.

"I need you," I whispered, my body humming with anticipation.

James looked up at me, the sweetest smile stretching his lips. "I'm all yours," he said, burying his head in the crook of my neck.

With trembling fingers, I reached between us and positioned his bare cock at my slit. I gasped as his throbbing head stretched my entrance, warm and impossibly hard. James gripped my hips as I lowered myself on his bare cock, his gaze focused on his length disappearing inside of me.

I sucked in a shaky breath as pleasure overwhelmed my senses. My only focus was his silky hard cock stretching my inner walls, filling me, claiming me. There were no barriers between us now. Physical or otherwise. It was exquisite, and I wanted more. I dug my nails into his shoulders as I dropped my hips, our gazes locked as my pussy eagerly swallowed his entire length. I gasped and shut my eyes, biting my lip as a shudder went through me.

Once I was fully seated, James released a throaty groan, my inner muscles clenching around him in response. I opened my eyes to take in his parted lips and glazed over eyes, an expression of pure bliss of his perfect face.

"Fuck," he growled, "this is beyond anything I ever imagined."

"Good?" I whispered breathlessly as I undulated my hips.

James groaned, fingers digging painfully into my hips. "Perfect, Cassie, you're fucking perfect." He thrust his hips, once, twice, our heavy breathing the perfect soundtrack for our reunion. "You're so warm and wet. So snug, like we were made for each other." He gripped the back of my neck and pulled me down for a bruising kiss, his dick twitching inside me. "Ride me, gorgeous."

Pleasure coursed through my veins like liquid fire when he wrapped a hand around my throat and squeezed. I slowly rocked back and forth, still getting used to his thick cock. It was different without a condom, less smooth. I moved my hips in a circle, the ridges of his cock grinding deliciously against my inner walls.

"You feel so good inside me," I breathed, beads of sweat dampening my hairline as I rode him.

James nibbled on my ear, his mouth lowering to suck on the sensitive spot on my neck he always found so easily. "Let me make it even better." He planted a foot on the mattress and lifted his hips to meet me halfway, driving even deeper inside me while his hands explored my body.

My skin felt like a live wire, every little touch bringing me closer to the edge. With each thrust, my clit brushed against his pelvis, sending waves of sizzling pleasure all over my body.

I planted my palms on his solid chest for balance, running a thumb over one round nipple, and started bouncing up and down. "More," I panted, needing him harder, deeper.

James rolled my pierced nipple between his fingers, then pinched it. It was as if he'd shot an arrow straight to my clit. My pussy pulsed in response and I squeezed around him, and he did it again.

"If you keep doing that," he grunted, "I'm not going to last."

"That's okay," I said in between pants, "we can always go again."

I shifted a little to the right and found my G-spot, and a high pitched moan erupted from my lips.

James moaned and pulled me for a searing kiss. "That's it, gorgeous. Take your pleasure."

I rode him with abandon, grinding my hips, chasing my orgasm as his expert hands teased my breasts. Then his fingers slid down my body to circle my throbbing clit and I screamed, the pressure in my core releasing all at once.

"Fuck, yes," he breathed. "Come all over my cock."

Fireworks exploded behind my closed eyelids as pleasure tore through me. My pussy clenched around his dick, and I mumbled incoherently as raw pleasure licked a fire on every nerve ending. Trembling, I opened my eyes to find James's glazed eyes on me, his expression almost pained.

We stared into each other's eyes for one long, feverish second before his mouth crashed against mine. His hands moved in a frenzy, caressing and squeezing whatever he could as my pussy continued to spasm around his dick.

Once the initial waves subsided, James cupped my ass and flipped us so he was on top, his dick never leaving my pussy. I wrapped my legs around him, my heels digging into his ass, urging him to move.

"Take what's yours," I moaned.

James released a guttural growl. Whatever control he was holding onto vanished as he pounded into me, the hunger in his eyes almost feral. It made me feel so desired, so hot. A primal urge took over me and I clenched my pussy around him in time with his thrusts, wanting him to explode inside of me.

The wet sounds of flesh pounding against flesh, our heavy breaths and loud moans, were bringing me closer to the edge. I didn't think I could come again so soon, but I reached between us to rub my clit.

"Cassie, fuck," James groaned, his eyes wild. "Let me feel you come all over my cock again."

"Yes," I moaned, my hips flying off the mattress as each exquisite stroke of his cock brought me closer to the edge.

James stared down at me as pleasure consumed me, his eyes never leaving mine as my body imploded again. I became a trembling mess, dragging my fingernails down his back and biting down on his shoulder as a mind-blowing orgasm shattered reality.

All I could feel was James inside me, on top of me, and pure ecstasy as he slowed his strokes. But I didn't want him to slow down. I wanted him to come apart with me. I squeezed him tight, gasping as sharp pleasure shot up my spine.

"Come inside me," I groaned as I locked my ankles around his waist.

James shuddered, his warm gaze unfocused as his movements became more erratic and his breath heavier as he reached his own orgasm. "Cassandra," he growled.

"Please. Deep inside me," I moaned as he shot rope after rope of hot, sticky cum in my pussy.

James collapsed on top of me, his hard body trembling with the aftermath of his climax. I hugged him tightly to me, running my hands up and down his muscular back, threading my fingers through his hair. We stayed like that for the longest time, our bodies sinking into the mattress in our post-orgasmic bliss.

After our breathing returned to normal, James propped himself up with an arm, a dazed look on his face. I smoothed his hair back, taking in his flushed cheeks and magnetic eyes.

He was beautiful. And he was mine.

"I missed you," I said, my voice hoarse.

He beamed at me, dark eyes shining with adoration. "I love you," he said. "That was the second thing."

His lips brushed against mine in the softest caress as I panicked under him. The words were there, on the tip of my tongue. But I couldn't say them. I hugged him tighter, trying to convey how I felt.

James smiled against my lips, as if he knew exactly what I was trying to do. "You don't have to say anything, gorgeous. I just wanted you to know." He dropped a loud kiss on my forehead and moved to watch as he slid his softening cock out of me.

I felt his cum leak out of my pussy and sat up a little to take in the sight.

"That's the hottest thing I've ever seen," James said, his deep, husky tone causing goosebumps to rise all over my body. He spread his cum all over my pussy, my breath hitching as his fingers brushed against my sensitive clit. "I'm debating carrying you to the shower, or leaving you covered in my cum." He lay down beside me, and I shifted to face him. "I think I prefer the latter, makes me feel like a caveman. Thoughts?"

I chuckled and shuffled a little closer to him, pressing my breasts against his chest. "I'm not ready to move yet. Can we stay here a little longer?"

"As long as you want, gorgeous," he replied, brushing my hair away from my face. "I like your haircut."

"Yeah? You're not just saying that to get in my pants?"

He shook his head a little as he stroked the shorter strands. "The longer hair made for a great leash," he said, the corner of his lips lifting into a sexy smirk. "But this length brings more attention to your gorgeous face."

"The girls said I look like Dora the Explorer."

James's eyes narrowed as he examined my face for a second before he burst into laughter. "I knew those big brown eyes looked familiar."

I punched him playfully on the arm, pursing my lips at his teasing. The sound of his laughter echoing around the room was like a balm to my soul. It had only been a few hours, but being with James already felt so right, so natural. People say it takes losing something to appreciate it, and that was entirely true. But I never realized how much someone walking into your life could shift your perspective.

For the longest time, I genuinely thought I was living my best life, working over sixty hours a week to make partner and volunteering at the shelter. Keeping busy so I didn't have time to stop and question if that was the right path for me.

But James brought me back to life, in a way. He helped me understand that feeling *something* was better than being numb all the time.

"Penny for your thoughts?" James asked as he caressed my cheek with the back of his hand.

I smiled, and for once didn't overthink at all. "You, and how alive you make me feel. It's like I'm fully awake for the first time since—" I stopped, frowning a little as the realization dawned on me. "Well, since my parents were alive."

James's lips lifted into a smile so dazzling that it made me a little light headed. "You make me feel alive too. When it's just us, nothing else matters. Not the company, the stock market, or any of the thousands of tasks I need to get done. It's just you and me."

"You keep leaving me speechless," I said, scooting closer and pressing my body flush against his. We hadn't stopped touching since we left his office, but somehow it wasn't enough. "But you just reminded me I forgot to tell you I quit my job."

James shifted to lie on his back, and I got comfortable with my head against his chest, listening to his steady heartbeats. "What brought you to that decision?"

I toyed with the little hairs on his chest as I said, "Turns out making sure privileged white men stay out of jail isn't very rewarding. I spoke with Marie, the shelter's director, and she's willing to hire me. Compensation will likely be drastically reduced, so money might be tight, but I'll still manage to support myself."

"I see," he said, his fingers tracing a line up and down my spine. "I know you can take care of yourself, financially and otherwise, but we're partners, Cassie. And that means I'll do anything in my power to support you in whatever you want to do."

I sighed against his chest. "I think I'll forever be trying to prove to you that I'm not after your money."

"Forever, huh?" He flipped us over so he was on top, his weight settling deliciously against mine. "I like the sound of that." He brushed his lips softly against mine before adding, "You don't have to prove anything to me, gorgeous. I trust you."

"How are you so perfect?" I said, giving in to an overwhelming feeling to squeeze his cheeks.

James's shoulders shook with laughter at my unusual gesture. "I could ask you the same thing." He then proceeded to pepper my face and neck with kisses, tickling me with his beard as I squirmed and giggled under him.

My stomach growled loudly, and he froze, hovering over me. "I guess we skipped lunch," I said, pressing my hand down on my stomach in a futile attempt to stop the noise.

A devilish smirk appeared on his lips before he said with a wink, "Oh, I had plenty to eat."

I rolled my eyes at that, but couldn't help chuckling at his cheeki-
ness. "What time is it?"

He flicked his wrist to glance at his watch, his brows lifting in
surprise. "It's almost four p.m. I guess time flies when we're having
fun." He lay on his side next to me, tracing a line up and down my
stomach with the tips of his fingers. "I have a game at eight, but I
can skip it."

"Don't," I said, turning on my side to face him. My insatiable
body wanted more, but there was always tomorrow. We had time,
now. "I'd love to see you in hockey gear."

James offered me a shy smile as he tucked my hair behind one
ear. "Would you like to come to the game? My parents and my sister
will be there, but you don't have to sit with them if you don't
want to."

"I'm not afraid of your parents, James."

He grinned widely at that, and said, "Good, because I don't
know what you said to my mom, but she won't stop asking about
you."

"That's weird," I said, frowning. "We talked briefly about
gardening, but I don't have a green thumb, so the conversation was
very short."

"Either way, she'll be glad to see you. And my father will be nice,
I promise." My stomach growled again, and he smiled. He rolled off
the bed in all his naked glory and offered me his hand. "But first, I
need to feed my girl. Is takeout okay? I don't think I'll have time to
cook."

"Take out is perfect. Do you think we have time to stop at my
place? I'd like to change," I said, pointing down at my ripped
stockings.

James fetched his smartphone from his suit jacket, pulled up the
delivery app, and handed it to me so I could choose something to
eat. "Sure. We should also grab whatever you need for the next few
days, and we can pack up the rest this weekend."

I nodded but said nothing. Living with someone was scary and
could make or break a relationship. But being with James was totally
worth it, and I would do my best not to screw it up this time.

We decided on Chinese food, chow mein for me, and dandan

noodles for James. I made a mental note that he liked the dish, eager to memorize every nugget of information about him. His likes and dislikes, fears, hopes, and dreams.

I wanted to know it all.

"We made a mess on your bed," I said as I handed him his phone.

"Our bed," James amended, "and I'll clean it up after we take a shower."

With that, he tossed his phone aside and scooped me off the bed. He carried me to the ensuite bathroom and set me down on the double vanity. "I don't think this is shower safe," he said as he unfastened the necklace.

Unfortunately we didn't have time for more funny business, so we took a quick shower. My underwear was soaked, so James loaned me a pair of boxers. I left him in his walk-in closet to pull on the clothes I'd discarded on the bedroom floor. We really needed to stop by my place because boxers and pencil skirts did not work together.

As I tried to smooth the lines on my skirt, my watch lit up with a text from the girls, wondering how everything had turned out. I had dropped my purse by the elevator, and I didn't like typing on my watch, so I sent them a bunch of emojis, including an eggplant and water droplet that painted a complete picture. And hearts, lots of hearts.

When James walked in, looking yummy in black sweatpants and matching hoodie, I was halfway through stripping the bed. "Where do you keep your sheets?"

He bent down to help me, a soft smile on his face. "There's a linen closet downstairs, by the laundry room." I gave him a puzzled look, and he scratched the back of his neck. "I guess I never gave you a proper tour of the place. Come on," he said, offering me his hand.

I followed him and tried not to balk as he showed me room after room. There were six bedrooms, along with seven and a half baths. Downstairs, he showed me his office, the formal dining room he never used, a library, and a fully equipped gym. Then he showed me another two rooms that were sparsely furnished, with only a couple of armchairs and a coffee table. Having this much space in the middle of the City felt unreal.

"I guess I don't really use all the rooms," James said, wrapping his arms around me from behind as we stood on the threshold of one of the empty rooms.

I leaned back against his chest and smiled up at him. "I don't see how you could."

He chuckled and disentangled us to offer me his hand. "Come on, let me show you why I got the place."

He led me to the elevator and, to my surprise, we went up instead of down. The doors slid open to reveal a rooftop terrace, complete with a long pool surrounded by sun loungers. To the right was a covered area with a bar and lounge chairs.

"Are you kidding me?" I said, turning back to face him. "You have a pool."

"Yes, we do," he said casually. "Do you enjoy swimming?"

"My parents took me to Lake Erie every summer," I said as I stepped towards the edge of the roof to take in the view. The sun was still high, shining on the canopy of reds and browns below. Beyond the park, the Hudson River glimmered in the distance. It was incredible.

"I really like this view," he said. "It's the reason I bought this place."

"Watching the sun rise and set from up here must be unbelievable."

"It is," James said, smiling widely as he pointed his phone at me.

I frowned, lifting one eyebrow in question. "What are you doing?"

"Just capturing the moment." He bent down to kiss my forehead, a look of pure adoration shining in his eyes. "Food's here, come on."

I followed him to the elevator, my heart so full it felt too big for my chest. Once I owned my mistakes and apologized, James had welcomed me with open arms. For the first time in my life, I believed a relationship could work. It was terrifying and exhilarating, and I planned to make the most of this second opportunity.

CHAPTER THIRTY-SEVEN

We stopped by my apartment so I could change and grab some essentials for later, though if we hadn't been in a hurry, I got the feeling James would have packed the entire place. I walked out of my room wearing skinny jeans, a black hoodie, and white sneakers, emulating his casual style.

He stared at me with a shit-eating grin as peeled off his hoodie and the jersey he wore underneath. "Will you wear my jersey? I have another one in my bag."

It was such a boyish move, straight out of high school, but I nodded enthusiastically, excited to wear *his* jersey.

"You can keep the hoodie," he said, as he pulled the shirt over my head. "It's cold in the rink." He stepped back to admire his work, a self-satisfied smile playing on his lips. "Now everyone will know you're mine."

My heart skipped a beat and, as usual around James, I didn't know what to say. I stepped closer and hugged his waist, tilting my head up for a kiss. Words failed me, but my actions were loud enough. Or at least I hoped they were.

Somehow, I filled two suitcases in the space of fifteen minutes. Just as we were about to leave, James walked back in. "Can't forget this," he said, holding up the framed photo of parents.

"Thank you," I murmured, clutching the frame to my chest. He had no idea how much that small gesture meant to me. And I had no clue what I had done to deserve him.

This time, when we made it to the ice-rink, the parking lot was dotted with cars.

We walked in through the back, then down a long corridor with doors on either side. James dropped his large duffel bag in front of the locker rooms before walking me to my seat. I wiped my clammy hands on my jeans as we approached his parents. To my surprise, they were sitting in the center of the stands, not in a private suite.

His parents and sister were sitting together, all three wearing Walton Corporation jerseys and casually sipping beer. When she saw me, Elisabeth jumped up and hugged me, shooting a knowing look between me and her brother.

James wrapped an arm around me and pressed me against his side as he turned to his parents. "Mom, Dad, you remember my girlfriend, Cassandra?"

Girlfriend. The word made butterflies rave in my belly.

"Miss Leigh, it's lovely to see you again," the senior Mr. Walton said as he stood to shake my hand, eyeing my jersey with curiosity.

I offered him a polite smile. "Please, call me Cassie."

"Cassandra!" Mrs. Walton exclaimed as she kissed my cheeks. "Have you finally come to see our boys play?"

My eyebrows drew together in confusion. "Boys?"

"Yes, Elias is part of the family," Elisabeth explained, "but we only adopted him because he's good at hockey."

"Speaking of Elias, I have to go," James said. "He'll throw a fit if I'm late." He gave me a peck on the cheek, and although I wasn't exactly a prude, my cheeks burned.

"Good luck," I said, as I waved him off and sat next to Elisabeth.

Mrs. Walton asked me about the fundraiser, and I was glad to have a subject I could speak about. As we chatted, it didn't surprise me to discover that she was on the board of several charities. Marie had suggested the Waltons were generous donors, and I realized I still had to thank James for his sizeable donation to the shelter.

A few minutes before the match started, Mr. Walton stood and asked if I liked beer. I said yes, and he sauntered off, returning with four fresh beers. It was an olive branch I gratefully accepted. The last thing I wanted was to cause a rift between father and son.

As the game started, I had more questions than answers. I knew the puck going in the net was good, but the game itself was so fast-paced and the puck so small, I could only stare on in confusion. Elisabeth was clearly a fan of the sport, and her behavior was my only clue about who was winning. She shouted insults at the other team and the referee, peppering them with sports jargon that flew over my head.

Fans on both sides made up little songs poking fun at their rivals, and James's family chanted along with them. Despite how tense I felt about hanging out with his family, I was having a good time. Granted, I would have to do some heavy research when I got home to understand the game, but I still had fun.

I focused on number seven, but even without the number I could easily have recognized James from his build and the confident way he carried himself, even in skates. He smashed against one of his opponents, stealing the puck and passing it to another player.

It was insanely hot. I had to surreptitiously cross my legs and press my thighs together. When I relaxed my muscles, I felt incredibly wet down there, too wet. A flush crept over my neck and I had to cover my open mouth when I realized it was James's cum leaking out of my pussy.

In that moment, Elisabeth turned to me and started explaining that James played defense while Elias was center and team captain. I barely registered what she was saying, and couldn't look at her without bursting into laughter, so I faced forward and focused on the game.

James and Elias flew over the ice, their movements graceful and powerful. I had no idea what being center meant, but Elias was on a whole different level. He maneuvered around opponents, passing the puck back and forth between his teammates as easily as breathing. I watched enthusiastically as they zipped across the rink, but my mind kept wandering elsewhere.

Elias scored and the crowd on our side erupted in cheers, but before I knew what was happening, the other team had scored. The game was more hectic and violent than I expected. Every few minutes a player would be smashed against the glass wall, penalties were called left and right, and players jumped on and off the rink in a way that made little sense to me.

During the short break after the first period was over, Elisabeth explained the rules of the game to me. I still had questions, but it definitely made watching the rest of the match more enjoyable. In between periods, James's father freshened all of our drinks, and when Elisabeth asked for nachos, he brought some for me too.

"Thank you," I said, smiling openly. The last conversation we had flitted through my mind, but he had already given me a peace offering. I just had to reciprocate somehow. When Elisabeth and Mrs. Walton went to the bathroom, I saw it as an opportunity.

I hated confrontation, but if things with James were to progress smoothly, making peace with his father was necessary. "This is exciting," I said, pointing at the ice. "I've never been to a hockey game before."

Mr. Walton smiled, and it was so much like James's smile, I blinked. "You should see a professional game. It's even better. I'm sure James will take you now that the season's started."

"I'm looking forward to it. Is there a team your family roots for?"

"The Rangers, except for that traitor Elias, who's a fan of the Islanders." He watched me for a second, then cocked his head to one side and said, "I gather you don't follow sports?"

"No, not really," I admitted with a smile. "I'm clueless about sports, but if James likes them, I guess I'll have to do a little research." My words were carefully selected to communicate that I'd be around longer without explicitly saying it.

Mr. Walton didn't miss a beat. "Oh, we have a private suite at The Garden. I'm sure he'll drag you to all the Rangers' games."

A look passed between the two of us, and it was enough. There was no need to address our previous conversation. After that, I was finally able to truly relax and enjoy the rest of the match. When the game ended, James and Elias walked off the ice and came up to celebrate their two-to-one victory, along with their other teammates.

I noticed that most of the spectators seemed to be family and friends of the players, which made sense for a corporate league. When James reached us, the wide grin on his face made my heart skip a beat. He engulfed me in a hug, my feet dangling in the air. Laughing, I linked my hands around his neck, his musky scent making my pussy throb. Plus, I was still leaking his cum.

"Congratulations," I said, wondering if that was the right thing to say after a game.

"Thanks, gorgeous. Did you have fun?"

"I did. It was entertaining, to say the least." When he bent down to kiss my cheek, I couldn't resist whispering in his ear, "I'm leaking your cum."

His hand tightened around my waist, and I leaned back to take in his wide eyes. He glanced quickly at his family and Elias, and whispered, "Fuck. You're making me hard."

Smiling, I stood on tiptoes and planted a kiss on his scruffy cheek. "Your boxers are soaked," I whispered back.

James growled deep in his throat, the sound raising goosebumps all over my arm. "You are wicked."

Elias interrupted us, slinging an arm around my shoulder. "I see you found a way," he said, looking between us. "I like a girl who doesn't give up."

James shot me a puzzled look, and I told him I would explain it later. Then he kissed me on the cheek again and followed Elias to the locker rooms. I stood there, grinning stupidly at his retreating form, until Elisabeth abruptly linked her arm with mine and declared we were going to meet the boys.

Puzzled, I followed her lead and said a hasty goodbye to his parents. Meeting them again was fine, but I was glad there wasn't much opportunity for conversation. It had been an emotional day, and I still needed a little time to adjust to this new reality.

I have a boyfriend, I thought, a goofy smile fighting to take over.

Once we were out of earshot, Elisabeth said, "Sorry for the abrupt exit. Minnie Huntzberger was coming our way. Unless you want to answer a thousand personal, very invasive questions about when you're getting married and procreating, stay away from Minnie."

"Noted," I said as we reached the locker rooms. "Thank you for today. I wouldn't be here if it weren't for you."

"No need to thank me," she said, waving it away. "My brother's been miserable without you. He tried to hide it, but he just seemed so forlorn. I'm glad he's happy now."

I wasn't exactly an affectionate person, but I drew Elisabeth in for a quick hug. "Thank you," I repeated. It was sweet how much she cared about her brother. We chatted for a bit about the fundraiser, and she told me about grad school and her aspirations of becoming a writer.

Booming voices interrupted our conversation as the players sauntered out of the locker room. James walked out with his duffel bag swung over his shoulders, his hair still dripping wet from his shower.

"Hey, I was just going to meet you." James threw an arm around my shoulder and deposited a kiss on top of my head. "Where's Mom and Dad?" he asked Elisabeth.

"Minnie Huntzberger was approaching, so we carefully retreated before she could spot us."

"Good, otherwise who knows when we'd be able to leave."

"Speaking of leaving, I should get going," Elisabeth said. "I still have to get back to school."

The three of us walked out together and said our goodbyes. James watched Elisabeth until she was safely inside the town car with her driver, then led me back to his own car. As we drove to his place, he patiently answered all of my hockey questions.

I wanted to tease him some more, but it had been a long day and he was surely tired from playing hockey. Back at the penthouse, I took my shoes off and picked them up to put them away.

"You don't have to take your shoes off," James said.

"I don't like wearing shoes inside. Is that okay?"

James tilted his head to the side, his brows furrowed. "Wear whatever you want, Cassie," he said softly. "Maybe we should get a shoe cabinet for the entry hall." He grabbed my shoes, tucked them under his arm, then lifted my suitcases and started making his way upstairs.

I followed him to help, but he refused to let me. He placed the suitcases in the closet, and I retrieved my toiletries bag and comfortable clothes before disappearing inside the bathroom. When I was done with my skin care routine, I found James on the living room couch, scrolling through his phone.

"Are you hungry?" he asked as I curled up next to him. "We had a late lunch but no dinner."

I shook my head. "Your father bought me nachos. I think it was an olive branch of sorts."

"I'm glad to hear it. My family's not perfect, but I'd love it if you became close."

"Your sister helped me sneak into your office, so I think we're already getting there," I said with a smile. "But aren't you hungry after all that skating and shoving men against a plastic wall?"

He chuckled at my poor description of a hockey game. "I think I'll just have a snack while—" His phone rang and he frowned as he glanced at the number. "It's work. I have to take this," he said apologetically.

"That's okay. I'm not a good cook but I'll make you a sandwich while you take the call."

He paused for a second, as if that wasn't what he expected me to say, then his mouth split into a huge grin. "I'd love that."

Smiling, I jumped to my feet and got started on the sandwich. It was a little silly, but the idea of feeding him set my pulse racing. I carefully assembled two sandwiches, trying to remember how Amelia layered the ingredients. When I returned to the living room with a plate and the watermelon soda he liked, James was still on the phone, his brows drawn together in concentration as he listened intently.

He smiled when I walked in, then his attention was back to his call. I sat next to him and browsed for something to watch, but my focus drifted to James and how confident and knowledgeable he sounded.

Whatever issue he was resolving, he was clearly an expert. Watching him give clear, concise instructions and speaking so intelligently had butterflies raving in my belly.

He wrapped up his call and released a deep sigh before reaching for his sandwich and immediately biting into it.

"Everything okay?" I asked, wondering if he liked the sandwich.

"Yes," he answered in between bites. "One of our subsidiaries failed to warn us before they updated their security software, which led to a massive breach. Now they're contesting the liability clause and trying to shift blame towards us to avoid the thirty-five million fine."

"I'm assuming you had extremely competent lawyers draft the contracts?" He nodded while he chewed. "As long as there's no ambiguity, they shouldn't be able to fight it."

"Precisely," he said. "Although, on top of that, the breach caused big investors to back out, costing us around eighty million, and another twenty from potential investors that lost confidence in us."

"So you're suing them?"

"Yes, and backing out of our multimillion-dollar contract with them. Their mistake will most likely bankrupt them."

"I don't know why, but the idea of you destroying a business that tried to screw you over is so hot," I said, fanning myself for effect.

James chuckled as he reached for his second sandwich. "Had they apologized and quietly paid the fine, I would've let it go. Mistakes happen. Now they'll have to suffer the consequences of their hubris." He finished his food in two bites and pushed the plate aside before settling next to me. "Thank you," he said, wrapping an arm around my shoulders. "That was delicious."

"You're welcome," I said, tucking myself against his chest. It was such a pleasure watching him devour something I'd made. I liked the idea of caring for him this way.

We snuggled on the couch and started watching a movie. It had been a long, tumultuous day, and enveloped by James's warmth and familiar scent, my eyelids started drooping.

A while later, his deep voice pierced through my drowsy brain.

"Earlier when you said I was being too gentle," he said, his fingers trailing up and down my arms. "I wanted to clarify that while I enjoy spanking you, it's not something I *need*. I don't want to do anything that makes you uncomfortable."

All the warmth seeped from my body at his words. I knew where he was coming from, but I didn't want my past with Andrew to affect our relationship, especially our sex life. Mostly, I didn't want James to see me as a victim, or act like I was made of glass.

I cleared my throat, afraid my voice would come out as broken as I felt. "What we do is consensual, James. I enjoy being spanked." I placed my hand on top of his, twining our fingers together. "Honestly, I would probably enjoy paddling too, but that's a discussion for a different time."

James was quiet for a long time, and I let him sift through his thoughts. After a few moments, he released a deep breath, holding me tighter against him. "I don't know how to walk that line," he said, his deep voice heavy with emotion. "I don't want to hurt you."

I sat up to look up at him, needing him to see my face. "You've never hurt me, James. I would have used the safe word if you had."

He cupped my face, brushing his thumb over my cheekbones. "I hope you never have to use it, but I also don't want you to hesitate to use it. Ever. Promise me?"

"I promise," I said, holding his gaze.

His returning smile made my heart skip a bit. The poor organ wasn't used to dealing with this many emotions. I wondered if you could have a heart attack from being too happy. Because this warm feeling that filled my chest and etched a permanent smile on my lips could only be happiness.

We decided to call it a night, and I buried my head in his neck as he carried me upstairs, bride style. I climbed into bed and fought sleep while James brushed his teeth.

He flipped off the lights before cuddling behind me, and draped a hand over my waist, sighing contentedly. "Goodnight, gorgeous," he said, pressing a kiss on top of my head.

After cuddling his pillow for the last couple of weeks, it felt surreal to be here. To know that he still wanted me. That he loved me. A content smile appeared on my lips as bliss washed over me. "Goodnight, James."

The next morning, I woke up facing a sleeping James. We hadn't drawn the curtains last night, so I watched the sky change color, the retreating shadows dancing over his skin. I had missed waking up to his perfect face, and now this was a privilege I'd never take for granted again.

Warmth blossomed in my chest at the sight of him, his sharp features relaxed, full lips slightly parted. I wanted to run my fingers over his bedhead, feel his scruffy beard under my palm, but I didn't want to wake him.

So I lay there, watching him, wondering if this was real. If I could truly be this happy. The part of me that was always waiting for the other shoe to drop was alive and kicking. Living with Andrew had felt like walking a tightrope, never knowing when the wind was going to change.

"Having second thoughts?"

James's voice startled me. His sleepy gaze was focused on me, and not for the first time, it felt like he could see into my mind.

"No second thoughts," I said, finally reaching to thread my fingers through his hair. He pulled me towards him, my breasts pressing against his solid chest.

"Good morning, gorgeous," he said, brushing his lips over mine.

"Good morning," I whispered against his lips.

His alarm rang just as he cupped my ass, grinding my pussy against his morning wood. He groaned, pulling back with a disappointed look on his face. "We need to get up before my brain stops functioning and my dick takes over. Do you want to shower while I make you breakfast?"

"You don't have to make me breakfast, James."

"I don't *have* to do anything, Cassandra," he said, matching my tone.

I rolled my eyes, and he pinched my waist playfully before literally jumping out of bed.

He stood there, his dark gaze roaming over my body, a smile slowly stretching over his lips. "You're so beautiful." His Adam's apple bobbed up and down, and he shook his head. "I'm going downstairs before I lose control."

I laughed, thinking he was kidding, but he rushed out of the room, sparing me a quick, heated glance before he disappeared down the hall. Smiling, I rolled off his comfy bed and made my way to the bathroom, my pussy aching exquisitely with each step.

After a quick shower, I dressed for work and did my makeup as my thoughts drifted. James was nothing like Andrew, and living with him would be nothing like it had been with Andrew. In the space of a few hours, he had already made his place feel like home. I didn't miss how he kept calling things ours—our bed, our pool—and I knew his word choice was deliberate.

By the time I made it downstairs, James already had scrambled eggs, bacon, and avocado toast perfectly plated on the kitchen island. "It smells delicious," I said, taking a seat.

James handed me a cup of coffee and kissed my cheek. "Not as delicious as you."

"You're not eating?"

He shook his head. "And before you say anything else, I love making you food and I will do it even when I can't eat with you. I have a breakfast meeting." He lifted his shirt and flexed his abs. "Unfortunately, I can't have two breakfasts and keep the abs."

I rolled my eyes, but didn't protest. It was nice of him to cook for me, and I really shouldn't complain. He was a big boy and could do whatever he wanted. "The abs are a priority," I joked instead. "I love watching your muscles tremble when you come inside me."

James froze with his cup halfway to his mouth, and I fought a smile. "Jesus, Cassandra. I'm going to be thinking about that all day."

"Then we're even. I can still feel you, especially when I walk."

His eyes darkened as he let out a shaky breath. "I'm going to go have a cold shower now."

I laughed as I watched him go up the stairs, feeling so light it scared me. But I wouldn't let my fears get in our way, not this time. James had left the newspaper on the counter, so I read the news while I ate the breakfast he had cooked just for me.

He had already cleaned everything else, so once I was done, I rinsed my plate and put it in the dishwasher. I reached for my coffee cup and my elbow brushed against a glass, knocking it off the island. It shattered loudly on the marble floor, shards flying in every direction.

Of course I had to break something, I thought as I crouched to gather the larger pieces in my hand.

Before I could finish cleaning, James came bounding down the stairs, already fully dressed. "What are you doing?"

"I'm so sorry, I dropped a glass," I said, unable to look up.

James picked me up and placed me on the counter. "I meant, why are you picking up glass with your hands? And you're barefoot, gorgeous. You could've hurt yourself." He opened a lower cabinet door, took out a dustpan, and quickly swept all the glass away.

"I'm sorry," I repeated, completely frozen.

He gave me a curious look. "It's just a glass, Cassie. No big deal."

I watched him scribble a note for his housekeeper and stick it to the fridge. He wanted to make sure she knew there might be broken glass so she wouldn't cut herself. James was so thoughtful, so kind, I could only stare at him with wide eyes.

After that, I finished getting ready, and he dropped me off at work. I was quiet, but he didn't push me. Andrew had made me feel so inadequate, especially when it came to house chores. I was messy, clumsy, a lousy cook. And God forbid if I ever broke anything.

But James had cleaned up for me, more concerned with my well-being than a broken glass. I was sure even if I broke something valuable, he would react the exact same way.

Shaking my head, I decided Andrew didn't matter and I should really stop comparing the two. James was kind, generous, and since we met, he'd done nothing but take care of me, even when I pushed him away.

Now that he was mine, and I was his, I caught myself dreaming of our future. Vacations, meals with his family and my girls, supporting him through stressful times, and knowing that if I stumbled, he'd be there to catch me.

And for once, those thoughts didn't scare me at all.

CHAPTER THIRTY-EIGHT

Now that I had put in my two weeks' notice, work was blissfully uneventful. The partners had assigned my cases to another lawyer, and I was mainly assisting them with witness interviews or researching precedents. It was the detective part of the job I enjoyed the most, so the days flew by.

Living with James was blissful, but by no means uneventful. He cooked me breakfast every morning and insisted on driving me to and from work. Granted, Paul was doing most of the actual driving, but I liked listening to James on the phone with his assertive and professional tone, his hand on my thigh. It definitely made for an excellent start to my days. And at night, he made dinner, or we got distracted and ended up ordering in. It was the honeymoon phase, I knew that. But it felt so easy, so effortless.

I was *almost* not terrified this would be snatched away from me.

I was dying to tell the girls everything, but it had been a busy week for all of us. We were going to Oasis tonight, to celebrate this new leaf I had turned over, and I couldn't wait to have some fun with my girls.

Right before lunch, Olivia called me to sign for a package. I stepped out of my office, dreading another gift from Andrew. As I approached Olivia's desk, a fragrant blend of spices tickled my nose.

Confused, I accepted the bag the delivery guy handed me, eyeing the restaurant name printed on the side.

I tipped the guy and peered into the bag, looking for clues. My rigid muscles eased when I saw James's familiar handwriting.

Can't wait to come home and bury my face between your legs.
James Walton

My cheeks burned as I read it, and I bit my lip to stop from grinning like an idiot. I wondered how he got the note inside the bag and how many people had seen it.

"Maybe I should quit, too," Olivia said. "You look happy."

"I am," I answered softly.

"I'll miss you. No one else here thinks it's okay to have ten cups of coffee a day."

Olivia and I weren't exactly friends, but we could be. "We can still meet up for coffee," I offered.

Her smile widened, and she leaned forward as she said, "I heard about this little coffee shop in Queens. They have over a hundred different coffee beans from all over the world."

"I bet no one there would bat an eye at ten cups a day. Sunday?"

She agreed, and I returned to my office, my steps light.

I set the bag down on my desk and opened it to find several containers filled with fragrant food. Without hesitation, I pulled up my phone and tapped on James's number. He answered on the second ring. "Hey, gorgeous."

"I got your package. Now I can feed the entire office."

"It's Moroccan," he said, his words muffled by voices and utensils clanging against dishes. "Yesterday you said you'd never had it before, and I'm having lunch at Miel et Safran. I thought you might like it."

"Thank you. It smells delicious. I just hope Olivia likes it too or we'll be eating leftovers for a week."

He chuckled, the sound rich and warm. "Did you get my note too?"

I figured he was in a lunch meeting, so it was the perfect time to tease him. "I did, and I was thinking you should sit on my face tonight. We've never done that."

"Cassandra," he said, a warning in his tone that sounded more like a promise.

"We haven't used any of the toys on you, either," I said, my tone casual, almost distracted. "I'm thinking vibrating butt plug while you fuck my face."

James groaned low in his throat and sounded strained when he said, "We'll discuss this later. I'm hanging up now."

"Maybe I should get a strap on on my way home and fuck you properly."

It thought I heard James murmur 'fuck' before the line went dead. Two seconds later, he sent me a picture of his bulge under the table.

James: I love it when you misbehave. It means I get to
punish you.
Me: Maybe you should misbehave so I can punish you.
James: I'm ignoring you before I come in my pants in front
of a dozen executives. Pick you up at six.

Biting my lip, I unbuttoned my blouse and snapped a quick photo of my breasts and hit send. He didn't open it, so I put my phone aside and went to ask Olivia if she liked Moroccan. We had lunch together, chatting easily before returning to our work. I still had a few strings to tie up before I finished my notice, and since I wanted to part with the firm on good terms, I didn't want the quality of my work to decline.

A couple of hours later, my phone vibrated on my desk, catching my attention. I smiled when I saw it was the group chat with the girls.

Rina: Pregame at your place, Cassie?
Me: I have to check if it's okay with James first.
Amelia: Can't wait to see his kitchen. Bet it's fancy.
Me: He does have lots of shiny appliances.

I wasn't sure if James would be okay with the girls coming over and wreaking havoc at his penthouse. The place was always so pristine, not a fleck of dust on the furniture or a mug in the sink. He never said anything about the clothes I left here and there, or the shoes I abandoned by the elevator, but I wondered if it bothered him.

Shaking my head, I reminded myself that James was an excellent communicator. He would let me know if my messiness was a problem and until then I wouldn't worry too much about it.

I liked how tidy and organized he was, though. In the morning, I was always rushing to get ready, looking for my phone or my earrings and running upstairs because I forgot something. Meanwhile, James always put everything in the exact same spot. Every night he took off his watch and placed it on the nightstand along with his phone and headphones.

He was a creature of habit, and it was so cute.

Pushing thoughts of James away, I focused back on work. The hours flew by, and soon I was in need of more caffeine. I pushed off my desk and pondered going to my favorite coffee shop around the corner. But these days, even with security around, being out in public put me on edge.

Settling for regular, free coffee, I made my way to the kitchen. As I passed Olivia's desk, she stopped me with an apologetic half-smile on her face. "The associates screwed up the motion to compel discovery in the Ventiglio case."

"How bad?"

"I counted twenty-two adverbs in the first two pages," she said, showing me the highlighted words on her screen. "Plus, the phrasing is unnecessarily convoluted and the argument is all over the place." When I glanced at my watch and released a deep sigh, she added, "Sorry, I know it's late, but Mr. Feldman wants it first thing Monday."

"It's alright," I said, wondering if I could get it done before six. "Coffee? I was just about to refuel."

I got us both caffeinated and returned to my office to look over the motion. After skimming it, I quickly realized I couldn't get it done before James picked me up, so I shot him a text. He insisted I text Paul to pick me up and not walk home alone, and even though it would take me fifteen minutes now that I lived in Manhattan, I readily agreed.

The elevator's door slid open and I raised my eyebrows in surprise when I noticed a shoe cabinet in the foyer that hadn't been there this morning. Smiling, I slipped off my flats and placed them on a rack beside James's loafers. A thrill went through me as I padded around the penthouse searching for him.

I found him in the gym doing squats with a barbell over his shoulders. Like a perv, I stood in the doorway, watching his muscular ass contract and relax as he completed the move.

"Eyes up here," James said, meeting my gaze in the mirror.

"I think I'm going to stare at your ass a little longer. It's fuelling those pegging fantasies of mine." I stepped further into the room as I spoke and took a seat on a workout bench opposite from him.

He set the bar down before grabbing a towel to wipe away the sweat dripping down towards his collar. "I'm starting to like that idea more and more."

I bit down on my lip in excitement, the thought of pegging James really setting my insides ablaze. "You got some new furniture?" I asked casually.

"So you don't have to carry your shoes upstairs," he said, reracking the weights. As if the fact he had purchased a cabinet just for me wasn't a big deal. My heart swelled to twice its size, and I jumped to my feet to wrap my arms around him.

"Thank you for the cabinet," I said, pressing my lips to his cheek.

He wrapped his hands awkwardly around me, his shoulders shaking with laughter. "I'm covered in sweat, gorgeous."

"I don't care." Leaning back, I traced his lips with my tongue before smashing our mouths together in a passionate kiss. When I pulled back, we were both panting.

"I'll get you furniture more often if this is how you thank me."

He bent down to kiss me again, but I pressed my finger against his mouth and pushed back a little. "Before we get carried away, I have something to ask you."

James gave me a curious look. "Ask away."

It was a simple question, but the more I delayed, the more nervous I got. James had said he didn't like people in his space. Maybe he really wouldn't like the girls coming over.

I'm not sure how I would respond to that.

Andrew had made it very clear my guests were not welcome. Not that I *had* any friends to begin with, but even on the rare occasion I needed to bring someone over for a group project or just to study, I wasn't allowed.

The girls were important to me; they were family. Whether or not James liked them, they were part of my life. It was important to me that both of us maintained relationships outside of our couple, and if he wasn't okay with that, I doubted this would work.

"Hey," James said, propping my chin up with his thumb, "what's on your mind?"

"It's girls' night and my friends usually come to my place for drinks before we go out, so I was wondering if they could come here."

He frowned, as if that wasn't what he was expecting to hear. "Are you asking me for permission to bring your friends over?"

"Yes, it's your place."

James sat astride on a bench and patted the spot in front of him. I obliged, hiking my pencil skirt up to mimic his position, and met his warm gaze. "It's *our* place, Cassandra. I appreciate the heads-up so I don't accidentally walk in naked, but you don't need to ask permission to bring your friends over."

"But it's not my place," I said. "It's not like I pay rent."

"What kind of asshole would I be to charge you rent?"

"It's not about you being an asshole or not, James. Even if you did charge me, it's not like I could afford it, especially with my new job."

His face fell, and he ran a frustrated hand through his hair. "Then what is this about?"

I frowned, trying to sift through my thoughts. "Despite the shoe cabinet and everything else you've done, I guess it's hard to see a place as your own when you're not paying rent."

James released a deep sigh. "I still don't want you to pay rent, Cassie." He took my hand in his, the contact immediately soothing me. "I understand that you suffered at Andrew's hands, and that financial control is one aspect of abusive relationships. That's not my intention, gorgeous." The expression in his dark eyes was completely unguarded, and it completely disarmed me. "I love that you're hard working and independent, and I would never try to take that away from you. We can keep our bank accounts separate, so your money will always be your own. Whatever you need. But I don't think it's fair for you to pay rent. Maybe we can find some other way to make this place feel like home."

"How do you do that? I didn't mention Andrew at all, and it's like you read my mind. You always know exactly what to say."

"I *see* you," he said as he tucked a strand of hair behind my ear. "Money has always been a non-issue for me, so purchasing something isn't necessarily what grants me a feeling of ownership. When I bought this place, it didn't feel like mine until I remodeled the kitchen, and added artwork to the decor. What would help make this place home for you? Do you want to change the decorations? We can get rid of everything and start from scratch."

He was so sweet, I just wanted to squeeze him. "I don't want to change anything. I'll get used to living here with time. It's just all very new, and I don't know what the rules are."

"There are no rules, gorgeous," he said, pushing to his feet. "Come here, let me show you something."

I grabbed his hand and followed behind him to a sitting room next to his office. But when he pushed the doors open, the room was empty, the smell of fresh paint lingering in the air.

"I thought this could be your office," he said, turning to face me.

"My office?"

"Yes, I figured you might like a room that's entirely yours. Plus, working hunched over your laptop on the kitchen counter is bad for your back."

My eyes started to water, so I wrapped my arms around his waist and buried my face in his neck. His scent calmed my wild heartbeat enough that I was able to form words. "This is too much."

James leaned back and propped my chin up with a finger. "You're it for me, Cassandra. I want this place to be our home, and there are no rules except the ones we make together." He brushed his lips against my forehead, his heart beating steadily beneath my palm. "I know your life hasn't been easy, and you worked hard to get where you are. It takes a lot of strength to walk away from an abusive relationship, and I admire you for doing it. I'm in awe of how strong and brave you are."

"I'm not sure I'm any of those things."

"You are also generous and kind, intelligent and funny. Sometimes you smile at me and you're so beautiful it's hard to breathe," he said, his eyes crinkling at the corners.

I swallowed the lump in my throat, and squeezed my eyes shut. Tears flowed freely down my face, and James stepped closer to brush them away.

Wrapping my hands around his waist, I pressed myself against his chest. He hugged me tightly and whispered into my hair, "I hate that he made you believe you're hard to love. Because you're not. And I'll keep repeating that until you believe it."

I sobbed in his arms, only mildly embarrassed at my outburst. He rubbed my back and whispered comforting words until I stopped shaking.

Once I had calmed down, he said, "On second thought, I actually do have a rule, but I think you'll agree with it. Elias is not allowed to throw parties on the roof. There was so much trash in the pool last time, so many condoms stuck to the filter, the cleaners had to drain it."

Laughter bubbled in my belly, despite the swirl of emotions pressing against my chest. "I think I can agree with that," I said, smiling softly.

"Now go text your friends to come over, and I'll make dinner."

"You don't——"

"Gorgeous, I already told you I don't *have* to do anything. But I'd love to make your friends dinner and get to know them better."

I nodded, unable to speak past the knot in my throat. James

probably sensed I needed a minute, because after claiming to be in desperate need of a shower, he dropped a kiss on top of my head and left. I sat in the middle of the floor, staring out at the New York skyline through the floor-to-ceiling windows of *my* office.

It was the culmination of all my ambitions and I hated that my first thought was that I didn't deserve it because I hadn't earned it. But I refused to engage with that. James wanted to take care of me, and there was nothing wrong with that. I didn't have to *suffer* to deserve every good thing in life.

Pulling out my phone, I texted the girls to come whenever.

Once I'd showered and slipped on a sundress, I joined James in the kitchen. His dark eyes surveyed my every move as I walked in, causing a flush to creep up my neck.

"Any dietary restrictions I should know about?"

"Nope," I said, taking a seat on a high stool.

"I was thinking mushroom risotto with pan seared scallops."

"That sounds perfect. How can I help? I'm not completely useless in the kitchen. I can chop things."

James poured a glass of wine and leaned against the counter to slide it in my direction. The sight of his muscles bunching as he supported himself on his elbow set my pulse racing. Living together had yet to diminish the effect this man had on me.

"I don't really need help," he said, as he pulled ingredients from different cabinets, completely at ease in his kitchen. I watched him pull out pans and pots, and line up all the ingredients in a way that reminded me of Amelia.

I narrowed my eyes at him, the corner of my lip lifting into a smirk. "You don't like help in the kitchen."

"I don't," he said, rubbing the back of his head. "I'm sorry, I just have my way of doing things…."

"That's okay. I enjoy watching you cook."

"How about dessert?"

"Oh, Amelia said she's bringing something. I bet you'll like it.

328

She's a talented chef. They should be here by nine," I added as I read their messages.

We chatted easily while he cooked, enjoying a quiet moment of simple domesticity. A little before nine, I got a call on my phone from the concierge and went downstairs to meet the girls.

"Holy shit," Amelia said as I punched my personal code into the elevator's security pad, "this place is really fancy."

"I know, right? Wait until you see the view. I don't think I'll ever get used to it."

"So, this is permanent?" Rina asked, a knowing look in her eyes.

I couldn't stop from grinning even if I wanted to. "Yeah, I think so."

Daisy squealed in delight, clapping her hands before she threw her arms around me. "I'm so happy for you."

"I think I'm happy for me, too," I admitted as I wrapped my arms around her. The elevator doors slid open, and we headed towards the kitchen. "James, you remember Daisy, Amelia, and Rina."

James was busy chopping something green, but when he heard us, he turned around with a bright smile on his lips. "Of course. It's nice to see you again."

"Likewise," Rina said politely.

I watched with bated breath as my friends interacted with James, waiting for the initial awkwardness to fade.

"I brought dessert," Amelia announced. "Cherry clafoutis and crème brûlée."

James brightened, clearly impressed. "Do you want to put the crème brûlée in the fridge?" The way he said crème brûlée in a perfect French accent had me pressing my thighs together.

Jesus, this man will be the death of me.

Amelia hesitated for a brief second before carrying her dish to the fridge. "This kitchen is incredible," she said, gesturing towards his shiny appliances.

"Thank you," James said, as he lined up cocktail glasses on the island. "Cassie says you're a chef. I'm looking forward to dessert."

"Oh, I'm not a chef, but I am saving up to open a bakery someday."

"That's exciting. What kind of bakery?" Amelia happily explained it all to him while he poured gin into a metal shaker, shook it, then strained his concoction into the cocktail glasses. "Ladies," he said, once he added a decorative leaf to each cocktail.

I took a sip, mint and lemon with a dash of gin coating my tongue. "What is this?"

"Southside cocktail. It's like a mojito with gin," he explained.

"It's delicious," Rina said. "You can barely taste the alcohol."

"That makes it dangerous for us," Daisy added with a laugh.

Amelia set her glass down and turned to James. "Before we become useless, can we help with anything?"

James shot me a pleading look, and I took a sip of my cocktail, completely ignoring him. Maybe it was mean to let him fend for himself, especially since Amelia was a bit of a control freak in the kitchen. But I wanted him to be himself around the girls, state his boundaries.

"That's not necessary," he said. "Why don't you give your friends a tour of the place, Cassie?"

"Are you sure?" Amelia eyed his preparation, and added, "I can take over the scallops so you can focus on the risotto."

His face turned a light shade of pink and I had to hide my smile behind my glass. "That's okay," he said, then turning to me, he added, "Actually, do you mind setting the table in the dining room?"

Rina burst out laughing. Daisy and I joined her a second later. "That's a slick way of getting us out of the kitchen," Rina said. "Amelia would have just screamed at us."

James shot a confused look between the three of us and Amelia. "Amelia hates it when someone's *in the kitchen* while she's cooking," I explained. "Bodily injuries would be involved if we offered to take over."

His lips stretched into a small smile, and his shoulders drooped with relief. "Too many cooks spoil the broth," he said, winking at Amelia.

Amelia shot daggers in our direction, which only made us laugh harder. "They're being dramatic. I'm not that bad."

Ignoring Amelia, Daisy turned to me. "Remember that time at

Thanksgiving when her cousin added salt to the gravy, and she stabbed his hand with a fork?"

"Or the time her grandma came to visit and lowered the oven temperature?" Rina chimed in.

"That was actually hilarious because everyone could see how much you wanted to punch your abuela," I added.

"I wanted to strangle her," Amelia admitted, "but abuela is sacred. She can do no wrong." Then she turned to James. "And the fork barely punctured my cousin's hand."

James laughed at our antics as he moved around the kitchen, that quiet confidence I loved radiating off him.

I smiled at him and stood. "Let's leave James alone with his cooking before he turns into Amelia." I grabbed plates and cutlery from the cabinets while Rina and Daisy carried the glasses to the dining room. Amelia followed behind us with our drinks.

"Babe, this place is insane," Daisy whispered as soon as we were out of the kitchen.

Rina shot her a look. "It's not like you're not used to it."

"Please, I walked away from that world almost a decade ago."

"You look comfortable here, though," Amelia added.

"I am, sort of," I admitted. "He gave me an office today. Well, it's an empty room with a view of the Upper East Side. I have half a closet upstairs and today he got a shoe cabinet for the foyer."

"Because you kept leaving your shoes scattered?" Rina teased, her eyes crinkling at the corners.

I shot her a pointed look. "No, I mostly carried them upstairs to the closet. But I guess now I won't have to because he got me a shoe cabinet."

Rina's all-seeing eyes scrutinized my every move as we set the table. "You seem very calm about all this," she said after a few moments of companionable silence.

"Yeah," Daisy said. "No urge to run for the hills?"

"No running," I said with a sigh. "He's literally making room for me in his home, in his life. And it's terrifying. I'm scared to screw up and lose him. But this feels right."

Rina held my gaze, and like always, it felt like she saw right through me. "Better to have loved and lost?"

I grinned. "Something like that."

Daisy wrapped an arm around my shoulders and ruffled my hair. "Look at our little commitment phobe, finally committing."

We set the table, and soon after, dinner was ready. It was a casual affair, filled with laughter, good food, and lots of alcohol. My heart couldn't possibly be fuller as I watched James and my friends getting along.

I might not have a blood family anymore, but my chosen one was just as real, just as loving.

After dinner, the girls and I insisted on cleaning up, and for once, James conceded. He told me he was meeting up with Elias and a few other friends, so he disappeared upstairs while we did the dishes. When we were done, I went upstairs to check if the coast was clear for the girls to come up.

He was in the walk-in closet, wearing black trousers that hugged his ass and nothing else. I wrapped my arms around him from behind, basking in his smell, his presence.

"Hi," I said. "You look handsome."

James's chest vibrated with laughter. "I'm half-naked."

I brushed my lips against his soft, warm skin. "Exactly."

"Cassandra," he growled in warning, "your friends are here."

"Spoilsport." I let go of him and sat on the settee. "They like you."

"I like them." He held up a shirt for me to inspect. "Do you think this shirt is okay for Euphoria?"

"You'd fit in better shirtless," I said, pushing to my feet to look at his options. In a sea of solid colors, Versace's bold patterns stood out. "This one will work."

He lifted the shirt and stared at the pattern as if it were offensive to his eyes, but slipped it on anyway. "This was a present from Lizzy. She said I needed to mix up my wardrobe." He looked in the mirror as he did his buttons. "It's ugly, but I guess it will do."

"It is ugly," I agreed, biting my lip to stop myself from laughing, "but you'd look hot in a paper bag."

"Thank you," he said, his cheeks turning pink. "I'll make another round of cocktails before I leave. Is Southside okay or do you want something else?"

I wanted to say that he didn't have to make more cocktails, but I bit my tongue. "Southside is perfect," I said instead.

James kneeled in front of me and cupped my face, his eyes lingering on my lips for a second before he stared into my eyes. "Paul is all yours tonight. Just text him when you're ready to go. Security will tag along from a distance, but please text Paul when you're ready to come home." His eyes were pleading, so I nodded in agreement.

I called the girls upstairs, and since it was pretty late, we finished getting ready in record time. Most of my clothes were still at my place, so I only had a couple of options. I chose a tight red dress that stopped right below my ass and grabbed the strappy Jimmy Choo sandals James had gotten me on his birthday.

When we made it downstairs, James was in the living room talking on his phone. A fresh round of cocktails was waiting in the kitchen, so we grabbed our drinks before joining him.

As I stepped into the living room in my short dress and bare feet, James's eyes darkened. A slow smirk crept over his face as he drank me in. "Gorgeous," he whispered, his husky tone sending shivers down my spine. I grinned like a fool and did a little turn, but he seemed to catch himself and turned to the girls with a soft smile. "You all look lovely."

"Maybe we should give these two a minute," Daisy joked as she wiggled her eyebrows.

Rina glanced between the two of us. "I think if we do, we'll never make it out of here."

"I'm actually leaving now," he said with a chuckle, then turned to me. "Walk me to the door?"

I nodded and ignored the girls' hoots and teasing.

When we reached the foyer, James turned around and pinned me against the wall, pressing his hard cock against my abdomen. His mouth was on mine before I could react, his expert tongue drawing a moan from my lips. "Fuck," he groaned, leaning his forehead against mine as we tried to catch our breath. "That dress should be illegal."

"You should see it with the shoes."

He sighed and stepped back to put some distance between us.

"I'm going before my cock takes control and I fuck you right here with your friends watching."

My eyes widened and I bit my lip. Maybe I was already tipsy, because the idea wasn't unwelcome.

"Cassie," James warned, "don't give me that look. Do you know your security code?"

I nodded and recited it for him.

"And mine?"

I hadn't wanted to know it at first, but James insisted in case I ever forgot my own. "Yes, I know yours too. And I texted Paul."

"Good. Elias is waiting for me downstairs." He stepped closer and placed his hand firmly on my hip. "Will you be a good girl for me?"

"Yes," I breathed.

"Have fun, gorgeous," he said, then brushed his lips softly against mine before stepping into the elevator.

"You too," I whispered as the doors closed.

When we got downstairs and spotted the limo, we all squealed like teenage girls. At Oasis, there was a table in the VIP section waiting for us. James was spoiling me rotten.

"You're glowing," Rina whisper-shouted in my ear.

I offered her a big, genuine smile. "I'm happy." My heart was too full to pretend otherwise. "Let's dance. Celebrate!"

The four of us danced the night away, round after round of cocktails appearing on our table. While we were on the dance floor surrounded by sweaty bodies, I noticed Ford and Ivan, my bodyguards, watching us from a safe distance. They offered me a chin salute, and I returned it, feeling safe under their watchful eyes.

By the time we left, Oasis was already half empty, and we were all slightly drunk. We piled into the car and apologized profusely for keeping Paul up so late. He dismissed us with a wave and didn't complain as we sang loudly in the back. After he dropped the girls off, he drove me to the penthouse, then made sure I was safely in the elevator before leaving.

I punched my code into the elevator and leaned against the wall, my fuzzy brain happy beyond belief to come home to James. Once the doors slid open, I gingerly removed my heels, trying not to make noise. Upstairs, I slipped into our bedroom, eager to crawl into bed next to my man. My steps faltered when I saw him lying on his side, sound asleep with his mouth hanging open.

The sight of him brought a smile to my lips. He was adorable.

After a sweaty night out, I was in desperate need of a shower, but I didn't want to wake him up. I tiptoed to the bathroom to grab my toiletries, then quickly snatched my pajamas, before going into one of the guest rooms. I removed my makeup and showered, then stumbled downstairs to appease my growling stomach.

In the fridge, I found what was left of Amelia's cherry dessert and some apple juice, and settled on the island with the container and a fork. For a short second, I thought about drinking directly from the bottle before I summoned the energy to grab a glass. Midway through my second slice, I heard footsteps, then James's sleepy face appeared in the kitchen.

"Hey, gorgeous," he said, walking over to kiss the top of my head.

"Did I wake you?"

"No, I just woke up and wanted to check if you were home. Did you shower in one of the guest rooms?"

"Yes, I didn't want to wake you up. I'd offer you some dessert, but this is the last piece and you have those abs to look out for."

He pinched my waist playfully at that. "Did you have fun?"

"Yes. Drinks kept mysteriously showing up at our table. I'm still a little tipsy."

"I can't take credit for that." He turned to close the drawer and cabinet I'd left open, then took a seat beside me. "Elias knew you'd be at Oasis and he said he'd take care of it."

"I have a habit of leaving every door open," I said, running my fingers up and down his forearms. "I'm sorry."

"Don't be," he said, stealing my fork and helping himself to a big bite of my dessert. It's cute."

"It's cute now, but I bet it won't be in ten years."

He lifted his head, his eyes shining with happiness, a bright grin on his face. "You think we'll be together in ten years?"

My face burned, but he looked so happy, I couldn't look away. "Maybe," I said, shrugging casually.

"You love me."

It wasn't a question, but I answered anyway. "I do."

He tucked my still wet hair behind my ear, looking at me as if he wanted to memorize me. "I love you, too."

I bit down on my lip, a tingle of excitement rushing through me. He had always looked at me that way, like I was precious. I'd just been too scared to acknowledge it. We stared into each other's eyes for the longest time, both of us sporting goofy grins.

I wondered how many good things I had missed out on because I was too afraid of getting hurt.

Not anymore, I thought, as I leaned against his shoulder and wrapped an arm around his biceps. My pulse slowed, a weightlessness setting over me as I melted into him.

"Come on," he said, scooping me up in his arms, "let's get you to bed."

I wrapped my arms around his neck and sighed contentedly as he carried me upstairs. We brushed our teeth standing side by side, and I couldn't help staring at our happy reflections in the mirror.

We snuggled on the bed, his solid body pressed against mine under the soft blanket. It was heaven.

"I've never thought love could be like this," I said as my eyelids got heavier.

"Like what?"

"So freeing."

I thought he had fallen asleep, but after a while, his hot breath tickled my ear. "Cassie?"

"Yes?"

"Are you going to remember this tomorrow?"

I turned around in his arms and scratched his beard. "Yes."

He smiled and pressed his lips against my forehead. "Goodnight, gorgeous."

CHAPTER THIRTY-NINE

I woke up to my watch vibrating softly against my wrist. The room was still dark, and James was sprawled on his stomach, peacefully asleep. I glanced at the little screen and suppressed a groan before swinging my legs off the bed and slipping out of the room.

My phone was on the kitchen island and I raced to pick it up. "Hi," I said as I answered, my voice deep with sleep.

"Morning, kid," Monty said, unusually cheerful for this time of day. "Sleeping in?"

"It's six a.m. on a Saturday, Monty."

"Alright," he said, laughing, "let's cut to the chase then. I went over the last ten years of Andrew's life. On the surface, he seems like a regular guy. He bought an apartment in your hometown a few years ago, opened an architecture consulting firm. Nice, stable job. Good income. "

I started making coffee while he spoke, my brain cataloging all the info.

"He's had a few girlfriends on and off, nothing too serious. His criminal record is clean, no charges were ever filed against him, but," Monty paused, "I went through the girls' medical records."

That's illegal, I thought, as I finished setting up James's fancy coffee maker and stumbled toward a stool. I had a feeling I should sit down for whatever came next.

"In the year they were together, one girl had two broken ribs and a dislocated shoulder. Separate incidents. Another girl had a sprained ankle. I guess that could be easily explained away, but then in the space of two months she came into the emergency room missing two teeth and with a broken nose, then once more with a deep laceration to her skull and several bruises."

It felt like all the air had been sucked from my lungs. "Do you know where he is?"

"As far as I can tell, he hasn't returned to your hometown and we weren't able to track him down. He's a real shit pump, Cassandra."

I almost wanted to laugh at his choice of words, but I was starting to panic. Monty rarely used my name, so I knew he was serious. "Thank you, Monty."

"There's not much else to report, but I've got a bad feeling about this one. Watch your six, kid."

"I will. Send me your bill? You got a massive tip coming your way."

Monty laughed and hung up, and I stayed frozen in place, focusing on my breath. Accessing medical records was illegal, I knew that, but I was still glad to know. I couldn't make excuses for not going to the police anymore.

Over the years, I had documented my injuries, including the last time he assaulted me in my apartment. It might be enough for a restraining order, but not much else. Still, there would be a record of the abuse, and if he did it again, to me or someone else, maybe having charges on his file would make it easier to stop him.

I sat there in silence, mapping out my next steps. Once my decision was made, I jumped to my feet, grabbed my laptop, poured myself a cup of coffee, and got to work.

Dear Bill and Patricia,

I have been putting off writing this because I know my words will give you pain. After my parents died, the two of you stepped in when I needed a family the most. And for that reason, I couldn't bear to tell you who your son really is, but now it has become necessary.

When I left Andrew years ago, it wasn't a mutual decision. We fought, and he beat me so badly I ended up in the hospital with a concussion and a fractured arm. I was terrified of him, terrified of what he would do the next time he 'lost his temper'. So I packed my stuff while he was at work and left. I changed my name and started a new life.

A few weeks ago, Andrew found me in New York under my new name and broke into my apartment. He seems to be under some sort of delusion that we'll get back together. That will never happen.

I didn't go to the police then, out of love for you. I feel like I owe you a debt of gratitude for all the love and support you freely gave me when I lost my parents.

But I can no longer do this. I'm filing a police report and getting a restraining order. If Andrew comes anywhere near me again, I will call the police. I will do anything and everything I can to protect myself and my loved ones.

This might be hard for you to read, but as I understand it, I'm not the only woman he has hurt. Maybe you'll doubt my words. That's ok. He's your son. I understand the urge to defend him. Attached you will find pictures from when we were still together, and from his recent visit to New York.

I've never wanted to hurt either of you, and I will forever be grateful for everything you've done for me. But I can no longer protect your son at my expense.

I hope you understand.

Best regards,

Cassandra Leigh (or as you knew me, Samantha Decker)

I quickly proofread the email, tears freely flowing down my face, then pressed send. The second it was done, my shoulders sagged and all the tension seeped from my body. I had been dreading telling Andrew's parents for nearly a decade. Now that the cat was out of the bag, it felt like weight off my shoulders.

It was still early, but I was fully awake now, despite only getting a couple of hours of sleep last night. James wasn't going to the office today, so I let him sleep in while I answered some emails.

A little after eight, I made him a coffee, black with one sugar, and climbed the stairs to wake him. I nudged the door open, and my heart skipped a beat when I caught sight of him sprawled on the bed, wearing nothing but black boxers, his dark hair sticking up in all directions.

He was beautiful.

Smiling softly, I tiptoed in and set his coffee on his nightstand before slipping in next to him. He groaned and wrapped his arms around my waist, pulling me to his chest. I melted against him, inhaling his intoxicating scent. Then I tilted my chin up and peppered his jaw and throat with kisses.

I felt his chest vibrate beneath me as he chuckled, and his hand traveled down my spine to cup my ass. "Hmm," he murmured, "now this is a perfect way to wake up."

"Good morning," I said, smiling against his neck. "I brought you coffee."

He let out an appreciative hum and pressed his lips against the top of my head. "Marry me."

I chuckled and tugged at the little hairs on his chest to tease him. "Is that all it takes to become Mrs. Walton? A little cuddling and coffee?"

Suddenly, he flipped us over so he was hovering over me, and I let out a high pitched squeal. "It helps if your name's Cassandra and you have gorgeous big brown eyes." He brushed his nose against mine and kissed me softly before sitting up against the head-board. "Thank you," he said as he reached for his coffee. "You're up early."

I sat up next to him and grabbed my phone to pull up the email. "I got a call this morning from my PI," I said, handing it to him. "Andrew's hurt at least two other women, so I figured it was time his parents knew. It wasn't exactly easy to write."

James was silent as he read the email, his jaw tense. I nestled against his side and waited until he was done. "How do you feel now?"

"Relieved. I didn't want to blindside them. Today I'm making an official report against him, then I'm filing for a restraining order."

He put the phone aside and finished his coffee, then gently cupped my face. "I'm very proud of you, you know that?"

My eyes filled with tears, and I desperately tried to blink them away. Before, it was easier to run away because I had nothing to hold on to. But now that I had the girls, James, and my new job at the shelter, I would fight to keep it. I wouldn't let Andrew take it from me.

"What else did the PI say?"

I filled him in on everything Monty had said, then added, "Andrew's not back in Ohio yet, so he might still be in the City. Monty told me to watch my back."

"I agree with Monty," James said, rubbing soothing circles on my back. "Please don't go anywhere without security."

"I won't," I said firmly.

"Good. I've been meaning to ask you, why Cassandra Leigh?"

"This old lady sat on the Greyhound next to me and when she got off, she gave me her book. She said it might cheer me up." I smiled as the memory came back to me, clear as day. It was a small act of kindness when I needed it most. "It was *Pride and Prejudice*. I read it cover to cover on the way to New York, and in Jane Austen's bio I saw her mother's name, Cassandra Leigh. I thought it sounded cool."

"It suits you," James said, beaming at me. He pressed a kiss to my forehead and stood. "Since you were eating clafoutis at five a.m., I'm assuming you're not hungover. Pancakes for breakfast?"

"I'm going to have to start using the gym if you keep feeding me like this."

"No need for that," he said, squeezing my ass. "I like to watch your ass jiggle when I fuck you from behind."

I burst out laughing at that, my sour mood completely dissolving. "Pancakes it is. I think I'll probably nap after, then go to the shelter in the afternoon."

"I'm golfing with a client around eleven," he said as he slipped on a pair of sweatpants. "We should sync our calendars so we can carve time out for each other."

I bit down on my lip, my heart racing with excitement. "We should," I agreed, smiling ear to ear. All the walls I had built to protect myself were necessary at the time, but letting James in was one of the best decisions I ever made.

Later that afternoon, Paul dropped me off at the shelter. Marie was busy sorting through donations, while Sheila went over some documents. We exchanged small talk, and then Sheila updated me on a few cases while I made a fresh pot of coffee.

The shelter had connections with the local police department, so it was relatively easy to make a report and file for a Protective Order. It felt surreal to be working on my own case, to see my name on the paperwork. But once it was done, I felt a weird satisfaction, like I was finally ready to move on.

I grabbed a pile of files and bent my head to work, excited at the prospect of this being my full-time job soon. It wasn't the easiest job, but just knowing that after a long day of work I would come home to James and cuddle with him on the couch or just chat while he cooked dinner.... I couldn't imagine life without him anymore.

Or I guess I could. I just didn't want to.

A couple of hours later, Sheila left to grab a snack for the three of us. I needed to stretch my legs, so I grabbed a few bags and headed to the basement to throw them in the wash before distributing them. There was still a lot to be done for the fundraiser. I had little experience throwing an event like this, so I really appreciated Elias and Elisabeth for helping.

If it went smoothly, then I could organize a couple of events a year to fund the shelter and maybe even open a new shelter with better facilities. I was separating the colors from the whites, dreaming of the future, when I felt a hard object press against my back.

"Hi, baby."

Panic flared in my veins and I whipped around to find Andrew standing a foot from me, a gun aimed at my chest. On instinct, I backed away from him, my hands raised in front of me.

"Andrew," I breathed, my eyes zeroing in on the gun. "What are you doing?"

He stepped toward me, his lips twisting into a threatening sneer. "I missed you. You didn't think I'd give up that easy, did you?" He smiled, but his eyes were cold and flat.

Andrew kept moving towards me, and I stepped backwards until my back hit the wall.

"Now, you're going to follow me, and do it quietly." He pressed his whole body against mine, pushing the muzzle of the gun against my stomach. "If you try to run, I will shoot you. And when I'm done with you, maybe I'll go on a little killing spree. Blame it on a mental breakdown and get out in two years with good behavior. Maybe I'll even hire someone from your firm to represent me."

"You can't afford us," I said, regretting the words the moment they escaped my mouth. It was the middle of the day. I thought of the women upstairs, the small kids playing around, Sheila and Marie in the office. So many lives were at risk because of me.

He chuckled darkly against my ear, the sound causing bile to rise in my throat. "You're funny." He pressed the gun so hard into my stomach I could feel the hole where the bullets came out. "Keep being funny and you won't live long. But if you listen to me, everything will be ok. I promise, baby."

I nodded to buy time and to put some distance between us and the shelter. Andrew tucked the gun into the waistband of his jeans, but my relief was short lived. A wave of nausea washed over me as his hands roamed my body. I recoiled from his touch, flattening myself against the wall, but there was nowhere to go. Tears pricked at my eyes as he squeezed my breasts. I swallowed, trying to focus on my breath—I needed to keep my wits about me if I was going to survive this.

I shuddered when he slipped his hands in my back pockets—he was patting me down, maybe looking for my phone, I realized. But my phone was upstairs, useless on my desk.

"Put this on," he said, handing me a parka from the laundry basket.

As I slipped my arms in the sleeves, I felt my watch press against my wrist, safely hidden beneath my sweater. I blinked, trying not to give anything away.

"We're going to walk out hand in hand, and you're going to look happy about it," Andrew said, leaning down to stare into my eyes. I resisted the urge to look away, taking in the deep, purple-blue circles under his eyes, the dark gleam in his gaze.

Andrew grabbed the back of my head, his fingers digging into my skull, and led me towards the basement door. He retrieved the gun and pointed it at my head, making me shudder with fear. "Now, I'm going to open this door and if you scream, if you try to run or do anything suspicious, I start shooting. You don't want anyone to get hurt because of you, do you?"

Before my horrified brain could form a reply, he threw an arm around my shoulders and pulled the door open. I stumbled forward and he pulled me to his side, while his other hand held the gun buried deep in his jacket pocket.

Fresh air whipped against my cheeks as I looked around, trying to find a familiar face, anyone from my security team. But they were at the front of the building, probably waiting patiently for me to leave. The basement door didn't open from the outside, there was no reason for them to watch it.

A chill ran down my spine when I realized he must have been hiding *inside* the shelter, waiting for the right time to strike.

We joined the flow of people walking on the sidewalk, and I trudged beside him in a panicked daze. *This isn't real. It can't be.* Andrew abducting me at gunpoint in the middle of the day had never crossed my mind. All of this felt surreal, impossible.

He'd always cared about his appearance, but now he was walking around New York with frumpy clothes, unwashed hair, and a gun casually hidden in his pocket.

This wasn't the Andrew I knew, which made my panic rise even higher.

He led us through a small park near the shelter. I kept trying to make eye contact with someone, anyone, but people were minding their own business, not paying us any attention.

I stumbled on in a daze, my legs heavier with each step I took. The scenery blurred around me as we walked, and I kept hoping that I'd soon wake up to James pulling me out of a nightmare. But Andrew walked beside me, the tight grip of his hand on mine anchoring me to reality.

He surveyed his surroundings, his red-rimmed eyes alert, awake in a way I'd never seen before. I needed to focus. To calm down and collect my thoughts.

My chest burned with each breath I took, but I forced the air into my lungs, ignoring the way my chest compressed in on itself. Gradually, my surroundings began to come into focus.

If anyone noticed I was missing, they could use my watch to track me. Rina had access to the app. With any luck someone would call her.

It will be okay, I told myself over and over. I just needed to buy some time.

We walked for a few blocks, the buildings around me familiar. About a block away from my place, Andrew veered left into a dark alley and led me down the stairs into a basement apartment.

It was dark inside, and the pungent smell of stale alcohol drifted to my nostrils, causing acid to rise up my throat. When he flicked on the lights, I noticed he had covered the windows so no one could see inside. *He planned this.* The thought chilled me to the bone.

I looked around me, trying to find an escape route, but there was only one other door and I assumed it led to the bathroom. Despite the limited space, the place would have been nice with its exposed brick walls and open floor plan. But discarded beer cans, empty liquor bottles, and takeout containers were scattered all over the floor. The scent of sweat and stale beer lingered in the air, along with a mix of old food.

The only clean place in the apartment was the bed pushed against the far wall. It was neatly made with crisp white sheets and fluffy pillows, a pair of handcuffs placed ominously in the center of the mattress.

Andrew used the muzzle of the gun to push my hair behind my ears, and I didn't dare breathe. "You cut your hair." He circled around me, planting his free hand on my shoulder, his face inches from mine. "Why?"

I lifted my chin, measuring my words carefully as I faced him. "I accidentally burned it on a candle," I lied, knowing how much Andrew liked my long hair. "It was too uneven, so I had to chop it."

He studied me for an eternity, and it took everything in me not to look away. When he nodded, I realized I wasn't the girl Andrew had known, not anymore. That girl could have never lied unflinchingly to his face, let alone gotten away with it.

A spark of hope ignited in my chest. I could do this. I could keep him talking until someone noticed I was gone.

"Take a seat," he instructed, gesturing towards a small table littered with bits of paper and takeout containers.

There were only two chairs, so I chose the one closest to the wall. "Andrew what is this about? Why did you bring me here?" While I spoke, I removed the coat and draped it over my lap. I needed to keep the watch hidden, and I was afraid he'd see it under my thin sweater.

Andrew casually took the gun from his pocket before throwing his jacket over a chair. My eyes followed the gun in his hand as he waved it around. "I missed you, baby. Our last reunion got cut short." He placed the gun on the table, facing me. "Where are you staying? You haven't come home for days."

"I have a cockroach problem, so I'm staying with a friend until the exterminators take care of it." The lie flew from my lips before it had a chance to fully form in my head. If I hesitated, he might think I was lying. Telling him I moved in with James was out of the question.

He leaned back in his chair and stroked his beard. "That's funny. I haven't seen anyone go in."

"They're coming on Thursday. I couldn't get an earlier appointment but I didn't want to room with cockroaches, so I'm staying away until they're gone."

He pushed to his feet, grabbed the gun, and tucked it into his back pocket. "It's not really surprising *you* have cockroaches. I'm more surprised you don't have rats." While he spoke, he made his way to the fridge. "This city is filthy and you've never been the best housekeeper. Beer?"

Carefully, I unfastened my watch and placed it in one of the coat's pockets. "Yes, please," I answered, ignoring his little jibe. He was trying to get a rise out of me. I knew that. But I wasn't going to bite. If we argued, this situation might escalate, which I wasn't sure I could survive. "You're right about the city. It's even worse during the summer. You can't even open a window without feeling like a trash stink bomb went off in your apartment."

He handed me an unopened beer bottle, and I hoped he wasn't clever enough to spike it without opening it. "Maybe that's why all the rich people like your little boyfriend take off for the summer."

"Do you mind?" I asked, handing him the bottle. He cracked it open on the edge of the table, then did the same for his bottle. I sipped my beer in silence, barely wetting my lips as I tried to steer the conversation to a safe topic. "Do you remember summers back home? We used to catch tadpoles at Moor's creek. The air was so clean, especially compared to New York."

"Do you miss it? You haven't been back since we left for college."

"I do," I said honestly. "Sometimes I wonder if things still look the same. If the creek is still there, or if that old lady still sits on her porch every day to spy on the neighbors."

"The old lady died." Andrew downed his beer, tossed the bottle aside, and fetched another one. "And me? Did you miss me?" he asked as he sat across from me, placing the gun on the table again.

I kept my features schooled, relaxed, even as my heart pounded heavily in my chest. "I do. You were my first love. My first every-thing really," I added with a small chuckle. "Nothing and no one could ever erase that."

"That's right," he said, smiling. He dragged his chair closer to mine and placed his hand on my thigh, his fingernails digging into my skin despite my jeans. "This time it will be different. I promise."

My breath caught in my chest, blood rushing in my ears. I took a sip to disguise my reaction while my brain scrambled to find some-thing to say in response. "I heard you opened an architecture firm, that you're doing really well back home."

"I'm not a millionaire," he said with a sneer, "but you won't have to work anymore. You can just stay home and take care of the children."

I wasn't sure if he was delusional, but if that was what it took to keep him calm, I would engage in his fantasy. Marie must have noticed I was gone by now. Unless she thought I left without telling her for some reason…. My stomach sank at the thought.

No. Someone would notice.

"You have no idea how much I missed you. All these years without you…. I tried to find someone else, but no one ever loved me like you did." He started stroking my leg, my body immediately tensing at the contact. "I need to feel you again, to be inside of you and feel that connection." Andrew leaned in to whisper against my ear. "I never felt that with anyone else. It's only you, baby. It's always been you."

Panic seeped into my veins, chilling me from the inside out. My chest rose and fell, but my lungs burned as if I wasn't breathing at all.

"Can I use your bathroom?" I asked, pushing to my feet on shaky legs. If I had a panic attack now, there was no way I'd be able to control this situation. "You know beer always makes me pee."

He shot me a disdainful look, his jaw clenching dangerously. I waited with bated breath for a few long seconds as he stared at me, before he pointed towards the bathroom. With a grateful smile, I ignored my preservation instincts and turned my back on him as I hurried to the bathroom.

I almost whimpered when I saw there was no lock on the door, no windows either. *Shit!* Planting my palms on the filthy sink for support, I shut my eyes tight and focused on my breath. The countless abductions cases I had read and worked on flashed in my mind.

The victims were almost always beaten to a pulp, raped, murdered. Usually a combination of all the above. Some were tortured, sodomised.

When we were still together, he had wanted me to cower, to hang my head in fear and keep my eyes low to the ground. He liked it when I cried, when I begged him to stop.

Fuck that. If he really planned to rape and murder me, I wouldn't give him the satisfaction of seeing me shake with fear.

I would bite his fucking dick off if I had to.

You can do this. Just keep him talking.

After flushing the toilet, I washed my hands and schooled my expression in the mirror. When I opened the door, Andrew was leaning against a wall, waiting. He stalked towards me until we were toe to toe, cold eyes fixed on mine.

"Do you think I'm stupid?" He pressed the tip of the gun against my temple before slowly dragging it down my nose, past my chin and my neck, until he reached my breasts. "I pour my heart out to you and you run off to the bathroom. Is it about *him*?"

His face was inches from mine, and the alcohol on his breath made my eyes burn. The gun pressed harder against my chest with each ragged breath I took. "Please, Andrew. I can't think with a gun pressed to my heart."

The corner of his lips lifted into a creepy smile, and he backed away, still pointing the gun at me. Then he laughed, as if I had made a great joke. He backed up and placed the gun in a kitchen drawer, out of reach from me, but also from him.

I breathed a sigh of relief. At least without the immediate danger of the gun, I might have a fighting chance.

Andrew strode towards me, a vicious smile on his lips. "Now that's out of the way," he said, wrapping his hand around my throat. He nuzzled the side of my neck, and it took all of me to remain still when every fiber in my body wanted to lean away from him. "Fuck, I've missed you, Sam."

He smashed his mouth roughly against mine and I forced my lips to relax. But then he plunged his tongue in my mouth and, try as I might, I couldn't make myself kiss him back. He pulled away, his nostrils flaring slightly as he looked at me.

Even after all these years, beneath the layer of booze and unwashed body, his taste, his smell—it was familiar. I shuddered.

"I've missed you too," I whispered, "but do you think we can take things slow?" I stroked his arm to keep him calm, anticipating his reaction to my words. "Remember when we were kids? How much fun we used to have, just the two of us? We could spend hours just talking in your car, listening to music…. I miss that."

"I see." His hand closed around my wrist, stopping my touch. "You have no problem letting the billionaire fuck your brains out, but when it comes to me, you just want to chat."

"No, it's not like that," I tried, but he forced my hand to his crotch. I felt his dick hardening in his pants, and alarm bells clanged inside my head as I internally recoiled in disgust. "Of course I want to have sex with you! But I've missed *you*. I want to hear all about your life. I want to get to know you again before we get intimate."

"That's very sweet," he said, releasing my throat to cup my jaw. "But we have all the time in the world for that later." He leaned forward, brushing his lips against mine. Bile rose in my throat, my heart beating wildly in my chest as he stuck his tongue in my mouth again.

I forced my eyes shut, knowing he'd be checking for that. He was still holding my hand against his growing penis, forcing me to stroke him over his pants. The bitter taste of alcohol assaulted my senses as he swirled his tongue in my mouth, causing bile to rise in my throat.

"Please, can we take it slow?" I tried moving my hand away from his crotch, but he held it firmly.

"Baby, it's been seven years. I don't think I can wait much longer." Andrew pressed his forehead against my neck before sucking my skin hard into his mouth. All my muscles begged to recoil as his wet mouth latched onto my skin, pain radiating from the spot he sucked. "There, now everyone will know you belong to me."

Andrew kissed me again, clearly unconcerned with the fact I wasn't kissing him back. He pushed me backwards towards the bed, twisting my arm behind my back at an awkward angle. Tears pricked my eyes, each hard-earned breath stinging my lungs.

This can't be happening. Not now. Not when everything was falling in line.

He made me want to crawl out of my own skin, but I dug in my heels and stared at him with what I hoped to be defiance. Although he had clearly snapped, I knew Andrew well enough to know that he thrived on fear. The more I gave him, the more crazed he would become.

"Please, Andrew. Can't we just talk first?"

He pressed his hard cock against me. I shut my eyes, wishing I could be anywhere but here. Andrew didn't answer me, he just continued kissing a path down my neck, groping my breasts. Then he froze when he felt my nipple piercing underneath my sweater.

"This thing," he said, poking my piercing with the tip of his finger. "It marks you as a whore. That's what you are. You open your legs for everyone, but now you just want to talk? That's not happening."

He pulled roughly at my nipple piercing, sharp pain shooting all the way down my spine. I moaned in agony, which, judging by the feral look in his eyes, Andrew mistook for pleasure.

"Andrew, stop. You're hurting me—"

"But you like that, don't you? You like it rough, so I'm gonna give it to you."

"Please, stop. I don't want to—"

He cut me off by sticking his tongue in my mouth again as he rubbed his body against mine.

I just wanted to curl up and cry. But that wasn't an option. I had survived him before and I would survive him now. Either that, or I would go down fighting.

This time, when I felt his tongue push past my lips, I welcomed him in, reciprocating the kiss to lure him into a false sense of safety. Then I bit down hard, as hard as I could.

Blood filled my mouth as it poured out of his, and I coughed it back into his face. He let go of my hand to tend to his wound, and I used the opportunity to scramble away from him. I raced for my beer bottle sitting idly on the table, but he grabbed my hair and yanked me back towards him.

He held me against him with one hand wrapped around my throat, my back pressed against his front. "Oh, Sam. You never learn, do you?"

I struggled against him to get free, his grip on my throat tightening. I elbowed him in the gut, but not with enough force to get away.

"You bitch!" Blood mixed with saliva came sputtering out of his mouth when he spoke. He threw me on the bed with so much force I landed awkwardly on my wrist. He spat on the floor, a gob of crimson landing on the linoleum with an audible splat, and said, "I'm going to have a lot of fun reminding you how to behave."

I grimaced in pain and rushed to find my footing and get off the bed. But I wasn't fast enough. The moment I stood, he body slammed me against the wall. My head smashed against the drywall and my vision went dark. Pressure exploded in my skull, a blinding pain radiating from the point of contact and expanding until another sharp, searing pain ignited across my face.

My body collapsed on the dirty floor as I cradled the back of my head, trying to calm the pain. I brought a hand up to my cheek, and felt a gash over my cheekbone. Confusion clouded my thoughts, the room spun, and I feared losing consciousness.

Andrew didn't give me a chance to get my bearings. His knee landed heavily on my chest, constricting my airway, and he wrapped his hand around my throat. I squirmed under him, kicking and punching, but he kept squeezing, tighter and tighter. It became harder and harder to breathe. My lungs burned and stars danced in my vision.

This is it. This is where I die.

I kicked him as hard as I could in a frantic effort to get him to stop. His fingers loosened around my throat. I gasped, taking big gulps of precious air, my head still swimming.

"I want you awake for this," he said, pushing to his feet. He swung his leg and kicked me hard in the stomach.

What little air I had in my lungs wheezed out as I coughed violently, trying and failing to catch my breath. Still trying to recover, I felt his grubby hands touching me, and something snapped. I went completely wild, kicking and screaming, hitting him anywhere I reached. I only lasted a few seconds before his hand pressed against my mouth to stop me from screaming.

"Shut your stupid mouth or I'll fucking kill you!"

I was too enraged to care about his threats. If this was how I went down, I'd go down swinging. I clawed at his face with my fingernails, then stuck my finger in his eye as hard as I could. Andrew cried out in pain as he lept off me, pressing his palm against his eye.

He glanced towards the kitchen, where the gun was, making my heart stop for a second. I crawled as far away from him as I could, frantically searching for a weapon. Anything I could use to defend myself. But I couldn't see past the tears and blood trickling down my face.

I screamed as loud as I could, hoping someone outside might hear me. Then his foot landed heavily against my ribs, and I collapsed again, gasping for air. He kicked me again and again, and all I could do was bring my hands up to protect my head.

My vision went dark as excruciating pain overwhelmed my senses.

I didn't have much fight left in me.

Finally, he stopped and leaned closer to me, panting hard. "This is all your fault. All I wanted was a pleasant reunion. Now look what you made me do." He ran a hand roughly through his hair and kicked one of the kitchen chairs, knocking it over.

Groaning, I tried to lift my head, but the movement was too much. The room started spinning, and my mouth was so dry. I lay back down, frantically searching my mind for something I could do. Then something glimmered under the bed. A beer bottle.

Everything hurt, but I reached under the bed and almost wept when my fingers grasped something solid. I held the bottle in front of me, and Andrew laughed.

"And what are you going to do with that?" he taunted, standing over me.

I dragged my arms and legs under me, adrenaline pushing me to at least sit up. The bottle shook in my hand as I tried to hold it up. My arms and legs felt like noodles, but every time he tried to get near me, I crawled away, brandishing the bottle in front of me. Suddenly, he pounced, and I smashed the bottle over his head with every ounce of strength I had.

He stumbled back as shards flew around us, but it wasn't enough to stop him. He lunged for me and gripped my wrist, easily snatching the half broken bottle from my hand. The moment he pulled me to my feet, I kneed him in the balls.

But I wasn't strong enough. All it did was anger him. He slammed me against the wall again, and I felt all the air whoosh out of my lungs as I slumped to the ground. He kneeled beside me, pure hatred in his eyes as he wrapped both hands around my throat and squeezed.

I felt something sharp digging into my hand, so I frantically spread my fingers to grab it. It was a shard of glass, a weapon. I closed my fingers around it and aimed for his eye. I missed, but I knew I would. So I stabbed him again and again, as quick and as hard as I could, until he jumped back.

He screamed in pain, clutching his bloodied face. If I'd had the physical capacity to laugh, I would have. As it was, I clutched my sides, my mouth gaping as I tried to breathe.

But then I watched as he stumbled to the kitchen drawer for the gun and pointed it at me, squinting to aim with his good eye. The door suddenly flew open, and a looming shadow tackled Andrew to the ground.

I blinked fast as stars clouded my vision, darkness closing in as blood dripped from my skull. My mouth was so dry. A ringing noise invaded my senses, increasing the already overwhelming pain.

Then there was nothing.

CHAPTER FORTY

The machines beeping next to me were driving me insane. I wanted to open my eyes, to end the noise so I could go back to sleep, but my eyelids wouldn't cooperate.

My whole body felt heavy, sore but not really painful.

I focused on the sounds around me, trying and failing to make sense of reality. The sharp smell of disinfectant burned my nostrils. Muddled thoughts floated around my brain. Something about Andrew, the shelter... I couldn't make sense of it. Every time I thought I could follow the string and piece something together, it fell apart.

I fought to open my eyes, but the effort resulted in a sharp pain on the side of my skull. It was enough to make me give up.

Either sleep or unconsciousness took me, I couldn't say which. At least it seemed like time had passed since the last time I was aware of my own existence. The beeping was still there, punctuating my pain. I just wanted it to stop. I needed it to stop.

This time I managed to open my eyes, but I only lasted an instant before the pain overwhelmed me. I fell into a restless slumber, my dreams dotted with flashes of mean caramel eyes and the glowing glint of a gun.

More time must have passed, because the next time I came to, I could feel someone touching me. I panicked, trying to push them off but failing because I couldn't move my limbs. It came back to me all at once.

Andrew.

No. It couldn't be him. That didn't make any sense.

I felt so confused. I was ready to give in to my body and sink into sleep again, but a familiar voice reached my ears.

"Cassandra."

The voice whispered over and over. I knew that voice, but I couldn't place it.

Thinking hurt, so I sank back into the soft pillows and let sleep take me.

I was just so tired.

I wanted oblivion, anything not to feel.

The next time I came to, the familiar beeping of the machines was still there to greet me. I lay with my eyes closed for a long time, trying to understand what was happening to me. That same disinfectant smell tickled my nose again. It was fainter now, but decidedly familiar.

Andrew.

The beeping.

I'm in a hospital.

Tears brimmed in my eyes when I realized I wasn't locked up in some basement with Andrew. Someone had come for me. The shadowy figure I had seen just before everything went black was real. *I didn't imagine it.*

All at once, I felt all the tension release from my muscles, even as I tried to grasp the reality of what I had survived. My eyes fluttered open when I felt a hand near my face. A bright light blinded me for a second, then a voice far away told me to cough. They gently repeated the order until I complied, and I gagged as something slid up my throat.

I struggled to breathe for a second, my vision going dark as a thousand needles pricked my throat raw. Then the pressure was gone, and a wave of relief washed over me as I sagged against the mattress.

But the relief was short-lived. There was so much pressure against my skull, my head felt like it was going to explode. I tried to bring my hands up to hold it, but my arms were too heavy to move. The light was too bright. Everything was wrong.

It felt like a garbage truck had run me over, then backed up to make sure they got the job done.

I just wanted to go back to sleep.

But then I heard that voice again. "Cassandra."

James. It was James.

I wanted to smile, but my body gave up and darkness took over once more.

I felt him before I heard him this time around.

James.

I blinked my eyes open slowly, but the room was dark, so it was easier this time. James's head rested against my arm, his hand firmly clasped around mine. Rina was on my other side, sitting on a chair at a weird angle with her head near my feet. Amelia and Daisy were squeezed together on a couch across the room.

Despite my confusion, seeing their faces around me immediately put me at ease. My eyes darted around the room as I tried to put the pieces of the puzzle together. Slowly, fragments played in my mind like a reel, the memories grainy and disjointed like an old movie.

Andrew finding me at the shelter. The basement apartment. The gun glittering in his hand. I squeezed my eyes shut, trying to relieve some of the pressure in my skull. None of it felt real, but the pain anchored the fuzzy memories in reality.

Memory was a cruel thing. I could barely picture my mom's face, but Andrew's expression when he came at me with the gun would forever be burned into my brain.

A shudder went through me, and I squeezed James's hand, basking in his warmth, his presence. It was enough to calm my racing heart.

James's eyes snapped open, and he quickly sat up. "You're awake," he whispered, wrapping my hand in both of his before bringing my knuckles to his lips.

"What—?" I started, but my throat was too dry, too scratchy.

"It's okay," James said reassuringly. "Don't try to speak yet. Andrew's in jail, and you're okay. That's all that matters right now. You're safe."

He reached over the bed and nudged Rina awake. She immediately shot up from her chair, her wide blue eyes quickly finding mine.

"Cassie!" Tears threatened to spill over as she smiled at me, pressing a hand against her heart. As if she'd sounded an alarm, Daisy and Amelia sprung from their awkward position on the couch and surrounded my bed. "The doctor—" Rina started.

Amelia wiped at her eyes with the back of her hand. "I'll go get them."

My eyes darted from face to face, a warm glow casting over me as I took in my friends and James. "Hi," I croaked.

"Hi, babe," Daisy said, resting her hand on my leg.

A nurse walked in, accompanied by a doctor, and everyone except James gathered by the couch to give them room to work. James stood at the foot of the bed, his hand on my ankle.

"Good evening, Miss Leigh," the doctor said. "I'm Dr. Kepner. How are you feeling?"

"Been better," I whispered painfully.

The nurse smiled knowingly at me, automatically moving to fill a glass of water. She brought the straw to my lips, and I almost moaned as cool water slipped down my throat, soothing my sore vocal chords.

"How long have I been out?" I whispered.

"Two days," the doctor replied. "You suffered severe head trauma and internal bleeding, and we had to take you in for surgery." She asked me a bunch of questions while the nurse checked my vitals, then smiled reassuringly at me. "Despite your extensive injuries, we expect you to make a full recovery. For now, you should rest. We can talk some more in the morning."

I nodded, and soon they were gone. The interaction was brief, but left me completely drained. "I'm tired."

"Go back to sleep," Rina murmured. "We'll be right here when you wake up."

My eyelids were so heavy, I couldn't even pry them open to look at her. I fell into a deep, peaceful slumber before I could form a reply.

The sun was peeking over the horizon when I blinked my eyes open, painting the still dark skies in shades of orange and pink. It took me a few minutes to situate myself, but the fog was slowly lifting. I glanced down at my body and took a deep breath, grateful to be alive.

According to the clock on the wall, it was just before seven a.m. I glanced around at the private room, complete with a small but comfortable looking couch, and my lips lifted into a faint smile.

James, of course.

He had pushed his chair against the bed, his upper body resting close to my legs while his butt was firmly on the chair, his legs folded under him. It seemed like the most uncomfortable position ever.

Rina and Daisy were curled up together on the couch, sound asleep. Amelia was nowhere in sight, although I was sure I had seen her last night.

As if he sensed I was awake, James slowly blinked his eyes open, a smile stretching his lips when he caught me staring at him. "Morning, gorgeous," he said, his voice groggy with sleep.

"Hey," I squeezed out. He was still wearing the same clothes I'd last seen him in. His hair was all over the place, and his usually tidy beard was overgrown. Deep, dark circles lined his eyes, but he was still a sight to behold.

"How are you feeling?" Slowly, he stretched out his legs and straightened his back, grimacing as his tight muscles complained from the awkward positions. "Should I go get the doctor?"

"No, I'm okay," I whispered, squeezing his hand. "I'm glad you're here."

"Nowhere else I'd rather be," he said, his voice thick with emotion.

"What happened? How did I get here?" I had to catch my breath before I could continue, but James waited patiently beside me. "Last thing I remember, Andrew was…." I stopped because I couldn't finish the sentence.

Andrew on top of me. Blinding pain as my head smashed against the wall. Beer bottles. It was all confusing and terrifying. My chest burned as I tried and failed to draw in enough air, tears clouding my vision as the memories flooding my mind overwhelmed me.

"Hey, it's okay, you're okay," James said over and over as panic gripped me and my heart rate skyrocketed. "He's in jail. You're safe. He's never getting anywhere near you again. I promise." He clasped my hand in his, anchoring me to reality.

The girls rushed over to the bed and promptly repeated James's assertions. Gradually, my panic subsided, and I blinked away the tears to take in the worry on their faces.

"I'm a little confused," I said, bringing a hand up to press against my eyes.

"That's completely normal," Rina said, pushing my hair away from my face. "Do you want to know what happened?"

I offered her the faintest of nods.

"When you didn't come back from the basement, Marie went to check on you. She sensed something was wrong, especially when she noticed your phone was still there. Then she called me, and I called James while I tracked your watch." She released a deep sigh, a soft smile shaping her lips. "There's more to it, but basically the police found you and brought you to the hospital. What matters is that worthless piece of trash is in jail, and you're here, safe with us."

There was no stopping the tears flowing down my cheeks as she spoke, but some of it was relief. I always thought my situation with Andrew would never be resolved, that I'd always be looking over my shoulder. But now it was over.

"I knew you'd track my watch," I said, my voice wobbly with emotion. "Thank you."

Rina's eyes swam with tears as she smiled at me, then leaned down to press a kiss against my cheek. "No need to thank me, Cassie. You're my best friend. I'd do anything for you."

A sob from across the room got our attention, and we all turned our gazes to Daisy. "Sorry," she said, sniffing loudly. "I tried to hold it in but you guys are so sweet and I'm so happy Cassie is alive! I don't know whether to smile or cry."

"A bit of both?" I offered lamely.

James chuckled softly beside me, along with Rina, while I basked in the overwhelming love present in this room. By the time the nurses came in with the doctor, I felt a thousand times lighter, but I still wanted to know exactly how extensive my injuries were.

"Good morning, Miss Leigh," the doctor started. "I'm Dr. Kepner. We met briefly last night. How are you feeling this morning?"

"A little fuzzy, but better."

"That's great to hear." Then she turned to my visitors and added, "I have to examine Miss Leigh now. Could you please wait outside?"

My eyes widened at her request, and I gripped James's hand tighter.

I didn't want to be alone.

"I'm not going anywhere unless Cassie tells me," James said firmly.

The doctor looked between us and silently agreed. Rina and Daisy stepped outside after assuring me they would be right back. Dr. Kepner proceeded with her examination, checking on incisions I didn't even know I had.

"What's the damage?" I asked. Judging by the way the nurse gazed at the floor and the doctor's serious expression, I figured it wasn't pretty. "Give me a summary. I'd like to know, please."

Dr. Kepner shot me a sympathetic look before she said, "You came in with two severe head injuries that caused some brain swelling. My colleagues in neuro drilled a small hole into your skull to relieve the pressure. The procedure was successful, but we're monitoring you closely in case there are any changes."

I stared blankly at her, waiting for her to continue.

"I operated on you to stop the internal bleeding in your

abdomen. The incision looks good and we'll keep monitoring you. You also have severe contusions on your upper body and bruised ribs, which will take time to heal. There's a fracture in your radius, and bruises and lacerations to the face, the latter of which should heal with minimal scarring."

"Did you perform a vaginal exam when I first came in?"

"Yes, we did. There was no sign of sexual assault, no tears or any other sign of penetration."

"Thank you, Dr. Kepner," I said in a measured tone. I should have felt relief. Joy. Something positive. But all I felt was numbness.

"Now that you're awake, the police will probably want to interview you. Do you feel up for it?"

"Yes," I said immediately.

Once the doctor left, I turned my attention to James. "Hey, handsome," I said, "how are you doing?"

James smiled and brought my hand to his lips. "Don't worry about me, gorgeous. Just focus on resting and healing."

"I can't help it. You look like crap."

His eyes lit up as he raised one eyebrow. "Two seconds ago I was handsome."

"You still are," I said, lifting my hand to caress his face. "But you look tired."

"Oops, sorry to interrupt, lovebirds," Daisy said, lingering in the doorway. "The cops are here."

I nodded, and two police women walked in. Their eyes widened a fraction as they swept over my battered face, and I wondered how bad I looked. I shouldn't care, but hiding the evidence of Andrew's abuse was still a knee-jerk reaction.

The detectives conducted a detailed interview, and I appreciated their thoroughness. I answered their questions to the best of my abilities, refusing to shy away from the excruciating details that managed to pierce through my foggy brain.

James stood quietly beside me, his solid presence giving me courage to go on. Once I finished my statement, he held a cup of water to my lips and I gratefully sucked on the straw. The detectives left, assuring me they would be in touch, and I sagged against the mattress.

"How are you feeling?" James asked, as he stood beside my bed.

"Tired. But I'm glad it's all over, even if it had to end this way."

"Security should've prevented this," he said almost to himself. He rubbed a hand over his face and shook his head a little, as if he was trying to shrug off whatever thoughts plagued him.

"We did all we could, James," I said, stroking his hand with the tip of my finger. "We were careful and took precautions. I refuse to wonder what else I could've done to prevent this, and I don't want you to question yourself either." My voice was raw with emotion and physical pain, but I needed him to hear me. "Andrew did this, and he's the only one who should be held accountable."

James brushed his lips against my knuckles, his magnetic brown eyes shining with adoration. "I love you so fucking much," he said. "When Catarina called me… fuck, I never knew what true dread was until that moment. And then you were in the hospital, unconscious but alive. You're the strongest person I know and I'm so grateful you fought so hard. I can't imagine my life without you, gorgeous."

"I guess it's lucky you don't have to. You're stuck with me now," I said, smiling through fresh tears.

"There's no one else I'd rather be stuck with."

Before I could say anything else, a knock on the door interrupted us. Amelia came in with a soup thermos and set a tray with a spoon in front of me. "I checked with the doctors, and this is safe to eat. It's just broth, but it's probably better than whatever they would serve you here."

Eating was the last thing on my mind, but Amelia had gone home to make me this, so I gratefully sipped the chicken broth. "It's delicious," I said, "thank you."

Once I ate all I could manage, my eyelids started drooping. But before I succumbed to sleep, I wanted to see what I looked like.

"I need a mirror."

Amelia and Daisy exchanged a weary glance, but Rina understood and handed me her phone with the camera open.

There was no bracing myself for what I was about to see, so I just held the phone up and stared blankly at the face looking back at me. My head was wrapped in a bandage mummy-style, which for a second got me worried about my hair.

They had probably shaved it.

I let that information sink in before moving on to the rest of my face. It was bruised and swollen, my lips cut up and dry…. It was bad, but nothing that wouldn't heal overtime.

"Okay," I told Rina, handing her back the phone. "I can handle this."

"Of course you can," Amelia said.

Daisy nodded in agreement, and added, "Yeah, you're a bad bitch."

The girls and James exchanged an amused look, but that was the last thing I heard before sleep took over once more.

This time, I awoke to laughter.

I peeled my eyes open, searching for the source, only to find Elias importuning a very flushed Amelia right outside the door.

"Hey," James said softly from his spot beside my bed. "Elias and my sister are here, but I wasn't sure if you were up for visitors."

I looked awful, but the fact they cared enough to come visit me was enough. "It's okay."

James shot me a dubious look, but nodded when I didn't say anything else. Elias walked in carrying an enormous bouquet, followed by Elisabeth. For the first time, I noticed the array of flowers, balloons, and baskets scattered around the room. It warmed my heart to realize that so many people cared about me.

"I'm so glad you're alive," Elisabeth said earnestly, taking a seat by my bed.

I tried to smile, and whispered, "Me too."

Elias sat at the foot of my bed, almost crushing my feet. "I heard you did a number on the guy. Blinded him in one eye."

"Elias!" Elisabeth said, shooting daggers at him.

"That's okay," I assured her. "It's good to know I did some damage."

"Mom and Dad wanted to come," Elisabeth said, "but they didn't want to intrude or impose on you."

"Clearly, we have no such qualms," Elias said, patting my knee. "By the way, darling, no need to fret over the fundraiser. Lizzy and I will take care of it and run everything by you."

"Thank you," I said. James was quiet, too quiet. It was worrying me. He stared down at our entwined fingers, deep in thought. He was clearly bone-tired. "Elias, can you take James home? He needs a nap and a shower."

James finally looked up and straightened his posture. "I'm fine."

A look passed between Elias and Elisabeth. Then she said, "We've tried. He won't leave your side."

"I need some stuff," I told James. "Comfortable clothes, my toothbrush and toiletries, maybe my laptop. You could go home, eat something, take a nap, and bring my things when you come back."

"I can just send someone—"

"No," I said, glancing at the others for help. "All of you look like you could use a shower and a long nap. I really appreciate all of you being here, but I'm tired and—" I had to pause for breath, a little annoyed that speaking had me panting like I had just ran a marathon.

"Are you trying to kick us out?" Daisy asked, raising a perfectly arched eyebrow.

"You're stuck with us, Cassie," Rina told me before turning to James. "But what about a compromise? We'll stay here while you go, then leave when you come back. That way all of us can get some rest."

Perspective was a funny thing, and so were the events that altered it. I would never be grateful to Andrew for assaulting me, but his return to my life had opened my eyes and forced me to stop lying to myself.

The thought of going through all of this on my own was unbearable, and as I glanced around the room at my girls, James, Elisabeth, and even Elias, my heart ached in the most beautiful way. For once it was full of love, and that love spilled over into this room, into my life, into all of our lives.

It took a little help from Elisabeth and Elias, but we finally convinced James to go home. He left along with his sister and Elias, and the girls kept me company as I drifted in and out of sleep. Hours later, I woke up in the darkness. Fear flared in my heart for a split second, but James squeezed my hand and it was gone.

He had showered and changed into loungewear, but he hadn't shaved his overgrown beard, and the dark circles remained under his eyes.

"Go back to sleep," he whispered. "I'm here."

"I love you. I'm sorry I didn't say it before, at least not in so many words."

"I love you too," he said, brushing a kiss against my knuckles. "I've never been so scared in my life." He swallowed, his Adam's apple visibly moving up and down. "I thought I'd lost you for good."

"I'm right here," I said, pressing my palm against his cheek, "and I'm not going anywhere."

I punched the code of our rental into the security pad, struggling to push the door open without dropping my groceries. This morning I'd left James sleeping soundly in our bed and slipped out for some fresh bread and pastries.

It took some sneaking around, but I had managed to convince his executive assistant to block three weeks off his calendar. Since I wanted it to be a surprise, she had filled his schedule with bogus appointments.

James has been nothing but supportive, patient, and loving since I met him, but even more so after I was assaulted. Between taking care of me and heading his company, he was stretched thin. He needed a vacation, so I had planned this little tour of Italy.

Everything was arranged so he wouldn't have to lift a finger, but he still insisted on cooking me breakfast whenever we didn't eat out. This morning I had gotten up at the crack of dawn to get his favorite pastries and the fresh bread he'd been obsessed with from a local bakery. I left the groceries in the kitchen and tiptoed to our bedroom to see if he was awake.

I found him on his back completely naked, sound asleep with the sheets tangled around his legs. He'd stretched an arm over my side of the bed, as if he was looking for me. Today marked the anniversary of the first day we met at Oasis, and even after everything we'd been through, the sight of him still made my heart skip a beat.

It hadn't exactly been smooth riding getting here. After I was released from the hospital, and spent weeks on the couch or lying in bed physically recovering, my mental health, which was already not stellar, had taken a nosedive.

Elisabeth and Elias had taken over the fundraiser almost entirely. And although they included me in everything and the event had been a complete success, it made me feel useless, worthless.

That had pushed me to go see a therapist, and it had only taken one session to realize I had a lot of unpacked trauma. I learned healthy coping techniques, and that rationalizing my emotions wasn't the same as allowing myself to feel. As my therapist put it, I was the sky, everything else was just weather. Feelings, good or bad, ebbed and flowed, and that was okay.

When I couldn't cope or had nightmares, James was there to hold me in his arms. Sex had been off the table for months, not only because of my physical injuries but because dealing with the trauma of being abducted and assaulted wasn't exactly an aphrodisiac. Sometimes I worried he would grow tired of me if I couldn't satisfy him. But since I was in a better place, I communicated those doubts to him. He reassured me that would never happen, and we had agreed to attend therapy together to have a professional input.

Now I was glad we had, because our Italian vacation would be entirely different without sex.

And we liked sex, a lot.

I stared at his chiseled, naked body, my gaze drifting down his taut stomach to that delicious V leading to his cock. Smiling, I sat gingerly between his legs, careful not to wake him. Then I bent down and placed his soft cock in my mouth.

James shifted but didn't wake, so I swirled my tongue over his head, teasing the underside of his dick. I felt him grow and harden in my mouth and smiled to myself. Sliding him out of my mouth, I fisted his cock and wrapped my lips around his head.

My grip was loose, but when I sucked on his head, his hand landed on the back of my neck.

"Cassie," he groaned, still half asleep.

I looked up at him and felt his dick twitch in my hand as his eyes met mine. Awareness slowly crept in, and to help him along, I relaxed my jaw and tightened my lips around his head before sucking his dick into my mouth, my gaze still locked on his.

A strangled groan escaped his lips when his cock hit the back of my throat, and his hips bucked, wanting more. I delivered, bobbing my head up and down, taking him as deep as I could. Wet sounds filled the room as I slobbered all over his cock, saliva dripping down my chin.

"Jesus, gorgeous. You're driving me crazy."

The familiar salty taste of his precum coated my tongue, and it drove me wild. I craved his pleasure, his thick cock pulsing within my lips as he emptied himself down my throat. Wrapping two hands around his cock, I worked him up and down, while I sucked his balls into my mouth and massaged them with my tongue.

"Fuck! I love it when you do that," he said, his voice strained.

I could tell he was close, and I wanted him to come in my mouth, so I wrapped my lips around his cock again. Stroking him with one hand while I massaged his balls with the other, I picked up speed, my tongue paying special attention to his frenulum.

It didn't take long for him to mumble, "Cassie, fuck. I'm coming." He fisted the sheets as he exploded in my mouth, his abs flexing and relaxing as sticky, salty cum slipped down my throat.

I welcomed the sensation of his cock pulsing in my mouth, ropes of cum sliding down my throat as I swallowed. Feeling James come undone under my touch made me so horny, my skin felt like it was on fire and my soaking pussy wanted more.

James propped himself up on one elbow and cupped the back of my head. He watched through dazed eyes as I slowly stroked his cock, milking him into my open mouth. "I love how you take my cock," he said in between heavy breaths.

I smiled up at him, a mix of cum and saliva dripping down my chin, and slowly twirled my tongue around his head. "I love your taste."

He groaned and grabbed the back of my neck, pulling my hair with enough force to make me meet his gaze. "Are you wet, gorgeous?"

I nodded, biting down on my lip. "Yes."

James gripped my waist and pulled me to him, using the sheets to wipe my face and neck. "Let me see how wet you are," he said, letting his hands drift down my ass to my cotton thong. His fingers brushed over my slit, and he groaned against my ear when he felt how soaked I was. Then his mouth crashed against mine, his expert tongue drawing a muffled moan from my lips.

"Wait, I got you breakfast," I said, pulling away.

He raised an eyebrow, a lazy smile stretching his lips. "You did?"

I nodded. "I got that bread you like. It was still warm."

"Bread can wait," he mumbled against my neck. He licked and nibbled his way to my chest, pulling the straps down to reveal my naked breasts. His mouth wrapped around one breast as he sucked on my pierced nipple. I arched into his touch, pushing my bosom into his eager mouth. "Sit on my face, gorgeous."

I didn't have to be told twice. Bunching my dress around my waist, I climbed onto my knees and positioned myself on top of his face. I reached down to push my panties to the side, but James tore them apart and discarded the shredded cotton on the floor. He gripped my hips and pulled me down, sucking my clit into his mouth before I had a chance to breathe.

"Jesus, James," I groaned, my pussy clenching in response.

My moans filled the room as I rode his face, his mouth giving my clit relentless attention. Gripping the headboard, I gasped as he blew on the sensitive bud. Sharp pleasure shot up my spine and my pussy spasmed against his lips, my orgasm quickly approaching.

James gripped my hip firmly with one hand, keeping me in place, while his free hand cupped my ass. I was so wet, my arousal dripped down my thighs. He used my natural lubrication to massage my asshole, the new sensation driving me closer to the edge.

"Please," I moaned. My thighs trembled around his head, and I groaned with frustration when he ignored my clit and started making out with my pussy. His mouth caressed my lips as he swirled his tongue all over, igniting all those erogenous zones at once.

I closed my eyes, strangled cries escaping my lips as my climax approached. A scream echoed throughout the apartment when he sucked my clit into his mouth, then swiped his tongue up and down a few times before sucking on the sensitive bud again. He continued this pattern until my muscles tensed, then suddenly relaxed, my limbs trembling as raw pleasure lit my insides on fire.

"Oh God," I whimpered as my hips bucked wildly, trying to escape his touch on my sensitive clit. But he held me down, brushing his tongue against my throbbing clit, stretching my climax until it stopped aching and started to feel good again.

"James," I groaned, trying to lift myself. His grip on my hips loosened, and I swung a leg to the side to lie down next to him. I cuddled against his side, gazing up at his glistening lips and his beard, covered in my cum. "You're so handsome."

He smiled and turned onto his side, facing me. "And you're absolutely gorgeous," he said, tucking my hair behind my ear.

I lifted one leg over his hip, and he cupped my ass to pull me close. His cock was hard against my pussy, and I reached between us to place him at my entrance. With one rock of his hips, he slowly entered me. I gasped and bit down on my lip as his bare cock stretched my walls, filling me until I couldn't breathe.

Wrapping my hand around his throat, I squeezed lightly as he thrust once, twice, my pussy clenching around his hard length. He peppered my face with kisses, his strokes shallow and lazy. I raked my fingernails down his back and reached down to cup his muscular ass, laughing as his dick twitched inside me.

"Remember that strap on I got last month? I think we should go for it." As I spoke, I brushed a finger against his asshole, feeling it pucker against my touch.

James moaned against my throat and thrust a little harder. "I'm game if you are."

I smiled and shifted my weight to climb on top of him. "Yeah?"

"Anything you want, gorgeous," he said, gripping my hips and pulling me down on his cock.

"What if I want you hogtied on the bed, wearing a vibrating cock ring while I pound your ass?" I said, panting hard as I rode his cock.

James growled, his chest vibrating underneath my palms. "Jesus, Cassie," he said, pinching my nipple as he lifted his hips to fuck me deeper. "That sounds really hot."

When his hand drifted down to circle my clit, I nearly lost it. I rode his cock with abandon, supporting myself on his chest as warmth pooled in my core. My legs started shaking, making it harder to ride him like I wanted. James noticed and tightened his grip on my hip, bouncing me up and down his thick cock.

Suddenly it all became too much. A loud moan flew from my lips as he pressed down on my clit, and another orgasm tipped me over the edge. I collapsed on top of him, burying my face in his neck as my pussy squeezed him like a vice, barely aware of who or what I was.

James pulled out for a second to flip me on my stomach before he entered me from behind.

I groaned, clutching the sheets as my insides melted and turned to goo. He smacked my ass, a stinging sensation mixing with the pleasure coursing through my veins. All I could do was moan and whimper as he set a punishing pace, chasing his pleasure.

His movements became jerkier and faster as he lost control, fingers digging into my ass almost painfully. "Cassandra," he cried, as he came with a shudder.

Warm cum filled my pussy, and I clenched around him. He groaned and draped his body over mine, kissing the back of my neck as he emptied himself. His body was warm and hard and deliciously heavy on top of me, but he was still careful not to crush me.

We took a moment to recover, our heavy breaths and the birds in the distance the only sounds in the room. Then he slowly slipped out of me, his cum dripping towards my vulva and the sheets beneath me.

I whimpered, pressing my legs together as soon as he was gone. "Do you know it's been a year since we met?" I asked as he tucked me into his chest.

James ran his hands up and down my back in a soothing motion, his lips stretching into a breathtaking smile as he gazed down at me. "You remembered," he whispered, his eyes still dark with lust.

I tugged on the little hairs on his chest in indignation. "Of course I remembered. I got a very good pounding that night."

His chest vibrated with laughter. "As much as I'd like to give you another unforgettable pounding, I have plans for today." He wrapped his arms around me and pushed into a seated position before swinging his legs to the side and getting up with me in his arms.

The bathroom was too small for both of us to shower, but he sat me on the sink and cleaned between my legs with a warm towel. "Want to shower first?"

I nodded and gave him a quick peck on the lips before jumping in the shower. James brushed his teeth while I washed, then we switched. In the bedroom, I put on a clean sundress before padding to the kitchen.

Italian coffee was something else. I smiled as I made a pot, the smell of freshly ground beans making my mouth water. I had already told James I planned to sneak some back home. He joined me a few minutes later, wearing only black boxers.

Wrapping his arms around me, he rested his head on my shoulder. "You made me breakfast."

I chuckled as I plated the pastries and some fruit, trying to make it pretty. "I didn't *make* anything."

"Thank you," he said, planting a wet kiss on my cheek.

We carried our breakfast to the small terrace of our rental. I had planned this trip as a surprise, which meant I paid for everything. My new job at the shelter was fulfilling, but the pay was modest, so we weren't in the fanciest of places. James didn't seem to care at all, even when the rental didn't look exactly as advertised.

This one was my favorite. It offered a dramatic view of Lake Como's blue waters and the surrounding greenery. It was breathtaking. I stared at the magnificent scenery as I sipped my coffee, completely at peace with James next to me.

"We should go away more often. I like to see you relaxed," he said, as he spread real butter on a slice of bread. He'd been truly obsessed with Italian bread, eating it plain or with a little butter on most days.

I found it adorable that such a simple thing made him so happy. "Your birthday is coming up soon. We could plan something."

"Do you like skiing? We could go to Aspen."

"I've never skied but it sounds fun."

"We have a house there," he said casually, "so maybe we could invite the girls, and Elias?"

I laughed and shook my head a little. Of course he had a house in Aspen. "Sometimes I forget how rich you are."

He shrugged, sighing contently as he bit into one of the pastries. "What's mine is yours."

I raised an eyebrow and shot him a look. "You do know that when we get married we're getting a prenup, right?"

He lifted his gaze and grinned. "Is this a hint I should be shopping for diamond rings?"

I shook my head, my pulse wild at the thought of becoming Mrs. Walton. "I don't think I'm ready for marriage right now," I said cautiously, "but when it happens we will sign a prenup."

James laughed and leaned back in his chair, balancing his coffee on his knee. "So we're not even married and you're thinking about divorce?"

"I'm just thinking about protecting your assets."

He leaned forward and pinched the side of my asscheek. "I'd like to protect this asset."

Laughter bubbled in my belly. "You're impossible."

A serious expression took over his face, and he grabbed my hand, drawing lazy circles on my palm as he spoke. "I know we're not there yet, but you said *when* we get married, not *if*. And I want you to know that I can see it. The two of us building a life together with two point five kids, teaching them to skate and traveling the world as a family."

My eyes widened and I swallowed, unsure of what to say. I wasn't ready for kids yet, and this relationship still felt new. I wanted it to be just the two of us for a while longer, but I also needed him to know we were on the same page.

"Two kids, no point five," I said, squeezing his hand. "But children change things. I want to enjoy us for a while. We won't be able to have sex all over the house when he have kids."

He grinned at me, his expression so happy I could hardly breathe. Dragging my chair towards him, he cupped my face and brushed his mouth against mine. "I love you," he whispered, and just like they always did, his words filled my heart, expanding it until I marveled that it still fit in my chest.

Once, those three little words had terrified me. But life was too short to be scared of loving and being loved. Living didn't come with guarantees, but I knew that every time I stumbled, James would be right there holding me up. And I'd do the same for him.

Scooting closer, I gazed deep into his magnetic brown eyes and whispered, "I love you, too."

ACKNOWLEDGMENTS

Thank you to my editor and savior, LP Tvorik. This book wouldn't be nearly as enjoyable without your brain picking it apart and stitching it back together. A big thank you to ACourtofSpicyEdits for the invaluable feedback.

Maï, I couldn't have done this without you. Thank you for the cover, the website, and the insane amount of social media posts. No one else would've put up with my endless nitpicking and font indecision. I owe you mountains of gold.

To Wallis, Maï (yes, you're here a bunch) thank you for listening to my ramblings about this book for over a year. I couldn't have asked for better friends, and I'm infinitely grateful to have you in my life.

To my brother V, who loaned me his monitor when my back gave out. And bought me an office chair to help with my knee tendinitis. You believed in me enough to invest in an office set up, and I will never forget it. (I'm sorry you'll never experience any of my stories spoiler free because I kept rambling about them.)

And finally, many thanks to my mom and stepfather, thank you for letting me live in your house rent-free so I could pursue my dreams. Even though you don't really understand what I'm doing, your support has never wavered.

This book, this dream of mine, wouldn't be possible without each of you. I'm eternally grateful.

RESOURCES

If you or a loved one needs help, here are some resources. You are not alone.

USA
    https://ncadv.org/RESOURCES
    https://www.domesticshelters.org/help

Canada
    https://www.casw-acts.ca/en/resources/domestic-violence-resources

France
    https://arretonslesviolences.gouv.fr/
    https://arretonslesviolences.gouv.fr/
    https://cfcv.asso.fr/

Bea Miller was born in Brazil and grew up in the heart of Europe. She planned to be a neurosurgeon, but after reading Pride and Prejudice for the first time, and recognising that maths weren't her forte, she changed her mind. After getting a bachelors in English Literature, she dabbled in teaching before realising writing was her true calling. These days her tastes have evolved from the classics to contemporary romance, the spicier the better.